SLOW
DANCE

A NOVEL

by

Melissa McDaniel

Bloomington, IN  Milton Keynes, UK

AuthorHouse™
1663 Liberty Drive, Suite 200
Bloomington, IN 47403
www.authorhouse.com
Phone: 1-800-839-8640

This book is a work of fiction. People, places, events, and situations are the product of the author's imagination. Any resemblance to actual persons, living or dead, or historical events, is purely coincidental.

© 2007 Melissa McDaniel. All Rights Reserved.

No part of this book may be reproduced, stored in a retrieval system, or transmitted by any means without the written permission of the author.

First published by AuthorHouse 07/25/07

ISBN: 978-1-4259-6390-3 (sc)

Printed in the United States of America
Bloomington, Indiana

This book is printed on acid-free paper..

I dedicate this book to George, Lisa, and Wayne, the three most important people in my life.

For their help and encouragement my heartfelt gratitude goes to Monika Kirkpatrick, Patti Sullivan, Lynn Carver, Jamie Jeremy, Shirley Lynn, Kathy Gaston, Jonellen Heckler, Chris McDaniel, Anne Steiner, Wendy Preo, Shirley Branch, Violet Yadegar, Nicki Lloyd, Colleen Karr, Brenda Rice, Kaytee Packer, Joanna Sebelien, Lynn and Brenda Matthews, William and Constance Roberts, Bob and Rebecca Owen, Beth McCall

And for their inspiration: Ava Acree, Leona Anglin, Mary Dees, June Glass, Shirley Mulvaney, Marlene Reid, Pam Williams and Kaye Tipton.

CHAPTER 1
It Begins

Sheila Branford is good to the bone. She's never strayed from the narrow path of her life. Why risk it? This one led her to a good job at a prestigious college; it got her a husband who's a good provider and two precious children. That she's miserable shouldn't enter into the equation

Eyes mostly male, turn her way as she enters the opening breakfast of a conference for higher education executives. Their appraisals are positive, but for a forty-two-year-old wife and mother, it matters not. She bites her lower lip, takes a deep breath, and affixes the smile that makes her appear more confident than she really is. It's her first time at this meeting and she knows few of the hundred-some college and university types in attendance. Two women, crisp, almost neuter in appearance, are inviting her to join them when someone grabs her arm. It's Roy Fitzgerald, a Southerner she'd met at an earlier conference.

"Hey darlin', come add some class to this table. Y'all, this gentlewoman is Sheila Branford, she heads the Community Affairs Office at Riel College, somewhere up here in the frozen North."

"Roy!" Sheila laughs, "Do you see any ice on this perfect summer day? And Riel, just FYI, is about an hour south of here, near Milwaukee."

"Wherever it is, darlin', it's a better place when you're there! Now, these folks have the good sense to hail from locales where this kind of weather isn't just a July thing. Ron's from Mississippi, Mike is from Arkansas, and Alabama's lucky to have Betty. As you know,

Melissa McDaniel

I'm a Georgia peach, and that rough- rider across from you is Florida through and through."

The career woman, wife and mother smiles professionally from one to another; her mask is compromised, however, when she gets to the Floridian. *What lucky woman gets to look at this every day?* Pleasantries are exchanged as she imagines the family such a face must have. *It's big: the fruits of a fabulous sex life, loving, too, because his warmth seems to be pulling me into his arms in a sort of virtual embrace.*

His name is T. Earl Langley and he hails from Pine Springs College, located in north central Florida. "A place," he says, "where towering pines and ancient oaks have room to stretch and yawn."

Sheila flashes on her lifelong love for the Sunshine State. "It's not for us, dear. We belong in Wisconsin," had been her mother's reply whenever little Sheila proposed they live in Florida.

He doesn't just belong in Florida. He owns it! Something stirs between her thighs. Frightened by the sensation, she steers their conversation to the sexless issues of higher education. Only once does she reveal anything personal. It's a self-serving remark about the critters on Earl's cap.

"Oh! I just realized those funny little guys are armadillos. My son, Chase, loves armadillos. He'd be trying to peel those off your hat, even as we speak!" Try as she might, it's impossible to go for long without talking about one, or both, of her precious children. "Is your school mascot really an armadillo?"

"No, they're the moles 'cuz they can't see to catch anything!" Roy cuts in.

"Darlin', we're the Attacking Armadillos."

"Yeah, they think they can play football," another buddy chides.

"I see," Sheila says, pausing for effect, "so do we!" Everyone laughs, understanding her college is better known for brains than brawn.

When the colleagues adjourn to a conference room for the first session Sheila selects her usual seat in the front row. She's gazing out the window, wondering what her children are doing, when a belt buckle embedded with something's teeth blocks her vision. Tilting her head all the way back she finds Earl's eyes. They're focused on an array of armadillo paraphernalia which he holds in two huge hands.

Those eyes! They're the same color as that duck...what's it called?

"For Chase!" he proclaims.

"Thanks," *Teal. They're teal green.* "I'll see he shares them with his sister."

"You've got a little girl, too? You're so lucky! I'll get some for her." He rushes off to return with more armadillo stickers, whistles, squirt guns, and erasers.

"Wow, how generous!" Her silver blues meet the teal greens.

You stir me, too.

It's the message he's been seeking. But Sheila finds the attention embarrassing. The queen of conversation has nothing to say. Feeling stupid, she looks away. Earl, understanding more than she does, moves on. Something has passed between them, and experience tells him a possibility exists, a possibility of what? He has no clue, but the beautiful blonde from the Midwest is worth knowing.

Neither lunch nor the breaks framing the sessions bring the two together again. From a distance, Sheila observes the Florida guy as he floats from meeting to meeting like a Spanish galleon in amid an armada of fiberglass dinghies. He isn't here for professional education alone. While others labor at working the room, he spends time on the few he really likes. In turn, their greetings to him are the kind bestowed on a lifelong friend.

As the sessions conclude, Sheila runs to her room to phone home. Talking to Allie, six, and Chase, four, always works like a tonic. After several minutes of lively kiddie-talk, Sheila checks in with Mara, their Polish sitter. "*Tak, tak*, all good," the woman confirms.

Confident all's well, she relaxes, content in her mommy-hood. *I have everything in this role. It's the crowning achievement of everything I ever hoped to accomplish. God, how I love them! A deeper, more complete rapture I've never known.* She pauses; knowing there's trouble in her next thought. *So why am I so miserable? No! I can't do this; this isn't the time to get into a funk!*

She stalks into the bathroom to confront the woman in the mirror. "You have everything." she scolds her reflection. "Can't you just be happy?"

The face doesn't buy it. *If having it all is what you've spent your life pursuing, why, when you have so much, are you so empty?*

"Stop it!" she screams in a stage whisper. Turning her back on the mirror, she escapes into the shower. The warm water feels wonderful on her skin. *This isn't a bad conference. That session on crisis management will come in handy, the town and gown stuff too. The people are nice. Those Southerners are a riot.* As she's thinking, slippery hands slide from neck to shoulders, arms, and chest, they encircle her breasts once, twice, three times. Pinching her nipples, she thinks of *him* and her breath grows shallow. With this arousal comes a deeper, more meaningful one. Earl's perfect face fixes in her mind's eye, and soapy fingers move downward ... *No!* She halts what she's about to do. *What the . . . ? How dare that man enter my mind and try to make love to me? How dare I let him?*

Furious with herself, Sheila exits the shower, dons her most conservative outfit, and trudges to the hospitality center for an Earl-free evening. Later, she gives herself high marks for the distance she's kept between herself and Mr. Langley.

He got the message, all right, perhaps too well, because the next morning she doesn't seem to exist for the man from Florida. *Rats! I hadn't intended to alienate him to the extent we can't be friends. Besides, the most enjoyable people at this conference are his buds. To steer clear of him would mean missing the good spirits of the entire Southern contingent. That's just not acceptable. O.K., so maybe I should work at establishing a purely professional liaison with Mr. T. Earl Langley.*

The bond forms instantly as Earl returns Sheila's businesslike attention. At lunch, the two chat politely, and by dinner, they are inseparable. Sheila's enjoying herself so much that when Roy asks who wants to go out for a farewell drink, she steps forward saying she'll join them as soon as she calls home. Her husband, Charles, answers the phone with a checklist of information. "The nurse called. Your mom's hallucinating again. Allie's invited to Meridy Carty's birthday party next Friday, and Mara wants to take off the day after tomorrow."

"O.K. Charles, tomorrow I'll call Dr. Black to get Mom's meds readjusted. And I'll arrange for a student from the college to stay with the kids so Mara can take the day off. Gosh, Meridy's party is the fifth one Allie's been invited to this month! Our six-year-old has a better social life than we have." Silence "I said Allie goes out more than we do!"

"Uh, yeah." He seems preoccupied, probably doing paperwork or watching television.

"I'm about to join some folks at a place called the Boilermaker. It's our last chance to commiserate. See you tomorrow, hon."

An accountant in a big Milwaukee firm, Charles is familiar with such get-togethers. "Fine, have fun, She." He clicks off.

As they pull into the Boilermaker's parking lot, Sheila realizes it's the kind of drinking establishment located in any rural U.S. town. The Southern contingent laughs to see a Wisconsin tavern so closely resembling its own watering holes. Even the pool-playing clientele looks familiar, with T-shirts stretched taut over beer bellies and jeans hanging off butts. Their girlfriends, too, make the Southerners feel at home as they adorn the bar in their Yankee version of redneck chic. Sheila watches them with interest. They don't turn her off; in fact, she almost envies their enjoyment of the here and now. Staring at them, she remembers her summers in the small resort town of Water Haven. *What fun I had before I became politically correct and sexless!*

Earl comes up, putting a beer in her hand and an arm around her shoulder. *This,* she thinks, drawing dangerous energy from his touch, *this is anything but sexless.* They stand close, each sensing the electricity swirling around them. Sheila loves the rush and wants to prolong it, but within that smoldering shiver is an entire universe to be denied. *Come now, I'm forty-two years old; nothing's going to happen.* This thinking gets her out on the dance floor, and into Earl's arms. The Righteous Brothers throb, "You've Lost That Lovin' Feelin'" while slow fingers caress the small of her back. Suddenly, the sensation feels provocative and cheap. *This can't be happening! I'm too good, too normal, and way too married to be doing this. What, besides this guy's killer good looks, pulls me to him so?* She draws back to consult the teal greens. They validate her confusion with a Rhett Butler twinkle. *He's laughing at me!* Angered, she pulls away, feigning interest in the jukebox.

In a heartbeat, Earl is at her side, and as she pretends to scan the song titles, this object of who-knows-how-many-women's dreams, grabs her hand. She stands paralyzed as the circuit is completed. *No way! I won't go there! I can't. But what if I do?*

Earl, sensing her panic, hands her a dollar. "Here, pick some tunes."

In no time, she's selected five country songs. The choice earns her a long, slow smile. "I didn't have you figured as a country music gal."

"I love country, but I never listened to it until six years ago when my car radio scanned to a country station. I've been hooked ever since. My husband hates it though. He says something happened to my chemistry when I was pregnant with Allie to make me love it as I do."

"People sell country short. There's more to it than they'd like to admit."

"Yeah, like a message. For me, it's causing some pretty disturbing thoughts to surface."

"How so?" Now she really has his attention.

For the first time, ever, Sheila decides to give credence to something she's been denying for years. "I'm a much simpler person than my lifestyle allows me to be. Somehow, the sophisticated nature of my life just kind of evolved. It's more the product of circumstances than planning."

"That's easy to let happen, but there's a danger that some day you'll wake up inside a life you hate."

"True." Sheila's voice sounds flat. She's thinking about something to do with her mom.

Sensing another mood change, Earl steers her to a barstool where he introduces the topic of his only son, Ryan. Pride flows from his description of the young man tough enough to play international soccer yet sensitive enough to write poetry in his spare time.

So he doesn't have a large family! Sheila's dying to ask about his wife, but that subject's better left alone. Instead, she volunteers more than enough information about Allie and Chase and what it's like to be the oldest mom on the playground.

Suddenly, one of the locals is all over Roy for moving a cue ball. What had seemed to be an abandoned pool game was really one waiting for its players to return from a trip to the bar. No big deal, for most, an apology would suffice, but these rednecks have their own form of retribution in mind. A fight seems seconds away.

"Ya no good motha'fucka! Ya think ya's'much better'n us? Y'need ta learn a lesson! We'll teach ya t'break up our game!"

Is there a code of conduct for pool players everywhere never to interrupt someone else's game? In the drama, Sheila sees laborers retaliating against the unjust treatment of a fancy tourist. Profanity aside, she can understand their rage.

The underdogs show their true colors, however, when they demand, "So asshole, what ya gonna do about it? How ya gonna make it right?"

Roy looks from one to the other as their agenda sinks in. Swallowing his anger, he drawls, "I'm so sorry, how 'bout I buy you boys a round, nah, make it two rounds of drinks?"

The boys, as Roy calls them, relax visibly. Straining to hide their satisfaction, "Well, O.K., but it ain't right."

"No, it ain't," now he's toying with them, "but it's just something I gotta do, know what I mean?" He smiles and ambles over to the bar where he plunks down the bills that will buy his way out of a fight.

Sheila is transfixed. She's never, before, seen a sting. "They set that whole thing up, waiting for the game to be interrupted, then feigning indignation!" "Believe so, sweet pea, probably do it every night, at least when tourists are around."

Sheila feels stupid for initially sympathizing with the locals. Then, angered by their con her thoughts turn to Roy. *Would he have been so conciliatory on his own turf? I think not. But in the midst of his associates, especially females, this Southern gentleman turned the other cheek.*

The excitement has cooled Sheila's fever for Earl. Evidently it did the same for him as he's accepting an invitation to play pool at one of the truly unoccupied tables. Sheila looks around and decides to join Erica and Kelly, two colleagues who are neither men's women nor women's women. Each is able to walk the narrow line between the two and be liked by both sexes.

Someone is showing them an e-mail device about the size of a pocket watch. Kelly grabs it to send a message to her husband. From the way she talks about him, it's easy to tell they're crazy for each other. Sheila wonders what x-rated text her friend is digitally whispering to her guy. While Kelly's involved, Sheila turns to Erica, wondering if she's noticed the current flowing between her and Earl. If she has, she isn't letting it show. Instead, the lovely, Irish-featured brunette is forthcoming with information about herself. She's married to a great guy who has a daughter from a previous marriage. No, she has no children of her own, and yes, sometimes she wonders if she's missing something. But most of the time, her husband and stepdaughter make her so happy that having a baby of her own doesn't seem important.

"Gosh," Sheila interrupts tactlessly, "my children are the only worthwhile things in my world. Without them, my life would be, as my hero, Henry David Thoreau would say, 'frittered away by detail.'"

"Really? What's so tedious?"

"Oh... nothing, really," Sheila backpedals. Then, struggling to resurrect her glass half-full identity, she adds, "I shouldn't have said that. My life is great, it's just a little frantic right now."

"I hear ya!" Erica raises her glass to Sheila. "Here's to the quiet times, moments when we can sit and think, and put everything into perspective."

Sheila smiles and drinks to the toast, but silently concedes, the quiet times are my enemy too. They're when I'm hardest on myself for not loving Charles the way I should. How stupid I was to think I could light my passion through the sheer will of wanting to love him that way!

A merry band of colleagues swaggers their way. Southern Comfort, having flowed in abundance, manifests itself in the group's high spirits. Someone suggests the revelry continue in the hot tub at the lodge. Most think it's a great plan.

A communal hot tub session with this group might be innocent enough, but Sheila's not sure. Riding back to the lodge, she inventories all the good things in her life: great kids, super job, nice husband. Nothing is worth losing all that.

"I'll get the key to the pool area," someone calls. The rest of the group stands on the sidewalk like children waiting for a school bell.

"We might as well stay here to be sure we can get the key before we get into our bathing suits," Erica observes.

"Suits? Are we supposed to wear suits?" Roy's whining puts Sheila's instincts on high alert. They intensify as the conversation moves on to the subject of spouses. None are allowed at this conference. What would they do if they knew skinny-dipping were on the agenda?

"Don't tell me you married folks don't skinny dip!" Earl protests.

"I do, with my hubby!" Kelly volunteers.

"Well, I'm not married, been single going on fourteen years." Earl stares at Sheila and gets real quiet, leaving his thoughts to everyone's imagination.

Single? He's single, free, and clear? And I'm in big trouble. In an almost psychic way, she knows this is a man for whom she could leave her husband. The key arrives and all make haste to change into their suits.

CHAPTER 2
Home

"No way are you going to that hot tub! He's slime, his jokes are dirty, he doesn't use good grammar, and you're married!" Sheila is ordering, almost begging the woman in the mirror to stay in her room.

The face doesn't agree. *He uses good grammar when he wants to and he has a fantastic sense of humor. Admit it, in one day you've had more fun, felt more alive than you have in years.*

"No, I'm not made that way. I won't stray from the path that's been laid for me, not ever!" Too uptight to sleep, Sheila paces around the room wishing she'd had a lot more to drink. And, damn it all, she'd forgotten to pack her Unisom. She has nothing to help her escape this night. Her thoughts fly to the hot tub. *They're there now. Is he pissed I didn't show? Does he think I treated him like a boy toy, leading him on then ditching him when the mood passed? Why do I care what he thinks? Duh, it's because I do feel something, and this was a really narrow escape.*

There'll be no sleeping tonight, so she decides to lie on the bed that faces the window. *At least, I'll be able to watch the pageantry of dawn.* For the next four hours, she does so, summoning the good forces within to put down the feelings that threaten her reputation, her job and, most of all, her family. At 6:00 AM, an embattled Sheila gropes her way to the shower. *Sweet Jesus, I'm going home in worse shape than I arrived!*

Out of the shower, she spends little time on her makeup and even less dressing. Her packing is haphazard; conference materials and

SLOW DANCE

dirty laundry share the same compartment of her carry all. She chuckles at the irony of this and slams the door to her room. After a night of tossing, only an omelet, loaded with the works, will do. In the breakfast line, two arms wrap around her from behind. It's Durwood, a man from a college out East. "Sheila, doll, we were worried about you last night."

"Worried? Why would anyone worry about me?" she asks, irate that someone she hardly knows would call her doll.

"Well, you know, you left with a pretty rough crowd," the Easterner stammers.

"And you feared I'd be led astray by the leader of the pack? For God's sake, Durwood, I'm forty-two!"

"Come on, Sheila, don't misread this. It's just that we care about you."

"Well, please thank the 'we' for their collective concern!" By now, her omelet is ready, so she dumps on enough hot sauce to match her mood and heads for the table where the self-appointed worrier is sitting. As she devours the spicy feast, she regales him with details of the outing to the Boilermaker. Ironically, she's defending the group, and particularly, Earl, for being the fun loving people they are. *I'll take them any day over this guy, so ready to accept stereotypes as valid indicators of behavior.*

Most of last night's players have made it to breakfast, but Earl is missing in action. Is it a response to her snub or too much Southern Comfort? Bloodshot eyes confirm the latter theory when she sees him in the lobby.

"You weren't at breakfast," she observes.

He nods, "I could say business kept me away, but you'd know better. Anyway, good luck this year." With a sad smile, Earl heads for the door.

He does think I led him on! He's a colleague, yet I treated him like a pickup. He's not slime, I am. I'm a sleaze with latent family morals, and I turned a potentially good friend into a cool acquaintance.

To keep her guilt from hitching a ride, Sheila decides to be proactive. She'll call Earl the very next day. From the safety of her office, over a thousand miles away, she'll explain she's committed to her marriage, but if he agrees, they can still enjoy a professional relationship. *And the gentleman in Earl will concur.* With this assurance, Sheila speeds away from the lodge, wanting only to get home where her little ones will make everything better. *Everything except this undertow that's been dragging me down all summer!* She's pretty sure it has something to do with her mother. It's not the sadness of Mom's Parkinson's disease, nor is it the time it takes for Sheila to run the support systems that enable her to stay in her home. What is it that's causing Sheila to see her mother in a less loving light? She remembers, as a child, being deeply, madly in love with her mother. Her beautiful, talented mother was the font of everything wonderful. None of her little friends had moms who did as much, gave as much, or were as much fun as her own sweet Mommy. As the years passed, she and her mother became entwined in the closest and least healthy of mother-daughter relationships. Through positive and negative reinforcement, little Sissy had learned that the price of her mother's addictive love was obedience in the most absolute sense, even to the extent of marrying her mother's — not her own — choice of a husband.

Sheila wonders what's triggering such hostility about something her mother did so long ago. When it comes, the answer ricochets off the pavement almost shattering the windshield with its force. *Earl! Earl is the embodiment of all that I gave up to keep Mom's love!* She speeds on for a good ten minutes, stewing in contempt for her mother's maneuverings. As usual though, she forces herself to reign in her anger. *This isn't good. I shouldn't allow this to bother me so. I'm in my fifteenth year of marriage to a good man, and, if I love him like a brother, so what? I have wonderful kids, great in-laws, and soon, we'll be moving into a brand new home on the shore of Lake Michigan.*

Sheila is depending on their upcoming move to solve everything that's wrong with her life. Long ago, she'd bought into a lifestyle to which she was ill-suited. Prior to that, it had been her dream to "pull a Thoreau." As in her hero's own words, she'd wanted to "live deliberately, to front only the essential facts of life." It had meant that, upon graduating from college, she'd leave her hometown of Richmond Heights for a place away from possessions and money. There'd be no TV, telephone, labor-saving appliances, but certainly, there would be a dog, books, and plenty of paper and pens for writing. Her objective would be to escape the details by which she'd seen others "fritter their lives away." But the pride of being offered a great teaching position cooled the flames of her Thoreau dream, and before long, the demands of teaching, her father's untimely death, and her engagement to Charles snuffed it out. Sheila rationalized that a cabin her grandfather had built on a lake was a worthy substitute for the real thing. When the children were born, she and Charles bought their own cottage on the same lake. To investigate places on other lakes never occurred to Sheila. Her mother's pull was that strong. Even so, when she informed the matriarch they'd be moving to a place within a five-minute walk, she was treated, yet again, to the negative reinforcement of her mother's withdrawal. The guilt this caused had driven Sheila to spend even more time at her mom's cottage, caring for her, but really, yielding to her control.

What's wrong with me? Why couldn't I see what was happening? How disgusted Thoreau would be to see me now! Not to worry, soon I'll be living on Lake Michigan and it will fill me with all the nature and solitude I need. Maybe Charles and I will kindle flames of our own with fires on the beach! Until then, I must do whatever it takes to keep my disgruntled psyche in tact. And in just five minutes, I'll see Allie and Chase!

Homecomings, whether from business trips or a day at the office, are joyous occasions. Having had her children after years of trying makes her covet each second she can spend with them. These days, thoughts of quitting her job to have more time with them dart in and out of her consciousness. Once, employment at the college provided challenge and fulfillment. Now, after a twelve-year climb to the directorship of her department, she feels consumed by the minutiae of politics and protocol.

"Mommy! Mommy's home!" A noisy confusion greets her as she climbs from the car. When the screen door is finally unhooked, the only two reasons any of it is worthwhile spill into her arms. Four-year-old Chase, in his black and white striped Oshkosh B'Gosh overalls, looks like a miniature engineer with platinum blond curls. Six-year-old Allie, with wide green eyes and honey-blonde braids, is cuter than Heidi ever was. Behind them is Mara, eager to go home after a long day.

"Mommy, we made booberry cake!" Chase announces.

"Blueberry *crisp*," Allie corrects, "and we did hopscotch."

"Neat!" Sheila says, savoring the sweetness of home. She perches her little ones on the kitchen counter so they can talk at eye level. "Tell me about camp."

"I got a blue ribbon because I finished all my crafts. That means I'm a Super Fruit Loop!" Allie proclaims with pride.

"That's great, honey-pie!" The camp has taken its division names from the cereal aisle at the supermarket. Cheerios, Wheaties, and Cocoa Krispies are all worthy competitors. Sheila smiles as she envisions Allie's future job résumé featuring Super Fruit Loop as an outstanding achievement.

"I'm proud of you, too, little buddy! How was your day?"

"Bad," Chase frowns, face grimacing with remembered pain.

"What happened?"

"I got hurt," he says, trying to sound pathetic.

Allie interrupts before her brother can arouse too much sympathy. "He fell off the glider."

"It bleeded!" Chase protests, chagrined that big sister thwarted his theatrics.

"Not much!" Allie's ready for battle.

"Whoa, now," Sheila separates the siblings, wondering when this rivalry escalated so.

Chase pulls up his overalls to expose a fresh bandage. Sheila peeks at the wound. "That looks nasty. How did you fall? Were you sitting down?"

"Yes...really!"

Sheila looks suspicious.

"I was sitting, but I had to make it go fast."

"Uh, huh," Sheila gives her son a haven't-I-told-you look.

Chase, adorable in his guilt, "I'm sorry, Mommy!"

Hugging both kids, she feels the regret of not being there, wherever and whenever the "there" is. *Tradeoffs, it's all about tradeoffs.*

Thirty minutes later, they're in her Seville, on their way to Grandma's. Allie fingers the Indian doll Mommy brought her while little brother aims his new slingshot toward oncoming cars. "Good trip treats?" Sheila asks, and receives adamant nods. "My treat is I get to be with you two! I'll bet Wookie will be thrilled to have her playmates back." She mentions her mom's adorable terrier to ease the kids' disappointment at having to go to Grandma's so soon after her return. As her mother's health has declined, these thrice-weekly visits have hardened into tedious obligation for her and for the kids, too. Parkinson's disease has disabled her mother to the extent that she now requires twenty-four hour care. On good days, Sheila understands her desire to remain in her own home. On bad ones, she grits her teeth with resolve. *If this is what Mom wants, I'm the one who has to make it happen. And making it happen is like running an exclusive nursing home for one.* Sheila is the chief administrator, overseeing quality control and the hiring and firing of the caregivers. Over the years, these employees have evolved from the licensed practical nurses they really couldn't afford, to cleaning women with no medical training but tons of warmth and common sense. The job is hard but the pay exceeds what they'd make housekeeping. It's three days on and two off. Two or three women rotate the schedule, and Sheila tries to be present for the changing of the guard, to dispense paychecks, and deal with whatever issues have arisen.

Louada is Mom's favorite caregiver. She's an attractive African American whose strength matches her size. "Mz. R.'s doing fine," she assures Sheila. "But those people she sees put the fright in her. It makes my hair stand up when she screams at them." Sheila reminds herself to call the doctors about adjusting the meds. "And, we need stronger bed rails, the front door won't shut tight, and the toilet in your ma's bathroom runs all the time." Louada checks to see if Sheila has heard. She nods, nerves tightening as the to-do list grows. Moving through the ideal kitchen of the fifties, she wonders when it was her childhood home became such a time capsule. Crossing the speckled linoleum floor to a tired aqua hall, she spies her mother hunched sideways in her favorite chair. Over time, it has grown enormous as her mother's size has diminished with age and disease.

"Hi, Mom!"

"Honey, where've you been? Did you see that little girl?"

"Allie? She's right here." Sheila brings her daughter forward.

"No! The one who keeps tearing around the house, I have to call the police but Louada won't let me. She isn't nice, she won't take me to the bathroom, and she..."

"First, Mom, let's visit. Would you like some tea?"

"No. Where's my grandson? Chase!" Her voice is screechy thin.

The little boy appears. He's been roaming the house, looking for the girl. "If I find her, Grandma, I'll get her with my slingshot!"

Both children approach their grandmother for the kisses they know are mandatory. She loves them deeply and there was a time when they loved her back without hesitation. That was when she shook less and smiled more. Now Grandma's wheelchair, her jumpy cold hands, and rigid body are scary. Hating to see their affection growing distant, Sheila insists they always give their Granny a hug and kiss. If they were to refuse, it would shatter what's left of her mother's self-esteem.

After their last visit, she and the children had discussed the changes they were seeing in Grandma. Sheila wasn't sure they'd understood. Now, when she sees each plant a kiss on her mom's withered cheek, she prays, *Thank you, Lord*, all the while hoping she's not putting them through any trauma. As mother and daughter chat, the grandkids entertain Wookie with a game of hide and seek.

"Dan called; he's back from a trade show so he and the boys might come to visit on Sunday," her mother says.

"Great." Sheila means it. She loves her older brother as a relative and likes him as a friend. The fact that he lives two hours away and is unable to participate in much of the hands-on care for their mom is not an issue. He's plenty busy as a single parent raising two teenagers. Besides, she's nearby, and isn't it usually the daughter who does these things anyway?

The visit is going well; her mother seems more alert than usual. After a while, Sheila excuses herself to check on the state of the house, her mother's clothes and grocery needs.

Louada, having overheard the earlier complaint, begins her defense. "I didn't do anything wrong. We were up all night, having to use the toilet, and every time she sat on it, nothing happened. So all I said was, 'let's wait and see if you really need to go.'"

"I understand," Sheila assures her. There are two sides to this ongoing story.

When such a scenario first played itself out, Sheila would over-react. Over time, she's learned to listen to both parties then trust her instincts. The caregiver's job is the hardest she could ever imagine. It's lifting her mother's dead weight up and down, moving her from one room to the other, to the bathroom and back again, cooking meal after meal and feeding every bite to her so she won't choke. At what point does the monotony and stress become too much? She wishes she knew. But just as the caregivers have their side, so does her mom. The humiliation of having to be dressed, cleaned, wiped, and fed is more than any once beautiful, refined woman can bear.

Privately, Sheila asks her mom what she meant earlier.

"I just want her to take me to the washroom when I have to go."

"That's fair," Sheila notes.

"And call the police to arrest that horrid girl," her mother adds.

"I'll speak to Louada about more visits to the bathroom. But Mom, you know sometimes your medicine makes you see things that aren't there, right?"

"Maybe, but this was real, as real as you standing there. Oh, I hate this! I'm not me any longer. I'm just a shell of the person I was." Sheila rushes to her mother and the two women rock each other as they work through feelings of mutual loss and anger.

The visit concludes, and Allie and Chase, so eager to leave, run to the car. Their mother buckles them in, lingering to catch Louada as she comes out to walk Wookie.

"You handled Mom's hallucinations well. Thanks for not letting her call the police. We don't need them searching for an invisible girl!" The nurse laughs. "And, unfortunately, with her illness, Mom's not always sure when she needs the bathroom, so it's best to take her whenever she asks. I know it's hard, but she's the one who pays you, not I." This last part, Sheila has learned, goes a long way in maintaining the caregivers' respect for their patient. Louada nods, vowing to do her best. Sheila knows she will.

As they drive off, the daughter pays silent homage to her mother. Even into her sixties, Dora Ronson could draw stares. Her face, with its Nicole Kidman nose and Bette Davis eyes, portrayed an alluring mix of intelligence and high spirits. Chic in glamorous hats and stylish outfits, she'd created a million-dollar look from the sale racks at Saks. Yes, her mother had more style than most women dream of. Although she struggles to maintain it, it's impossible for her to resemble the magnificent person she once was, and she detests the creature she's become.

Sheila remembers the diagnosis of Parkinson's disease coming shortly after her mother's seventieth birthday. "I'll do anything to lick this," she had sworn. So with good doctors, medicine, and sheer strength of will, Mom maintained the status quo for five years. But eventually, she came to realize that no one licks Parkinson's, and as stronger doses of medication are unable to combat the weight loss, muscle dysfunction, and difficulty swallowing, blinking, speaking, even, smiling, the person she once was has started to go.

Sheila feels she's already accompanied her mother through the five stages of death, going through denial, anger, bargaining, depression, and, now, mournful acceptance of the infirmity. *My confidante, greatest fan, and best friend are gone and in their place is a frail invalid who needs me to be the mom.* This thinking makes the anger she felt toward her mother earlier in the day seem shallow and selfish. She parks her car in the garage and helps Allie and Chase out of their safety seats. As she does, she hugs each, finding rapture in the one role she loves.

Charles arrives home to find his wife putting the finishing touches on their favorite last-minute supper, Kraft Macaroni and Cheese and smoked sausage. Sheila smiles to see her husband's thick, black curls blown every which way from the wind. It adds to the boyishness of his short, stocky frame. She leaves the stove to give him a flirty French kiss and a squeeze on the buns. *All these years I've played this part. Will I ever feel it? What about you, Charles? Why do you hold back so, always making me be the one to flow into you? Where's your passion? Maybe you don't feel it either. Wouldn't that be a bitch if, all these years, I've been doing this not to hurt you and you've been doing the same? I'll have to ponder that sometime, just not now.* Dismissing the thought, she calls her family to dinner.

Sheila's tired to the bone. It's been a long day after an almost sleepless night. *Was it really yesterday when all that occurred? Then there was the drive home and the visit to Mom's.* Wanting dinner to be fun, she strains to maintain a lively repartee. Charles mostly listens though, and Sheila feels frustrated that, as usual, she is the one making the effort.

As the meal concludes little Renatta and Colby from next door invite Allie and Chase to spend the last hour of daylight outside. Sheila accompanies them, reminded of her own childhood in the then-wide-open spaces of Milwaukee's brand-new suburbs. At dusk, she and her friends would roam free in the young neighborhoods. They'd search for arrowheads in their backyard cornfield, and pretend to be pioneers or wild horses in the soon-to-be-bulldozed woods.

Now Allie and Chase's adventures are confined to the crowded blocks of an aging suburb, where every square inch seems built upon or paved over. *Does the evening beckon to them with the same promise of freedom it held for me? Freedom, such a faraway place!* During these last thoughts, darkness has conquered the summer dusk. Renatta and Colby scamper home, and she and the kids go inside to find Charles in the family room. This is Sheila's favorite place in the whole house. The co-mingling of books with action heroes and Barbie furniture always warms her heart. Here, Allie and Chase spend the last minutes of their day stowing away their toys. As she helps, she looks at their father, gazing intently at the TV. *He's so serene and centered; things don't trouble him the way they do me. He's calmed me, tamed what he used to call my wild and reckless side. That's good, I guess.*

When the ten o'clock news concludes, Charles rises and turns off the TV; time for bed. The ritual of everyone sharing the same bedtime is the product of Sheila working full time. Being gone so much, she craves every second she can spend with her children, and they yearn to be with her too. If gleaning more time together means letting them stay up until Mommy and Daddy go to bed, so be it. Tonight, Allie and Chase stretch their bedtime preparations to the limit. By the time they settle down, Mom and Dad are numb with fatigue. In bed, they chat lazily, then with conviction, about getting the house ready to be sold. What could be intimate snuggle time becomes a meeting of the board. *And I let this happen, not just this night, but every night. Why?* The question gnaws at her consciousness until she enters shallow sleep.

At 2:30 AM, she awakens abruptly. *Right on schedule,* she thinks, looking at the clock radio. *When did this habit begin?* No, she's not going to lie here waiting for her anxiety to confront her, and no, she won't get up and expend it with a flurry of memos to her staff. Instead, she finds her way to the bathroom to locate the sleeping pills she'd have traded her soul for the night before. Taking one, make that two, pills from the bottle, Sheila gulps them down with water. Next, she pads downstairs to the liquor cabinet to survey the selection. Since she does this often, her beverage choice is based on whatever will be least missed. She takes two stiff belts of Tangueray. Its warmth relaxes her, and the fogginess it induces helps to seal out what's really bothering her. There's also the effect the booze has as

Melissa McDaniel

it mingles with the pills, promoting a thick, "it-doesn't-matter-anyway" feeling. *Yep, here it comes,* Sheila thinks as she returns to bed, next to the sleeping husband who hasn't a clue.

CHAPTER 3
Powerful Feelings

"It's after seven, better get up, see you tonight, hon!" Charles calls upstairs before heading out to catch the 7:10 commuter train.

Sheila makes her way to the medicine cabinet, *only Excedrin can dent this headache.* Then it's down to the kitchen for, as Dolly Parton would say, her cup of ambition. Two heaping spoonfuls of Taster's Choice go into a mug of water. Popping it into the microwave, she thinks, *I could stay home. There are women, (and guys too) who would take time off to plan how to use their newly acquired knowledge. Yeah, right! When did I become such a diva? But just this once, couldn't I move more slowly into harried reality? Maybe spend a whole day doing kiddie things?* It's starting to sound good when Sheila realizes it is Friday, the day of the all-important cabinet meeting. It's critical to her department's visibility, and only she is allowed to attend.

"Shhhhit!" she hisses, gears kicking into overdrive. In seconds, it's business as usual. The boiling brew she removes from the microwave is cut with cold water and consumed in gulps. Then upstairs she bounds to wake Allie and Chase. The shower is next. As she finishes her lather-up, there is combative chatter on the other side of the curtain. Wrapped in a towel, Sheila sneaks out to surprise her little ones. "Whose munchkins do I have here?" her wicked witch voice demands. Screams and giggles pierce the air. "Hey, how about a picnic when I come home for lunch? Then Amy, the student helper you like so well, can take you to the beach when I go back to work."

"Yippee!" they exclaim, and Sheila wonders if she ever was so exuberant.

"O.K., we'll do that. Now let's dress fast! Who can be ready first?" All three scamper in different directions. Sheila, certain she'll be dead last, surveys her crowded closet. *Does owning too many clothes really mean a person feels unloved? Why I crave these lifeless pieces of cloth I don't know, but buying them does seem to nourish something inside. Thank God for resale shops! Without them, I'd be broke or incredibly frustrated.* The Liz Claiborne suit she chooses may be on its second or third generation of ownership, but its "don't-mess-with-me" style has seen her through many a tough meeting. Pulling her hair up also conveys a sense of power. To that, she adds gold earrings and enough makeup to set off her eyes.

Chase and Allie slam into her simultaneously. "We have a tie in the speediest dresser contest. Wow! You two look great in your camp shirts, and you made excellent choices on what shorts to wear." A fan of Maria Montessori, Sheila believes children should make their own clothing choices. It's probably a backlash to her own mother's dictatorship over what her little Sissy could and couldn't wear.

Next comes breakfast. This meal, on weekdays, is a study in efficiency. Allie and Chase choose their cereal and pour it into bowls. To add milk, they use a duck pitcher that pours it through its mouth.

"Look! He's barfing!" Chase laughs.

"That's nasty!" older sister scolds. "Yeah Mommy! Honeydew's my favorite!" Allie makes a happy face smile as Sheila sets a bowl of freshly cut melon on the table. All three down their Frosted Flakes in contented silence, Mommy, guilty about the sugar overload guides a chunk of cantaloupe toward Chase's mouth. Allie knows she's next so she grabs a piece before Mommy does that to her.

Beeeeep! The camp mini-van announces its arrival, and Sheila herds her campers down the sidewalk. Mega-hugs later, Allie and Chase are on board with their respective pals. In four hours, they'll be delivered back to her with new adventures to tell, but now she must make haste.

"Dishes, you can wait!" She slams the kitchen door and hustles off to work.

Ninety minutes later, she emerges from the cabinet meeting grateful the session was more relaxed than usual. Even the higher-ups seem intoxicated by the midsummer weather, but come autumn, reality will set in, heavy with the demands of a new academic year. Sheila loves the fall, but she faces it with mixed emotions. It means her community relations office will be expected to perform at a perfect (albeit fevered) pitch. Labor-intensive town-and-gown initiatives as well as a national media campaign await the attention of her already overworked staff.

As she enters her building, Quincy and Samantha — her right and left arms — warm her with their smiles. These two women are as much a part of Sheila's life as Charles. Their skills in keeping the details of the department afloat are matched only by the emotional support they provide. Sheila has no doubt that she loves them.

"Hi, guys! How's it going?"

"Great! Not even a little glitch this time." Sam informs her.

Quincy adds, "People leave us alone when they know you're gone, so maybe you could go away more often?"

"I'll keep my bags packed!" She opens the door to her office and cringes at the papers overflowing her in-box. Even more will be in her e-mail. At least there are no appointments on her calendar. This should be a quieter day than most.

By her desk is a window with a view of Lake Michigan. The beach is covered with, what Sheila calls "sun people." *Do you ever work? What do you know that I don't?* She frowns, eyes moving from one hard body to the next. The paunchy, yet muscular frame of someone in his middle years catches her eye. *Earl,* the name beckons seductively from a place where things are best left alone. *Oh please! This can't happen every time I'm reminded of the man.* She sits, eyes fixed on the stranger. *How can I rid myself, my life, of this stupid infatuation?*

Diffuse it. Her bossy inner voice is whispering. *Acknowledge it, deal with it, and take away its power.* She waits patiently as her mind and her heart come to terms with a plan. Her brain says it could work. Her heart, not so sure, says it's at least worth a try. Sheila pulls out the roster of attendees from her conference materials, picks up the phone, and eleven touch-tones later, she's ringing Earl's direct line.

Melissa McDaniel

"Earl Langley," the baritone voice melts Sheila's resolve. It waits patiently for a response as she agonizes over her message. In her haste to rid herself of the problem, she'd given no consideration to the text. "Hi, Earl, this is Sheila Branford, from..."

A low chuckle interrupts. "I know where you're from, Miss Sheila."

"Miss Sheila," how Southern! Then she remembers why she's calling. To gain control of the conversation, she inquires, "How was your flight home?"

"Safe, that's the best kind. I did see an awesome orange and blue sunset. It made me think how great it is to be alive."

"Mmmm, I've seen some of those," Sheila says, noticing Earl's use of good grammar with only a hint of a drawl. *He sure can switch it on and off!* Enough stalling, with a deep breath, she jumps into the reason for her call. "Earl, you know the other night I kind of disappeared?"

"Really?" he's not about to help her with this.

"Yes, I decided not to join everyone at the hot tub because," *there's no socially correct way to put this*, "well, because I was heated up too much already. Do you know what I'm saying?"

"Yes, I do, blossom. Those were powerful feelings moving between us." He pauses to see where Sheila will take this.

"Exactly, that's why I left. I'm married, happily married," she lies.

"I understand, but that doesn't mean we can't be friends."

Here it is! This is what I wanted all along.

He continues, "Maybe the next time I get up your way, I could drop by, see your shop, meet your staff," Earl's voice trails off.

"Great!" she agrees too quickly. "Just let me know when." Suddenly self-conscious, she wants to end the conversation. "Well, I'm sure you're busy so I'll let you go. Thanks for understanding about the other night. You're a class act."

"No, darlin', you are."

They exchange good-byes and click off. Sheila takes a deep breath and looks out at the beach. The man with the paunch is gone, as is the threat Earl had posed to her psyche. *I handled that just right. Truth is always best.*

Not ready to let go of the conversation, she recreates it word for word.

"Those were powerful feelings moving between us." *He put that well. This ego fix should carry me for some time.* She stashes Earl's words and the memory of their encounter in the keepsake corner of her brain. There they'll reside like a fine set of books, enjoyed, and given a place of honor on the top shelf. With this done, Sheila doesn't think of Earl again, not until his "personal and confidential" note arrives three days later.

CHAPTER 4
Psych 101

Professional words with provocative undertones. Between the lines, Earl is a man wishing he hadn't had to settle for a professional relationship. In a postscript, he writes, *"I'll respect your wishes and corral the feelings you've stirred in me. But should your situation ever change, please make me the first to know. In the meantime, a professional liaison can, and will, exist between us. I'm an e-mail away."*

Earl gets no reply. Instead, Sheila does diligence to forget her Southern gentleman as she spins from work, to home, to outside activities. Her life is a spinning wheel of obligation. The instant one spin is completed, another begins. There's a benefit to all the spinning; it consumes time, and without time, Sheila cannot think. Introspection is a luxury to be denied when there are budgets to do, employees to manage, a mother to look after, and a house to sell.

"If we can make it to Christmas, we'll be home free," she tells Charles. "Once we sell this house, and move into the new one, we'll be able to relax." Things seem more doable when they're streamlined into a fast-forward manner.

The house sells quickly and as the December moving date approaches, Sheila confides in Samantha Scott, "It'd be easier to move across the country, moving ten minutes away doesn't provide enough incentive to throw things away. Lately, I've become a major pack rat. I have trouble parting with the most insignificant things!"

"I know what you mean," Sam commiserates. "My husband calls it *DPB*: dreaded possession buildup! Why we do it requires a review of Psych 101. Good luck, and before you throw anything out, let me look at it first! Just kidding, I've been there, done that, then I got therapy."

Sam's comment about therapy hits home in the midst of Sheila's moving day mess. A scrawny, little man from the moving company, having just dragged himself upstairs to confront yet another carton of Sheila's possessions, confronts her. "Ma'am, you got too much stuff."

Who are you to criticize me? Do you have a clue how needy I am? Do you know all this stuff is a reaction to some quiet, no, some raging desperation? Do you? Well, do you? No, I thought not! That's what Sheila would like to say; instead, she sarcastically thanks the little man for his observation, and turns to fill another carton, regarding each item in a new and harsher light. As the physical manifestation of what's wrong, she may never have enough. She works on in angry silence as the small movements of her packing propel a greater movement within.

Self-realization takes time to crystallize. Until it's ready to announce itself, it can be ignored without much consequence. But when it's ready, it demands a prominent place one's persona. This is what's happening to Sheila. The sad little man has forced her to face the fact that she is truly miserable. How long has she used the accumulation of things to counter the anguish within? She's not sure, but she knows she's every bit as empty as her silent outburst had proclaimed. *Something is wrong with my life. It's like a fever, burning its way into my consciousness; an infection I must treat before it consumes me. In time, I'll have to deal with it. But right now, I just have to get us moved.*

CHAPTER 5
Christmas

The night of their move, Sheila unpacks cartons until dawn. It's December twentieth and she has to make enough order for Christmas to emerge from the chaos. In October, she'd purchased and wrapped Allie, Chase, and Charles's presents. November had her taking her mother shopping for the thirty-some gifts she insists on giving to friends and relatives. For over ten years, she's preserved her mother's gift giving traditions, taking her shopping, buying the presents, wrapping them, and orchestrating the occasions at which they are to be distributed.

"Oh, Mz. R, this is too much for Sissy! You expect too much from her," was Louada's observation during one of their shopping expeditions. They were in a TJ Maxx store. Chase, indignant at being confined to the child's seat of the shopping cart, was trying to escape. Allie, ensconced inside the cart amid clocks, toys, kitchenware, blouses, silk scarves, and men's ties, was also irate.

"We only need a few more presents, and, no, I won't consider giving money or gift certificates. They're too impersonal." From her wheelchair, Dora Ronson had angrily refuted her daughter's suggestion that cash might be welcomed by relatives who were tired of getting things they didn't need or want. The quest had continued with another shopping expedition and two lunchtime errands for the already ragged Sheila. Finally, it's her turn. Cookies get baked with the help of willing little hands, their tree is decorated, and four stockings hang from the mantle of the brand new fireplace.

SLOW DANCE

As Christmas Day concludes, Sheila collapses and reviews her efforts. She'd overseen a festive Christmas Eve for her mother and the grandkids before going to church with Charles's parents and back to their apartment for more presents. In the morning, they'd opened gifts from Santa in their new home, returned to her mom's for early dinner with her brother, then over to the in-laws for another dinner with that side of the family. Somewhere between the move and all this, she'd staged a tea for Mom's neighbors and a luncheon for the caregivers. Along the way, she'd wondered if anyone realized how much behind the scene work had to occur to keep it all going. Still stewing, she retires and succumbs to sleep until 2:30 AM when she's roused by the discontent that has been stalking her all fall. *I might as well get this over with.* Since the thinking she's about to do requires the breadth of all outdoors, she rises and pads to the utility room to don the clothes usually used for shoveling her mother's driveway or playing in the snow with Allie and Chase. Layered against the cold, she heads outside and down the stairs that lead to the moon-drenched beach. There she's greeted by the spectacle of a glowing white canyon of ice, the product of waves incessantly pounding the frozen beach. It's breathtaking, but full of danger, so Sheila opts to study it from the base of the stairs. After brushing a foot of white powder from the last step, she sits, and waits for her inner voice to speak first.

O.K., so you're finally ready to admit you're unhappy — no, not unhappy, you're miserable. Something is horribly wrong and if you don't fix it, you'll surely get sick. All that positive mental attitude crap hasn't been working for years. You've run yourself ragged; achieving a life you neither needed nor wanted. And what you do need, you don't get from the nice, but passive man, you married.

Sheila shivers and it's not from the cold. This honesty is leading her to the edge of something too horrific to contemplate, let alone do. Stalling for time, she scuffs at the snow with her boot. The woman of action is paralyzed with indecision and fear. In the distance, she sees a luminescent ice flow bobbing on liquid black. It seems gloriously free as it rides the waves, but it isn't free at all. It must go where it's pushed. It has no choice but to endure the ride.

"Nor do I have a choice!"

The proclamation is uttered aloud by the little girl who, for years, was conditioned to put the feelings of others first. "It's a done deed.

I'm married, with two precious children, a career, and a sick mother. I have no choice but to endure so no one else will be hurt." It's the obedient child's utter dread of hurting others that tricks Sheila into believing more is right with her world than wrong. "What I must do is rally my forces to find happiness in my here and now. 'Gentler, sweeter, kinder' will be my battle cry; I'll be less the efficient machine, and more the caring daughter and wife. First thing I'll do is have Mom over for a nice lunch. It will bring us closer when she sees how many of her ideas I used in decorating this house. Yes, that's what I'll do and I'll invite one of her old school chums to make it extra fun."

In accordance with this gentler, sweeter, kinder campaign, the very next Sunday, the dutiful daughter drives her mother and Louada to her new home for a luncheon with Miss Worthy, a devout Christian Scientist. Eighty-one-year-old Miss W, as she likes to be called by younger generations, hops from her car and almost skips to the house, making Sheila grieve for her Parkinson's ravaged mother. *Is this living proof that faith and positive attitude can directly impact one's health?* Sheila dives further into this thought as she wheels her mother into the house. *Mom's always been a nervous, almost angry person. She kept the "glass half-empty" side of her personality hidden from most, but Dad and I saw it. I don't know if Dan had knowledge of her dark side. Mom's so crazy about him she becomes a different person when he's around.*

"Sheila! This is soooo purty!" Louada declares, and Miss W pronounces it the loveliest living room she's ever seen.

Her mother mmm's her own reaction through tight lips. Even the Parkinson's mask doesn't camouflage the severe look on her face. Sheila's shocked. This isn't what she was expecting. Hurt, she watches her mother survey the room, lips pursed and eyes cold as the snow outside.

Miss W understands what's going on; pulling Sheila into the hall, she whispers, "She's jealous, that's what this is! She's jealous of her own daughter! Dora's always been that way."

Struck dumb by the insight, Sheila looks at her mother being wheeled around the room. Louada's praise continues but Mom isn't listening, something fierce is raging behind the Parkinson's mask. Ignoring the drop in temperature, she continues the tour, moving her guests through the study, guest bathroom, dining room, and kitchen.

As the tour concludes, she attempts to pay homage to her mother. "This woman, right here, taught me everything about decorating." When the complement is ignored it hits Sheila that the cold front really means she's become too successful for her mother's liking. *How ironic! The life I chose to please my mother is now the source of her contempt.*

At the luncheon's conclusion, Miss W hugs Sheila. "Don't let her get to you; I never did." With this, the octogenarian bounds to her car, waves, and drives off. Sheila watches until she's out of sight, grateful someone else knows the real Dora Ronson.

After taking her mother and Louada home, Sheila reflects on the afternoon. *What a waste, or maybe not, considering what I just learned. It certainly proved how stupid I was to have allowed her to control my life. Well, I'm in charge now!*

Get real! A stronger, angrier voice challenges from within. *You'll live out this script exactly as she's planned because the pain that looms in a rewrite is too frightening to contemplate.* The voice, she concedes, is right, so with no possibility of change, Sheila seeks refuge in her gentler, sweeter, kinder resolution. The next step in her campaign, she decides, will be to focus on creating the romance she's sure must exist in other marriages.

CHAPTER 6
Danger

In February, Sheila's gentler, sweeter, kinder battle cry reaches a climax when she plans an escape that, she hopes, will save her relationship with Charles. On a Friday afternoon, they leave work early to drive to Chicago for Presidents' weekend. Sheila is delighted with their room at the Sheraton. Its view from high above the Chicago River makes her fantasize about making love next to the window. *We'd feel like we're soaring above the water and through this canyon of buildings! But I'm too sleepy for that; I'd choose a nice nap over any afternoon delight.*

Apparently, Charles isn't in the mood either. He wants to scout out the neighborhood, maybe walk until they find a place for dinner. The thought of a hike makes her weary, but not as much as having to manufacture an interest in making love. *What's wrong with me? I used to enjoy sex. Now, unless I've had a couple glasses of wine, I'd rather go without. But that's thinking for another time. This weekend, I'm going to live in the here and now. It's good I arranged not to have to check on Mom so I can give this weekend my best shot. But God, I'm tired!*

They leave the hotel and walk briskly toward Lake Michigan. *O.K., you great lake, you help couples fall in love all the time. How about this indifferent twosome? Can you make us crazy in love with each other? Will you please, pretty please, make me mad for this man, and him, nuts about me?* But why would the lake honor her wishes here when it ignores them three hours to the north? Sheila's learned to expect nothing more than a pretty backdrop from her lake.

It's all up to her. But she's tired, so tired. She looks at Charles striding several steps ahead. Skipping to catch up, then falling behind again, she realizes her husband doesn't know or maybe doesn't care that he's outpacing his wife. This makes inner Sheila sigh. *Perhaps in another time, another place, especially, another life, you two could be right for each other, but in this life, you have too much inside that wants to come out, and Charles, whether it's intentional or not, makes you hold it in. And you need more than he's inclined to give, like a spontaneous kiss or two arms encircling you from behind. You need too much and he gives too little. You're not attached to one another; there's the rub!* This makes Sheila wince.

"Something wrong?" Charles asks, noticing the strain on her face.

"Oh, I was just thinking." It's a response begging for discussion, but Charles trudges on in silence. The brisk pace does make her feel better, hungry, too. Dinner, at a Navy Pier café, is delicious, but the conversation is sparse. When they do speak; the topics range from the children, Sheila's mom, Charles's parents and the logistics of upcoming activities. It's a board meeting, not a lovers' repast.

Sheila racks her brain for a topic that will trigger some meaningful conversation. She picks one she's been pondering for a while, "Charles, has it ever occurred to you we could sell our house, invest the money, and move away from our high-priced environs to a simpler, more economical place? Then we could find less stressful jobs and have more time for the kids and maybe even each other!"

Her husband sits in silence. *Is he savoring the idea or does he think I'm crazy?* Neither: the accountant in Charles is calculating their net worth and, just as she's done, he's arriving at a figure that's surprisingly high.

"Yeah, I guess so," he says with indifference.

"Yes! We could find a place in the country, something with wide-open spaces for the kids to range around."

"That doesn't appeal to me at all, She, and I'm surprised you'd even think about it. You, Ms. Dynamo, would wither and die in such a place." Her silence makes him think he's getting through so he continues. "What about your mom? And don't you want our children to grow up with the same advantages we had? You want them to go to the best schools possible, don't you?"

Melissa McDaniel

Exhaustion is enveloping Sheila. *He's dug into this lifestyle, plus he'd never give up his partnership at the firm, and I shouldn't expect that of him. It hurts, though, that he brushed off my idea with no thought as to what's going on in my head. It's like he's not interested in me personally. He has no desire to look into my soul.*

And back in the room, Ms. Dynamo has no desire to make love to her husband. "Sorry," she tells Charles, "I planned this to be an evening of torrid sex, but I'm way too tired." She turns over and pretends to be asleep until she really is.

Room darkening shades and the absence of their kiddie wake-up brigade allow Sheila and Charles to sleep gloriously late on Saturday morning. Breakfast in bed is considered, and nixed by both. Charles wants to see Chicago, and Sheila quickly agrees because she's too tired to spend the day making love as she'd originally planned.

The weather, milder than usual, is in the high thirties with only a slight wind. This prompts them to stroll along Michigan Avenue before taking a double-decker bus tour. The beautiful and expensive storefronts are inviting, but Sheila resists. There's no point going in. She never shops in stores like these and she'd be especially uncomfortable with Charles along. Early in their marriage, she'd conditioned herself to be the thrifty wife she knew he wanted. This made her intensely self-conscious about spending money. Even now, when a shopping fix is needed, she only goes to fifty percent off sales or consignment shops. Acquiring things for the least amount of money is the game she plays. Looking in the Neiman Marcus window, she remembers a time, in their first year of marriage, when Charles took her in a similar store and bought her an outfit. She'd worn it, feeling elegant wrapped in its quality. When people complimented her on it, she'd proudly tell them her hubby had given it to her. The continuous reminder of his love had been a wonderful thing, and Sheila has never forgotten that gift.

That was long, long ago, she thinks as they stroll past more stores, yet, even now, if Charles were to pull me into one of these stores and buy me something, anything, my gratitude would abound. He won't though. He loves the cost-effective woman I've become.

She's tired, so tired. Rather than energizing her, the day of fresh air and sightseeing has made her wearier than ever. To rally for dinner, Sheila downs a couple of Excedrin, hoping they will stimulate her. And they do the job well enough to render her a so-so dinner companion. She upholds her part of the conversation as it again focuses on the minutiae of their life, and not at all on their feelings. When they return to their room with stomachs too full, Sheila realizes she hasn't drunk enough to make her feel the least bit sexy. She's bloated and exhausted and wants only to go to sleep.

But wait, this was to be a romantic weekend! Remember gentler, sweeter, kinder?

All right, all right. First I do this. Then he does that. Then I do that, and he does this. Their lovemaking proceeds along these lines. Later, when Sheila recalls the weekend, it's not a romantic interlude she remembers, but a slow, tedious coming to terms with things as they are. For Charles, seeking a deeper relationship with his wife is not part of the equation, nor does he see anything wrong with their frenetic lifestyle. *Must I resign myself to forever running in circles like Allie's gerbil does on its exercise wheel?*

The voice she's been trying so hard to beat back manages to be heard loud and clear. *Even a gerbil stops running when it senses danger.*

Chapter 7
Water Haven Retreat

"You know, honey, it's almost March and we haven't had our winter retreat." Dora Ronson grows silent as she watches her daughter for signs that her hint is taking hold.

"I can't do it Mom; it's too risky going to Water Haven in the dead of winter. I don't like driving for hours across mile upon mile of frozen farmland. Then there's opening the cottage and unloading the car in potentially deep snow." The arguments, she knows, sound weak and selfish to her mother's ears.

"We did it last year just fine, and we had such a good time."

Arrrr! Maybe you had fun. For me, it was hell on wheels, all that *schlepping in and out of groceries, suitcases, the wheelchair, you, and my babies, after first shoveling a driveway buried in two feet of snow.*

"It wasn't that easy, Mom, with the kids and all."

"I know dear, but they're a year older now, more manageable."

And you're a lot worse, Sheila wants to say, but hasn't the heart.

"I'm afraid this may be my last retreat." That her mother said the same words last year doesn't matter. For several years now, Sheila has gone the distance to insure that her mother's memory bank will be full for the time when she cannot create new ones.

"O.K., we'll go," she concedes, and when her inner voice flips out about her giving in she shushes it with *remember gentler, sweeter, kinder…relationships count.*

One week later, she's steering the crowded Seville through snowy farmland. The night above is freckled with stars. "Starlight, star bright, do you see the stars tonight? Let's make a wish!" *My wish is to find happiness in the here and now.*

From the back seat, "I want a — mmmm!" Chase's wish is smothered by big sister's palm.

"Don't tell or it won't come true. Ouch! Mommy, he bit me!"

"O.K., that's enough, kids. Why don't you put on your hand puppets, and do make-believe to some Raffi songs?" Two wee hands become polar bears, and two more are kitties. They bow and swoop with each other in time to the music until the soothing tune makes the puppet masters sleepy. Soon, they've joined Granny and Wookie in a snooze allowing Sheila to trade Raffi for her favorite country music station. She ponders the meaning of a song about second chances as she takes the Water Haven exit.

This is a town she's known since birth. There's Byrd's Drugstore, once the classiest store in town. Next is the movie-theater. It had been a wonderfully dark and cozy place for her dates with Sonny, the first, and maybe, best love she's ever known. A boarded up drive-in restaurant reminds her of the summer she worked as a carhop. *My character crystallized in this town. Why ever did I choose sophistication over simplicity? In doing so, I left something behind to wait for me here. Like Paul Simon says, "The nearer your destination the more you're slip sliding away." But that's the last thing I should think about now.*

"Hey sleepyheads, we're here!" The car lumbers across a wooden bridge onto the ruts of an icy road. Frosty drifts guard the trail. Beyond them, darkness is everywhere. *This would be one hell of a place to get stuck.*

Finally, the Seville's high beams settle on a cedar cottage standing proudly in the snow. *There you are!* it seems to be saying. How she loves this place! It seems to embody all the happiness she's ever known. Thankfully, the wind has blown enough snow off the driveway to make it possible to pull in without shoveling. Sheila puts the car in park, and mercilessly turns on the interior lights. Four waking passengers groan and blink. Wookie is the first to act. She jumps onto Sheila's lap, begging to be free of her confinement. As the door opens, the terrier swan dives into a snowdrift. Soon she's tunneling through the whiteness for the perfect place to pee.

Now, it's Sheila's turn to get out. In firemen's boots and a down-filled parka that makes her look like a stuffed pig, she trudges to the cabin's only door. Thankfully, she has no trouble with the lock. Inside, she switches on a light and ups the thermostat. Outside again, she clears a path through the snow for Allie and Chase to maneuver. Once in the cabin, they race each other to their toy corner. They love playing with their treasures, so new after months of separation. "Stay in your coats until the cabin warms up," she tells them before going out to rescue her mother.

"O.K., Mom, we'll get you inside now, sorry for the delay." Mom nods. Parkinson's disease has taught her how to wait. With the door wide open, Sheila carefully swivels the frail form to the edge of the seat. With one hand in the small of her mother's back and the other holding her arm just above the elbow, she brings her to a standing position. Sheila braces herself, knowing this will be like walking with a life-sized Raggedy Ann.

"All right now," she puts her left arm completely around the thin waist and holds her mother's right hand in her own. "Here we go, Mom, right, left, right," Sheila is trudging but her mother is not.

"Wait waaaaait!" Mom screams.

Sheila stops, "Can you move your feet?"

"I don't think so."

"Let me push the snow out of the way, then you'll be able to move your feet while I do our bear hug grip; that usually works." Her fingers interlocked behind her mother's back, she starts again. "Here we go! Mom! Move your feet!" Nothing happens. She half-carries, half-drags her mother's limp form around the car. To reach the storm door, she must stretch. She can reach it if she holds her mother with one arm. The door swings open as Mom buckles and falls. Lunging to save her, Sheila crashes on the cement step. *Thank God for looking like a stuffed pig!*

She's fine but what about Mom? *Please, Lord. Make her O.K. We're all alone here. Don't let her be hurt.* In Sheila's mind, she's always run with the angels. What else can explain her good fortune in almost everything? Now she needs all the luck those divine beings can muster. In the seconds it takes to crawl to her mom, she experiences fear, anguish, and then anger with herself for thinking she's such a super being she can pull off a weekend like this.

Wookie appears from nowhere to lick her mistress's face. "Mom! Are you O.K.?"

"I think so; nothing hurts."

"Thank God!" Sheila gushes as she hugs the woman on the ground. *Really, I mean it, Lord: thank you.*

Above them, the storm door opens and Allie peeks out to see her granny in the snow, looking as if she's about to make a snow angel. "That was exciting," her granny quips. Both women laugh. Mommy rocks Grandma in her arms and it looks like she's crying.

Not sure what's going on, Allie takes charge. "Mommy it's cold down there, bring Grandma into the house!"

"Yes, sweetie, I'll do that right now." Sheila wishes her daughter's little body could match the size of the woman inside; then the two of them could get Grandma into the house.

"O.K. Mom, this time we'll do it!" Energized with adrenaline, and sounding like a football coach, she makes a plan. "I'll support you from behind with my arms under yours. If you can stand up, great; if not, I'll pull you up the steps." Sheila wonders where all this confidence is coming from. "Up we go." She stands, managing only to raise her mother to a forty-five-degree angle. Mom tries to move her feet but the snow allows no traction. Fortunately, it's so slippery her heels glide smoothly as Sheila drags her to the stairs.

"One, two, three…up!" They ascend one step, then the next, and finally, the third. Years of water skiing, and, more recently, toddler toting are paying off. "Ta da!" Sheila heralds the last heave that hoists her mother into the cabin.

"That was easy," Mom observes.

"Piece of cake!" her daughter lies as she steers her mother into the living room and eases her into a chair. Mom's eyes close as exhaustion sets in. Leaving her to rest; Sheila checks on her little ones. They're engrossed in play so with everything peaceful on the kiddie front, she unpacks the car. It takes seven trips to transfer everything into the cabin, which has become warm enough for all but Wookie to remove their coats and get ready for bed.

The next day is Saturday. It's frigid all day with single-digit temperatures and howling winds that force them to stay inside, playing board games by the fire.

On Sunday morning, the outside thermometer registers a balmy twenty-six degrees. With the sun shining and no wind, it's time for a snow romp! Sheila puts her mother's wheelchair by a window overlooking the yard. The frozen lake provides the perfect backdrop for Mom to watch them enjoy the winter wonderland. They pelt each other with snowballs as Wookie chases from one to the other, attempting to catch the icy spheres. When she does, they hit her muzzle and explode, giving her an adorable white face.

"Wave to Granny," Sheila coaches. Both kids hail their grandma. A wobbly wrist acknowledges the gesture, and on the once-beautiful face, a quivering smile appears.

They roll one huge snowball for the base of a snowman, and two smaller ones for its torso and head. "Now, let's find some pebbles and sticks for the eyes, nose and mouth." Before long, they have a face.

"He needs a hat," Chase observes.

"O.K., but maybe he should be a she if this is the hat we use." Pulling off her hot pink beret, she styles it on the snowperson's head.

"Cool!" Allie loves it. "We'll call her Frostina."

Chase wrinkles his nose. "Snowmen are boys!"

"Tell you what little buddy, the next snowperson we make will be a he. We'll alternate, how's that?"

Chase agrees, so they put the finishing touches, including twig eyelashes, on their creation. Frostina, strong and erect, stares straight at Grandma. Sadly, of the two, the snow woman is in better shape.

With huge appetites, all but Frostina scoot indoors for lunch. It's at the conclusion of this meal that Sheila's mother introduces a topic best left alone.

"Sonny Lawson came to see me yesterday."

"No, Mom, not yesterday, maybe last summer?" Lately her mother's merging past and present.

"No, it was yesterday; we sat and talked in my kitchen. He's sure a cute boy. Whatever happened to you two?"

This has come out of nowhere. Sheila's summer love for both high school and college is often in her thoughts but she'd assumed, for her mother, he was most deliberately forgotten.

"He's as adorable as ever. Such personality! So talented!"

"Loads of personality, tons of talent, but still, he wasn't good enough for me, right, Mom?"

Dora Ronson looks up, shocked by the contempt in her daughter's voice. Whatever is she talking about? She faintly remembers some maneuvering she'd done to pull Sheila from Sonny's reach, but that was for her own good.

"I loved him, Mom! It was the kind of love every mother should pray her daughter will find. What did you see as so wrong with him?" Decades of regret are spilling forth. "Why were you so certain he wasn't right for me?"

Dora returns Sheila's angry stare. How dare her daughter talk to her this way!

"Was he was too provincial for your taste? Was that why you worked your ways to get rid of him?"

Still, her mother sits in cold silence. The Parkinson's has dulled the sharp tongue she used to use to pierce her daughter's convictions.

Sheila understands this, she knows that right now she could make up for all the times she'd wanted to open fire on her mother but hadn't dared. Now, as this woman who controlled her for so long sits, listing sideways, she could barrage her with two decades' worth of swallowed words and choked-back tears. She could lead her mother through the propaganda campaigns she'd waged, first against Sonny, and later, against Ed Willard. But bullying this invalid will fix nothing.

Allie comes in wanting attention. Sheila scoops the little girl into her arms so they can share a love-fest of hugs and kisses. *Lord please,* Sheila prays, *don't let me depend so much on my daughter's love that I keep her from living the life she chooses.*

And yet, something inside her observes, *Allie and Chase already are all you care about in this world. Are you starting to live through them, the way your mom did through you?*

Shhhh! I'll think about that later, right now, I've got to get us packed and on the road before dark.

CHAPTER 8
The Mirror Knows

"Do I really have to do this?" It's a Monday morning in April and Sheila is scowling at her appointment calendar. In March, a very professional T. Earl Langley had called to say he had business in Milwaukee, and when he was there, would she show him her department? She'd agreed, but now, her feet are icy cold. Maybe, she could plead an emergency. *No, he'd see through it. Just get it over with,* she instructs herself as she heads to an appointment across campus.

The meeting runs long and Earl is kept waiting at least half an hour. When Sheila returns, the receptionist meets her at the door, "A perfectly adorable man is here to see you. He smiles like Clark Gable and, oh my, what charm! Just wait until you hear his accent!"

"Really?" Sheila asks, noticing a flush on the woman's neck.

"Yes! I wonder if he's married. My daughter could really go for him."

Sheila smiles, *like mother, like daughter, like me? No, not like me!* She thinks as she deliberately saunters into the lounge where Earl is waiting.

"Hello, blossom!"

What did he call me? With her pulse quickening, she manages, "Hi, I'm sorry to be late, I was across campus. You know how it is."

"Not a problem, your receptionist gave me a tour of the building, then she put me in this glorious room where I could watch the lake, and enjoy the best cup of coffee I've had in a long time."

"O.K. then," she's all business, "Let's go to the conference room where you can meet everyone."

As her entirely female staff comes through the door, Sheila sees the same nanosecond gush that she, herself, experienced upon meeting the handsome Mr. Langley. Even the coolest woman of the group seems to be energized by his good looks and warmth. *Does he get this reaction from all females? Is it his looks? His drawl? His size? His charm? Maybe he gives off strong male pheromones.* Whatever it is, she decides his allure is a good thing. It's the turn off she'll need to get through the day with her fidelity in tact. As the meeting winds down, Earl revs up, entertaining everyone with stories about his own department. Sheila hates to interrupt, but time is growing short. "I'd better conclude this meeting before I lose you all to the Sunshine State! Besides, if Earl's going to catch his plane, we have to leave this instant."

Outside, she steers her guest toward her Seville for a ten-minute drive to a cute Aussie restaurant. There a hostess in khaki shorts, halter-top, and outback hat shows them to a table. Sheila judges Earl's indifference to the attractive young woman to be more shrewd than genuine. *He knows I'm watching.*

Despite her resolve, and without even the benefit of an adult beverage, Sheila relaxes in Earl's presence. Totally professional, he makes no reference to last August. Sheila hears about his experiences buying a new home and counters with anecdotes on her own recent move. Although she talks about her children, there's no mention of Charles. It's none of his business.

"This has been delightful," Sheila realizes that, apart from being with her children, nothing she's done in the past ten months has been so enjoyable.

"Darlin', we could have fun in a cardboard box." Then, fearing he might be misunderstood, he adds, "We're buds; that's all."

Sheila pays the check, hoping it will give her the upper hand, for what, she does not know. And as they approach the airport, she chatters way too much about urban sprawl. Certain the police will insist on a quick farewell, she double parks in the arrival lane outside the Delta terminal.

"Last stop before Florida! Thanks for coming by to meet my staff."

"No, sweet pea, I'm the one to say thank you. I appreciated lunch too. When you come South, I'll return the favor."

"Absolutely," she lies. Avoiding his eyes, she pops open the trunk, and hops from the car. A moment later, Earl is by her side, joking with the skycap who takes his luggage. *He has the capacity to make everyone's day better.* She thinks this while noticing how great he looks in his navy blue suit. *His tanned face seems to glow next to that crisp white shirt. God, he's handsome!*

"Well then, I'm off!" He's cheerfully aloof but Sheila knows better. Offering her hand, she looks defiantly into the teal greens. Earl takes it and raises it to his lips. Kissing it slowly, he looks up, letting the warmth in his eyes melt the ice in hers. The pressure of his lips on the back of her hand is nice, but Sheila is not prepared for the wild sensation that rips through her when he kisses her super-sensitive palm.

"Thanks for everything," he says with one, last, killer smile.

"No problem!" Sheila grins and escapes into the car. Only when she's behind the wheel does she allow herself to stare at Earl's departing form. He disappears but her body continues to revel in the sensation of his kiss. Amid the glow, Sheila wonders if she's letting something important slip away. *Too much stuff is swirling between us to allow the professional friendship I'd envisioned. Instead, we'll be the skittish superficial colleagues we were today. I felt his desire all morning. Did he sense something from me? If he did, it doesn't matter. My behavior communicated what he came here to find out. I proved there's no messing with Sheila Branford!*

For the rest of the day, Sheila moves in a pious glow. And why shouldn't she? She's proven to herself that she can withstand major temptation. When she greets Charles in the evening, her inner being screams, *Please, oh please, grab me, kiss me; show me I mean something to you! You have no idea what I did for you today.*

Unfortunately, the afterglow of her chastity is short-lived. By May, there are daily alerts to hazardous going ahead. This happens in a big way when she and Charles host a dinner for their neighbors. Much of the conversation centers on a couple about to send their young children on a six-week camping trip with their grandparents.

"It's a great way for them to bond with Gammy and Pop-pop," the man smiles with assurance.

"Yes!" his wife concurs, "And we, also, hope it will instill them with a reverence for nature."

"That's true," her husband cuts in, "But we really have another more selfish agenda. It's the opportunity for my lady and me to reconnect romantically. I miss the woman I married!" He pulls her wife closer so he can kiss her cheek and she, in turn, affectionately nuzzles his neck. For a moment, they are the only people in the room.

Sheila observes this in dumb silence. What she'd contribute to the conversation would be too embarrassing to Charles and humiliating to her. She looks at her husband, so intent on cutting his steak. *When did it happen? When did you and I stop being husband and wife?*

Later, doing the dishes, she reflects on her reaction. There's no way I could tolerate Allie and Chase being gone that long. Without them, what would I have? I'd have this house (which I find isolating), my mother (who's draining me dry), my job — no, the job would have me, and I'd have my husband, a man who seems to be emotionally divested of me. Being alone with him is like… being alone!

Wait, are you saying the life you've worked so hard to achieve is nothing without your children?

All I mean is they're the center of my life. Is that so bad?

What's bad is that being the nucleus of your own mother's universe is what got you into this mess. Will you put Allie and Chase through the same ordeal? Will you influence their decisions so the lives they choose will satisfy you too?

Sheila scratches at a glob of baked-on casserole. That inner voice is raising an uneasy truth. Should she once and for all acknowledge it, or push it back as she's always done? *Lord, I keep praying you'll tell me what to do but I don't seem to be getting any answers. Are you letting me mush through this mess as a learning exercise on the way to some profound truth? If so, I don't think I'm smart enough or deep enough to figure it out. Please Lord, won't you please help me fix what's wrong, now, before I do to Allie and Chase what Mom did to me?*

This thinking plagues her all weekend. It even follows her to work on Monday, so much so that she tries to escape it the only way she knows how, by going home to spend her lunch hour with Allie and Chase. After dining on tomato soup and Mrs. Paul's fried clams, the children run outside to pelt each other with bubbles from their bubble blasters. Sheila laughs as she watches them arch and fall when the bubbles hit their marks. From window to window she runs, recording the battle on her camcorder. But when they spy her, they break character and run from sight.

"Gotcha!" she yells through the glass. Turning from the window she's struck by the reality that her posh, white-on-white living room looks cold, almost antiseptic. She remembers decorating it, the entire house for that matter, like she runs her staff meetings. "Efficient" is the only adjective she can find for the décor. It's fresh, new, and frigid in its perfection.

She crosses to a curio closet and studies the treasures within. *I see more of me in here than in this entire room.* Her eyes rest on a Limoges dish that once belonged to her father's mother, a woman she never knew. *What would she make of my discontent? Oh my God! What's that?* The mirror in the back of the curio closet has captured her forty-three-year old reflection in the harsh reality of midday light. Lines she's never before seen are taunting, *Middle aged, middle aged, you are so middle aged!*

Maybe, but I'm as old as I feel and I feel...

Old! The wrinkled reflection interrupts.

I guess I do feel old, and harried and tired. But there's nothing I can do about it. There's no time off for good behavior, just more work.

There's always time off for death.

What's that supposed to mean?

You don't get it do you?

Get what?

That at the end of your life, you're dead, done, gone from this world, how much time do you have before that happens? How will you choose to use it?

What do you mean, choose? Do you see a choice here? I'm expected to live out my days exactly as I'm doing.

The face winces, and an inner voice different from any Sheila has ever heard speaks up. *Before long, Allie and Chase won't want to be your own best buddies. They'll be off running with their peers, and you and Charles will be alone.*

This makes Sheila shiver. *He may want that even less than I do.* She stares at the reflection and it stares back. Neither one is happy with the other so they simultaneously turn away.

The grandfather clock chimes once, time for Sheila to comb her hair, freshen her make-up, and go outside with Mara to say good-bye to her children until suppertime. Although the career woman returns to her office, her spirit stays behind to commiserate with the visage in the curio cabinet.

CHAPTER 9
The Cat In The Hat

By July, Sheila's making nightly visits to the beach. On this particular night she's down there searching the sky for answers. As usual, the stars are diluted by the lights of Milwaukee. Feeling sorry for them, she lowers her gaze to the horizon. *The nights are blacker and the stars more visible the farther one gets from here. Even I am brighter the farther away I get.* She follows the lake into infinity, seeking the jubilant person she once was.

Long ago, I let others write my story. Now, I'm living the consequences, and this script, so unlike the real me, is more like an out-of-body experience. Is this the quiet desperation Thoreau warned me about? Yes, Mr. Thoreau, my life truly is frittered away by detail.

Gazing at her lake again, she silently addresses it. *Seldom are you so still. Your serenity is soothing, inviting even. How hard is it for a good swimmer to drown? With such cold water, it can't be that difficult. I could walk out until it's over my head and start swimming toward Michigan. Hypothermia would do the rest.* Seconds pass, the lake is daring her to do it. *Wouldn't it be easier for Charles to have a wife who dies rather than one who walks out?* More seconds, the lake is waiting.

Easier for Charles, but horrible for Allie and Chase! No, I would never do that to them. Still, is there no end in sight? Will it always be too much detail and too little love? How else can I get the frantic monotony to stop?

The lake beckons again. "No! This is not the answer I seek!" she tells herself firmly. With strange new resolve, Sheila turns her back on the promise of ultimate simplification and returns to bed. At 6:00 AM, she rises to drive to the same meeting that had fanned her discontent twelve months earlier. *No more escapist thoughts for me! I'm a being of action, not reaction. If something can be done about my situation I'll know it when I see it.*

It's at the opening session that Sheila looks for — and finds — her seemingly professional friend. He seems to be searching the room for her, too. When Earl finds her, the killer smile she was so suspicious of the year before spreads across his face. He cuts through a circle of colleagues, easing one right, another left, until he reaches her.

"Miss Sheila!" he pulls her to him in an embrace that is not at all professional and the kiss he places on her cheek reminds her of oral sex. Grudgingly, they pull away, but stand too closely, feigning interest in the quality of each other's travels. "And how's your staff?" Earl inquires.

"They're great. Every one of them wants to be remembered to you. You made quite an impression!" Sheila smiles as she tells herself *either I make a break for home right now, or wake up with this man tomorrow.* No amount of rational thinking can counter what's going on between her legs, and the real surprise is her total admission that she wants, no, needs Earl this very night.

Later, when she reflects on the two-second thought process that convinces her to bed Earl she'll realize the inner Sheila knew the outcome all along. While her guilt-ridden conscience had been struggling with the sin of it, her wiser sub-conscience understood what had to be. At this moment, however, all she knows is she's moving in one direction, and she's actually glad. For once, she'll write her own script.

Dinner is served at a nearby roadhouse. During the meal, Sheila and Earl's non-verbal foreplay intensifies. She hasn't a clue as to what's come over her she's operating on desire alone. The risk of being found out, and the fear of what it might do to her, doesn't hold her back. Her body burns with a need that's obliterating rational thought. When Earl mouths, "Want to go back?" she nods. Casually, they stand. With a growing sense of embarrassment, Sheila banters with colleagues as she moves toward the door. Earl is working the room from the opposite side. No one knows or cares what they're up to.

Melissa McDaniel

A steamy silence accompanies them to the lodge. Earl parks the car, and Sheila freezes in fear. Inside her head is the distant whir of a premonition. What this one is saying she doesn't know, but she acknowledges its presence with frightened animal eyes. Earl smiles sympathetically and pulls her hands onto his lap. They rest on something hard. Feeling it sends a thrill through her body. In a heartbeat, she's in his arms, and after several moments of wet, sucking kisses, their bodies demand more. By now, Sheila is all surrender, and in it, she takes charge.

"Let's go!" she says sliding to her side of the car and opening the door.

"Now, wait a minute, blossom. This is your call, if you want to think about it, I'll understand." Sheila can't believe what she's hearing. *Is this a Southern gentleman thing?*

"Get out of the car!" she commands.

Fueled by the promise of what's to come, Earl follows directions, moving as swiftly as his condition will allow. Sheila waits on the sidewalk, the same place where she'd ditched him the year before. Arms around each other, they trudge as one toward the lodge. Sheila wants to go to her room, Earl's buddies are next to his and she's afraid of being seen. He doesn't care; he just wants a room, fast.

The television in her room blasts tunes from CMT, and a lamp burns brightly to trick would-be burglars. Sheila decides to leave it all on, music and light should provide a great backdrop for what's to come. When they kiss, it's a kiss that seals their fate, for after it, nothing other than sex will suffice. She starts to undress, then realizes she's wearing less-than-sexy underwear. *Too late now!* She unbuttons her shirt to expose a sensible white bra. Earl watches, oblivious to its practicality. Her shorts fall from her hips, revealing French-cut cotton undies. Unaware of himself, Earl licks his lips. Encouraged, Sheila unhooks her bra. Her breasts spill out and Earl gasps, "Whoa! My fantasies were good but not this good."

By now, he's naked. Sheila looks and glances away, blushing. Just as she's wondering what to do next a lightning bolt from nowhere envelops her as hands that have craved her body for too long pull off the undies. Her thighs, hips, and belly all feel their fire. One hand holds her breast and tweaks her nipple while the other circles its way down her body and up again. Big, supple fingers find a place that's soft and surprisingly wet. Within seconds, she feels a magic current gaining strength. It grows and grows until the circuit is completed and she comes with supernova intensity. Paralyzed with sensation, Sheila has only one thought, *passion and skill run deep in this man!*

Having witnessed Sheila's exquisite climax, Earl draws back and looks at her as if he's seeing her for the first time.

"Miss Sheila, you're what I've always wanted!" He takes her hands and holds them over her head, letting go of one long enough to guide him into her. She does her part, and he groans approval. Eyes closed, Earl's in that zone in which man becomes slave to one drive alone. He pumps hard then stops as something shoots through him, transforming his expression to an almost painful one. His brows furrow and his mouth grimaces, but it isn't pain. It's the ecstasy he was seeking. He collapses, nestling his face between her breasts. Sheila breathes in the fragrance of the chestnut curls, and contemplates what to say.

"Wow!" is the best she can do.

"Mmmmm" is Earl's empathetic reply. He kisses her neck as she sleepily laps up the attention.

"Tell me about Sheila!"

"Huh?" She resents the assignment. To talk about Sheila means bringing up her family, her children, and the husband on whom she's cheating. Besides, the more impersonal they are, the less anyone will be hurt.

"What makes Sheila tick?"

His persistence is annoying, but she makes an attempt. "O.K., if I must. I grew up in a middle-class suburb of Milwaukee. My father is deceased, my mom's an invalid, and I have a nice brother who has two sons. The best things in my life are my precious children, Allie and Chase." She cannot bear to speak of their daddy. Sick with shame, she grows silent as everything about her turns inward.

Earl senses this, so without skipping a beat, he launches into his own, abbreviated, autobiography. Born in Flowery Branch, Georgia, he grew up the eldest of two boys in a working-class family. In high school, he'd had the good fortune to excel in football, baseball, and track. This earned him a scholarship to the university where he met his first and last wife. They had one son and divorced after eight years.

As Earl introduces his friends in the next chapter of his life story, Sheila wonders if all of his women get treated to this oral history. Really though, she's impressed that this hulk of a man speaks with such sentiment about his buddies. *Is it a Southern thing, or is it Earl?* She's not sure, but what she does know is when he describes his buds, his energy level rises, making him positively irresistible. In the middle of a depiction of crazy Sean Murphy, she can wait no longer. While he's talking about Murph and a pair of twins in the Bahamas, she begins again. Earl knows what's coming and grows quiet, letting Sheila transport him someplace wonderful. And so it goes with each new session of lovemaking. Nights like these bring people real close, real fast. At dawn, Sheila and Earl pry themselves away from the passion; but throughout the day, its memory keeps them in a state of mutual arousal.

At one point, Earl slips her a note, proposing an evening walk by the lake, "to talk." I'd rather our lovemaking speaks for itself. What could talking do, other than move us to another level? And really, there can be no other level. Despite this, she nods the affirmative to his querying eyes.

She's happy. God, she's happy! It's the sort of happiness she'd known long ago, when she was a different person. How she's missed that woman! Sheila never thought she'd see her again, but today she's catching glimpses of her. Finally, dusk announces their rendezvous time. Waiting for Earl on the path to a pond, Sheila tries to be realistic about what's happening. *This isn't good. I shouldn't be doing this. Will I be able to stop before things go too far? Can I box him up like "The Cat in the Hat" and wheel him off before Charles finds out?*

Earl's arms encircle her from behind. His body leans into hers, and as he lovingly kisses her neck, Sheila wonders how he knows this is what she's always wanted from a man. Still lingering, however, is the worrisome image of boxing up Earl like *"The Cat in the Hat."* Turning, she looks at her cat. His eyes seem to be chanting, "It's fun to have fun but you have to know how!" *If only he weren't so delightful, so handsome, and so right here! But maybe he's not so available. Although he's single, he's too adorable not to hold a place in some woman's heart.*

"Tell me about the women in your life."

Earl, in a playful, kissing mood, is caught off guard. Buying time, he steers Sheila down the path. "Other women? Hell, I don't want anyone but you."

"Surely your years of bachelorhood have rendered some close relationships."

"O.K., let's see, since my divorce, there have been two. One was nice, but her company transferred her to another state, where she met and married her boss. The other, well, let's just say she was nothing like you. You know the Garth Brooks song, 'Unanswered Prayers'? She was one of those; I owe him big time."

"Was she smart, fun, pretty?"

"She thought so. Look, Blossom, if I were in a relationship with either of those gals right now, I'd end it in a heartbeat. If you were available, I'd want you for all time. You know, don't you, I'm up to my eyeballs in love with you?"

"And I'm right there with you."

Shocked by what just came out of her mouth, Sheila's heart checks her brain for agreement. Begrudgingly it's given. *Yes, you do love him. He's perfect for you! What a tragedy,* her heart moans, *he's sixteen years too late. It doesn't matter,* her brain interrupts. *Your mom would have done him in too. What matters now is keeping this under control. Keep it light. Don't let this love thing carry you away. There's no future in it.*

Earl is ebullient. Hearing she loves him releases all inhibition. Emotion flows from the man, and Sheila is a thirsty recipient. Within seconds, an almost supernatural bond joins them together. But for the mosquitoes, they could sit under the stars all night. Instead they return to Sheila's room where the bond grows even stronger.

The exhilaration of what she's feeling wakes Sheila at dawn. *Oh my God! Is this what it's like to really love a man? What an enormous thing I've been missing! The worry, now, is how do I live without it? By tonight, this passion will have to be beaten back and caged. Don't think about that now,* she cautions as she turns to satisfy the man she loves.

Way too suddenly, her respite from reality is ending. With time, only, for a rushed goodbye, Earl hustles Sheila into the privacy of her room. "May I see you again?"

Sounding as noncommittal as her bursting heart will allow, she explains that, as a married woman, she can be there for him very seldom. *That's all I can do right now,* she tells herself. *Maybe, when I'm home and my feelings have dulled, I'll be able to end this all together.*

"Well, blossom, I'll send you a letter telling you what I don't have time to say. Now, one last hug and I'm gone."

Unlike last year, Sheila's drive home has none of the "I should try harder" and "I should do more" of her life. This time it's full of the six-foot-three, chestnut haired, teal eyed love of a man who has brought her back to life. At one point, she considers a "same time next year" approach. *But no*, she decides; *with it, would come a guilt, the depth of which, I've never known.* Still, the fact remains, she's let a man she truly loves into her life, and she wishes he could reside there forever.

CHAPTER 10
Filling in the Blanks

The words Earl hadn't had time to say arrive at Sheila's office via special delivery. His letter is an exquisite piece of writing, filled with deeper feelings than she'd imagined. *I thought he was capable of such sentiment, but to put it on paper demonstrates greater depth than I'd given him credit for having. What a man!* The letter, she leaves at the office under lock and key, but the memory of its words manages to rouse her from sleep one night when she awakens to the realization that Earl's feelings match her own. *This man is as real as his words and he's opening avenues of speculation I've never before traveled.*

It's at this point Sheila starts to wonder if the love Earl has to give is too good to pass up. Am I willing to go public with my fifteen-year-old lie? Am I ready to confess that I let my mother rule my life and I never grew to love my husband as I'd planned? Charles is a great guy but he can't become what he's never been: my true love.

Throughout August she moves in a daze of indecision, yet, when Earl asks if she'd like to see him again, she says yes without hesitation. By mid-September, some truth and a few lies have created a trip in which Sheila is to visit Sara Boudreau, an old college pal. The plan comes together so easily it seems preordained. In no time, Sheila finds herself in the Nashville airport with Sara by her side. Not many women would stand by her in this, but Sara understands. Having observed Sheila's marriage from afar, she's felt something like this was inevitable. Right now, she's providing an alibi. Before long, she fears, she might be rendering much-needed support.

She watches Sheila pull Earl from the crowd. The passion, evident in their embrace, says it all. This isn't a flippant infatuation. They grasp each other as if they're hanging on for life. Only when they've absorbed enough of each other's energy, do they separate to acknowledge Sara's presence. Noting Earl's warmth and good looks, she understands her friend's dilemma.

Three's a crowd, so as the baggage comes and the conversation wanes, Sara makes her good-byes. Looking wistfully at her bud, so overflowing with the energy of love, she wants to tell her to be careful. This could backfire with a magnitude of devastating proportions — Sheila could lose her home, her kids, everything. Instead, she suggests good restaurants and the perfect place for a stroll by the river, then she leaves and the lovers are alone.

In the privacy of their rental car, they fly together again. Fifteen minutes later, they pull from the curb. During the drive to the hotel, the air sizzles with the sheer joy of being together, and once they're settled into their room, bed becomes the sole order of business. Their lovemaking, at first urgent and needy, grows luxurious and comfortable as the afternoon wears on. All attention is focused on each other. The world, so full of detail and obligation, does not exist. Finally, in the glow of repeated satisfaction, they emerge from their hotel to take the stroll Sara prescribed.

They find a park complete with war memorials and long wooden benches. It's on one of these that some of their deepest secrets come out, like the fact that Sheila had been very much in love with two other men before she married Charles. She tells him how their demise and her husband's ascent were the result of her mother's maneuverings. Finally, she confides her unfulfilled dream of "pulling a Thoreau." It's important for Earl to know there are dreams in her yet to be lived.

When it's his turn, he talks of growing up on the wrong side of town, using athletics as his ticket out, and of the day he mangled his leg ending his dream of a sports career. Their differences are apparent, yet through the sighs and laughter, a bold unanimity springs forth.

Their letters have already acknowledged the inevitability of "being together." They've come that far that fast. Somehow, it seems to be in the natural order of things. Sheila however, must still be reassured about something. "Tell me again about your most recent love."

"You mean the unanswered prayer?" Earl asks this as if the finality in the words should be enough. Sheila nods, needing more. "If I'd married her, darlin', we'd be looking at two divorces, not one. You and I are meant to be together. I'd do anything to live the rest of my life with you, Sheila, anything." His words hit their mark, advancing their relationship another notch. In them, Sheila hears that Earl would go the same distance she would for them to be together. Of course, his declaration is hypothetical. He wouldn't have to move mountains the way she would.

If she does leave Charles, she'll be leaving the only life she's ever known, leaving her home, and her career. But she's certain of one thing: she will not be leaving her kids. She knows it'd be best if they start out with Charles, to help him through the first awful months. Then, when she's settled, and he's tired of full time daddy-dom, they could join her.

Still, why am I willing to risk everything for this man from a galaxy far, far away? Do I want to go that far away? Actually, yes, the breakup of my marriage would be too catastrophic to witness firsthand. Earl, in the middle of a story, doesn't sense Sheila's turmoil. What does he know of turmoil? He won't have to change a thing. He has no marriage to end, no mother to worry about, no job to leave, and, why no job to leave? What's more special about his job than mine? I've worked my entire life to get where I am.

Sheila's already spent hours pondering this. *It's not the job. It's the place. Some people, like some animals, cannot survive outside their natural habitats, and Earl is such a creature. He's so of the South, the thought of transplanting him to a large Northern city is positively repugnant. In no way do I feel about my home as Earl does about his. What is there to feel close to? Its subdivided congestion makes my eyes yearn to see farther than the house across the street or the gas station on the corner. How often have I dreamed of leaving it behind for a more rural place? There's no case to be made for Earl leaving a region he loves to join me in a place I'd love to leave.*

Deep down, Sheila knows her love for this man extends to his Southern backdrop. She can't explain her affinity for a region she's never seen, but she knows it's a place she and the children will cherish.

The weekend continues as long talks fill in the blanks of Sheila's concerns. Earl has planned a perfect retreat: walks in the woods, drinks on the riverfront, music at the Bullpen, and, best of all, a country breakfast at the Loveless Café. It's all new, all wonderful. She's laughed more in these two days than in a year of weekends with her husband. *Sad, so sad really, Charles deserves better. If there could have been this chemistry between us, I wouldn't be here now. Why couldn't there have been such chemistry? I certainly prayed for it. God didn't answer those prayers, so why will He help me now? Maybe He really is a laissez-faire God, winding up the universe like a clock and leaving it to run on its own. If that's the case, I'll have to fix things myself.*

At Sunday brunch, Sheila notices something like a fist tightening in her chest. *How can I ever face Charles acting as though I've spent an innocent weekend with Sara?* Everything about this disgusts her, yet the most despicable thing is the fact that almost two decades earlier, she'd put the dear man into the tragedy they'll soon be living. *And after all that time, I'm going to make him the victim of a naïve woman's poor judgment.* Sheila stops her introspection long enough for them to drive to the airport and say good-bye. Then, again, from the plane she whispers to the clouds, "Lord, I don't really think you're a laissez-faire God. You brought Earl and me together for a reason, so please help me make it happen and make it the best thing for Charles, too. He deserves more than the make-believe wife I've been." Inwardly she continues, *it'd be hateful to take Allie and Chase with me in the beginning, but please, I beg you, make it be that after the initial blow, he'll see Allie and Chase should be with me. Wouldn't that be best for everyone?*

When the taxi pulls up to her house, Sheila can see Charles and the children in the kitchen having dinner. With a pang, she realizes the lonely scene is what it would be like if she were gone. *No, Allie and Chase will be with me. Maybe not at first, but sooner, rather than later, they will be with me!*

CHAPTER 11
Fear and Worry

Who is so large of spirit she could understand what I am about to do? Sara's long distance support is wonderful, but Sheila craves the empathy of someone nearby. The two friends she trusts most in the world are Samantha Scott and Laura Tolafson. Sam can't be her confidante because she and Sheila work too closely together. Laura, however, is in another department of the college.

It's at lunch that Sheila drops the bomb on her friend. *Strange, she's not at all surprised.* "I'm relieved at your reaction, Laura; I was afraid you'd be shocked."

"Not really, I always felt you two were just co-existing."

"You saw that?" Sheila shakes her head, "How long have I been kidding myself that I've been fooling the world?

"A long time, I'm sure. And you've fantasized about leaving him for just as long. What else could explain the extent of your planning and your absolute readiness to change your life? You may just have decided this, but I see a woman who is already gone."

"I wished myself gone often enough, but I never thought I'd do it."

"But you are now, and if I hear you right, there's no chance of reconciliation."

"No, that would mean I'd be giving in yet again."

"It worries me that Charles hasn't a clue you're even thinking such a thing. He'll be blown away with shock and anger."

"I know. He won't believe I've been unhappy for so long. So determined I was, not to make him the victim, I bucked up and played the part of the happy wife and this is where it got me."

"No one's ever ready for news like this, even if you think he's indifferent to you, he won't accept it. Please, Sheila, be very careful!"

"Whoa! I wasn't expecting that, but you're right. This is going to be an ambush of the worst kind, but I think I can control the damage by initially letting the kids be with him. That will help him get through the roughest part."

"When will you tell him?"

"It's mid-October, if I can hold on until the New Year, it will allow Allie and Chase to have a good Christmas."

"Can you keep the charade going that long?"

"If Charles never noticed my unhappiness before, why would he now?"

"Maybe so, meanwhile I'll think good thoughts."

"Thanks friend!" Sheila hugs her pal as they depart, "I'll keep you posted and I promise I'll be careful."

Dan, Sheila's older brother, is another person she must tell sooner rather than later. This, she does in the end of October, when she and the kids take her mother to Water Haven. It may be the last weekend, ever, that she and her children will spend in their cottage. They make taffy apples and feed an abundance of bread to the ducks on the lake. After peewee golf, they scavenge for treasures in the local thrift store. Sheila performs each of these traditions with a sense of never-more.

Although her mom came along this weekend, she's staying in her own cottage with Louada and Dan. Saturday evening, when Allie and Chase are over at a friend's house, Sheila takes her brother out for a beer. The Sand Bar, a place she once frequented with Sonny Lawson, is where she drops the divorce bomb.

Don't you dare succumb to that little sister thing! Ten years earlier, she'd confided her unhappiness to Dan. "Don't be a "me-first" person; you can work it out." He'd advised this with such certainty she'd believed him. Feeling selfish and small, she'd taken the blame on herself and tried harder than ever to be happy. This time, little sister seeks no advice. She informs Dan that, as he knows, she hasn't been happy for years, but that's going to change. "And there's someone else," she blurts out. With the fist hammering in her chest, she outlines her intentions. She's doing it! She's actually telling her brother she will leave her husband.

Dan, divorced from one woman and separated from another, doesn't know what his role in this should be. His perfect little sister, the one who always did everything right — is about to cross over to the other side. Can she really be ready to leave her idyllic life and move into that other, less savory realm?

"It's a big step, honey."

"I know it is, Dan. That's why I've arranged to go to Florida next weekend, unless I see or learn something to change my mind, I'm going through with it."

"Your job?" Dan asks, still not believing this.

"I'll miss it, but it's time to do something different, don't you think?" Dan doesn't answer. He's still trying to fathom why this sane woman would do anything so rash.

She moves the discussion onto Allie and Chase and her certainty they'll eventually be with her. "It's not right for me to take them to Florida right away, but Charles will see they should be with me once he's healed."

Dan lifts his eyebrows in a response Sheila chooses not to interpret. After paying for the beers, the new, imperfect little sister and her big brother drive to their mother's cottage. As she drops Dan off, Sheila reminds him their mom doesn't know yet. "I hope my secret won't be a burden."

"That's all right, hon, it's what I'm here for." The tone of Dan's voice tells her more than his words.

This encounter, like the one with Laura, hasn't been all that encouraging; still, she's glad she told Dan. He deserved to hear it from her now, not later, in a light refracted through her mother's interpretation.

Sheila fetches Allie and Chase from their friend's house. Wanting to be alone with them, she passes up the offer to have a drink with the parents, Barb and Ron Considine. Through the years, this couple and the, soon-to-be un-couple of Sheila and Charles have been friends. She wonders what will happen when half of their foursome is no more.

Back in the cabin, she lights a fire in the fireplace so they can roast marshmallows. Every gooey bite gets washed down with hot chocolate. All this sugar may keep them up, but she doesn't care. Each smile and laugh is gilded in the reality that she may have to go without it for, how long? *Not too long, God, please not too long!*

At this moment, it seems her consciousness is intensified beyond human powers. For the rest of her life, Sheila will carry the details of this time with her children. It's her last flash of innocence: mother, daughter, and son — a trilogy of perfect love. She grieves, too, over the dreadful reality that's about to enter their lives, and she hates the sad, cruel thing it will do to their daddy.

Will you two ever forgive me? She wonders, as she watches them concentrate on their marshmallows. *How can I make you see I'm leaving your daddy, not you? Will you ever understand that if I don't leave, I'll be as grasping and possessive of you as your grandma was of me? If I don't do it now, there won't be a next time and you will be the ones to suffer as I escape through you.*

On Sunday, the drive home is an easy one. Still tired from their late night fun, Allie and Chase sleep soundly. Wookie is comfy in Louada's lap, and Sheila's mom naps in the front.

Finally, I've separated from you, Mom. No longer do you wield your awesome power. Why did it take so long to see the hold you had on me? If you'd remained healthy, and in full grasp of your manipulative power, would I be breaking away even now?

These aren't angry questions, just curious ones, asked when one is reaching to understand. If Sheila can comprehend her mother, she might understand herself, and in so doing, she might see why she's so driven to be with Earl. The silent, one-sided inquisition yields little insight. Maybe the upcoming trip to Florida will reveal more.

CHAPTER 12
Bald Nuts

"This place is as cute as a bug's ear, handy too!" Sheila calls across the tarmac of the tiny Pine Springs regional airport.

"Enough of your airport evaluation; come here to me!" Earl's arms open wide to give his lady the hugs and kisses to which she's become accustomed. Then he sweeps her through the single room airport and out to the parking lot. There's a lot to be said for simplicity.

On the way to Earl's, they stop at Alvira's Medicine Shoppe, Pine Springs's favorite middle-aged drinking establishment. Here, Sheila meets the infamous Sean Murphy, better known as Murph, and local legend, Mullet Moss. With their raucous good humor and storytelling talents, they shine in bold contrast to the bland correctness of Sheila's northern compatriots. Murph, a native of south Florida, is here to attend tomorrow's Armadillo football game. He's a real estate attorney who enjoys pissing off developers and environmentalists alike. His rogue attitude crystallized when, as a child, he traveled the carnival circuit with his parents and today, his rakishly handsome black Irish looks still draw women like a magnet. That may be why he's on wife number three.

Mullet Moss is a good ol' boy with bright red hair and the bluest eyes Sheila has ever seen. Born and raised in Pine Springs, he makes his living winning fishing tournaments around the state. Sheila's first impression of the man is that of an extremely fit Suma wrestler. His rotund physique seems not to harbor an ounce of fat. Upon hearing how he once ran through a locked door, she decides he's every bit as crazy as Earl portrayed him to be.

Such Faulkneresque characters deserve a great backdrop, and they have one in the scenery of north Florida. On the way to Earl's, Sheila is treated to neon green pastures with hundreds of cattle seeking shade under enormous Live Oaks. Next are dense forests of sky-high pines, and occasionally, a field of wild flowers. Sheila finds it overwhelming that such natural splendor is a part of everyday life for the lucky people of Pine Springs. *With all this, why would anyone live anywhere else?*

They turn onto a heavily wooded road lined with country-style homes. Earl's is the one at the end of the street. It's warm and inviting with an almost new car smell and a huge backyard for Mattie, his chocolate lab. A cozy rush hits Sheila the second she walks in the door.

She has the same sensation Saturday morning when Earl serves her breakfast on a deck overlooking Mattie's domain. The sycamore and sweet gum trees that shade the yard are a haven for birds. Their chorus is so soothing Sheila wishes she could sit and listen for hours. But the day is to be dedicated to college football, so she puts on her game face and accompanies Earl to the first of many tailgates.

It is here that Sheila realizes that not everyone in Pine Springs is glad Earl has a new lady. When he leaves her to fetch a cold beer she senses an aura of contempt emanating from someplace nearby. From behind a pickup truck, a woman is staring at her with dagger eyes. Only Earl, embracing Sheila from behind, breaks the hostile concentration. Then, as if a switch has been thrown, Dagger Eyes runs across the lot to pull Earl from Sheila. Shocked, she watches the woman smile beguilingly at Earl, begging him for attention like a run-over dog. He listens, nodding politely, then excuses himself to return to Sheila. When Dagger Eyes follows, he puts his arm around Sheila saying, "Satin, this is my new lady, Sheila Branford. You're going to be seeing a lot of her."

Belle Satinopolis is the name Earl gives when he introduces the woman. Satin, as she likes to be called, is anything but. She's in her forties, unless the wrinkles on her face exaggerate her age. *Ridden hard and put up wet* is Sheila's assessment. She was beautiful once, but years of sun, sorrow, or hard, hard living have left their marks. Satin's smile hisses *I hate you.*

Stunned, Sheila absorbs this, *Oh God, you really do!* Times like these often tell her more than she wants to know. She reaches to shake hands with the icy creature but there is no response, only the message, *Earl should be with me, no one loves him as I do; no one!*

You poor thing, Sheila shoots back. *You planned this to be your turn, didn't you? Well, it's not, nor will it ever be, because I'm here to stay.* Their eyes lock in a death-defying stare as Sheila is herded away by an anxious Earl.

"That was frosty," she quips, hoping he'll volunteer some information.

"Oh, that's just Satin. She's like that sometimes, but she's harmless."

Harmless like a school of piranhas!

Aside from Satin, the rest of Earl's friends are warm and receptive to the woman about whom they've heard so much. Sheila, feeling liked and accepted, is pleased to realize that, with or without Earl, she'd enjoy having every one of them as a friend.

Tad Pettigrew is the senior member of the group. Upon meeting Sheila, he's openly jubilant, announcing that Earl has "finally found a gal with class." Taking Sheila's arm, he escorts her to meet his wife, Leonora, whose auburn locks and honey-brown eyes are quick to embrace Sheila with their warmth.

"So you're the Sheila Earl can't stop talking about! Mercy, that boy's smitten!" Her drawl is as lovely as she is. "Listen up now, don't you be put off by any of these rascals. They get turned inside out on game days."

"And if they don't, we check to see if they're alive. Hi, Sheila, I'm Janice, Murph's third wife, and, if he's real lucky, his last. Welcome to Florida!" Sheila studies Janice's dimpled smile, and long tousle of black curls, wondering what beauty secrets these Southern women could divulge. There are no tricks, she decides, just raw beauty inside and out.

An arm encircles her waist pulling her close. "Hello gorgeous, I hope you're alone."

"Get your hands off my woman!" Earl grabs the man by the throat in mock rage.

"And if I don't?" It's Odom Dysart, Earl's old teammate going along with the joke. Odom stars in so many of Earl's stories Sheila feels as though he's already a close friend.

Melissa McDaniel

Murph and Mullet come up to express surprise that she's still in town.

"I'm not here for Earl," she explains. "I'm here because I like his buds!"

This wins her high fives. This North-South communication is not without confusion, however. Straining to keep up with the Southern dialect, Sheila gets the sense that most of what is said takes the form of one huge sentence in which dozens of words are slurred together. Their colloquialisms also leave her in the dark. To her, a "bad boy" is a naughty child of male gender. To Murph, it's a dangerous storm, a powerful pick up truck, a talented football player, and a stiff drink.

At one point, Mullet renders her speechless when he whispers, "Shiela, y'ont some bald nuts?"

Easy now, he's too good a friend of Earl's to be trying to gross me out. "Pardon?" she asks.

"Y'ont some bald nuts?"

What the hell? She inhales deeply, struggling for a less lewd interpretation than the one that comes to mind. *Do they shave their peanuts down here?* She conjures an unconvincing image of a peanut in a barber's chair.

Mullet, impatient with her slow response, jams a paper bag into her hand and shouts as if she's deaf, "Bald nuts!"

Sheila sees a soggy bag brimming with wet peanut shells. "Bald?" she asks.

"Yes, bald! We ball'em in wata!"

"We boy-all them in wa-ter," Earl translates, thinking this is hilarious.

"You boil them? Why would anyone boil a peanut?" But when she tastes one she knows, "Hey, these are good! And a lot better than the nuts I thought you were offering!"

Mullet doubles in hysterics, then proclaims, "This furtha convinces me, North'un folk'r kinda slow!"

After a victorious game, the fans reassemble to celebrate the win. Earl's son, Ryan, drops by to meet the woman his father says is "the one." At twenty-five, he's a free spirit, floating wherever his looks, talent and personality will take him. "Thank you," he whispers, "for making my dad so happy. The other night, when you two were talking on the phone, I actually heard him giggle. Do you know how great that sounded?" Sheila's touched by this amazing young man.

How wonderfully unselfish of him to express his gratitude to her! The two continue their chat, each making it clear to the other that Earl's happiness is a priority.

Somewhere in the conversation, Sheila decides if she were to have a twenty-six-year-old son, she'd want him to be like Ryan. Is this a fluke? Or does providence have something to do with how well everything is going? She wants to believe it really is God answering her prayers.

He especially seems to be present Sunday morning when Earl takes her for a boat ride on the Suwannee River. It's a crystalline day, chilly enough to make the air squeaky-clean. The Cypress trees that drape the river with Spanish moss seem to be welcoming her into nature's sanctuary. "This is better than church!" she exclaims.

"This is God's house, darlin'," Earl says in earnest. "Here, we worship Him with our fellow creatures; the buzzards up there warming their wings, that wild sow guarding her little ones on the river bank, and don't forget the Great Blue Heron fishing over there by the shoals..."

"What about the handsome creature beside me?" Sheila teases.

"I wouldn't go that far, but I do believe He'd rather be here with us, than walled up in some palace of a church." Earl takes her hand, and as he does, the clenched fist in Sheila's chest opens, and from its palm floats a peace she's never known. *There will be no more thrashing about for answers,* she thinks. *These woods, the river, and this amazing man are calling me home.*

As soothing as her time on the river has been, the minutes preceding Sheila's departure are riveted with dread. She's at the point in her dissonance where it would be better to get it over with than to tolerate the status quo. What first pulled her to Earl now draws her to this place. She is recovering what was long ago lost; to refuse it now will be suicide of another sort.

CHAPTER 13
Time To Tell

It comes to a head with Charles on a cold November night when Sheila pleads off the pillow talk she's always encouraged. With her back to him, she lies completely still, forcing her breathing to sound rhythmic and deep. When the breaths of her husband seem to match her own she rises to tiptoe from the room. *I plod through these days with the zombie heart of a person about to commit a heinous crime. To slumber beside my soon-to-be victim is too hard. He is my guilt personified.*

Ensconced in the family room, with office work around her, she hears the door slide open slowly, tentatively. When Sheila looks up, her husband's ashen face tells her this is the moment she's been dreading. It has been said when people face death, they see their lives flash before their eyes. On this occasion, Sheila's sixteen- year marriage parades by in a nanosecond. This will not be a happy Christmas.

"We need to talk," Charles's voice is pitched with caution. He doesn't enter the room straight away. Instead, he skirts along the wall, as if seeking its support.

"Yes, we do," Sheila finally replies. *This is it, Lord, please help us both.*

Charles stands waiting before her. He looks as though he's already feeling the pain. The fist in her chest clenches tighter, forcing her breath to grow so shallow she checks to be sure she's breathing at all. Next she notices her arms and legs seem to be deadened with Novocain. Charles is the last man on earth she wants to hurt. *Is there no other way?*

You know there isn't. He's waiting. It's time to bludgeon him with the mistake a silly girl made long ago.

"Charles, I've kept a secret from you for sixteen years," Sheila begins. To her surprise, relief flashes in her husband's eyes. He seems to be thinking no secret is so bad he can't stand it. "It's the fact that when I married you I didn't love you as I should have. I thought that would change. I was sure that over the years we'd fall deeply in love, but it never happened. You're a wonderful person, but I don't love you as a woman should love a man."

Still, he seems relieved, "Don't worry about that now, Sheila; we have a great relationship." The accountant in Charles is thinking whatever's wrong with his overly romantic wife is inconsequential to the partnership.

"Now? Don't worry about it now?" Sheila interrupts. "This didn't just occur to me; it has been tearing me up for sixteen years. I've been living a constant lie, so much so, it has made me unstable."

Repulsed, Charles takes two steps back then rears up, ready to fight. "Don't give me that shit!"

"It's true! You remember when I was deeply in love with someone else, and we planned to be married, but I broke the engagement for religious reasons?" Charles nods. "Well, that wasn't the real reason; it was a cover to hide the embarrassing truth of why I broke it off. I didn't care he was Catholic! It was my mother who didn't want me marrying one. And when she learned I'd agreed to convert, she went crazy. To this day, I don't know why it meant so much to her. In my entire life, I've seen her attend church less than a dozen times. Anyway, she came at me with the Armageddon of manipulative tactics. First, there was her phony logic: 'Look how rocky your brother's marriage is, and he's married to a Catholic.' When that failed, she screamed that I was disgracing my family. She knew I'd usually do anything to stop her rampages, but to her surprise, that didn't work either. I was that much in love with Ed. It was then that she did the thing no mother should ever do. She froze me out. Cold and formal, she'd look at me only when others were present, and then it was with the pain of the ages in her eyes. I doubt I could make you, or anyone else, understand how painful it was to be deprived of her narcotic love. I suffered for months, telling no one

Melissa McDaniel

what was going on. Always, I prayed she'd come around but she didn't. Her glacial treatment foretold a future of never-ending heartache with me always torn between the man I loved and the mother I'd lost. Broken, and pathetic, I succumbed, thinking I might find another man I'd love as much as Ed, but I'd never have another mother. I was too blinded with love for her to see what a mean thing she was doing. And because I told no one, I never had the benefit of a second opinion. Then once she'd pried me from the man I truly loved, she encouraged me in the direction of one I did not. You, Charles, were that unlucky person."

"I can live with that," he breaks in. "Things are good, we have a wonderful family, a beautiful home."

"And you have a sick wife, one who wants to be away from all of this, and especially, I'm afraid, from you." *That was way too harsh,* Sheila scolds, but curiously, Charles's reaction doesn't register the blow.

Still standing, he asks, "So, what are you going to do? Go look for that Ed person?"

"No, I'll never see him again."

"Then what? What do you want?"

"I want to stop pretending to be happy. I want a life not so cluttered with things and obligations that I have no time to live. I want a man not so detached that, in self-defense, I train myself not to feel. I need someone who can look into my soul and nourish me with love!"

Stiff and frozen, Charles can only stare at Sheila with the frightened eyes of a child who fears the worst is yet to come. Taking pity on her victim, she alters her approach, "Charles, we're so different. I know I'm emotionally needy, but that's the most authentic thing about me. For you, the agonies and ecstasies of life are things you'd rather do without, for me, they're at the heart of everything. I don't want to die, having only lived like this."

"You really are something! You have all this and you're whining about not having enough emotion in your life? Wake up, Sheila, this is the real world. You're not some heroine in a movie!"

"That's it exactly! I've played a heroine all these years because I felt I had to do right by you. I threw myself into the part of a happy wife, breaking character only when I was alone. But my façade crumbled when the heroine grew suicidal. Charles," Sheila takes a deep breath, "I want a divorce so I can marry someone else, I want-"

Before she finishes, Charles's legs buckle. He barely reaches a chair before collapsing. Underneath the silk robe the kids gave him for Fathers' Day, he's shivering like a feverish child. Now he's bending over his feet as if he's going to be sick.

"All I want is a fair settlement. I know you'll want to stay in this house, and you should. And it's probably best that," *for the time being,* her inner voice interjects, "the kids stay with you, because, the months after I leave will be difficult, and to take them away from you is something I cannot do." *But please, once you're healed, let me have my babies!* Throughout her oration, Sheila maintains a trancelike calm. Although the message is seven weeks premature, it has been well rehearsed. She kneels beside Charles.

Not wanting to look at her, he shrinks into the chair, "Oh God why is this happening?"

Lord, what can I say to make him hurt less? He's crying now, probably the best thing, and as his cries become shuddering heaves, Sheila joins him and they weep together. *This is a deathwatch. Our marriage is dying.*

Charles rises up again, "How can you be so final? Just boom! It's over? You're not even giving me a chance? You can walk away from sixteen years, just like that?" The anguish in his voice is proportionate to the pain inside. Any answer she gives will only hurt more. And softhearted Sheila, the gal who always caves in at the prospect of hurting anyone, knows she must do something drastic or she'll lose her conviction. She makes her "feeling self" leave her body and float above. Left below is a less emotional twin, a being, who, because of her conviction, is able to cause the kind of pain that is necessary.

"I'm sorry, Charles. To you, this seems sudden. But I realize now, it has been coming for years."

"You never told me!"

"There were signs along the way. Don't you remember me constantly suggesting things that could improve our marriage? And what about that time I told you I had seriously considered leaving you? Remember?"

"You'd said you thought about it but you didn't do it so I figured everything was all right. And you never said I should change."

"You're right. I was the guilty one so I figured I was the one who was supposed to change. But I do remember telling you I needed more from our relationship."

"Well, I don't! And now you're not even giving me a chance!" As anger overcomes pain, Charles starts to yell. "I thought things were fine! How can you give up like this? What kind of a mother are you? This is a midlife crisis! You need a shrink!"

This would have shattered the softhearted Sheila floating above, but her twin, below, is well intact. The remarks about "what kind of mother" and "needing a psychiatrist" don't seem to penetrate. Instead, she responds with a distant and sad, "Maybe I do, but nonetheless, this marriage is over."

The sparring continues until the living room has grown almost as cold as the November night. "We're exhausted. You go up to bed. I'll stay here awhile." To sleep beside Charles, now that he knows, is even less possible than before.

"We'll talk tomorrow," she promises. To her, it's a way to end the ordeal for the moment. For Charles, it's a promise, a hope with which he can allow the torture to slacken albeit, temporarily. He needs sleep so he'll have the strength to put an end to this madness.

"I love you She; I always have." His words bring the emotional Sheila back into her body.

"I know," she whispers, fighting off the sobs until he's upstairs.

Not only can she not sleep by her husband, Sheila can't sleep with herself. Who is this despicable creature? Have the seeds of such atrocity always resided in the sweet little girl? Were they swelling and growing inside her all the while she was trying to be everything to everybody? How can she do this to such a nice man, the father of her children? Wouldn't it be better to go on sacrificing than to reap the destruction that's sure to come? Is getting away from this life so very important? As a chalky dawn smudges the horizon, Sheila feels less certain than she has in weeks. The agony, the upheaval of it all may be more than she can bear. What she'll be doing to Charles is too terrible a ransom to pay for her freedom. For a while, the softhearted Sheila seems to be winning.

Wait! To spare Charles's feelings, you would acquiesce again? When will you learn it's not up to you to keep the world from hurting? It was to spare your mother's feelings that put you in this position in the first place.

There you are! Sheila hails her inner voice with relief. It is a consciousness she's learned to respect.

Go forward, it commands, if you retreat now you'll never get free. Surely you know this isn't only about being with Earl, it's also about leaving a place and a life style you find claustrophobic. At long last, the wheels are turning; keep the momentum going.

But what about Charles, my mother, and my children? I'm so frightened things won't work out. What if I hate it in Florida or with Earl?

Charles won't die, you can manage your mother's care from afar, and you are not leaving your kids. You will be with them in every way you can until their father lets them be with you in person. Florida and Earl don't really matter. The important thing is you'll have yourself to rely on, not the approval of others.

Fueled by the courage of her inner voice Sheila enters the surreal world she'll walk through for ninety-nine days. *This will be my purgatory, but if God is on my side, He'll guide me through the fires of Charles's rage.* Although she feels physically ill with the guilt of what she's doing to her husband, she no longer suffers from constant fatigue. She moves ahead with swashbuckling "let's-get-it-over-with" zeal. Her work, caring for her mother and the children are all accomplished with renewed energy and love of life.

She feels honor-bound to cooperate with Charles in his attempts to salvage the marriage. It must never be said she didn't try, so when he suggests they go to a marriage counselor, Sheila agrees. On the way to their appointment, the silence in the car reminds Sheila of the roar she hears in Allie's conch shell. Charles senses it too because, when they reach the counselor's home, he jumps from the car as if he's escaping something dreadful. They march, single file, up the sidewalk to what looks like a cozy English cottage. As welcoming as the house is, the man who answers the door is not. Sheila wonders if he is naturally cold or professionally objective. There is no warmth, no charisma around which she can rally. She sits down; worried the session won't go well. But actually it does. In a non-committal tone, the counselor delivers the sad statistics that few marriages survive a "mid-life relationship." For Charles, the appointment is over once he hears this. He resists the man's efforts to get him talking. To him, this is about Sheila, and her need to see the life they've built together mustn't be torn apart. Having banished the softhearted Sheila to the rafters, her less emotional twin endures the hour with a façade of impenetrable calm. At the appointment's end, they have accomplished nothing, Sheila's objective all along.

The drive home is even grayer than the day. To tolerate the tension, Sheila thinks about the weeks ahead. *Four weeks until Christmas and Charles already knows. What a surreal December this will be! And as for Thanksgiving, what has Charles to be grateful for? Never have I thought myself capable of the cruelty I now sow daily. When did the sweet, hard-working, overachieving wife, daughter, and mother become a selfish, cold-hearted bitch? From now on, every day will unfold with its special torment. There will be the torture of facing Charles, play-acting as if nothing is wrong for Allie and Chase's benefit, and then there'll be Mom's shock when she hears the news. The months ahead will be pure hell, but I have to march through those fires because my trip to Florida confirmed that retreat is not an option.*

Chapter 14
Thanksgiving

Sheila's news of wanting a divorce is too fresh to maintain any semblance of a happy Thanksgiving. The only way to avoid such an ordeal is for Sheila to withdraw. To that end, she had agreed to participate in a public relations workshop at the University of Florida. That done, she's now in a rental car headed for Pine Springs where she'll spend the holiday with Earl and his son. She'd love to have Allie and Chase with her but their daddy would never have allowed it. Besides, it is best they stay with him to unknowingly help him through this first holiday without her. *It's horrendous being away from them, but it might show Charles how little he's been involved in their daily care.*

They hadn't batted an eye when she'd told them she'd be away on business over the Thanksgiving holiday. Holding them in their traditional sandwich hug, she'd sensed her absence would be more painful to her, than them. *Is it the blessing of a great sitter or the curse of an overly demanding career that has created such adaptive children?*

Earl is working in his vegetable garden when she pulls into the drive. He rushes to her and is startled by the exhaustion evident on her face. It looks, to him, like the fatigue of terminal illness. Concerned, he pulls her into the house, makes her a drink, and draws a hot bath for her. "Darlin', I'll be on the deck. When you feel like company, come on out." Half an hour later Sheila feels good enough to join him on the porch swing. They swing in comfortable silence as Mattie chases lizards through the bushes. After a while Earl whispers, "I could sit like this forever, least 'til we die."

Melissa McDaniel

    Sheila understands, feeling that where she is, is exactly where she should be. If there's such a thing as a soul returning to its place of origin, this world of towering pines and Live Oaks is hers. "It's good to be home." she sighs, and she thinks she hears Earl's throat catch as he squeezes her hand.

    The time she spends in Pine Springs is a glorious respite from the battleground of home. Charles doesn't call, but she phones the kids daily. She imagines them basking in their daddy's attention; he's more available to them than he's ever been. With every call, she must beat back her homesickness. Not being with her family on Thanksgiving is so unnatural, were it not for the coming and going of Earl's friends, and the newness of her surroundings, she would be utterly miserable.

    The person most masterful in helping Sheila escape her self-pity is Earl's son, Ryan. She loves his company and is touched by the strong bond growing between them. Ryan, too, is at a turning point in his life. Upon completion of college, he'd spent a few years seeing the world as a professional soccer player. Now he faces the reality of finding a job and settling down to carve out a life. Already, Sheila cares enough for Ryan to worry for his future and she hopes he'll make better choices than she did in her early years.

    Thanksgiving portrays the Langley men at their best. Everything they do, from golfing to preparing dinner, to just sitting and talking for hours, presents them as a remarkably devoted father and son. It seems their struggles as a bachelor dad and only child provided a basis for mutual respect. Seeing this heartens Sheila for two reasons. First, Earl's instinctive fathering skills get high marks, and she sees him capable of a similar role with her own children. Secondly (and this is a "worst case" scenario), it consoles her to see that it's possible for a child to thrive without a mother on the premises.

    The holiday's greatest surprise comes in the form of its delicious Southern cuisine. The father-son team prepares a feast of smoked turkey and fresh ham baked in apple juice. The accompanying cornbread stuffing, orange and sweet potato casserole, pickled okra and fried green tomatoes are as Southern as the chefs. She's never seen two men work side-by-side to produce such excellent fare. It's rather intimidating to realize they've survived so well without female assistance. On the positive side, Sheila sees the independence of this father and son as an enormous plus — in no way will she be typecast for the kitchen.

Also invited to Thanksgiving dinner is the Wyatt McKee family from nearby Gainesville. Katelyn, Wyatt's wife, is a knockout. Her short, upswept hairdo elongates a sleek, 5'9" frame, while gold-flecked hazel eyes dance on the most perfect cheekbones Sheila has ever seen. And, best of all, she's a sympathetic listener! So much so that when she inquires about Sheila's children, she gets an earful. Having repressed so much for so long, Sheila can't stop talking to the caring stranger. Katelyn, having listened intently to Sheila's plan to leave her husband and eventually get the children, doesn't share her confidence.

"He'll use the children against you," she pauses to consider what she has just said. "Yes, I'm certain he'll use them to hurt you. I would if Wyatt ever left me."

"No, Charles isn't like that," Sheila's quick to say. "Besides, just the other day, a counselor told us both how destructive that would be to them. No, that's one thing I don't have to worry about." But even as she mouths these words, she's wondering if she doth protest too much.

The next two days pass much too quickly and by Saturday evening, Sheila can no longer beat back the sheer dread of returning to the chaos she's created. She looks at Earl and marvels that, for him, Sunday will be just another day. He'll take her to the airport, kiss her good-bye, and resume his life without a blip on the screen. She, on the other hand, will walk straight into society's wrath. How many people has Charles told by now? She pictures a tribe of hostile neighbors ready to throw stones. With her face buried in Earl's neck, she howls, "Nooooooo! I don't want to go back!"

"I know, darlin', your wagon's plenty full, isn't it?" He pulls her close, letting his power flow into her soul. If he'd been the greatest motivational expert in the world, he couldn't be handling this any better. The fact that he has to bear none of the shame or anguish doesn't matter. At this moment, he's inside it with her. Because of him, she'll find the strength to pillage and plunder the marriage she'd worked so hard to build.

Chapter 15
Telling Mom

Back in enemy territory, Sheila knows she must trade her spontaneity for calculated detachment. This way, Charles is less able to strike and wound. It also helps when she tells her mother she's leaving.

Objectivity is key here, the voice coaches as she approaches Dora Ronson's room. *Don't let her become the domineering mother and you, the chronically yielding offspring.* From the doorway, Sheila sees the tiny frame listing into the cushions of a chair. One wrist jerks up and down in time to music no one hears. The other hand would do the same if it weren't lodged between a bony thigh and the arm of the chair. Her rigid neck pushes her face into a cushion, not because it's comfortable, but because she hasn't the strength to turn it elsewhere. Gently, Sheila rolls her mother's face outward, coaxing her neck and torso to follow suit.

"Is that better, Mom?"

"Not really, nothing's very good these days."

What must this advanced stage of Parkinson's be like? Here she sits trapped inside a body that doesn't work. She can think, but she can barely move, and all too often, her thought process is impaired by medication, poor Mom.

"Mom, I have something to tell you."

"Is Dan O.K.?"

"He's fine. It's about me. I'm not sick or anything, but if I were to continue like this, I would be. Do you remember ten years ago when I told you how unhappy I was?" Dry, tired eyes rally enough to fire a warning shot. *Ah yes, you do remember.* "When I confided that I was thinking about ending my marriage, you said I was the problem; that I wanted too much. And you coached Dan to say the same thing!"

Her mother's Parkinson's-riddled body rises up, tense and ready to fight. Fierce eyes almost extinguish Sheila's next sentence — almost, but not quite. She's cowered to that look too many times. This time, she answers it with her own angry power. "I listened to you and I stayed. But now, I know better." She takes the cold, rigid, shaking hands into her own, "Mom, I love another man, and this time, I really am going to end my marriage." Her mother says nothing, but Sheila knows she heard because the hands jerked away. "In three months, I'm moving to Florida to live with this man. His name is Earl Langley. I'll still manage your care, and I'll visit often. I'm sorry, Mom, but this is something I have to do." *And maybe if you hadn't manipulated my life so long ago, I'd be happily married to Ed and I wouldn't be doing this at all.*

With adrenaline pumping, Dora Ronson reaches back ten years to the issues they'd discussed. "You've always wanted too much. Every marriage gets dull."

"Maybe, but this time I'm deeply in love with someone."

Her mother isn't listening; she's dealing with the shock of what she just heard. Sheila waits for the argument to begin. *She's gone inside to plan her move, wondering what to say or do to keep me here. But knowledge is power, and, I'm on to her.*

The two sit side by side, each feigning interest in a public television crafts show. Sheila wonders if it's hard for her mom to watch such programs when she can no longer indulge her talents. *To sit day after day watching the boob tube is no life for someone so bright.* Sheila recalls a time when she'd asked her mother to consider moving into a nearby, five-star, assisted-care facility. For what they spend on twenty-four hour care and the upkeep of her house, they could afford it. Her mother has friends who live there and they give it high praise. A physical therapist would be available to work with Mom, and there's even an old-fashioned ice cream parlor where she could take her grandkids. But she'd nixed the idea from the get-go. Later, Sheila realized her mother's plan was to move in with her and Charles just as her grandma had moved in to share her little girl's bedroom. As Sheila's father once said, "Granny came to visit and never left." Most of Sheila's grade school years were spent with a geriatric roommate. She'd grown accustomed to falls during the night, and the sight of false teeth resting in a cup on her nightstand. Needless to say, her little friends seldom were invited to spend the night. But the worst part was seeing her grandmother's presence turn her beautiful mother into a haggard caregiver.

No, the little girl in her had vowed, *this will not happen to my children!* Fortunately, Sheila had seen it coming when her mom moved in to "help" after Allie was born." Then, with Chase, she'd repeated the attempt. Refusing to let her stay had cut Sheila to shreds, but her allegiance was to her children. Those were the only two times she'd ever really stood up to her mother.

Oh well, that doesn't matter anymore. What she must do now is make plans to manage her mother's care and run her household from over a thousand miles away. It can be done and Sheila will see that it is. She never, before, shirked her responsibilities as a daughter and she won't now. Will people accuse her of sloughing off her mother's care on her brother? Probably, but she'll know the truth. *After all, for twelve years, who's done the visiting every few days, the grocery shopping, the doctor's appointments? Who hires and fires the caregivers, does the payroll, handles the bills? No, that's wrong. Until now, Charles has been a prince paying the bills, submitting insurance claims, and doing the taxes. I'll do that from now on. Nothing more will be expected of Dan other than his current visits. If he wants to increase them, that'll be nice. It's his presence she pines for, not mine.*

As the crafts program draws to a close, Sheila feels guilty about her last observation. Dan's isn't an easy life. A stressful sales job keeps him traveling, but he's good to his mother, sending her postcards and candy from various places. When he visits, he always does his share of lawn or house chores. *It isn't his fault he's out of state. I, on the other hand, have always been the close-by daughter, and the one who, even though she does so much, always feels like it's never enough. And, although I'll soon be the long-gone daughter, I'll bust my buns to make everything just right for her. That's the way I'm made and after all, she is my mother!* Softening, she takes one of the bony hands into hers. "I love you so much, Mom. I hope, somehow, you'll understand what I'm doing."

Mom looks away, her power has weakened, and somehow her daughter has found an inner-self strong enough to loosen her grasp. Finally she rallies, "You would do this to your children?"

"I'm not divorcing my children; even though we may have to be apart for a while, they'll know I'm always with them." Her assault hadn't had the impact she'd intended so Dora Ronson chooses to ignore her daughter, turning her attention to the television.

Go ahead, freeze me out; this time, I don't care. As she leaves, Sheila pulls Louada aside and, again, drops the divorce bomb. "The only difference is we'll be talking more over the phone than in person, and I'll come back at regular intervals. Everything will be fine," she assures the nurse as well as herself.

On the drive home Sheila congratulates herself on the successful encounter. *Something has gone tilt in our mother/daughter relationship. This probably happens to most women in their twenties. Oh, well, better now than never. What's next? I have to sell my jewelry to support me through the transition, and give away the woolen suits and sweaters I'll never wear again. This, I'll do in the midst of buying Christmas presents, putting up decorations, and pretending for Allie and Chase that we'll have the best Christmas ever!*

Chapter 16
Ambush

December is horrific. Pretending for the kids, and the world, that nothing is wrong extracts a huge toll from both Sheila and Charles. Since they never discuss things in front of the kids, it is routine to stay up, talking long after the little ones are in bed. For a decade and a half their life plans have been identical, and now, they couldn't be more disparate. Charles's goal, in these discussions, is to locate the problem and fix it. Sheila's objective is to accommodate Charles: he's the victim and should be given every consideration, so night after night they sit by a fire sipping whatever alcoholic beverages they have in stock. Sheila likes the fires, and thinks her husband's attempts to create a romantic atmosphere are painfully sweet. But it's sad to think of all the fires they haven't had throughout the years.

One night, Charles confesses to having had an affair ten years earlier. He does so hoping to convince Sheila that she should continue in the marriage just as he had done. His news isn't really that surprising. The timing of his affair was concurrent with the gaping void that had loomed in their marriage. It was what had prompted those conversations with her mother and Dan, the ones in which she'd been accused of being a "me-first" person.

If Charles thinks his confession will work, a furious Sheila proves him wrong. "Charles! If you didn't love me enough to be faithful, you should have told me and freed us both! Ten years ago, we could have parted without the tragedy that's unfolding today!" The waste of it all disgusts her; still she's torn with the thought that if he had done that there'd be no Allie and Chase.

Undaunted that his strategy backfired, Charles tries a different approach the next night, and the next, and the next. His words stroke, and eventually brow beat his wayward wife. She sits, and listens but won't be budged. Yes, they've had what people would call a good marriage. Yes, there have been good times. No, she won't try to work things out and reconciliation is out of the question. Sheila's best defense is to get drunk. The more intoxicated she becomes, the easier it is to take the insults. It also increases the likelihood of going to sleep later. But the sleep that follows these sessions is that of a small animal, expecting to become something's prey. And the nights are so short; she awakens in the morning still inebriated. Worst of all is the fact that this slow, torturous murder of their marriage must continue for another twelve weeks. For the first time ever, she prays for the minutes, hours, and days of her life to pass quickly.

Years from now, she senses, she'll recall this time with reverent appreciation of Charles. She has dealt him the worst possible blow and he is bearing the trauma with dignity and restraint. With all she's putting him through, she's coming to understand how murder/suicides can happen.

On a Sunday in mid-December, she drives to Milwaukee to attend a conference for private school professionals. Her recent bedlam has allowed no time to prepare a presentation she's expected to do. *Not to worry,* she thinks as she inserts her hotel key card in the door, *I'll write it in the solitude of my room. All I need is a few undistracted hours and I'll be good to go.*

"What? Who? How the hell did you get in here?"

Charles is unpacking his valise. He throws Sheila a charming, mischievous smile, but it fades when he sees his wife's fury. "No! You can't do this! I have a presentation tomorrow and I haven't even begun to prepare. You have to go. How did you get in here anyway?"

"I told the desk I was your husband."

"And they just gave you a key?" Angry tears are forming fast.

"Sure, I showed them my driver's license. We do still have the same last name."

"How dare they? They had no idea I'd want you in my room."

"Well, husbands and wives are generally on good terms."

"We're not!"

"I'm trying to change that," straining to sound playful, "I've ordered dinner, shrimp cocktail, prime rib, chocolate mint pie — all your favorites."

"Great! I'll be too full and too sleepy to even care about writing a speech. This is wrong, Charles! If I don't have time to myself, I'll crash and burn tomorrow."

"You never crash and burn, you're such a natural. You can pull off anything."

Sheila is stunned by this remark. Can it be her husband has no clue how hard she works on her seemingly effortless presentations? Does it mean he's never understood the energy her job extracts from her? Did the superwoman in her ever let it show? She thinks not.

Escaping to the bathroom to splash cold water on her face, she marvels at the reflection in the mirror. *Look at this! These lights actually make me look radiant, on this, the worst day of my life!* For a second, she looks up to see what kind of bulbs can do such a thing. *Correction: The day I told Charles I wanted a divorce was the worst day of my life. There have been so many lately, it's hard to keep track. I should sue this hotel. How dare they give him a key? What if he came here to kill me? No, not Charles, he's a saint for the way he's handling what I keep shoving at him. Still, they should have made him sit in the lobby until they got my permission. Then I could have refused and told them to send him on his way. Oooh! It makes me crazy to think of all those years when a night like this would have been lifesaving water to a woman dying of thirst.*

The rosy reflection cuts in. *Yes, it's the pits, but you must go out there and make him to go away.*

I've hurt him so much already, would sending him away be too humiliating?

Allowing him to stay would be too encouraging.

He'd think I tried.

The time for trying is over. His staying will only accomplish one thing: It will make you look really stupid in front of your peers tomorrow.

The bathroom door opens, and Sheila crosses the room to Charles. Looking anywhere but than into his hopeful eyes she demands, "Get out, now! I don't want you here!" With this, she collapses into sobs.

It's her crying that brings Charles to his senses. He considers his options. She doesn't seem to want him here, and who knows? Maybe he really is jeopardizing her speech. If she does crash and burn it will be his fault. At this thought, he hurls his things back into the valise, heads for the door. Without looking back, he says, "I'll cancel room service on my way out."

As the door slams shut Sheila wipes her tears and tries not to think about what just happened. *All right then, I might as well get at it.* In a file folder, she locates the sparse outline she'd compiled when she was first asked to do this presentation. *I wrote this half a year ago, long before I became the scum-bag I am today.* She struggles to pull organized thoughts from an unfocused mind; then she tries to rehearse the little she's done in front of the mirror. But the stranger she sees there won't let her do more, and when she attempts to find sleep, it evades her. Charles is there, in bed with her, just as surely as if she'd let him stay.

The next morning, with an acid stomach from too much coffee and a body aching from too little sleep, she tries to be the "natural" her husband had described. An excruciating ninety minutes later, Sheila's certain she has, indeed, crashed and burned.

Chapter 17
Mom's Rebuttal

Thankfully, Sheila must leave the scene of her crash to attend a board meeting in Milwaukee. Such meetings are her forte; for these, she's always prepared. It's during the treasurer's report that she's handed a memo. Reading it kicks her into overdrive. "Mother taken to hospital." Always, in the back of her mind is the worry that someday her mother will die before she can get there. Sheila stares at the memo, cursing its lack of information. Her mom has a history of going to the hospital for what her caregivers call, "sinking spells." *Is this one of those or is it life-threatening? No sense debating it!* She passes the message to the board president. He gives her a sympathetic nod as she gathers her things, and scoots from the room.

On the way to her car, she phones the hospital. They confirm that Dora Ronson is in the emergency room, but no further information is available. Half an hour later, she spins through the revolving door of the E.R., positively terrified of the news on the other side.

"My mom's in there. Can I go in?" she points to the curtain barring entrance to the emergency room.

"Yes, dear, the nurse at the station will direct you," a motherly receptionist explains.

"Thanks." No stranger to the E.R., Sheila knows what to do. "Dora Ronson?" A nurse points to a cubicle. "Her condition?"

"Stable."

Relieved, Sheila pulls the curtain aside to see her mother stretched out on a gurney. She winces. *Mom always looks so cold on those things.* A young woman, evidently a resident, is checking her pulse.

"Sissy!" Eunice, another of her mom's caregivers, rushes to her. "Girl, I'm so glad you're here! Your mama wasn't responding to anything I did. I thought she had a stroke."

Sheila nods to Eunice, then cuts to the intern for her assessment. "It's possible your mother had a trans-ischemic attack. Do you know what that is?"

"Yes, I've been told it's like a mini-stroke. She's had them before, is she O.K. now?"

"I've been better," her mother whispers, eyes still shut.

"Mom! I was so frightened!" Relief is gushing from Sheila.

"Were you?" The ice in this reply doesn't keep Sheila from pulling her mother's hands into both of hers. She bends to kiss the cold, thin lips. Dora Ronson opens her eyes and fixes them on her daughter.

"Do you know what happened?"

"No," Mom pauses, "Do you?" This time the sarcasm is so obvious, Sheila looks at Eunice who is, in turn, regarding her employer with amazement.

Sheila tries again. "Did you hear the doctor say you may have had a T.I.A.? One of those mini-strokes like you had when you went to the hospital two years ago at Christmas."

At this point, the doctor breaks in, "Mrs. Ronson, someone will take you to your room in a few minutes." Turning to Sheila, "Your mother is very dehydrated, so we'll keep her on an I.V. and do some tests to be sure nothing else is wrong."

"How did she get so dehydrated?" Sheila's careful not to look accusingly at Eunice.

"That can happen to people in your mother's condition." The doctor's referring to Mom's advanced stage of Parkinson's disease. "It's difficult getting them to ingest enough fluids. O.K. Mrs. Ronson, I'll check on you later." She pats Mom's shaking hand, gives Sheila a sympathetic smile, and leaves the cubicle.

"Mom, since you'll be here overnight, I'll take Eunice home so she can get her things and leave. Then I'll take Wookie to my house, and I'll be back to see how you're doing in an hour or so." Her mother nods with cool indifference.

Melissa McDaniel

On their way to the parking lot, Eunice unleashes her anxiety. "Woo whee! Your ma gave me such a fright! It seemed like she was dead. About that dehydration thing, all the time, I'm asking if she wants a drink. I hold the glass to her lips, and sometimes I put the straw in her mouth, but that makes her mad. Last few days, she hasn't wanted to drink at all."

"I know it's hard. Maybe when she gets home, we'll try telling her it is doctor's orders that she drink six glasses a day."

"Six?" Eunice asks in disbelief.

"I know it won't be easy but it has to be done, actually it should be more."

Something occurs to Eunice and she laughs. "You know what? This is the second time your ma's spent Christmas in the hospital. You s'pose she likes having Christmas in there?"

"Christmas is still a few days away; she'll be home by then." Sheila tries to sound confident, but it has crossed her mind too. *What does it matter? This already promises to be the holiday season from hell.*

At her mom's, she packs the dog's things, and gives Eunice instructions on locking the house. The caregiver, in turn, tells Sheila she'll go to church to pray for her employer. Wookie dashes to the car thrilled to be going anywhere with Sheila. "What do you think, Wook? Did your mistress do this on purpose? Is this her way of saying, 'See what you're doing to me?' If so, she still can deliver a frightening blow!"

Chapter 18
Christmas Eve

The days preceding Christmas are bittersweet as Sheila and the kids make cookies and decorate the house as if they'll always be there, together. But even these moments are tarnished by her mother's attempts to regain control from a hospital bed.

Thank you, Lord, for finally showing me what she's capable of doing. It gives me a power I've never had. Thanks, also, for Earl's phone calls. Without them, this week would have been unbearable. He's my something worth suffering for. He's what was missing ten years ago. The difference, this time, is that I have the love of all loves waiting for me on the other side of the trauma. How much easier this would have been if Earl had appeared around the time Charles had his affair! But fate didn't oblige, and, now, I toil in these sad trenches as I put everything on the line for this man, my "something-worth-suffering-for." Tonight, I'm as deep in the trenches as I'll ever be!

It's Christmas Eve. Sheila, Charles, and his parents are in church, watching Allie and Chase perform in the Christmas pageant. *We look like a "Far Side" cartoon as we kneel, here, in prayer. Charles is imploring the Almighty to make this nightmare go away. His parents are praying for their daughter-in-law to come to her senses. And I'm begging God to help me get gone without causing too much pain to Allie and Chase, and, once the trauma is over, to make their father see they should be with me, their hands-on Mommy.*

On and on she prays, paying attention to the pageant only when Allie and Chase are on stage. *No, she won't pray for her mother who* is still in the hospital. Instead, she silently addresses her. *Mom, you deliberately put yourself in there this time. And you're still there because you told the doctors you didn't want to go home. What gives? Do you think this will actually keep me from leaving? Can't you see I'm saving my life here? If my actions deep-six our relationship, so be it. I loved you so much there would have been plenty of love for you. Why did you insist on keeping me all to yourself?*

As the congregation recites the Lord's Prayer, Sheila's struck by its relevance. "And forgive us our trespasses as we forgive those who trespass against us." *Mom, I can forgive you for loving me too much, but never for what your manipulation did to Charles and me. You really didn't give a damn that my love for him wasn't near what I'd felt for Ed!*

The service ends, and as arranged, Charles is taking Allie and Chase to his parents for dinner and their gift exchange. Sheila isn't joining them on grounds that she should be with her mom.

She'd love to congratulate her little ones on their performances, but she mustn't, for she'd certainly burst into tears. Nodding to her in-laws, she exits out the back. Outside, she turns and walks backwards so she can train her eyes on the church's golden glow. The light, shining through the stained glass windows, is cozy; loving, even. Yet, the people inside would judge her brutally if they knew what she's about to do. *Who, in their right minds, would not?* Before her hot tears can turn icy cold, she dives into her car to get out of the wind and away from her thoughts.

The engine starts and the sounds of her favorite country music station fill the silence. How she loves this music! The lyrics speak straight to her. With spirits somewhat restored she heads to the hospital.

"Hi, honey!" is her mother's surprisingly cheery greeting when Sheila appears in the doorway. She seems genuinely glad to see her derelict daughter. "Where are my grandkids?"

"They're with Charles and his parents. They'll be here tomorrow. Want some Christmas music?" Sheila clicks on the c.d. player she'd brought in earlier. "And let there be light!" she proclaims, plugging in the artificial tree she'd made the first Christmas Mom was in the hospital. "It's good this other bed is unoccupied, tomorrow we'll have a lot of people here, and we'll need the space. You'll have your own private Christmas party! Dan and the boys are coming so I'll bring the presents for them and the ones for Allie, Chase, and Charles too, ok?"

"That's fine." Her mother sounds agreeable; maybe she's coming around.

"Merry Christmas, Mom!" Sheila sets a gaily-wrapped present on her mother's lap.

"How pretty," she says, letting her daughter unwrap it to reveal a pink bed jacket.

"I want you to have this to wear when everyone arrives."

"Are you sure I have presents for everyone?"

"Yes; I finished your shopping this morning. I even found that computer game for Dan's boys, and I wrapped up a nice blouse for you to give me." (As she's often done, Sheila has taken an almost-new shirt of her own and wrapped it to serve as Mom's present for her. The gift of more time with her children is what the ruse accomplishes.)

"Charles's parents came by today," her mother says, smoothing the bed jacket with shaky hands. When Sheila doesn't respond she snaps, "Your in-laws came by!"

"I heard you, Mom. That was nice; they're the best in-laws anyone could have." Sheila means it with all her heart.

"They told me Charles really does love you, and they can't understand what's happening."

"I'm sure they can't."

"I said Charles loves you!"

"Mom, it's more than that, it's that I never loved him, as I should have."

"That's no reason to, to…"

"End the marriage? Mother, I'm layered with reasons."

"I met him, you know, and I don't care for him at all."

"Who?"

"Your young man; I don't like him."

"Where did you meet him, Mom?"

"I met him after the play. He was Julius Caesar."

"He's an actor?" Sheila prompts.

"Yes, he's shallow, full of himself."

The meds are responsible for this; still, Sheila remembers long ago, Mom used those exact words to sabotage yet another beau. An old tape seems to have rewound itself inside her mother's head. Deciding to play along, Sheila says, "He thinks you're wonderful. I'm sure, when you get to know him, you'll like him."

"No! He won't make us happy!"

So revealing is this retort that Sheila wants nothing more to do with the conversation or her mother. She switches on the television to locate a Christmas special into which they both can escape. An hour later, she leaves her drowsy mother to get home in time to put Allie and Chase to bed on this night before Christmas.

When the children are asleep, Sheila and Charles fill their Christmas stockings. This accomplished, she excuses herself to finish wrapping her mother's gifts. "Solitude!" she whispers to herself as she closes the door to the study. Soon, she's engrossed in the rhythm of the work. Cutting, folding, snipping, taping, Sheila's no stranger to this task. When she was little, she loved wrapping presents, but it ended when her mother asked her to wrap all of the family's presents, even her own.

"Don't peek!" she'd say. But of course, Sheila did. She knew it ruined any chance of a surprise, but she did it, every year, to spite her mother. *Why did Mom do that? Was she really so tired?* Sheila sticks a tag on one of Allie's presents as the memory of her mother's weary sighs cuts the solitude. *Few others heard them; they were reserved for Grandma, Daddy, and me. "Look what you're doing to me. Look what I've become,"* they seemed to say.

Blaming the fatigue on housewife boredom, the little girl had vowed it would never happen to her. *When I marry, I'll have a job with lots of excitement, so I won't ever be a drudge like my mother!* That conviction became Sheila's career-woman charge from junior high on. But that sort of fatigue finds busy career women, too. Remembering her lethargy of recent years, Sheila wonders if depression plagued her mother, as it must have her. *Just as I donned an energetic front for my public, so did Mom. Did Dan know? Probably not, but if he did, neither he nor I would have discussed it. That would have been like criticizing God.* Deep in thought, Sheila hasn't noticed the door pushing open. Startled, she jerks up to see Charles.

"May I come in?"

"Charles, this is Christmas Eve. Let's not fight."

SLOW DANCE

He enters with exaggerated caution. As an attempt to be cute, it wins no points.

"No talking tonight, please!"

"No talks, I promise. I just want to give you something."

"You shouldn't be giving me anything." Then, more gently, "Not with what I'm doing to you."

"Well, let's say it's something I should have done a long time ago." With this, he draws a blue box from behind his back and lowers it to her level.

Sheila cringes downward. If she takes it, a scene is sure to follow.

"Please, Sheila!" The pain in her husband's voice causes the involuntary reaction of her hand reaching for the box. Still not looking at her husband, she pulls off the ribbon, and lifts the lid, to see a black leather case. Inside is a diamond-and-platinum watch. If such a gift is a measure of Charles's desperation; he's in bad shape, so she'd better tread softly. Trying to sound more appreciative than offended, she says, "It's beautiful, it's more than beautiful, it's exquisite. But it would be dishonest of me to accept it." Putting the case back in the box, she starts to hand it back.

"No, sweetheart, it's my gift for you."

"I can't."

"Yes, you can. You deserve it. You've been a wonderful wife and a great mother. Please take it."

"I can't accept it." Then, before Charles can patronize her further, "I don't want it!"

"Fine!" He swipes the case from her hand and storms from the room, pulling the door shut with such force it bounces open. Charged with nervous energy, Sheila decides to tackle wrapping a huge box for Chase. Pushing it over, under, and around, she manages to disguise its contents with almost an entire roll of paper. As she slaps on an adhesive bow, Charles reappears. "How much do you think I can take?" Rage glistens in wet eyes. "What do you think I am? I'm not made of iron!"

Sheila's throat catches, "I know the gift meant a lot to you, but..." she breathes in deeply. *Should I tell him what I really think or let it go?*

Tell him, the inner voice commands, *he needs to know.*

Melissa McDaniel

"This is too much, too late. It's not even like you. It's as if someone advised you to do this." She realizes she's treading as softly as a Sherman tank, so she stops. To say she used to pray he'd demonstrate his love with much smaller pieces of jewelry would flatten him. So she sits, waiting for the rage to come. And it does; every hurtful thing Charles can think of is hurled her way. She's deceitful, conniving, and selfish. She's never been honest and doesn't deserve anyone's love. She's a sick and unfit mother!

"Go to hell!" This time, it's Sheila storming out. In the refuge of the dark living room, she lets the tears come. *We're two good people. What evil inspires us to behave so?*

Chapter 19
Christmas Day

"Santa came! He was here!"

Allie and Chase shake their parents awake with no clue their Mommy spent most of the night on the living room couch. At dawn, she'd crept upstairs to be lying next to Charles when they burst in. Sheila rises to follow her little ones as they creep back downstairs to confirm what they'd seen seconds before.

Chase peers cautiously over the railing. "They're there! Our presents are there!"

Jumping over the last step, he tears into the living room where the Christmas tree gloriously spans the width of a picture window. Sheila and Allie are right behind, and Daddy follows close by.

"Ta-da!" Sheila clicks on the tree lights, then, sitting cross-legged on the floor, she motions to Allie and Chase to scramble into her lap. All three savor the moment, suspended in time and resting in God's palm. Forever after, in times of despair, Sheila will resurrect this instant as the single, most perfect moment in her life.

Having drunk their fill of Mommy-love, Allie and Chase spin around to survey their presents.

"Give Daddy a hug," Sheila whispers, steering them toward their father. Charles has been standing nearby, witnessing the love passing between his children and the bitch responsible for dismantling his life. He kneels down to embrace Allie and Chase. It isn't a luxurious hug. He's too focused on the she-devil in his midst, and the children are impatient to get to their presents.

Allie and Chase get the lion's share of the gifts. Every so often, Mom or Dad gets one. When Sheila opens hers from Allie and Chase, she's touched to see that Charles had taken them shopping and let them pick out something all by themselves. It's a warm-up suit that's obviously expensive. As with the watch, Sheila wonders if the price tag was part of a plan. It's feels good though, to be surprised with something so nice. It's as if someone thinks she's worth it. But the good feeling erodes when inner Sheila reminds her how long she'd wanted a gesture like this. Later, when she exchanges the suit for one half as costly, she realizes she'd actually felt the outfit was too good for her. With them both making excellent incomes, she still is most comfortable shopping in thrift stores. *Why, ever, did I allow myself to be conditioned like that?*

Throughout Christmas morning, Sheila and Charles tiptoe through a series of polite but cool encounters. *Ignorance is bliss*, she thinks watching Allie and Chase, so happy amid their treasures. They're truly oblivious to the fact that something is wrong between Mommy and Daddy. *Maybe it's because they've always seen us being civil to each other, but without a lot of hugging, kissing, hand holding, or even paying attention to each other. Is that what we've taught them marriage is like? Oh, Sheila! Do you think you can mess things up anymore than you already have? It really is time to get yourself gone!*

At noon, Sheila goes to the hospital for the Christmas soirée with her mom and Dan's family. As she expected, her brother and teenage nephews have already arrived. Bradley, his youngest, is perched on the windowsill. Jason, two years older, is lounging in the recliner, and there's Dan, standing attentively at his mother's side. Surprise of all surprises! Annette, Dan's first wife, Brad and Jason's mother, is sitting on the other bed. Over the years, she and Dan have worked as a team to raise their boys. Now, happily single, it seems a wonderful gesture she's made the effort to be here.

Sheila has thought of Annette more this fall than she had in all the years since the divorce. As she's awakened to the manipulative role her mother has played in her own life, she's identified similar maneuverings in her brother's relationships. Her mother had been viciously jealous of Annette. She was, after all, direct competition for the love of her son. Such tension there'd been! Family gatherings, which should have been fun, were stiff and artificial. And always for Sheila, they were pockmarked with her mother's behind-the-scenes Annette bashing. *Poor Annette,* she thinks, rushing to hug her ex-sister-in-law. *You were always made out to be the bad guy. And whom did I believe? Mom, of course! If Mom told me something, it had to be true.*

"It's wonderful to see you!" Sheila whispers between hugs. Annette, surprised by the warmth, returns the embrace. Jason and Bradley watch in amazement. They have no memory of their mom and Aunt Sheila together.

Sheila moves about the room greeting her brother and nephews with the usual Christmas clichés. When she gets to Mom, she recognizes the stony, saccharine smile that had always graced her face whenever Annette was around. Mother looks at daughter, eyes screaming *what's "she" doing here?* Ignoring the inquiry, Sheila holds a glass of sherry to her mother's lips with the express purpose of getting her tipsy. *Maybe this will cheer you up so the rest of us can relax.* And it does. A bubbly happy sugar high sticks with her mom for most of the afternoon. Sheila's portable *hors d'oeuvres* are downed as the sherry continues to flow. Her nephews, two really nice kids, stick it out, with the assistance of Dr Pepper, Cheez-its, and Christmas cookies. It helps, too, that Sheila brought two plastic garbage bags full of presents.

When Charles and the children arrive, he joins in the celebration with an excellent show of gaiety. His good spirits seem to say he's a man who has it all. Annette, uninformed on recent developments, wants a photo of Sheila and Charles. "The lovers!" she proclaims as she poses them leaning toward each other. With this, Sheila decides she must confide in her former sister-in-law and newfound friend.

Soon, it's time for Charles and the children to leave for Christmas dinner with his relatives. "Yes," Sheila promises, she'll stop by later. She's certain jumping through a hoop of fire would be easier, but she owes this to Charles.

"You men stay and visit with Grandma. Annette and I will see when her dinner's coming." Strolling down the deserted corridor, Sheila gives the woman beside her an appraising look. "You're still beautiful, Annette." Her ex-sister-in-law is an Italian Goldie Hawn. Huge brown eyes complement a gangbuster smile, and her thick black hair is something Sheila's always envied. "The years haven't left a mark!"

"The same can be said for you, Sheila. And you've done so well for yourself. You seem happy too!"

"That's what I'm best at, *seeming* happy." The sarcasm snaps Annette to attention. "Listen, I have to tell you something. I've done a huge injustice to Charles and myself all these years. I shouldn't have married him, and then I shouldn't have tried for so long to make it work. Brace yourself Annette: Charles and I are getting divorced."

Annette stops walking. This news is too shocking to absorb and move at the same time. Perfect Sheila with the ideal life is not happy? Who could have guessed? She searches her brain for any encouraging cliché that might be appropriate, but the pain on Sheila's face warns her it would be trite. Instead, she pulls her former sister-in-law into her arms as one would a child who'd tried hard, yet failed. They hold each other closer than they ever did as sisters-in-law.

"Thanks. I'm not getting many hugs these days." Sheila steers Annette toward a windowsill where the two can sit and gaze at the winter day. When Sheila feels like talking again, she gives a quick sketch of the past ten years. The subject of Earl comes up, not as the reason for her departure, but as an incentive. "I've finally come to realize that leaving this life I was never meant to live is vital to my well-being. Earl is making the change more bearable but he's not the reason. I am!"

"Well, my dad used to say life should never be wasted. Maybe it's important you salvage what's left of yours; and Charles's too. I'd say go for it!"

Sheila appreciates Annette's brutal empathy. Not since she told Sara and Laura has she felt anyone so completely on her side. The heart to heart brings the two women so close neither wants to break it off to return to her mother's room. But it's late, Annette has to get back to the city, and Sheila must fulfill her promise to drop in at Charles's parents. Fortunately, her brother and his sons can linger a while longer. The high spirits of her departure are as phony as they can be. The surreal nature of what she's planning is starting to have its way with her. Once, she hurt because she couldn't stand the life she'd made for herself. Now, she hurts from all the pain she's causing others in ending it.

Like what I'm doing to these good people, she thinks as she pulls the car up to her in-law's apartment. Her thoughts continue as she walks to the door. *This is too, too awful. These people have been my family for sixteen years. They're the nicest people I know, yet I'm breaking their hearts.* Sheila can almost touch her mother-in law's strain as she opens the door to her philandering daughter-in-law. Always a class act, the senior Mrs. Branford pulls her inside with a welcoming embrace. Then Charles's dad, as good an actor as Sheila is an actress, gives her his usual, "Hello Babe!" greeting and hug. Charles is warm and solicitous of her every need while Allie and Chase dance around their mommy, coaxing her to enter into the Christmas fun. As she greets Charles's aunts, uncles, and cousins she wonders if they know what's happening. They must, because after the initial hello, everyone gives her a wide and respectful girth. Being horrid makes one powerful.

Allie and Chase are delighted when she seeks refuge in a board game on the floor. Their daddy comes over to kneel beside them. Having put aside the wrath of their Christmas Eve offensive, he places gentle hands on his wife's shoulders. Sheila pauses to revel in the sensation. *Touch is such a glorious thing, so little effort for so much joy.* Before it feels too good, she reminds herself they'd gone years without much touching.

"Yeah Mommy!" Cheers interrupt Sheila's reverie as Chase gleefully moves her pawn up a ladder. Charles, realizing his presence is achieving nothing, gives her shoulders one last squeeze and stands to join the adults. *Just as well,* Sheila thinks, relieved to be alone in her children's world.

As the evening draws to a close, Sheila feels almost nauseous saying good-bye to her in-laws. These are dear, sweet people and this is the last time she'll be with them. In one week, her mother and father-in-law will leave to spend the rest of the winter in Arizona. Their emotional investment in her has been great, but it is ending and they'll have little to show for the years they put in. Making inane small talk, Sheila rivets her attention on zipping the children's coats. At the door, she hugs the one she's called Mom for a decade and a half, understanding fully that this woman will never, ever forgive her. Her father-in-law comes forward with sad, knowing eyes. "We have to talk," is all he says.

Melissa McDaniel

As the Branford family exits they look every bit like a normal family, tired and happy after a busy Christmas Day. *How appearances lie! That's O.K. In three days, I can escape to Florida for some glorious — albeit temporary — inaccessibility.*

Chapter 20
A Fatherly Chat

The respite in Florida is to be hard earned. First, Sheila must move her mother home from the hospital, and arrange for the caregivers to resume their schedules. Then, with Mom's care in place, she feels obliged to have that talk with Charles's father. *So no one will ever be able to say I didn't cooperate!*

The meeting is another out-of-body experience. Floating above, Sheila watches a warm but aloof daughter-in-law field questions about her behavior. She's obliquely honest, wanting to spare her father-in-law's feelings whenever possible. Yes, she's leaving Charles to move to Florida. No, she's not entirely certain she'll stay. Yes, the children will remain with their father; she could never leave him and take his children away at the same time. Yes, she deeply loves "this Earl person" and no, it isn't infatuation. Yes, she and Charles had problems before Earl. No, it isn't a sex thing.

Her father-in-law says problems are universal to all marriages. This can be worked out, fixed even. He fishes for the disclosure of a deep, dark secret that may be destroying his son's marriage.

What about your own son's infidelity? No, that's not fair, I mustn't go there. It didn't cause the demise of my marriage. It's only one link in a long chain reaction.

"The problem is with me. It has always been my nature to keep on going as if everything is fine until I finally explode. That's happened and now the prognosis is zero."

Melissa McDaniel

"Do you mean the prognosis for your marriage to Charles is zero? You're that certain of this guy?" Her father-in-law can't believe it.

Sheila whispers the one word he doesn't want to hear. "Yes." At this point the only one who could shake her belief in what she's doing is Earl. She's his to lose. Only if she were to learn he'd misrepresented himself somehow, would she even begin to doubt her decision.

The meeting moves toward its conclusion as courteously as it began. Charles's father tries to end things on a positive note. "We love you, Sheila. You'll always be part of our family, no matter what."

"I love you, too, Dad." *What a shame*, she thinks, *to divorce a person, one must divorce the parents too.*

Home again, she tells the bathroom mirror, "When all this is over, you'll be one tough broad."

The mirror commiserates, *each day brings a new ordeal, but it's so worth it! Now, go pack for some hard-earned R & R.*

Chapter 21
Respite

The plan is for Sheila to fly into Atlanta where Earl has spent Christmas with his brother's family. He'll pick her up at the airport and, together they'll drive to Pine Springs.

Looking good as ever, she muses upon seeing her guy. *Am I such a sucker for a handsome face?* When Earl breaks into his killer smile, she knows it's true. She buries her face in his chest, a little girl hiding from the world. When he starts to let go, Sheila holds fast. For this, she's just spent the most torturous month of her life and, for this, an even worse one is in the offing. Still, she holds tightly to his bulk, letting his strength pour into her. She drinks what she needs and then drinks more. Earl wants to move away from the crush of travelers cutting a wake around them. Her grasp says no. She needs more now, not later. For the first time in a month, she's able to take deep, luxurious breaths, not the nervous wisps to which she's become accustomed.

Finally, after one more devouring kiss, she allows him to steer her toward baggage claim. They shuffle with others like the legs on a massive centipede. Sheila's still curled into Earl's chest. His head nuzzles her hair. Anyone looking at them might assume she's just returned home from an ordeal of sorts. She looks worn, and battle-fatigued, but relieved to be back in her love's arms. To a candid eye, it looks as though all is right with her world.

It's not so! This isn't some sweet reunion! She silently scolds a woman's sympathetic smile. *I'm an adulteress who's going to leave her sixteen-year marriage for her lover of six months. I'm wild and*

Melissa McDaniel

reckless and I wreak havoc wherever I go. I'm worried to death about my children and feeling vengeful toward my mother. I don't deserve to ever be happy again.

What do you know about it? Her thoughts address a man who lets them pass. *Do you think we're some innocent couple who's found love in mid-life? Ha! Ask Charles about that!* By now the centipede has curled around a conveyer belt.

Whew! inner Sheila cautions, *Get a grip before you self-destruct.*

Just as she's climbing out of her funk, Earl says casually, "Hey blossom, someone else is hitching a ride with us back to Pine Springs."

"Not a problem!" She'd been craving the time alone with Earl, but she'll rise to the occasion. "Who might that be?"

"It's Satin, one of the gals you met last fall. She's flying in from Charleston. We'll pick her up at the next terminal."

"Oh," she says, realizing he never really sensed the vibes Satin had spewed her way. *O.K., if Satin is a friend of Earl's, I'd better give it a try.* And she does. For more than an hour, Sheila tries to chip away at the icy aura in the back seat. Her inquiries about Satin's holiday are genuine: she'd like to hear what a Charleston Christmas is like, but the response is terse. In no way will Satin give the Yankee bitch a glimpse into her world.

Sheila decides it's time to cut bait. *If I persist, you'll pull me deep into the muck of your contempt. Why do you dislike me so? Are you that in love with Earl? I feel you back there, straining to weaken me with the force of your hatred. But guess what? I don't like you either and I know how to make you suffer.* With this, Sheila commences to arouse Earl in full view of her adversary. It's discreet; she won't give Satin anything lewd to gossip about. But it's enough to charge the air with unspent lust. First, her fingertips play with the curls at his neckline. From there, they move across his shoulder, down his arm, and on to his thigh. Earl winks at her as she traces little circles on the inseam of his jeans.

"Mmm!" Stifling his delight, he checks the rearview mirror. "She's asleep," he mouths with a "please don't stop" look in his eyes.

Sheila doesn't believe it for a second. *Satin, you just keep on pretending you don't know how much your boy wants me. Keep those eyes closed all the way home!*

When they finally pull up to Satin's condo, she grabs her bags, and mutters a curt "good-bye" without looking at Sheila. Earl shrugs his shoulders at the behavior then speeds home to complete two hours of foreplay. Ten minutes into their lovemaking, the phone interrupts their rapture. The shrill rings count three then stop.

"Think that was your husband?" Earl pants.

"No," Sheila's certain. "That's Satin having the last word."

The next morning, she sits on the bathroom counter, watching Earl brush his teeth. He must go out for a while. Mullet has called to complain that Satin was at his house all night, "Drunk as a billy goat, and talkin' crazy."

Sheila's instincts sound an alarm. Is this Satin's next blow in their point/ counterpoint repartee? She studies Earl. He's definitely more annoyed than alarmed at her behavior. Especially aggravating to him is the fact that Mullet's demanding he stop by. "If you don't, she ain't gonna leave!"

"What I can't figure out," Earl tells Sheila, "is what got into her over the holidays."

"Come again?"

"When I dropped Satin off at the airport, she was happier than I'd seen her in ages, bubbly even. Then, coming back, she did that sulking thing, and now this."

Sheila watches her guy. *Is he really so clueless? Should I fill him in on the facts of life or let him muddle through it from a male point of view?*

"Do you think she has feelings for you?" Sheila can't believe this is first edition news.

Earl scrunches his nose. "Naaaaaah," he scoffs at her reflection in the mirror.

"Yeaaaah!" Sheila mimics back. "What do you think are the chances that she figured once you'd run through your stable of women, you'd finally get to her? And now she's pissed because I came out of nowhere to lay claim to what should be hers?"

Earl examines a fingernail so he won't have to look at Sheila. *What truths are those teal eyes concealing?* Not wanting to dignify this soap opera any longer, she drops the subject and snuggles Earl from behind. Realizing how much of this huge man there is to love both outside and in, she wonders, *how many Satins are still in your life? I want to know about every one of them — or do I?*

"Come on, Mattie!" She and the lab go outside where Mattie finds a tennis ball to drop at Sheila's feet. Squatting, she engages the old, wise eyes, "Girl, I hope from now on, you and I will be the only women in our guy's life." The lab's tongue swipes at the nice lady's cheek. "You've witnessed a ton, haven't you? I wish you could tell me about it; how about a hint?" Mattie, bored with the conversation, is fixated on the ball. Sheila chuckles at the honest communication and gives it a heave.

Was I too rough on Satin? Her rebuffs made me want to get even. Did she get plastered just to get Earl's attention? If so, it worked. Looking up she sees him, dressed and ready to rush to Satin's aid.

"I'm fixing to be at Mullet's for only a while. Then I'll high tail it back so we can head for Clermont." Earl treats Sheila to a Rhett Butler twinkle as the full wingspan of his arms envelops her. What a sensation it is to be surrounded by the all of this man! Their embrace is prolonged, just as it was at the airport. This time, it's Earl refusing to let go. He's savoring how good it is to have her in his home, hoping, praying maybe, that before too long, this will be permanent.

"I want this too," she whispers.

Earl's exhale is a shudder of emotion. He still can't believe this woman has chosen him, especially with what she soon will be going through. Keeping his arm around Sheila, he steers her into the house. "Feel free to call your kids, your mom or your staff. And if you take Mattie for a walk, you'll have a friend for life."

"Don't worry, I'll keep busy. Now go, you heartbreaker, render whatever aid is necessary, but make it quick!"

Earl turns for one last good-bye. This time, it's to Mattie. Kissing her on the top of her head and rubbing her ears, he says, "Bye girl, take care of Miss Sheila, she's important to us." Leaving his womenfolk to entertain each other, he speeds off.

"O.K. Mattie, we'll take that walk, but first I want to call my kids."

"Mommy!" jubilant cries crowd through the receiver. Allie and Chase are each on separate extensions.

"Hi punkie-pies! How're you doing?" Sheila releases herself to the wonder of her children, as she leads the conversation with her questions. *It may have to be like this for a while,* she tells herself. *When I arrive here in March, I'll have to depend on Ma Bell to keep us close.* She pushes the thought away, letting the happy chatter of her children flow through her. She reminds them of the activities they have planned over the next six days; maybe with something to look forward to, they won't miss her too much.

They seem fine, although they, again, want to know where she is, why she's there, and when she's coming home. Riddled with guilt, Sheila explains that she's in Florida visiting a friend, and she'll be home in six days. "The time will pass quickly, and this way, you'll have Daddy all to yourselves. She hopes Charles shares her enthusiasm, but maybe, she'll get the kids sooner if he finds the role of hands-on-Daddy to be tedious. Sheila marvels at the length of the conversation. Who says children have short attention spans? When it's time to say good-bye, she's the one to cry. To hide her sniffs, she soothes them with words of love and praise. Savoring the adoration coming through the phone, they listen. "You're my own sweet darlings, and I love you with all my heart. Be sweet to each other. I'll call again tonight, and we'll have another good talk." Tears come fast as she listens to the chorus of goodbyes. "Good bye, Allie. Bye-bye, Chase, I'll talk to you soon, mmwah!" Blowing loud kisses into the phone, she makes sure they hang up first. Then, utterly alone, she clicks off. *This is how it will be. Can I stand it, even temporarily? How can I, the Goody Two Shoes of all time, be in such a position? What brought me to this point? What...*

Stop! Her inner voice cautions, *If you're not supportive of yourself through every step of this process, you will, indeed, go mad. Later, if this proves wrong, you can change your mind.* This thought tags along as she takes Mattie for the walk Earl prescribed. The two stroll through the golf course community of attractive rustic homes. Sheila loves the way their contrast of stone and wood is highlighted by thick backdrops of pine, oak, and magnolia. The people are nice, too; every single passerby waves or stops to greet her. *This place is like a warm, easygoing friend.*

"What's the matter, Mattie?" The aged dog is sitting down and gnawing at her paw. "You've got a sand spur, don't you?" Sheila recalls Wookie's bouts with the prickly atrocities. The terrier, familiar with the drill, has learned to stand still and lift her paw so Sheila can take it out. But Mattie's ten times larger and her teeth are huge. She kneels beside the dog, remembering the lab she and her brother had as children. Buckshot had been the best dog in the world, but he'd suffered an untimely death under the wheel of a landscaping truck. Her next dog, Thor, was a rage-filled cocker spaniel, capable of attacking anyone without warning. Living with that crazy pooch had conditioned her not to get too close to any dog.

But Mattie's not like Thor, and it's in a lab's nature to be sweet. Hoping the stereotype applies to this eighty-five pound canine, Sheila bends down to the retriever's level. "Mattie-girl, I can help you." Wise honey-brown eyes search Sheila's silver blues. "If you let me, I'll get the nasty thing out."

Sheila scratches the dog's ears and, as she's seen Earl do; she blows tiny kisses within inches of her mouth. "Good girl." Slowly, she lifts the wounded paw. Don't get your face so close to the dog! Her father's admonition calls from decades past.

"Here it is. Ouch, that's sharp!" Sheila examines the spiky orb impaled in the pad of her index finger. She flicks it away, and feels two more in Mattie's paw. "Hold still, girl, we can do this. There's one, and here's the other. We got 'em! Look at these." Mattie sniffs the culprits. "What a brave girl you are!" Sheila hugs the dog with the distinct sensation she's being hugged back.

They return home to find Earl already there. "All's well," he announces.

Sheila's dying to know the details of his encounter with Satin, but she'd seem nosy, worse yet, insecure. "I'm glad. I was afraid we might not be able to leave."

"Darlin', nothing could keep us from leaving. As they say in the Bahamas; 'not my problem, mon!'" His words, sharp with aggravation, make Sheila feel better about whatever, past or present, has transpired between Earl and Satin.

What follows is the happy rushing around of two people, unaccustomed to each other's ways. They move through the house packing for their car trip, first to overnight with friends in Clermont, then to drive to Conch Cay, Sean Murphy's Jupiter home. Finally, they're on their way, with Mattie stretched across the entire back seat of Earl's Jeep.

The first stop is at the home of Jack Randolph, one of Earl's oldest buds. Throughout their college careers, they studied, played sports, and partied together. In the years following graduation, their friendship saw them each married, with families, and then divorced.

Alana, Jack's second wife is what Southern men call "fuckin' gorgeous." Her face is spellbinding and her figure seems too perfect

SLOW DANCE

to be of this world. Sheila listens to the couple regale her with stories of wild days gone by. Ravenous for information about her man's past, she gnaws at each anecdote as a starving dog would a bone.

Alana discloses the most. Her female opinions are woven into every one of her "he said, she said" stories. In an earlier life, Jack had played professional ball. The experience carved a lifestyle, the tales of which challenge Sheila's perception of right and wrong. It bothers her to think Earl was a willing participant.

As the stories flow, Earl leans back, balancing his chair on two legs. He stares at the table, silently imploring his buddy to shut up.

Not to worry, Sheila consoles herself. *These people have seen more of life than my own myopic, work-dominated existence has shown me. I like them, and God knows I appreciate them for not judging me. They provide a cozy fortress where the world can't get at me.*

It's mid-morning when they leave the Randolph's to head for South Florida. The scenery's lovely, but Sheila would rather look at Earl's tanned face. The blues and greens of his Hawaiian shirt make his eyes more teal than ever. She'll never get enough of that face, but there's more to it than that. He's the warmest, most soulful man she's ever met. To live in the radius of a soul like his is a worthy goal.

Conscious of Sheila's scrutiny, Earl begins to talk. He tells her how he spent the summers of his childhood with his grandparents in the factory town of Chicopee, Georgia. There he and his cousins were never at a loss for things to do because all their games came from their imaginations, not from the external props kids need today.

In her mind's eye, Sheila sees little Earl conquering the countryside in handed-down dungarees and faded, striped T-shirt. Next she looks at the self-made man by her side and whispers a prayer of thanks that he's in her life. For the next four hours, they volley childhood stories back and forth, each learning and loving more about the other. By the time they arrive at Conch Cay, the Loxahatchee riverside home of Sean and Janice Murphy, they've climbed even deeper into each other's souls.

Chapter 22
New Year's

Sheila likes Conch Cay, the Murphys' Loxahatchee River home. In it, they live the good life; the good life doesn't live them. She knows this is true, because Murph is one uncompromising individual. He won't let anything or anyone dictate how he lives. That's why he's on wife number three. It's also why this one will stick. As Sheila remembers from the fall, Janice is a psychologist who knows her man from the inside out. He isn't going to change, not even for her, so she lets him live the life he wants, and because of that, he wants her by his side.

As Sheila helps Janice get things ready for a New Year's Eve celebration, she can't help contrasting her to Alana Randolph. How fascinating it is that two pals of Earl's are attracted to such different women! She looks across the room at Earl, already engrossed in a bowl game. *What needs do I fill for you, my love? Cute and intelligent or beautiful and beguiling?*

Guests are arriving, so Sheila stays near the door to meet the cross section of humanity coming to ring in the New Year at Conch Cay. Earl comes by with a margarita for her. When he sees she's at ease mingling with the natives, he heads back to a game. After a while, Sheila moves out onto the deck where Chelsey Cook, a petite brunette, stands admiring the view. A man, about Earl's age, approaches, "You O.K., baby?"

"I'm fine, Sandy. Now go bond with the boys," she dismisses him with an affectionate kiss.

Instead of leaving, he announces, "You and Sheila have something in common; you're both here cheating on your hubbies." Zing! The reality in those words sears a red hot "A" on Sheila's chest. "Chelsey's fixing to leave hers, and I hear from Murph you are too."

To Sheila's Midwest way of thinking, "fixing to leave," is a not quite as horrible as "cheating." Her defenses relax some, and as they do, she begins to pour her heart out to this total stranger. Empathy flows, as the two grow close in their mutual plight. They'd both known their marriages weren't working yet they'd stayed, and in each case, it had taken "another man" to bring their unhappiness to a festering head.

"I'm such an approval seeker," Sheila confides. "Staying in my marriage seemed easier than facing the wrath I'd incur if I were to end it. Plus, I felt I deserved my unhappiness since my decision to marry Charles was at the root of it. But now that I know what I've been missing, I have to go through with the miserable deed. T. Earl Langley is way too good to pass up." Sheila thinks on this for a moment, "It's not just the man; it's this place and the absolute necessity to change my life that's taking me from the home I've always known. I wish I could explain it in some intelligent way. Up there, people will surely see my actions as those of a selfish, uncaring bitch. But I'm far from that."

"I know what you mean!" Chelsey choruses. People see this as a sudden whim when really, it's been building for years!" The two commiserate until midnight approaches. Then, with hugs of support, they adjourn to find their "other men."

The New Year is minutes away, so Earl guides Sheila back on to the deck for a panoramic view of the river. "I want us to greet the New Year under the stars. This is our year, darlin', this one's for us and no one else." Sheila is willing herself to look happy, but it's not working. Noticing this, Earl inquires, "Something wrong, blossom?"

"Everything! I dread so much what I have to do these next ten weeks! The coward in me says it's too hard, but a new voice in here," she points to her heart, "says I have to save myself. Earl, am I so worth saving?"

"Hell yes and you're saving me too sweet pea. You've made all the difference in my life." Reading the depth of Sheila's pain, he adds, "Darlin', nothing I say can help with what you've got ahead.

Melissa McDaniel

All I can say is I'm here for all time." His words make her feel less alone, but she has yet to commit the most solitary act of all, that of leaving Charles.

At midnight, Murph comes by to envelop her in a somber New Year's embrace. Sheila clings to him, knowing he's one of very few people who understand what she's going through. Their subsequent conversation will have great impact in the months to come.

"You and I have a lot in common," he begins. "We're good people who invested years in so-so marriages, until one day we realized we couldn't do it anymore. Now, Miss Sheila, I see guilt oozing from every one of your pores and that's your biggest worry. It's not what you're doing to your husband; it's what you're doing to yourself that's your enemy. Remorse is a destructive force. In fact, it will kill you, so you've got to be sure you're doing this for yourself, separate and apart from Earl. If you do it to be with him, remorse will eat you alive."

The light of the moon casts ominous shadows over Murph's face. His black Irish eyes look like two holes boring into his skull. *There's truth in what he says, the vision in those caverns is as deep as I suspected.*

Murph continues, saying he in no way wants to dissuade her from what she's doing. "God knows! I've never seen T. Earl so happy! But I hope you can develop a sense of balance to rely on when things get tough. And believe me, they will."

"For forty-three years, I thought I had a sense of balance, but then I learned the scales were off!" Sheila quips, knowing if she doesn't laugh this instant, she'll surely cry.

"Well, here's your chance to adjust the scales. My money says you'll do it."

"Hey, you two, what's going on?" Earl strolls up. Sensing the significance of the dialogue, he'd stayed away. The three share an embrace similar to the sandwich hug Sheila does with her children. She senses a wonderful bond of solidarity growing between them as they gaze at the river. Murph and Earl feel something too. It's their eager anticipation of the next day's fishing trip.

Janice, Sheila notices, is talking to two other weekend guests. The man looks like any other rough riding ex-athlete type, but Sheila knows his body is raging against him in the form of advanced colon cancer. He, his wife, and their twelve-year-old daughter are visiting the Murphys to escape the drudgery of his disease. Right now, he seems as hearty as any other "go-for-the-gusto" guy at the party, but this could be his last New Year's celebration.

She's heard it said that when a person has cancer, it's as if the spouse has cancer too. That may be true, but tonight, his wife — a striking brunette — is exuberance personified. She shows none of the wear and tear that lies below the surface. On this night, she is giving herself to the here and now, acting as though the ravages will never come. Sheila watches this woman, hoping to absorb even a little of her strength. *Time is precious and she's not about to waste what little they have left. That's what this is about.* She wonders how much time she, herself, has left and it scares her that she's already squandered so many years. For too long, she's served everyone's wishes but her own. *If I were facing certain death, what would I do? That's easy, I'd do exactly what I'm about to do. I'd let my newly awakened soul be the one to decide how I'd write the rest of this script. And no one, not even Earl, would have editorial input on the way it ends.* Rejuvenated by her declaration of independence from influences, real or imagined, she kisses her guy and runs inside to wish Chelsey good luck in the coming year.

Chapter 23
Slow Murder

Sheila's respite is ending. It's time to fly back and face the reality that awaits her. "Remember what I said about remorse," Murph whispers as they leave.

Sheila acknowledges his admonition with a mock salute. "No remorse!" she proclaims, forcing her voice to sound positive. Later, on the plane, his words return. Part of his agenda is to protect his friend. *He doesn't want me turning Earl into the bad guy. Murph doesn't know what a guilt-assuming person I am. If things don't work out, it will be my fault and no one else's.*

Enough introspection, what's the next step? It's moving out of the house and, now that her in-laws are wintering in Arizona, into their apartment. *Take it one day at a time*, inner Sheila advises. *First, move into the apartment to get everyone accustomed to you not being around all the time. Then, in nine weeks, move far away from the marriage, and the life — but never from your children, they will always be with you and you with them.*

Sheila pictures herself, unemployed in a new place with a man she loves but doesn't know very well. To have her kids with her would, of course, be best for her. But it wouldn't do to thrust them into a new home, school, and state with a man who isn't their daddy. *Why am I even thinking about this? I'd never leave Charles and take the children, too; that would kill him. Mom conditioned me, always, to be the one to sacrifice my needs for those of others, and for Charles to survive this ordeal, he'll need the focus, comfort, and sense of identity that Allie and Chase will provide.*

Sheila struggles to keep this in mind on a blustery Sunday morning in mid-January as she prepares for the most gut-wrenching experience of her life. On this day, she and Charles will tell Allie and Chase that she's moving out of the house and into their grandparents' apartment. With eight weeks before her departure this move is necessary to help Sheila and the children make the adjustment to being away from each other.

Immediately after church, she goes shopping to lay in a supply of goodies for the kids as well as a stash of convenience foods to help Charles through the next few weeks. The shopping goes quickly since she knows exactly what the kids and he would want. Among the short order dinners is Kraft Macaroni and smoked sausage. She chooses a particular brand of sausage because it's buy one, get one free. Funny, even now, she shops as though they're on a tight budget. *What will my spending be like down there, when I have no job? The proceeds from selling my jewelry will only stretch so far, but I won't touch the money Charles and I saved together, nor will I use any of my leave-of-absence paychecks. They'll go straight into the account Charles and I hold jointly. No one will ever be able to say I took off with more than my share!*

She pushes the cart to the check out stand. The mere act of placing Kraft dinners, chocolate doughnuts, and Kudos on the counter engulfs her in a wave of sentimentality. Here comes the fist, tightening again, as her eyes fill with tears. The store clerk asks if she's all right. Sheila nods but dares not speak. On the way out, she sees a public phone and rushes to it as if it were a dear friend. Through it, she'll find her courage. Picking up the receiver she punches the numbers that will connect her to her strength.

"Blossom! What a great surprise!"

"Earl, you're there!"

"Course I am. What are you up to this glorious Sunday morn?"

Glorious? Sheila gazes out at a monochrome world of ice and snow. "I need your support. In an hour, I'm telling Allie and Chase I'm moving into their grandparents' place without them."

Just saying this makes the fist in her chest seem to spring open and flatten her against the wall with its palm. Unable to move, she waits to hear Earl say something to make it all right. Nothing comes. "I'm at the grocery store putting in a supply of things they like to eat." No response. "Are you there Earl?"

Finally, a cautious voice, "That's my girl, you're doing everything you possibly can, aren't you?"

"Earl, this is so hard!"

"I know it is Darlin'. We've talked about this. You have to be sure you're doing this for yourself, not for me, otherwise you'll suffer remorse."

"Remorse?" Evidently her honey and Murph have been talking. "I know about remorse. What I need from you, right now, is encouragement, like hearing how much you love me and want me there, et cetera, et cetera!"

"Of course I love you and I want you here, but you have to do what's best for you and for the kids." Clearly, Earl will not take responsibility for luring her to Florida. Why, now, of all times, is he pulling himself from the equation? This makes it even harder; it means she no longer has an accomplice in the heinous deed. The horrible thing she's doing is hers, alone.

Switching to a more comfortable subject, Earl explains he's in the process of putting up twelve quarts of Ruskin tomatoes.

I'm on the verge of telling my children devastating news and he's canning tomatoes. Life is so lopsided!

With no words of "I need you, you're wonderful, and everything will be fine," Sheila loses interest in the conversation. "Time's short, I've got to get home to make Allie and Chase's favorite breakfast. Love you, bye!"

On the way home, she anguishes over what truly is best for the kids. Is it better to say, "Whoops, sorry Charles, I didn't mean it and don't worry about what I need. That's never been important before, why should it be so now?"

If you do that, the voice cautions, what happens then? First, you'll kill your love for Earl like you did for Sonny and Ed. Then, you'll prolong the role-playing another twenty, thirty, maybe forty years. You'll act the part of a happy woman, who lives with a man she doesn't love, working at a job she no longer loves, in a place she never loved. Happy, happy, joy, joy. Won't that be healthy? And what happens to the children of the frustrated actress? Will they know the tension of her passive anger? Of course they will — just as you suffered your own mother's unhappiness. Don't you remember how hard you tried to fill her half-empty glass?

SLOW DANCE

Is that what happened? Did I bond to her in my conviction to make her less tortured? Sheila pulls herself from the past as things come suddenly clear. "No! I mustn't do that to Allie and Chase."

Is God telling her this? Or is this her inner consciousness breaking through? Whatever it is, a humming, whirring "pay-attention-to-this" sensation is forcing her to take notice. *What's best for your children is to have a happy, fulfilled mother, not one who's neurotic from living a lie that's decades old.*

"I smell bacon! French toast? Yeah! That smells good, Mommy!" Happy voices pull Sheila from her thoughts, as Allie, Chase, and their daddy enter the kitchen. "We'll tell them after we eat," she whispers to a sullen Charles as they carry the food to the dining room. He sits at the head, Sheila, to his right, and Allie and Chase have their usual fight over who sits by Mommy. A while back, they'd agreed to a "me for lunch, you for dinner" rotation.

"You got her last night, I get her now." Allie shoves Chase from the seat.

"I get her tonight!" he snaps back, and for special effect, he crawls under the table to take the seat opposite Sheila. *Do you see this?* Sheila thinks, looking at her soon-to-be former husband. *How could you justify keeping them any longer than the time it will take for you to adjust to being single? Don't you see they need me more than they do you?*

But these are thoughts for another time. This breakfast deserves her full attention. Allie, Chase, and Sheila chatter about Sunday school, play dates, and what movie they want to see. Daddy's silent and still as a stone throughout the entire meal. As brunch concludes, Sheila looks into his eyes. They're staring at the middle of the table. *It's up to me, Lord. Send me the words, please!*

She looks at her children waiting to be excused. *They're so precious!* "Allie and Chase, Daddy and I have something to tell you." She pulls Allie onto one knee and waves Chase over to the other. Sheila has sought the advice of counselors on how to explain something like this. No words are right. Here they sit, her darlings, waiting for the news Mommy's about to share.

"Daddy and I love you both very, very much. That will never, ever change. Daddy's a good person and I am, too, but we aren't good together. That means we're not happy being married to each other. So we're not going to live together anymore. In a few weeks,

Melissa McDaniel

I'm going to move to Florida, and I'll be away from you for a while. But I'll come to see you, and be with you often. And we'll talk on the phone every day. Of course, you'll visit me lots in Florida, too."

That was awful. Sheila looks at Charles. He sits, eyes still fixed on the center of the table. "To help us get used to the feeling of being away from each other, I'm going to move into Grandma and Grandpa's apartment. We'll still see each other lots and the time we'll share will be more special than ever." Sheila, so afraid she'd cry, is instead calm and alert. That's because she's left her body and is floating above, watching herself deliver this information in third person.

Allie and Chase sit, wondering what it means. At seven and five, they understand nothing of this. She pulls each of them into their traditional sandwich hug then coaxes them to do the same for their daddy. As they hug, Charles whispers something.

"Huh?" asks Chase.

Daddy whispers again. Understanding the words this time, the little boy turns to Sheila, "I will miss you," he tells her.

"Oh my love, I'll miss you too, so very, very much!" Suspended above them, the other Sheila looks down at the scene, positive she's never made the acquaintance of the scumbag below.

Allie's bewildered; her rock, her anchor, her own true love of a mommy is doing what? She's going away? Where is she going and why? Sheila sees the concern in her little girl's eyes, but knows it may take time to reach her lips. As the counselor has suggested, they will have many talks in the coming days. Charles still says nothing. Worried his cold silence will frighten the children, she asks Allie and Chase to help her clear the table, then get ready to go to Grandma's.

Going to Grandma's is not what Sheila wants to do; it's what she *has* to do. Since her mother came home from the hospital, their relationship has continued to suffer. It has everything to do with her impending move to Florida. The less emotional Sheila watches from above as her mother practices the tactical withdrawal of years gone by. *That no longer works, Mom. Finally I see it for the emotional blackmail it is.* With her mother ignoring her, Sheila spends most of the visit playing with Allie, Chase, and Wookie. They dance to old records. Doing the Twist and Shout, the Bird, and best of all, the Monster Mash, helps her feel better. When her mom says the music makes her nervous they switch to the Sleeping Beauty Ballet. Allie and Chase copy Mommy's simple ballet steps, their faces, little studies in concentration. How she loves them! How she adores her precious children!

When ballet loses their interest, they decide to build a snow fort for Grandma. All three don their layers and run outside to wave at her through the window. *Less than a year ago, we were building a snowman for you outside the cabin in Water Haven. This is the closest we'll get to a winter retreat this year. In fact, we may never have one again. Did it ever occur to you, Mom, that one day your maneuverings might bite you back?* Soon, they stand, surrounded by their icy creation. It resembles a fence more than a fort, but who cares? Allie and Chase shout and wave to get Grandma's attention, but she's asleep, slumped in the wheelchair, looking utterly helpless. Guilt stabs at Sheila; she shouldn't be away from her mother, she shouldn't be so selfish.

Inner Sheila knows this is shaky ground. Her softhearted counterpart has been defeated many times at exactly this point. *Keep those blinders on! Don't you dare let your guilt talk you out of it; your life depends on this!*

Chapter 24
Moving Out

Sad to the bone, Sheila loads her suitcases into the car. This is the morning she moves into her in-laws' apartment. Charles is helping, thoughtful, and courteous. He's doing his best to make it known he'd welcome her back anytime.

Every cell of her body seems to be in mourning. It's as if a loved one or some beloved entity is no more. There's no doubt she still cares deeply for Charles, her roomie of sixteen years, and more importantly, the father of her children. He's part of her, and that will never change. Even more embedded in her soul is the family, that entity to which she has dedicated her life. From this day on, the family will never again be the same.

Charles remarks that the transfer of Sheila's luggage has been amazingly easy. He doesn't know she's already sent the bulk of her things to Florida. Before he can figure it out, she switches the conversation to the topic of his parents' generosity. They are allowing her to stay in their apartment while they winter in Arizona. "This is above and beyond," she observes, knowing they're hoping this separation will help her regain her sanity. *They don't know how gone I am already. This sojourn,* she thinks as she hangs her clothes in a guest closet, *is the next step in my plan. It's the purgatory I must endure before I begin my new life.*

She leaves the apartment to have breakfast with Allie and Chase. It's a tradition from which all three must slowly be weaned over the next two months. Each week she'll do one breakfast less, until the last couple of weeks when they'll be eating breakfast only with

Mara, their Polish sitter. *Will Charles rearrange his schedule to breakfast with the kids? I hope so.*

Soon, they're in the car for the short drive to school. Hugs and kisses later, she's off to work with a full schedule of meetings. The day concludes with a trip to the dentist to replace a worn filling. The small talk between Sheila and Dr. Scranton deliberately focuses on Charles's sisters. The news that she moved out this very morning is not chitchat for the dentist's chair. As she leaves the appointment with a temporary filling in place, Sheila thinks, *one more dental visit and I can check this off my "to-do" list.* So thorough are her departure plans, she's brainstormed on every dental and medical problem that should be corrected before her insurance runs out.

Although her mouth is swollen and numb, she manages a soup supper with Laura Tolafson. As she sips her hot and sour repast, she finds herself grateful for a friend like Laura. *She knows everything I'm about to do and she's still my friend!* Sheila explains that eight weeks stretch before her like a field of land mines. "The mines of public opinion, especially, will blow me to smithereens if I let them. With a heart as tender as mine, I have to take the offensive on damage control or it will wear me down until I lose courage. Hopefully, I can minimize the gossip with a tightly orchestrated schedule of announcements designed to say as little as possible."

"Will Charles cooperate with that?" Laura inquires.

"I think so. He's none too eager to make my intentions known. He's still hoping I'll come to my senses before the neighbors find out."

"Sheila, you are the bravest woman I know. You're also the kindest. I'll be the first to tell people that you had no other choice but to do this. I'll also tell them I know what it's doing to you to leave your children, even if it's only for a while."

Later, in the cozy darkness of her in-laws' guestroom, Sheila allows the memory of her friend's compassion to soothe her like a warm bath. Maybe it will help soften the ache of this, her first childless night.

Suddenly, she hears the apartment's front door click open and closed. Barely able to breathe, she gropes for the phone to dial 911.

"Sheila, are you here?" It's Charles.

For weeks, she'd longed to be free of her husband's late-night inquisitions. This was to be the day; this apartment was to be her safe haven.

"Damn it, Charles!" She runs out of the bedroom, "You scared me!"

"I'm sorry, sweets. It didn't occur to me you'd think it was anyone else."

He looks so hopeful, her heart begs her to be gentle, but it's too late. She beats the air with her fists and stomps her bare feet on the tile entryway. "No, no, no! This wasn't part of the deal; I'm here to be away from you, not available for your spontaneous drop-ins! You have to leave right now!" To make her point, Sheila jerks open the door.

Charles ignores the gesture and sits on a bench. He pats the place next to him indicating that she should join him there. "Sweetheart, I have to know something." She groans and stays by the door. "Is it your job? Are you burned out in your job?"

Lately, when Charles has come home with a fresh new approach to his wife's recalcitrant behavior, Sheila has credited it to the advice of a co-worker. *Which one of them helped plot this tactic?*

"Good God!" she screams in a stage whisper. "Next to Allie and Chase, my job is the thing I'll miss most. I wish I could take it with me! No, Charles, you're barking up the wrong tree on this one. Try this: I'm burned out in our marriage!"

Her husband's muscular frame caves in at the blow. "That was harsh. I didn't mean to be so blunt, but this drilled out tooth is killing me." Close to tears, she takes a shot at logic. "Charles, I'm over here to see what it's like to be separated from you. How will I know if you're here all the time? Don't you think it's in your best interest to give me some space?"

This makes sense. After a brief silence, Charles stands and moves to the door.

"You didn't leave Allie and Chase alone, did you?"

"Mara's with them."

Now it's clear. This ambush was to last the entire night. *Either Charles is turning out to be quite the romantic, or someone's giving him very good coaching.*

"Here," he pushes a bottle of Merlot at her. "Maybe we'll actually drink it sometime." She lets him kiss her the way she once wished he would, but her Richter scale registers nothing. The door closes after him. *Poor Charles, he's doing his best but it's like getting blood from a stone.* Just this morning, the disc jockey on her country music station had described a song as being one of the "snooze and lose" lessons in life. He could have been talking to Charles. *Maybe, what he's learning from all this will benefit some future woman, it's too late for this one.*

Chapter 25
Psychodrama

An important task on Sheila's "to-do" list is getting the Water Haven cabin ready to be sold. Both she and Charles agree it must go. Sheila loves it dearly, but it had become just another extension of her responsibilities at home. Over the years, the convenience of a two-minute drive between her mother's cabin and her own had come to mean a three- and four-visit day. Shopping, cleaning, cooking, and just plain doing for Mom were a big part of her weekend routine. Come Sunday night, she'd be wondering where the time had gone.

It will change nothing, but like many positive components in her marriage, she must say good-bye to her precious cabin. On a weekend when Charles takes the kids to visit one of his sisters, Sheila heads to Water Haven. Pulling into the driveway, she marvels that it's the first time she's ever been here without Charles or her mother nearby. Feeling unbelievable free, she runs into the snow-covered yard, spins like a dervish, and falls backwards on to the crispy whiteness. She studies the night sky, taking attendance, *Sheila Branford, are you present in this moment, really and truly, present?*

"Completely," she whispers. *How often did I perform this roping in of my consciousness when I was young? How seldom have I done it lately?* "Yes, Mr. Thoreau, you nailed it when you wrote, 'our lives are frittered away by detail.' And according to your definition of wakefulness, I've missed a lifetime of dawns. Wow, after all these years, I'm talking to you again!" She wonders if, in his day, Thoreau would have listened to all of her soul searching. *No, you'd have locked yourself in your cabin if you'd seen me coming. To your way of thinking, I must be a spoiled whiner who turned her back on her true self long ago.*

Sheila gets up and crunches to the edge of the frozen lake. It was here that she and Charles stood, considering whether or not to purchase the cottage. She'd so hoped moving out of her mother's cabin would help their relationship. "Ha!" Sheila laughs into the darkness.

The cozy cabin is almost as cheering as Earl's letters. If anything can cast out her memory demons, it's his sweet words. In fact, she thinks, opening one for an encore read, he writes as well as he makes love. *Before his letters captured my attention, I craved him physically, but my heart was my own. Now, even my heart belongs to the man in these pages. If the quality of our lives is determined by our relationships, the quality of mine is about to improve significantly. Even the most mundane things will be special.* These are the thoughts that guide Sheila to sleep in the cabin she'd shared with Charles.

In the morning, the first task is to meet with a real estate agent. Because the woman has known her family for years, Sheila chooses not to reveal her true motive for selling. Blaming a life that screams for simplification, she says it's time for her cabin to go. Although the agent suspects something, she's too professional to pry.

"By the way," she says, walking Sheila to the door, "did you know the Considines have separated?" This is news; Sheila remembers seeing them last fall when Allie and Chase went over to play with their daughters. At that time, all seemed fine.

"I'm so sorry," Sheila says while silently cheering her friend, Barb.

"We all hope they can work it out."

"Hmmm, I guess I hope for whatever's best for them. Maybe that doesn't mean staying together."

"Oh my!" the agent's taken aback, "Well, I suppose, but it would be such a shame, don't you think?"

Sheila knows this woman's generation truly believes this. Rather than widen the gap, she says, "I do wish them luck. And I wish you the same in selling the cottage! This is my card, call my office anytime, and here's an extra set of keys." With a smile and a hug, Sheila hastens out the door before things get too emotional.

Melissa McDaniel

That was disconcerting. I don't like lying, but what's really hard is the fact that I'm arranging to be rid of the one possession that's important to me.

Sheila spends her afternoon sorting through drawers, closets, and cupboards, stacking one pile for the Salvation Army and another for Charles and the kids. Around four o'clock, there's a knock at the door. At first, she doesn't want to answer. No matter who it is, she'll just have to tell more lies about being here alone.

"Sheila, are you in there? It's Barb. Open up! I'm freezing!" Sheila goes to the door. "Hi, I wanted to tell you what's going on with Ron and me."

"I heard, and I secretly gave you an 'atta girl', because I'm doing the same thing!"

Barb doesn't seem terribly surprised. "You know, Sheila, I kind of thought that might be happening!"

And they're off! Like horses leaving the gate, the two friends tear into a non-stop dialogue, spanning the next hour. Years of acting like happy wives make their "coming out" a celebration of honesty.

"It's Ron's weekend with the girls; want to get something to eat?" Sheila had wanted to spend the night alone in her cabin, but being with Barb is suddenly more important. They drive to the Sand Bar for a burger, some beers, and more commiseration. Barb admires Sheila's guts to actually be moving away, while Sheila says her friend is more courageous to be sticking around.

"This isn't the first time I've thought of leaving," Sheila confesses. When I considered it before, I realized I could never do it and stay nearby. It's better for everyone if I clear out. Besides, I'm going to a place that seems to be calling my name," her voice trails off then comes in firm again. "No, it's impossible to end my marriage and remain nearby. But I sure do wish you courage, Barb, as you stay to face the firing line." At evening's end, they hug, each growing stronger from the other.

As her friend drives away, Sheila wonders, *how many other women on this same night have shared secrets of unhappy marriages?* Pulling another beer from the fridge, she opens it, draws a slug, and walks through the cabin once so dear to her and Charles. She opens a closet that stores her husband's "summer grubs." These vestments have seen him through many a weekend. Sheila touches the old ones he used for working in the yard; and the not-so-old ones

SLOW DANCE

for relaxing later on. She fingers his red swimsuit as it hangs on a hook with a "same-time-next-year" expectation. But there'll be no next year. Reaching down, she lifts his sandals. *Oh, Charles, you wore these constantly!* She's mourning. This is a kind of death, her death, and his. The pleasant man who wore these sandals is gone forever. The summers of innocence are gone as well.

Careful, her inner voice warns. *Don't let this get out of control.*

Sheila ignores the admonition. She has to work through this. *Charles, I'm so sorry, I never meant to do this to you!* She goes to the kitchen for another beer. *You don't deserve what I'm throwing at you. All you ever did was marry the girl of your dreams. Some dream, huh? More like a nightmare! I was sure I was doing the right thing. I thought I would grow to love you as much as I had the others. The others?*

With this, Sheila focuses on the reality she's beaten back for years. Sonny Lawson and Ed Willard, how blessed she'd been to know the kind of love that abounded in either of those relationships! But she'd laid waste to each of them. *Why? Who in her right mind would turn her back on something so good, not once, but twice? And then turn around and marry a mere pal?* She grows still. Through the picture window, in the snowy darkness, her mind's eye sees a young woman, inexperienced in life and vulnerable to her mother's designs. *What was Mom's assessment of those delightful young men? Sonny was too country. Ed was too Catholic. Sonny, Ed, and then Charles.* Sheila whirls from the window to glare at the empty rocker where her mother would usually sit. With a full wind up, she hurls her empty beer bottle at the target. It ricochets off the corner of the chair and clatters across the fireplace.

"Damn you, Mother! You did this to me! You did this to Charles!" Sheila crosses to the bottle, lying on the floor. With the kick of an old showgirl, she again sends it soaring. This time, it barely misses the picture window. Her brain registers the near miss. *House isn't sold; best not trash it.*

Now, her rage finds words and they're coming fast. "Mother, how dare you manipulate the course of my life? I see you now — the summer before my sophomore year in college. We'd just arrived at the cottage and you could see how thrilled I was that Sonny had called to arrange a date. I was in the bathroom but you couldn't wait until I was done to accost me. You flung open the door and hissed,

'Is this what you want?' I sat, in shock, jeans and undies curling around my ankles. Disgust loomed on your face. Evidently your daughter was denser than you'd thought so you continued. 'I said, is this what you want? Would you be proud to introduce Sonny to your Richmond Heights friends? Don't you realize he hasn't the means to make you happy ten, fifteen years from now?' I felt sick as you bludgeoned me with your words. You'd never said such things or used such a tone, but it was to be the first of many such encounters. Words, they were only words! But they belonged to you, the one person in the world who wanted what was best for me. Because of that, I attached more meaning to them than they deserved. And, because you knew so much about what would make me happy, I ended it with Sonny. "Then, during my senior year in college Ed became your nemesis. We were so perfect together you had to reach to come up with something wrong about him, so you resorted to your prejudice. Ed was Catholic. So what? He was a Christian. But no, you — the one who never went to church — grabbed onto your Protestant faith and wouldn't let go. I thought you'd be happy for me when we became engaged. What a shock it was to hear your litany of stereotypes on Catholics. And when that didn't work, you set Dad on me. What a set up! We went to Howard Johnson's for dinner, and right before desert, he suggested I wait a while before taking such a big step. I rejected his suggestion and he said 'fine'. But later, when he informed you of his failure to hotbox me, you called with another tirade. 'How can you do this to your religious heritage? Think of Uncle Mike holding you at your christening; how would he feel?' It occurred to me my uncle, dead many years, wouldn't care."

Sheila stops to collect herself before she really gives it to the rocking chair. "Did I scare you that time? Were you worried you no longer had me to yourself? Is that why you did the unforgivable thing? The thing I pray I'll never do to my children? Was it premeditated or did it just happen? And why? Why, Mother, why did you withdraw your love from your only daughter? You froze me out; giving me a firsthand view of what living without your love would be like. You forced me to choose between a life with your love and one without. At twenty-one, I chose the love I'd known first, the love I needed most. There may be other men, I told myself, but I have only one mother. I gave in, and you won."

Sheila turns her back on the chair as she gathers her thoughts for the next attack. Stalking back to it, she leans heavily on its arms. "Beating back my love for Ed took a huge toll on me. It wounded me so much I became totally submissive to you. In no way would I allow myself to hurt like that again."

Sheila steps back from the chair, "Enter Charles: a good buddy, a man you didn't criticize, a man you actually seemed to like. As time passed, it became clear I could have Charles without losing you. We could live happily ever after as husband, wife, and mother-in-law. Did you approve of Charles because you knew I wouldn't love him more than I loved you? Because you were sure he would never threaten your dominion over me? That was so wrong! I hate you for what you did to me but I despise you more for what you did to Charles. It's over, Mom, you control me no longer!"

That Sheila screams these words at a vacant chair in an empty cabin doesn't matter. She feels she's finally confronted her mother, and she's won. One last beer and a stack of old magazines accompany her to bed. When she's mellow enough for sleep, she prays. "Please Lord, watch over Charles. Help him get through these months. Make him understand the mistake I made in loving my mother too much and him too little. And please keep Allie and Chase healthy, happy, and safe all their lives long. Amen."

In the morning, Sheila wonders if she'd had a kind of nervous breakdown the night before. *Kind of like a primal scream? Man! When did life get so hard?* Suddenly, the pre-Earl years seem almost golden. *Never mind the tedium, at least back then I wasn't ravaging Charles's life.*

You've always taken the wishy-washy way out. The only thing anyone could accuse you of is being too nice. Now it's time for a mid-life correction, and things will have to get worse before they get better.

She rises to face her last day in her beloved cottage. She dusts, vacuums, washes the kitchen and bathroom floors, and cleans the fireplace. Her last task is to check on her mother's cabin. Just looking at the outside of the log home is enough to tell her everything is fine, yet, the dutiful daughter parks her car by a snowdrift and gets out to check the cottage more closely. The wooden door groans open slowly, almost as if it resents the intrusion. *I won't disturb you for long,* she informs her sleepy pal. A musty scent makes her smile. This is the cabin's signature smell. With it, she conjures up a blissful childhood.

Moving through the kitchen, she enters the living room. Cozy and secure, it's like a womb. Within its warmth, she'd grown from an infant to a young adult. Since the cottage had no television, she and her mother had boarded their books each evening for destinations unknown. These were the roots of Sheila's romantic yearnings. It was also the cement that bonded mother and daughter together in a deep and destructive love. *No wonder you resented my friends, you must have hated it when I grew old enough to go out on my own. Dad was always away and Dan had things to do, but I was to be your companion for all time.*

Suddenly, she's in a dialogue with her mother some twelve years earlier. "My dear girl, I'm worried that if you postpone a family much longer you may never have a daughter with whom you can have the same wonderful relationship as we have."

What? So I can do to another the same thing you've done to me?

"I don't want you to miss loving her as much as I do you."

And demanding she love me tenfold in return? Making her feel obligated to be my girlfriend, my social outlet, and as I grow aged, to rearrange her own life to better serve me? Sheila remembers how these questions had hung in the air just out of reach of her tongue. She'd imagined her little girl awaiting conception, a sweet little nothing, destined to become a woman with feelings, intellect, and most of all, free choice. *I'll never steer your decisions to suit my agenda. You'll be free to make a life, independent of me, and away from your grandmother's manipulation. If I can't make that happen, I shouldn't be a mother.*

That episode had accomplished two things. It had worried Sheila about the manipulative tendencies she'd manifest were she to become a mother, and it underscored her negative feelings about her own mom. *I knew I wasn't happy back then. Why did I go on and on as if I had no choice in the matter? Now, twelve years later, I stand in the same room, ready to break up the family my mother pleaded with me to have.*

Sheila lowers the window shades, returning the cabin to sleepy darkness. Then, as she exits the cottage of her youth, she slams the door — partly because it's warped, but mostly, because it's so satisfyingly *final*. The rest of the day, she moves in high gear, closing her own cottage; then driving the four hours to be there when Allie and Chase return home.

Chapter 26
Countdown

"Just think, blossom, the next time we see each other, it'll be for all time." Over the phone, Earl's voice is full of happy anticipation. "It's less then a month now, and I'm counting the days!"

"I can almost smell the stable," Sheila quips, but she's unable to disguise her dread of the next twenty-eight days.

"I feel so bad for what you're going through, sweet pea. I wish I could go up there and take you out of that shit right now. But I know you've got to do this solo. All I can do is love you like you've never been loved before."

"That's what I need you to do, Earl." His words are nice but they don't soothe the open sores of the constant shame Sheila's feeling. *This is pre-departure anxiety*, she tells herself as she plots the logistics of notifying her boss and staff of her plans.

The first of these announcements comes at the conclusion of a regularly scheduled appointment with her boss. For a nanosecond, she wonders if she can do it. *Can I really announce that I'm leaving the job I love and worked years to attain? Watch me!*

"Bernice," she begins, "before we adjourn, there's something I must do. I haven't been personally happy for much of my adult life, and I have to correct that. To do so, requires I take time off. This is a request for a leave of absence although it's very possible I may not be returning. A lot remains to be seen."

Stunned, her boss takes the letter that Sheila has pushed across the desk. She scans the niceties then focuses on the request for a leave. It doesn't make sense. She searches her employee's eyes for an explanation and sees they sizzle with cheerful madness.

"I haven't been happy in my marriage for a long time." From the surprise on Bernice's face, Sheila knows her role-playing has been complete.

"You two always seemed so solid; I never heard you once utter a complaint about your marriage."

"I never said anything about it at all, wasn't that a clue?" Neither has Sheila shared her resentment of the way her mother dominated her life, nor has she expressed dissatisfaction with Bernice for keeping her department flattened under her thumb. Sheila, the positive mental attitude gal, has never put her discontent into words. Not until now, what would have been the point? Charles wouldn't have changed, her mother would have called her selfish, and her boss would have seen her as a weak and disgruntled employee.

"And you should know," Sheila says deliberately, "I'm involved with someone. I'd rather you hear it from me than the mob that will soon be forming!"

Her boss listens but doesn't want to hear. Sheila has always been one of her most reliable employees, dependable, easy to manage. How can she do something so rash, and with such short notice? It's out of character, so unlike her hard working, success driven nature. Why, Bernice wonders, is she deliberately derailing herself from a track that has it all? Her mind searches for some logic that might snap Sheila back to reality. But the mad, defiant eyes tell her nothing she says will make a difference. She reaches across the table, taking her employee's hand in her own. "I hope we won't lose you."

"That may not happen," Sheila assures her, but the conviction in her eyes says, *I'm in charge, and I'll do what I must.*

As she watches Sheila leave, Bernice marvels that the one employee to whom she'd never given a second's concern, the surest of sure things, is pulling the rug out from underneath her. Good natured, compliant Sheila may soon be gone.

Sheila is truly sorry to be ending a fairly satisfying employee/boss relationship, but she's also congratulating herself on successfully jumping through another blazing hoop. *That imagery is appropriate. The emotional energy I've expended on accomplishing each step of my departure has been huge. And there have been so many flaming hoops! They extend back to when I first revealed my plan to Sara. Then, there was that excruciating night with Charles, the time I told Mom, the meeting with my father-in –law, and worst of all, the Sunday I told Allie and Chase I'd be leaving. Now my boss and next my staff, I'm glad the fiery hoops only recently occurred to me. It would have been too daunting last September. Now the trail of flames behind me is longer than the one ahead.*

It's at the conclusion of her department's weekly staff meeting that Sheila announces her impending departure. Silent eyes scream, *Is this really happening? What does this mean for me? How can anyone, who so clearly has it all, be so ready to give it up?* Anger, disgust, and a hint of admiration are the next reactions.

Every one of these reactions is valid; I deserve them all. I seem to be running out on everyone who's ever been good to me.

Next hoop please! Her inner voice knows Sheila mustn't dwell too long on what she's doing. *Come on, what's the next hoop?* Getting no response, the voice continues, *It's that in fourteen days you'll load your car, clean your in-laws' apartment, and close the door on the only life you've ever known.* What once seemed far off is drawing near, almost too near, and Sheila's spirit seems to be missing in action. Knowing the reason why, the voice reminds her, *you'll see the kids just two weeks after you leave. They'll be with you in Florida for their spring vacation. Maybe by then Charles will see they should be with you!* This one, hopeful thought is an antidote for the utter dread threatening the next fourteen days.

Minute by minute, hour by hour, she mushes through each day with her "to-do" list keeping her on course. It's important she leave her work in good order. Her departure may seem abrupt, but really, for the past three months, she's been readying her staff to carry on in her absence. She never wants it said she just walked away.

Although it hurts like hell, Sheila must pull back on the time she spends with Allie and Chase. It is part of the plan she'd discussed with the counselor she and Charles have chosen for the kids. She's to see her children a little less each week until the day of her departure so two nights before she's to leave, Sheila, being unable to see them, spends the time with Laura Tolafson and Samantha Scott. They're the only guests she's invited to her in-laws' apartment. To have guests in their home seems tasteless, even for this one evening, but since Sheila's new life and limited income have already begun, her buds have insisted on a potluck of fresh fruit, cheese, crackers, and two bottles of wine.

For many years, the three have worked together in the trenches of the college. Now, both Laura and Samantha confess to a mild frustration at being left behind. Sheila understands exactly what they mean. With her departure two days away, she feels the thrill of a promising new future. *Life with Earl will be fun, but what about life without the identity of my job, and, especially, my kids? That will be tough, but I've always succeeded at whatever I've done. I can make it work.*

The evening ends with reluctant good-byes. When will they be together again? Is Sheila going to be O.K.? Still in her "make-it-work" mode, she swears she'll be fine, and she's confident Earl will provide the emotional support she'll need to land on her feet. Like a heroine in a potboiler novel, she buoyantly bids her friends farewell.

Chapter 27
Departure

For better or worse, tomorrow I leave. Thank God, Earl's flying here to make the drive with me. Without him, I'd be alone with my thoughts and that would be excruciating. Sheila gazes at the frozen, almost glacial beach outside her office window. It reminds her of that summer day when she'd searched it for answers about a Southerner she'd met. The sun people she'd watched then are somewhere else, bundled up and going about their winter business, but they'll come again, when the snow melts, and spring warms the sand. *Will my successor look out, as I did, and wonder what they know that he or she doesn't? I might just learn their secret as I embark on my new and jobless life. Will I ever find anything as fulfilling as this position? Will I even try? Maybe I'll be a stay-at-home mom!*

She leaves work in her already-packed Seville. Over the past few weeks, she's scrutinized her life to determine what is vital and what can be left behind. Essential clothes, toiletries, and vitamins will take the trip with her. Files to manage both hers and her mother's affairs also make the manifest, as does a selection of her favorite books, photographs, and memorabilia. Things that didn't make the cut are stored in boxes at her mom's. Each is marked, "Sissy's things. Do not remove."

On this last night, she, Allie, and Chase dine at McDonald's. Her little ones are in great spirits. They know Mommy's leaving tomorrow, but they'll see her in two weeks. Yippee! That makes it less final.

SLOW DANCE

As their Happy Meal feast concludes, she gives each a new backpack. Thrilled, they open the surprise to find framed photographs of them with Mommy. Next, is a photo calendar of puppies for Chase and kitties for Allie. "Now you can see all the times we'll be together." Hoping her worry doesn't show through her words, Sheila points to each month where she's penciled in the visits she knows will occur. The children watch silently as her finger moves through the markings; then they resume digging into their backpacks. Next come books of postage stamps, boxes of kiddy stationery, and address stamps to make sending letters easy. Finally, they get a pager with which they can beep her when they want to talk. "When I hear the beep, I'll call you right away. The telephone will keep us close." After dinner, the threesome romps in the indoor playground. *You may not remember any of this, but please remember my love!* Later, at their front door, she keeps the good-bye light, saying she'll be back to take them to school in the morning.

The next morning, she doesn't recognize the woman in her rearview mirror. *I'm the woman you have to be to get this done,* it answers, as her children come bounding from their house. Mara, unsure what's happening, follows close by. The two women hug, and Sheila struggles to convey that this good-bye is only for fourteen days. *"Tak, tak, yes, yes."* Mara answers, but she still cannot fathom why her employer must leave her home to live somewhere else.

On the way to school, Sheila does her best to fake a happy mood. What did they eat for breakfast? What are they doing in school today? What do they think of the playground's new swing set? Any one of these topics is better than the one that's so thick in the air. As she's always done, she parks near the rear entrance where they watch children come from all directions to disappear inside the school. With only a few minutes left, she can no longer take refuge in trivia.

"Listen, sweeties, you must remember, you're my own precious darlings and I love you very, very much. We'll be away from each other, but our phone calls will keep us close. Mara will be here every day to take good care of you, and Daddy will be with you every night and all day Saturday and Sunday. Best of all, we'll see each other in fourteen days! I'll drive up from Florida and we'll visit Grandma for two days then we'll fly to Florida for a whole week!" Tears swell in her eyes. *Lord, get me through this. I'll scare them if I fall apart now.*

Melissa McDaniel

As if in response to her prayer, the radio blasts forth with "Achey Breaky Heart." Oblivious to the pools in Mommy's eyes, Chase starts to sing. Allie, scrunching her nose at the song, chimes in anyway. Soon, all three are singing with Billy Ray Cyrus. By the song's conclusion, there's just enough time for Allie and Chase to scoot into school before the bell rings.

"I love you tons and I'll see you real soon!" Sheila fakes her brightest smile as the two people who matter most in her life move from her reach. They wave and blow kisses but they're already engrossed in greeting friends. *Keep them safe, healthy, and happy, Lord, and help them to someday understand.* They disappear inside the school. *And please make this timing be right.* Most of the research she's read, and the advice she's sought, seems to agree that the older a child gets, the more guilt he or she might internalize in a divorce. *That's why, if I'm ever going to do this, it has to be now. Even one more year would be too late.*

For maybe the last time ever, she pulls into her reserved space in her office parking lot. Her appearance today is to bid farewell to the most important women in her life. In the flush of good wishes, Sheila begins to feel better. One staff member pulls her aside, "I know you're doing this because you have to. I wish my daughter were as brave as you." The endorsement brings grateful tears to her eyes as she realizes these are not employees, they're family, and she's leaving this family as well as her own. Hugging Quincy, Sam, and so many others, she eases down the stairs and out the door. A huge part of her doesn't want to leave these people with whom she's actually spent more waking time than with her very own family. Getting into the car, Sheila waves to these relations made intimate through the bond of common cause. Backing from her reserved stall, she heads toward her last stop.

At her mom's, Sheila dishes out an early lunch of KFC fried chicken, mashed potatoes, and coleslaw. Louada joins them, fully aware of Sheila's impending departure. The two women have covered the waterfront on the details of the long-distance communication upon which they'll depend. "I have every confidence in you, Louada, you'll do fine, and so will the other nurses." It heartens her that Louada is so supportive of what she's doing. *Is it because she's been an objective observer of me since I was a* teenager? *Maybe she's sensed my unhappiness; that's why she's so willing to aid and abet my escape.*

"Sissy, you go do what you gotta do. You're a great gal and you shouldn't feel bad 'bout wantin' things different. We'll be just fine!" Sheila hugs Louada, feeling like a little sister in the glow of big sister's unconditional love.

The three share a nice lunch. In the course of it, Sheila realizes that, like her children, her mother is focusing on her only being gone for a couple of weeks. *O.K., smaller increments may work better for her as well.* Before she leaves, she gives Louada a box of envelopes, a roll of postage stamps, and an address stamp with her name and new address, "For bills and anything else you feel you should send me."

To her mother, Sheila gives a poem she's written and had done in calligraphy. When she reads it aloud, the final words, "and most of all, your love," make her voice crack.

"There, there," Mom says slipping into a role that's decades old. "You'll be back soon."

Sheila nods, fighting to keep her tears at bay. With a long hug for her mom, another for Louada, and a little one for Wookie, she leaves the house she's known since she was seven. *It's happening. I'm getting gone! At long last, I'm exiting the realm of my mother's influence. This was Mom's life, not mine. Her emotional blackmail kept me here, near her, working the long, hard hours necessary to achieve the affluence demanded by this overpriced lifestyle.* And she's leaving a marriage that should never have been. *Dear, sweet, victim Charles — he's tried so valiantly to keep me here. Will I ever survive the guilt?*

Such thoughts must stop or she'll be in a funk when she meets Earl. As she merges into the airport lane, the runaway wife forces herself to focus on what she's running toward. It's a wild rural place where she can be herself without the trappings of job titles and possessions. And then there's Earl. He has never communicated second thoughts of any kind. In Sheila's eyes, he's as stalwart as the live oaks that landscape his beloved South. She maneuvers to a less-congested area where she can park until the police tell her to move. Watching the automatic doors, she backpedals to her final minutes with Allie and Chase. *They seemed so fine, saying good-bye, and running off with their friends. Was that a good sign? Please make that a good sign!*

At this moment, a door swings open and her future walks through. Larger than life, Earl's bundled into his L.L.Bean parka, and Snowy River hat. Sheila chuckles, thinking he looks like a healthy version of the Marlboro man. She's treated to his killer smile as he crosses the street. By the time he pulls her into his arms, her breathing has grown deep and the fist is nowhere to be found.

"You ok with this?" The question is meant to appease his guilt.

"Yes. Sooner or later, I'd be doing this, even if you hadn't come along."

Relieved, Earl settles his frame into the passenger seat. "O.K., blossom, wagons ho!"

Off and running, they exit Wisconsin, bypass Chicago, and eventually cross the Indiana state line. As the distance grows between herself and her children, Sheila clicks on her mind control. *Focus on the positive, only the positive.* To reinforce these thoughts, she looks at Earl. He's doing the oddest thing! Something has made him sit bolt upright. His head is swiveling on a 180-degree axis, eyes huge with surprise. For decades, Sheila has driven through the Indiana countryside, never once registering the amazement she sees on Earl's face.

"It's so flat, it's so damned flat! I never knew Indiana was so flat!"

Sheila's charmed; his excitement holds the wonderment of a child. "Of course it is, the Midwest is mostly prairie."

"Sure, but I never expected this. It's flat as a hotcake, far as the eye can see. I reckon we never stop learning, do we, sweet pea?"

"No we don't, and I never dreamed I'd see forests of towering pines in Florida!"

Around 8:00 PM, they stop for dinner at a Cracker Barrel restaurant. In the fall, Earl had introduced Sheila to this fast growing chain of Americana. She loves it, as she does anything country. At this point, she doesn't care if she ever eats in an expensive restaurant again. *Simplify! Yes, Mr. Thoreau, I'm trying.*

They sit in the non-smoking dining room, where remnants of bygone days, washboards, rakes, old soap advertisements and cereal boxes keep Sheila's eyes entertained. Earl watches her absorb the scene. Their eyes meet, "You're so beautiful!" he blurts out almost unintentionally.

After twenty years of too few compliments from the most important man in her life, Sheila glows in the affirmation. "Thank you!" she beams, recalling the draught of loving communication that had existed between Charles and her. In the early days of their marriage, she's tried to set an example, always complimenting him on things, but when he didn't reciprocate, she'd felt like a chump.

Fortunately, with Earl, this skill seems already intact. But just in case, maybe she should say something. "You know," she confides, "when you say things like that it means a lot to me. Please don't ever stop!" Earl doesn't respond, and over the months ahead, this exchange — or the lack of it — will become an object of Sheila's intense scrutiny. At this moment, anyway, she feels she's taken steps to insure good communication between them.

After a dinner of fried catfish, okra, mustard greens, and cornbread, they strike out again, thinking they'll reach Louisville before stopping for the night. But by Indianapolis, they're wearing down, and having no desire to be too fatigued to make love, they pull into a Days Inn.

Sheila takes one last look at her car before entering their room. Every inch is loaded with things she'll need to start her new life. If someone were to steal her possessions, what would she do? Then she reminds herself she's already without Allie and Chase. *And they're more important than any possessions, but they're not my possessions, nor are they things that can be uprooted at the whim of their mother.*

"Looks like we're in for some bad weather tomorrow," Earl remarks; eyes fixed on the Weather Channel. Sheila chuckles. To her, "bad weather" is a Milwaukee blizzard, minus forty degrees wind chill, or a paralyzing ice storm. Driving south, the weather should only get better.

Earl clicks off the TV and turns to Sheila. Taking a shoulder in each hand, he gently pushes her down and backwards on the bed. Please God, Sheila prays, don't let this marvelous man ever change. When Earl kisses her, it's a kiss that penetrates her soul. It tells her he's the one who will give her what she thought she'd never have again. Their lovemaking is sweet, gentle, and pure. It lasts twenty minutes and as Sheila snuggles into Earl for some afterglow, he goes to sleep with the abruptness of a light that's been switched off. Hot snores blow across her face. *No big deal, he's beat. Still, on this night of the most colossal thing I've ever done, I do wish he'd held me a little longer.* Sheila rolls over to avoid the gusts, while still trying to keep her body close to his. But even with his belly nestled in the small of her back, she feels alone.

Then it comes, hitting her full in the face and washing over her from head to toe. The force of it swirls around and then stills, making her soak in its painful pool. *Allie and Chase, I love you. Feel my love!* She's aching and sick with separation. It's an unnatural thing she's done and nature is telling her so.

A digital clock clicks the minutes and then the hours away as her mind fights her body for control. Finally, she fixes her sights on the only sure thing she knows: She'll be with them in fourteen days. "Fourteen days" becomes a mantra. With it, and the help of two more Unisoms, she falls asleep until Earl awakens her with, "My, my, Miss Sheila, you certainly know how to sleep!"

Instinct tells her this lovely man would neither welcome nor know how to deal with knowledge of her pain. And the guilt he'd feel could drive a wedge in their tender, new relationship. *Best keep this private. Besides, I got through the night O.K. Maybe the worst is over.* She smiles, saying she slept fine.

A snow-laden sky prompts them to abandon thoughts of even a quickie. Sheila's certain they'll reach a more Southern clime before any snow can find them. But find them it does, halfway between Louisville and Nashville. By the time they reach Nashville, the snow reminds her of the blizzards up North. *It's following me. All the bad stuff is following me!*

"Penny for your thoughts," Earl says this hoping to interrupt whatever is going on in his lady's head. He's started to notice a tendency she has to go deep within herself for long periods of time.

"Oh nothing, I just want to put distance between me and weather like this."

"That we'll do; darlin', that we'll do," he assures her, eyes riveted to the highway. By now, the snow and slippery conditions are forcing him to drive less than thirty miles per hour on the interstate. When the radio announces that the storm has officially become a blizzard, Sheila quips, "This will be one last clear memory of the crap I'm leaving behind!" Earl chuckles but his full attention is on driving. Visibility is bad and traffic has slowed to a crawl. Several cars have pulled off to the side. Others peek out of ditches. Seeing this makes Sheila grow quiet.

It takes two hours for the bumper-to-bumper cars to snake their way toward Murfreesboro. During one long stand still, Sheila pops the hood of the trunk, and skates back to it. First, she surveys the contents of her life getting coated with snowflakes, then, pawing through garment bags and boxes of her children's art, she locates a basket of gourmet foods Laura had given her as a bon voyage gift. Clutching it, she slams the trunk and starts back.

"Looks good! Can we have some?" the kids in the next car call out. The decal on the rear window identifies them as University of Michigan students.

"Where're you headed?" she asks.

"Daytona, if we ever get there!"

"Good luck," she smiles, tossing them a bag of chips.

"Hey thanks! You're all right!"

Back in the car, a snowy Sheila announces, "Provisions!"

"Listen to this." Earl turns the volume up in time for her to hear that they're closing the interstate.

"How can they close a highway with hundreds of cars parked on it?" Both the radio and Earl leave the question hanging. The radio returns to its regularly programmed talk show. "The Storm of the Century" is the subject of choice.

The nasal-twanged drawls of Tennessee locals come through the speakers. One old boy is full of advice. "War ya gotta do," he says with authority, "is pull yo'chines otta th' shed and git'm on yo ties!"

Sheila looks at Earl. He smiles, and laughs as if it's a comedy routine.

"No b'dy' w'out chines on'er ties sh'be drivin'! So don ch'all go nowhar widou dos chines y'ear?"

"Did you get that?" Earl laughs.

"Let's see," Sheila begins, "chines on ties is the Tennessee version of Mullet's bald nuts, am I right?"

"You got it, darlin'!" Earl's relieved Sheila's good spirits are returning. Laura's goodies also help create a festive atmosphere as they creep along.

With the interstate closed, all cars must exit at Murfreesboro. They do so, driving past the newer hotels in hopes of finding a vacancy in the older part of town. The radio tells them emergency housing is available in a school gymnasium.

"So this is how it will be?" she ponders aloud, "Allie and Chase will see their mommy interviewed on TV, sitting on a cot in a gym, a victim of the Storm of the Century." Earl's laugh makes Sheila pull her next thought inside. *The announcer will say, "This is Sheila Branford from Wisconsin. So Mrs. Branford, were you headed south to escape the snow?"*

I'll respond, "No sir, I'm escaping my marriage of sixteen years, and the work-driven self I'd become. Spending tonight with hundreds of strangers is just another adventure in my new life. Would you like to meet the man for whom I'm leaving my husband?" With that, the flustered announcer will move on to find someone more to the liking of his Bible Belt viewers.

Happily, Sheila's vision doesn't become a reality. In the old part of town, a motel from the fifties beckons with a vacancy sign. After checking into their tidy time capsule of a room, they trek off on foot in search of food. They find a half-timbered building that, in its day, must have been a grand old roadhouse. It's reborn as a sports bar that claims to serve "the best wings in Murfreesboro." It also serves up the sexiest wait staff Sheila has ever seen.

Here, Sheila has two revelations about the South. First, its battered and deep-fat-fried pickles are delicious. Second, the female breast wields awesome power over Southern men. Even Earl's, *her* Earl's, eyes can't help feasting on the cleavage.

Damn! I want him to stare at my breasts, not theirs! This arouses Sheila so much that by the time they get back to their nifty fifties bedroom, she's ready to do a steamy striptease. *And why shouldn't I? After all, I'm stranded in a snowstorm with this gorgeous stranger. Yes, in many ways, Earl is still an unknown. This man with his unusual taste in food, and his obvious appreciation of the female anatomy couldn't be more foreign to my Midwestern psyche. If I'm ever going to know him, it starts here and now.* What follows is the best sex she's ever had and as Earl lies, spent on the bed, Sheila begs to do it again. Sex is now a priority of major proportions.

By late afternoon, the "storm of the century" dominates the TV programming, but when she calls her children, they don't know there is a storm, let alone one of the century. They've had a good

Saturday, busy with the play dates Sheila had arranged before she left. They sound fine, more than fine — they sound great. This eases a tension that has plagued Sheila all day. Finally, after a couple of scotches with Earl, her sleep-deprived body welcomes a full night's slumber.

Bright white morning awakens Sheila. Squinting at the snowy brilliance, she gives thanks for having escaped the prior night's demons. In a mood of celebration, she suggests they venture out in search of a great country breakfast. Earl, delighted she loves food as much as he does, heartily agrees.

At Granny's, they find a country breakfast buffet. "Granny's been busy!" Sheila exclaims, surveying the spread of cheese grits, country fries, scrambled eggs, thick-sliced bacon, country ham, pork sausage, corned beef hash, biscuits with gravy, and hot cakes served with sorghum molasses or pure Tennessee honey. Approximately one hour and three helpings later, the couple waddles from the diner in time to see an exodus of cars filing by.

"Highway's open," Earl mutters with a toothpick in the corner of his mouth.

"Best we get on our way," Sheila says, sad this vacation-within-a-vacation is coming to an end. It has been a respite from the reality of a life she ultimately has to face. It also is the place where she'd witnessed her own rampant sexuality. At breakfast, she'd been fantasizing about an afternoon of delicious sex. *Oh well, guess I'll keep,* she cajoles herself. Back on the highway, they zigzag slowly over the still slick Mt. Eagle Pass. Then it's on to Chattanooga, then Dalton, Georgia, and later, Atlanta. After that, they still have five more hours to Pine Springs, but they push on. It's Sunday and Earl wants to get home so he can go to work the next day.

Work? What will I do? But Sheila's not going to worry about that now; there's too much to be accomplished. She has to get a handle on the long distance management of her mom's nurses. Then she'll work on her own finances. She needs to open a checking account with what she has from selling the rest of her jewelry. And in just twelve days, she'll be driving back to get her children for spring vacation.

The horrible weather accompanies them to Pine Springs. "This can't be Florida," Sheila jokes. "Something beamed us down in the

Northeast. Twenty-six degrees with freezing rain is not Florida. I want warmth and sun, lots of sun."

Earl laughs, "Don't worry, darlin', they called this "storm of the century" because this shit doesn't dare come but once every hundred years."

Finally, they pull into Earl's drive. Exhausted from hours of dangerous driving, they leave the fully packed car in the driveway. It's too late to call the kids or check on her mom. Luckily, Sheila had reached Allie and Chase earlier; her mom is another story. The day before, when she'd called her from Murfreesboro, Louada had informed her, Mz. Ronson says she won't talk to you t'il you come home."

Fine, Mom, Sheila had thought, *your behavior proves more and more why I'm here.* "O.K., Louada, tell her I'm fine and I love her."

The beat goes on, she thinks, climbing onto Earl's waterbed. Lying next to him, she realizes it doesn't matter that her mother is still trying to work her ways. At this moment, there's a lot that's right with Sheila's world. She just made it through a horrible storm, the man she loves is sleeping beside her, and her children, although they're not with her now, will be soon. Little does she know "storm of the century" was nothing compared to the turbulence soon to come.

Chapter 28
First Things First

On this, the first day of her new life; Sheila waves good-bye to Earl fully aware she's the one with no place to go. And although she's just had a great start-of-the-day conversation with Allie and Chase, she feels blue, surreal, even. *It's like I'm somewhere between vacation and hell. These next few days will be critical. It'll take tons of self-counseling to pull this off without getting too deranged. O.K., where to begin?*

She has the morning to herself. Even Mattie is absent. She's at the kennel, waiting for Earl to pick her up on his lunch hour. First, she decides to don jeans and a sweatshirt to suit the forty-degree day. *Now it's time to unload the car, lest I get the urge to turn and run! The sooner I integrate this into Earl's stuff, the better.* As certain as she'd been about things last night, she's equally as unsure this morning. *Why's that? Nothing has happened, yet I feel I could leave at any time.* Maybe it's because unpacking means storing her things in boxes in the garage. To his credit, Earl has emptied a rod in his closet; but it's full after she brings in the first load. The next armful, she squeezes into the guest room closets, and the rest stays in a box in the garage.

Even with all the giving away I've done, I still have too many clothes. Was I that emotionally bankrupt? That's all right, I'll figure out what I need in my new life, then discard the rest. In the meantime, I'll rearrange the contents of the guest room dresser to accommodate my shorts and tops. And, for now, my lingerie will reside in a flight bag in Earl's closet.

When Mattie and Earl arrive at noon, Sheila is all moved in. The aged lab greets her new mistress with a wagging tail. "So Mattie, do you mind me moving into your territory? Are you willing to share your daddy?"

Not a problem! Mattie responds in licks and wags.

Checkers, a drive-in new to Sheila, has provided Earl with a feast of grilled chicken sandwiches and excellent fries. Sheila's unhurried frame of mind allows her to savor each bite, but her lunch partner appears tense. Earl's preoccupied and eager to return to the work that piled up in his absence. This is disappointing. Sheila had been hoping for some affection, maybe even a quickie to beat back her insecurity.

Oh please! The voice scolds. Less than two hundred hours ago you, yourself, were a harried professional, anxious to complete each day's to-do list. You, of all people, should understand the pressures of Earl's work. Turn this into a positive. If you don't, you'll become a drudge to whom he feels obligated and that will be the kiss of death.

Sheila, recognizing the wisdom of her inner voice, ushers Earl to the door. "Time for you to go, we've both got work to do." Earl smiles in grateful relief. So apparent is his desire to be gone, she winces and wonders if Donna Reed felt so abandoned.

"I guess it's you and me, girl," she says, scratching that special place behind every dog's ear. Luxuriating in the sensation, Mattie regards her new friend with wise eyes, *Get used to it, he does this all the time.*

"Want to come back to the bedroom and help me figure out where to put my stuff?" Agreeably, Mattie follows Sheila, plopping down close enough to watch every move the nice human makes.

"Brother!" Sheila exclaims to her new best friend, "This drawer is packed full!" She fingers through its contents. Much of it belongs to Ryan; the rest is an assortment of souvenirs and photo albums. *Don't look, don't pry, ask first.* "Oh, why not?" She whispers to Mattie who doesn't seem to care either way. "Even so, Mattie, I'm glad you don't talk." The pooch, enjoying their complicity, crawls even closer. Together, they look at the albums. They depict their guy from toddler-hood to almost present day. It's a good record of the growth and maturation of a jubilant, athletic, and extremely photogenic guy. How she loves that face! A small plastic album portrays a birthday celebration which, according to the date, was two years prior. Holding it toward the light, Sheila studies the face of Earl's date. She scrutinizes the woman from every angle. She's the sort who's attractive when she fixes up, but raw beauty is not apparent.

This could be the "unanswered prayer" relationship of Earl's recent past. *Is she that Carlene person?* This makes her appraise the visage again. *I thought she'd be prettier.* Sheila has been told about Carlene by several of Earl's friends. Cheap, ill-mannered, and unfaithful — she'd been characterized as all the above. Sheila had enjoyed the portrayal until the conversation got around to Earl. It was sickening to hear how her guy had been used and abused at Carlene's faithless whims.

How dare she? How could anyone do that to someone they love? "Never again," Sheila vows aloud to the photograph. "You will never again hurt this magnificent man." Recognizing the violent nature of her own conviction, she hopes, for Carlene's sake, she won't show her face again. It's after 4:00 PM. The photo viewing and drawer-sorting has taken almost three hours. When Earl arrives, Sheila shows him where she stored the albums. A few days later, she's gratified to see he's put the "Carlene" album in the trash.

On the fourth day of Sheila's new life, Louada calls to say they're at the hospital. Immediately, Sheila is planning her departure. "Wait now, Sissy. She's O.K. Matter of fact, they're sending us home. This is a false alarm." There's a pause, "You know what I mean?"

Sheila's not sure. Usually it's a T.I.A. that sends her mom to the hospital, and those can be serious. "What happened?"

"Your ma didn't want to eat or drink. Then, she says she wants to go to the hospital, so I believe her, right?"

"Right," says Sheila, "that's what you should do."

"Well, we get here and they can't find what's wrong, blood pressure's ok; she's not dehydrated. I'm guessing she thought it'd bring you home. She's real mad I didn't call you before the doctor checked her out. But we're fine now, and a friend of mine who works here will take us home when she gets off."

"That's great, Louada. Can I talk to Mom?"

Sheila hears voices, then her mother's thin "Hello?"

"Hi, Mom! I'm glad you're all right."

Melissa McDaniel

"Are you coming?"

"What? No, I'm not coming right now; I'll be there in a week. Remember? The kids and I will stay with you for two days so we'll have lots of time together. Then Allie, Chase, and I will fly to Florida for their spring vacation. In the meantime, Louada will take good care of you. I love you, Mom. "

This is said to no one because her mother has already hung up.

When Sheila calls later Louada admonishes her not to be upset. "Girl, your ma's got to realize you can't be here as fast as you used to. You're too far away!"

"That's what I needed to hear, Louada. Will she talk to me now?"

"She's sleeping. When she wakes, I'll give her your love."

"Thanks, you're the best!" Sheila hangs up. "I *am* far away, damn it!" The anger in her voice snaps Mattie to attention. "It's O.K. precious," she croons, realizing how deeply she loves this dog. Nose-to-nose, she confides, "Sweetie, I'm far from everything I've ever known, but I've got to make this work." She's not sure what the "this" is, but something tells her it will be worth it, besides, she's never been one to give up. "You've got to help me, girl. Can you give me some of your strength?"

I'm here for you, the steadfast eyes seem to reply.

Sheila moves through the next few days in third person as she watches herself trying to settle into a house that isn't hers. First, she attacks the dog fur that seems to be coating everything. As she vacuums and scrubs, the once-busy career woman marvels that an activity she's always hated is her first choice of things to do. *But really, what is there to do? I have no meetings to go to, no deadlines to meet. I'm standing on the edge of nothing with empty hours looming ahead.*

The high points of each day are phoning the kids, and spending a few hours in the evening with Earl. The rest of the time, Sheila floats above watching the person below slide through the minutes in an aimless, passive way. When she identifies this to be more destructive than healing, she decides to fill the void with useful work. But the work she's best at isn't here. The job she often cursed for frittering her life away is *up there*. And the important work, the blessed work, of caring for her children, is also over a thousand miles away. *Lord, I need you more than ever. I don't know what it is I should do, but you do. Please don't keep it a secret!*

The answer comes. *First things first, get ready for the kids' visit,* and so she does. She organizes a guest-room to be designated as hers. The other, she transforms into a room for Allie and Chase. She buys them new bikes, and sets them up with Florida wardrobes from Kids Wee Cycle. Finally, she plans a budget to pay for their vacation fun. *Thanks, Dad, and my boyfriends of days gone by, little did you know your gifts would buy my freedom!* Her promise not to invade the marriage's joint accounts now seems more foolhardy than heroic. In the long run, however, she'll be proud she took the high road. And, maybe in the future, Charles will appreciate what she's done.

Will a time come, too, when he'll realize what a sacrifice it is to let him start off with the children? Will he see I'm doing this to get him through the hell I've caused? He will see, won't he?

Chapter 29
Spring Vacation

Fourteen days had been the mantra that comforted Sheila on that first horrific night away from her children. Now, every one of those days is behind her and she's back on the road to Wisconsin. To break up the twenty-hour drive, she'll spend the night in Sara Boudreau's Nashville home. Before ringing the doorbell, she fights to resurrect her sunny persona. *Sara mustn't see the mess I've become since I jettisoned 90 percent of my identity!* The ploy almost works, but within seconds of seeing her bud, her happy veneer cracks. Sobbing in Sara's arms, she admits to her overwhelming loss of identity and complete panic at being without Allie and Chase. It gets worse when Sara urges her to fight for the children. Having recently entered law school, she's researched court cases similar to Sheila's, but rather than give her friend courage, they demoralize her further. They're cases of adultery, abuse, neglect, and worse yet, abandonment. None of it resembles the marriage she and Charles worked at for sixteen years.

"No, I can't do that to Charles, my children, or myself. Besides, as well-known and revered as the Branford family is in the Milwaukee court system, how do I know I'd get a fair trial? All I can do, Sara, is leave it in God's hands. He, better than any judge, knows what they mean to me, and I to them."

Sara can see it's no use. In one year, she's gone from providing an alibi for her friend to serving as a depository for her guilt.

The next morning, an artificially buoyant Sheila bids her chum good-bye. The visit has only served to strengthen her resolve to let no one, not Charles, the children, her mother, or any of her Wisconsin friends see the anguish she's suffering. *Happy, happy, joy, joy, I'll play the dauntless heroine. Can I do it? Of course, I can didn't I pull off being a happy wife all those years?*

The role-playing begins as soon as she crosses the Wisconsin state line. Fortunately, her country station is playing all the right mood-elevating songs. They steer her through Milwaukee in time to arrive at the kids' school a few minutes before dismissal. Sheila parks in her usual place, and watches, heart racing, as little people start to appear. When Allie and Chase emerge, her heart seems to jump from her chest. Allie pokes Chase and points to the Seville. Their little forms stand transfixed. They seem to be wondering if she's a mirage. *Lord, they're so small, so very small!* Chase is the first to move with Allie running a nanosecond later. "Mommy, Mommy, Mommy!" Sheila, out of the car, is running too. Meeting in the middle, they hug and kiss, over and over again. Other mothers stand watching. Her peripheral vision tells her that they know. Frozen with curiosity, or contempt, they watch. *You only know one side!* Sheila's eyes scream in protest. *Oh, why bother? You'll believe what you want. I guess this will prove who my friends are!* The threesome sandwich hugs for a long, long time. *They belong with me. Lord, can't you see they really do belong with me!*

"Ah, good, very, very good!" Mara's approval comes from behind. Tears forming, Sheila rises to hug the sitter. A flurry of run-on Polish tells her how glad Mara is to have her back.

"Allie and Chase, go to Grandma's." To make sure the sitter understands Sheila pantomimes driving the car. "First we go to house for suitcases, then vacation!"

"*Tak, tak,*" Mara nods, with glowing satisfaction.

She thinks I'm back for good and it will only come clear when I leave again, how awful! Sheila and the kids walk to her car as Mara runs to get their safety seats. The little boy's arms encircle one of Mommy's legs, and Allie hugs her waist.

"Sheila! What's up?" It's Alice, one of Sheila's favorite moms.

When she has both kids in the car, she approaches her friend to speak privately. "You've heard about Charles and me?"

"Yes, I'm so sorry, but I wish you well. Are you taking Allie and Chase to live with you?"

"Not right away; Charles needs them with him."

"I can imagine." Silent for a moment, she seems to be envisioning Charles without Sheila. "Well, let me know how I can help. I mean it, too — I'm not just saying that."

"I know, Alice, you're one of the true blues. Thank you."

Another mom approaches. Lorelei, a woman Sheila has cast as "the earth mother supreme" pulls her into a bear hug.

"You've heard?" Sheila asks.

"Yeah, I hurt big time for you and Charles too. But you need to know there's a slur campaign going on out there."

Sheila pulls back to check the earth mother's eyes for confirmation.

"Yes indeedy, and not just by your husband — it's your father-in-law. You won't believe what he did. Picture this, as my son's birthday party was ending, he came at me announcing you'd run off with some Casanova. Even though I wasn't listening, he followed me around the room proclaiming it loud enough for everyone to hear!"

Sheila regrets knowing this. She'd always felt a kinship with Charles's father and had hoped, in some way, he'd understand her actions. "Well," she stalls, still trying to put it in perspective. "He doesn't know all the facts, and of course, he's mad as hell."

"Yes, but he was forcing it on me, a total stranger!"

Sheila smiles and gets into her car. "Lorelei, you truly are the earth mother supreme! Thank you!"

"Listen, hon, anyone who knows you, realizes there's a ton of stuff under this iceberg. I'll remind people of that."

She blows Lorelei a kiss as she pulls into the stream of cars. As Allie and Chase chatter happily, she can't help but wonder what more is being said. No one, other than she or Charles, knows the whole story. And she's actually protected him with her silence. Out of some weird loyalty, she hasn't told a soul about his less-than-innocent past. *Maybe his dad would be less condemning of he knew his son, also, had an affair. So why do I keep protecting him with my silence? Why didn't I tell Lorelei just now?*

Flipping into flashback mode, she returns to a time ten years earlier when the already distant man was more so. She'd pulled into her driveway one night to find Charles sitting in a car with one of his employees. It was then she'd wondered if an affair had cooled his feelings for her. But it hadn't fit with the man. Charles, she'd

SLOW DANCE

thought, had too much character. Even with the truth staring her in the face, she'd surmised his distance was just his way. *Damn you, Charles! If your love for me couldn't withstand the allure of an extramarital tryst, why didn't you set me free? I may be at fault for marrying you, but you're to blame for holding me to my vows when you'd already broken yours!*

Sheila's rage is already off the meter when she pulls in the drive to see Charles coming out of the house. He startles at her fierce look but recovers enough to manage a flirty "Hello, stranger!"

"Spare me!" she spits in a fierce stage whisper, as she opens the door for the kids. They tumble out, hug Charles and run into the house for their things. "I've just been hearing how your dad is telling everyone I ran off with some Casanova!"

"If the shoe fits, wear it!" he smirks.

"That shoe fits you too, buddy!" she screams.

Charles's expression says only that he's sorry he ever brought up his affair. Deliberately turning her back on her less-than-faithful husband, Sheila runs to the house. "All aboard the Grandma express!" Happy giggles precede her little ones down the stairs. Each one jumps off the last step with a backpack and a cherished stuffed animal in tow. Their father appears with a suitcase. Sheila winces, thinking how hard it must have been for him to pack their things for a vacation without him.

"Thank you for getting them packed." She strains to smile.

Charles turns his back on her and walks outside to the children. "You guys have a good time now. I'll call you tomorrow, and on Sunday I'll come to see you before you leave. I'm going to miss you and I love you very much."

"I love you, Daddy! Love you!" Their spontaneous affection for their daddy makes Sheila's heart ache. In the car, she reflects — first, on her husband's, then on his father's hostility toward her. *Do Allie and Chase sense it? Are they safe with Charles? Of course, and they're better off in the stable environment he can provide. Down South, everything, the people, the surroundings, even the dialect would be foreign to them.*

Even she and Earl have misfires communicating on the simplest things. When he told her to "put up" the chocolate sauce, she put the bottle up, like he said, on the shelf for condiments. Later, Earl almost emptied the refrigerator in search of the sauce. When she located it

Melissa McDaniel

for him, he snapped, "Blossom, don't you know that stuff's supposed to be refrigerated!" Her confusion lasted until she heard Earl say he'd "put up" the leftovers. As they laughed, she'd wondered when their differences would backfire again.

At her mom's, Sheila embraces the woman she hasn't missed for a second. "How's my girl?" The thin voice sounds welcoming. *That's good; this visit needs to go well.* And it does. For the next two days, they share a better time than they have in eons. Sheila feels more like a daughter and less like a nursing home director. Her obligations are the same, but the everyday drudgery has diminished with distance. Allie and Chase, so happy to be with Mommy, are little angels. They love playing with Sheila but when she explains she must spend time with Grandma, they make Wookie their playmate.

Her mom's health, also, seems a little improved. Had they been dragging each other down? Even a doctor's appointment confirms that her vital signs are somewhat better. Back home, her exhausted mother promptly goes to sleep in her easy chair. Half an hour later, she awakens, racked with pain. Sheila administers a painkiller to quiet her mom's beleaguered nerve endings and tells the children they can watch television in the den. Then she sits in an armchair next to her mother and starts to shorten a skirt hem. *Around here, the length of this skirt is perfect, but down there, it looks frumpy.* Losing herself in the rhythmic in and out of her needle and thread, Sheila contrasts the Southern women she's met with her Midwestern cronies. Florida women have such style! It seems every one she's met has something scintillating about her. *They have a knack for accentuating the positive. Is it cause and effect? Does warm weather make them wear fewer clothes, demanding they be in great shape? If so, does it follow that being in great shape encourages one to show it off?* Whichever it is, she'd hate to learn that the fun-loving, flirtatious women she's found so welcoming are the same breed of sexual predator as Earl's Carlene. *All this is new to me; it's as if I'm being reborn.*

When Sheila looks up to check on her mother, a bittersweet smile comes to her lips. Mom, under the influence of her medication, is air sewing along with her daughter. She's doing the needlework she's done all her life. The fact that she has no needle, thread, or material, matters not. It's all there, in her mind's eye. They sew on together, chatting a little, but most of the time just enjoying each other's company as they partake of their crafts.

Allie appears in the doorway. When she sees Grandma's behavior, her green eyes grow huge like cat's-eye marbles. Too befuddled to speak, she looks to Mommy for explanation. Sheila nods and winks, hoping the old soul in her precious daughter will understand that everything is fine. Allie, bless her heart, nods and backs from the room with eyes fixed on Granny. Everything is fine, it's better than fine, for at this moment, the bitter, messed-up daughter and the mother who'd loved her too much are united in mutual activity.

Come Sunday, Sheila and Louada make dinner for Dan and his sons. Over dessert and coffee, she marvels that it doesn't feel the least bit strange not to have Charles with them. *Was he that invisible in my life?* She's pondering this when the invisible man appears in the doorway. Awkward pleasantries are exchanged, and Sheila excuses herself to walk outside with Charles and the kids. She watches as he makes a big deal out of the fact they'll be gone for a whole week.

"Voila! The instant hands-on Daddy!"

"You're a piece of work," he spits back, throwing a ball for Wookie and the children to chase.

"No, we're a piece of work. That's why we have to end this quickly."

"I'll go when I'm ready," he says, thinking she means they should end this encounter.

"I mean we need to end this marriage as soon as possible."

If during moments of extreme insight things seem to happen in slow motion, this is such a moment for Charles. The muscles on his face slacken as his heart seems to crack open. His spirit of denial is unable to thrive amid the horrid reality that Sheila really does want out of their marriage. How did this happen? Not so long ago, he'd had the perfect wife and home. Why him? What did he do to deserve this? His despair hushes Sheila. She's seen his pain in recent months, but not like this. He seems to be imploding before her eyes. She waits in anxious silence, but nothing more is said. Charles fakes a happy wave to the kids. In slow motion, he opens the car door, eases himself in, and starts the engine. The gearshift moves and the automobile slides back inch by inch.

Melissa McDaniel

Murder, this is murder in slow motion. How can I be so cruel!

The car creeps away. Its driver looks so racked with pain he dare not go faster. Finally, it inches around a bend in the road and is gone.

Feeling nauseous, Sheila tries to concentrate on the joyful antics of Allie, Chase, and Wookie, but the bilious feeling stays with her. It even accompanies her the next morning as they fly to Florida. Only when they land does she start to feel better, and as Earl greets them, the sadness lifts completely. The great big honey of a man is holding a sign welcoming Allie and Chase to the Sunshine State. Next to him is Mattie, looking adorable in a straw hat and sunglasses. Sheila smiles, *it's going to be a wonderful week!*

Chapter 30
Mommy's New Friend

Even though she's designated one of Earl's guest- rooms to be hers, and another to be the kids', Sheila decides it would be more acceptable for them to sleep at a nearby Holiday Inn. When they're not there, they are at Earl's, playing with Mattie and riding their new bikes. In the evenings, they all make dinner together. Allie and Chase like the big bear of a man who is their mother's new friend. He's warm but he doesn't push himself at them and he's respectful where their mother is concerned, never kissing or hugging her in their presence.

Toward the end of the week, Sheila and the children drive to Clermont for an overnight with Alana and Jack Randolph. Alana is a hit with the children. She's like a Southern Auntie Mame. "Now rememba, Chase," Alana drawls, "When y'all are in my house, you eat only what you like. If you don't like something, just leave it on your plate." Chase, eyes wide with surprise, checks her mother for confirmation. Sheila nods the go-ahead he seeks. As she watches her son push the beans aside, she realizes the three of them could spend a month here, basking in Alana's easy warmth. But time is growing short and they have to get back to Pine Springs to spend their last day with Earl before flying back to reality. It's spent with Sheila and the kids, accompanying him in a golf cart as he plays a round at his club. This simple activity seems to be one of the most exciting things the children have ever done. On each tee box, they search for tees, whole or otherwise. "They're our own little greens crew," Sheila says, marveling at their concentration on performing the task.

"The club should pay you two for the good work you're doing." Earl means this as a compliment, but Chase's five-year-old mind takes it literally.

"Really? How much will we get?"

"No, little buddy, I was kidding about being paid." Then, seeing the disappointment on the little boy's face; Earl makes it better. "But tell you what, to thank you for finding all these nice slightly used and broken tees I'll buy you each a hot dog and soda when we finish."

Allie scrunches her nose. "Earl, I don't want a hot dog. Can I get something else?"

"Blossom, you can have your run of the snack shack. Anything your mama approves of, you can have!"

Allie's little body straightens with pride as she beams up at Earl. She's never before been addressed as a "blossom" and she kind of likes it. This great big friend of her mother's is ok by her.

Damn, this week's gone fast, Sheila snarls to herself as she drags out of bed the next morning. The lazy days of Florida sunshine are behind them. She must now return Allie and Chase to their father. "Time to get up, honey-pie," she whispers in Allie's ear. Then to Chase, "Wake up little buddy, we're going on the airplane today!" The promised adventure of another airplane ride is enough to get him moving. All three scoot around preparing to emerge into the brilliant sunshine of another Florida day.

First, they stop at Earl's house for a quick good-bye. Sheila would give anything to know what's going on in her children's minds as they hug Earl and Mattie.

On the way to the airport, Allie confides, "I like Earl. He's nice."

"He's cool and so is Mattie!" Chase chimes in.

"I'm glad you like them, I do too!" Sheila says, relieved the visit has gone so well. Soon, they board the plane and four hours later, Sheila sees the Milwaukee skyline from the airplane window. *Damn! In only a few hours, we have to say good-bye. Is this what the future holds? Sad farewells hinged together by joyous visits and long absences?*

Hush! The inner Sheila cautions. *Thoughts like that will destroy you. Things will work out if you take them one day at a time.*

It's a shock to find that Charles is not home. After arriving at the airport, the threesome had taken a cab to her mother's. Following a brief visit with Grandma, they'd piled into the Seville to "go surprise Daddy!"

Coward! If you're such a caring dad, why aren't you here for your children when they arrive? Instead you've arranged to have Mara here? What will happen if I leave and you're still not home? Do you expect her to deal with the aftermath?

Although she'd promised her mother they'd have dinner together, Sheila calls to say she'll stay with the kids as long as she can, in hopes Charles will appear. *Not to worry, this means more time with Allie and Chase and that's a good thing.* The threesome plays in the yard and on the beach for the rest of the afternoon. By dinnertime, Charles is still nowhere to be found so they walk to a nearby restaurant. There, they share what Sheila realizes is their last meal for several weeks. *Don't go there. Don't you dare go there!*

"O.K., now we'll go back to your house," she explains as the last spoonfuls of ice cream are being downed. She mustn't say, "We'll go home," lest their little minds think it's her home too. But whom is she kidding? Of course they think that. They've never known it any other way.

"No, no Charles." The worried sitter informs Sheila. Her eyes seem to be spewing a string of anxious Polish words. Knowing something very bad has occurred in "her" family, Mara suffers from the same tension as her employers.

"That's O.K.," Sheila explains, "We'll unpack your things, have a nice bedtime story and I'll tuck you in. Then I have to go to Grandma's, and tomorrow I return to Florida." She hates saying this but she mustn't let her children think they'll see her in the morning.

"Do you have to?" The pain evident in Allie's seven-year-old voice tells Sheila her daughter fully understands her message. Five-year-old Chase, not really paying attention, doesn't realize what's about to happen.

"Yes, I must, but we'll be together again soon."

She tucks them into the twin beds of Allie's room, so they'll be together when she leaves. Then sitting between them, she tells the next installment of her "ongoing tales of Peter Pan." In the course of five minutes, she spins a plot in which Peter foils Captain Hook and cleverly saves the Lost Boys, "to face yet another, rip-rousing adventure!" Saying these traditional words is too much for Sheila. She bursts into sobs, something Allie and Chase have seldom seen.

Alarmed, they climb onto Mommy's lap. "Both kids!" But the words which always accompany their traditional sandwich hug only bring more tears.

Really frightened now, Allie and Chase begin to cry, too. "What's wrong Mommy?"

"Nothing, sweeties, everything will be fine. I'm just going to miss you very, very much. Let's pray. Please, Lord, help Allie and Chase feel my love wrapping around them always, let them feel me with them everywhere they go; protecting them even when I can't be here."

"No!" It's Chase now, sensing what's about to happen. "No, Mommy, don't go!" He buries his face in Sheila's breast and his little fingers grasp the sweater she's wearing as if to hold her in place. All the advice she's sought from counselors and friends is of no help. All she can do is wrap her babies in her arms and rock them, humming a song reminiscent of happier days. It calms the little girl and boy, and their crying subsides.

During the song's fourth chorus her guilty conscience breaks through. *Stay, they need you, and you need them. They'll be grown soon. You can go then. Make your break for it then, in, maybe, twelve or fifteen years. Stay. Endure.* But by the sixth chorus, the reality of this directive hits home. It would be twelve or fifteen more years of living someone else's life, in a place she's grown to hate, with a man she doesn't love, twelve or fifteen more years of working at a life which extracts too much of the wrong stuff from her. It will all be hers if she stays here tonight.

No! Don't you dare back down! You've made the change, now see it through. You'll be a better mother as the person you were meant to be, not as the frenetic, automaton wife, daughter, employee that everyone else would have you be!

But this is too hard! Lord, I need your strength! Ever since this started, I've depended on you. Please help me now.

Minutes pass. Allie and Chase have relaxed in the security of her arms. *Where the hell is their daddy? Why is he doing this? Doesn't he realize how hard this is on the kids, or, is this on purpose? Is his absence meant to prove a point?*

Suddenly it comes clear. *It's a setup! He's deliberately staying away to make sure this will be a horrible good-bye. How manipulative! How cruel!* Sheila's furious and it's this anger that drives her forward. She tenderly returns her children to their beds. Once they're snuggled in, she stands ever-so-slowly.

"Don't go!" Allie whispers.

"Stay!" Chase commands.

This will be a stand off; the children aren't going to go to sleep as long as she's here. She kisses each, saying, "I have to go see Grandma now, and you, my precious little ones, need to go to sleep. You've both got big days at school tomorrow." She rises and moves to the door.

"Mommy! Don't go, please don't go!"

"Everything will be fine, honey-pies. Mara will come up to sit with you until you go to sleep. I love you tons and tons, and I'll call you when you get home from school tomorrow."

"Mara!" Sheila calls as she runs downstairs. Amid tears she, pantomimes her instructions to be sure the sitter understands. "Go sit with Allie and Chase, hum to them until they go to sleep."

The two, who have spent seven years working as a mother and grandma team, kiss each other's wet cheeks. "Go," she whispers, pointing upstairs. "Go to them! They need you!" As she ascends, Mara blows her a kiss saying what Sheila thinks are the Polish words for "I love you." She disappears into Allie's room and Sheila hears the sweet sounds of her voice, assuring the little ones all is well.

Cursing Charles's insensitivity, she scoots out the back door with anger so intense it seems to propel her to her mother's house. On the way there, she makes a decision. She will act the part of a happy daughter, eager to get on the road, saying it will be infinitely safer she leaves tonight rather than in the morning rush hour as she had planned.

She'd originally looked forward to a good night's sleep in her old bedroom. But like Macbeth, Sheila hath murdered sleep. *What, with my anger at Charles, and my own disdain for the unnatural act I'm committing, there will be no blissful oblivion tonight. No, it's better I get on the road and drive as far away as I can.*

It is almost nine o'clock and her mother has just gone to bed. Her tiny, rigid form is propped up by a multitude of pillows strategically placed to soothe the contours of her aching body. As Sheila approaches her mother, she tries not to let the shock of what she sees register on her face. Parkinson's disease has all but displaced her lovely mother. She climbs onto the bed to get as close as possible.

The love Sheila feels for this woman right now is enormous. It's a little girl's love for her beautiful, all-giving Mommy.

"Mom!" she cries as she attempts to embrace the brittle body. Tears come again, but this time, they flow out of true and pure love for the woman who, for so long, had been the most important person in Sheila's life. That she sees her mother as having been so instrumental in her current predicament is irrelevant, "Mom, I love you, I love you so much! You're the best mother I could ever have."

"I love you, too, my precious little girl." Her arms reach out to pulse in rhythm around her daughter's neck. There's more passion in Mom's voice than Sheila has heard for a long time. She pulls back to search her mother's face. The eyes are dry; Parkinson's parched her tear ducts long ago, but the burning mother love of another time and place still glows there. It is rapture only a mother knows, and it bears testimony to a love neither time, nor illness, nor the pettiness of human nature can destroy.

Sheila kisses the mouth that can pucker only slightly. She presses her lips to her mom's cheeks, her forehead, and the top of her head. A love for all time is pouring from her soul.

"I'm sorry I have to leave now, Mom, but I'll be back in a few weeks."

"O.K., honey, be careful."

Infinitely relieved this good-bye is going well, Sheila lingers, savoring the tenderness of the moment, storing it for future withdrawals. "And you take care of yourself, Mom. Remember to drink lots of water." Again embracing the tiny form, "I'll call you tomorrow night to see how you're doing." With a quick hug for Louada, and another for Wookie, she's out the door before her happy façade can crumble.

Back in the car, the complete horror of the goodbye with Allie and Chase comes real. *It's good I'm putting this energy to use. As wild as I am right now, I'll be wide-awake all night.*

The roads are almost empty on this Sunday night, allowing Sheila to speed away from Wisconsin, down through Illinois, and on to Indiana. *Hot coffee will help,* she tells herself, *but what's really charging me is my wrath. How dare Charles not be there for the kids? If he wants them so much, he better face up to his responsibility, if not, I'm here, ready and willing!*

SLOW DANCE

It takes around six hours to get to Indianapolis, then it's onto Louisville, followed later by Nashville. *This is like being on a train, a very fast train.* Hour after hour, the stars roll by. Slowly, with every hundred miles, her spirits start to rise. Dawn is breaking by the time she reaches the Smokey Mountains so she pulls off the road to better absorb their majesty. Monster domes, sporting thick white mufflers of clouds, seem to whisper to her alone. *There now, everything will be all right. In the midst of your turmoil, something much greater watches over you. Let it guide you in your search."*

"In my search?" Sheila asks. *Yes, it is my search, but no one else sees it that way. They see a middle-aged woman who's gone gaga over some Southern dude. Not knowing the history of my discontent, they actually believe this happened overnight. How simple it is when people are only willing to see what's on the surface!*

She may be returning to the South, but it isn't so much for Earl as it is the act of getting away from the person she'd become. She'd borne it well; taught in childhood never to complain, she hadn't. *That's why everyone's so shocked now. If I hadn't already been crumbling, Earl may not have gotten through that protective wall I'd constructed around myself. To the world, it seems he seduced me away from a loving marriage. Well, the world is wrong. And now the world thinks I'm racing back to him, when actually, I'm returning to a part of the country I love, a place where there happens to be a great guy who loves me.*

There's a ton of healing to be done, but what healing can occur simultaneous to her committing three murders? There's the murder of her marriage, her career, and her life as she's always known it. The month is April, by fall she hopes to have the destruction behind her so the rebuilding process can begin.

Chapter 31
Settling In

Sheila's been on the road over twelve hours, awake for twenty-eight. Her body feels like lead and sleep won't wait. *I'm already past the most dangerous part; if only I could keep going! No, I may be dumb, but I ain't stupid!* She smiles, the Southern colloquialisms she'd found so quaint are now her own.

A motel, boasting cheap rates, lures her from the highway. Upon checking in, she goes straight to her room, bolts the door, removes her shoes, and crawls under the sheets. In seconds, this woman, so prone to wakeful worry, is asleep.

Hours later, the afternoon sun has found her room. Sheila considers pulling the blackout drapes, but further sleep is improbable, and she can still make Pine Springs by dark. She's up and out in five minutes. How she loves life on the road!

It's dusk when she pulls into Earl's driveway. He's sprinkling his vegetable garden, hose in one hand, a scotch and water in the other. A cell phone is wedged between his shoulder and neck. "Guess who just blew in!" his delight is genuine. Sheila had called when she'd stopped for gas so her early arrival is no surprise. "Yeah, can you believe it?" he asks into the phone. "She left Milwaukee last night and here she is. That's my gal! So I'll be fine for dinner, thanks anyway." He bends to kiss her.

"Who's that?" Sheila mouths.

"Callie," Earl responds.

Callie, short for Calliope, is a leggy redhead who frequents Alvira's Medicine Shoppe. She'd welcomed Sheila with open arms, saying she stood ready to help anyway she could. She'd even said she'd come by to check on her as soon as she arrived in town. Callie has yet to appear for Sheila, but in her absence, Earl gets a call. *What is it with these nurturing females who can't do enough for this man? First there was Satin, now Callie. How many others stand ready to fuss over him!*

To avert the cold front he sees forming, Earl starts bludgeoning Callie with praise for his Sheila. There's nothing his lady can't do. He's never known anyone like her. She's smart, funny, and a long haul driver to boot. He's never been so happy.

This is too funny! Sheila grabs the phone in mock protest. "Hi, Callie, Earl's being kind; the drive was no big deal. It's an easy eighteen hours. Besides, he's my carrot, if you know what I mean."

Callie, undaunted, reminds Sheila that Earl's birthday is only a few days away. "Last year, we had a party for him. We could do that again."

And the beat goes on! Sheila says she'll talk to Earl about it. Later, when she does, he thanks her for not committing to a party. "Darlin', I don't want to celebrate my birthday with anyone but you." It's exactly what Sheila needs to hear as she resumes this strange new life of hers.

But is this living? It doesn't feel like it; it's more like floating in suspended animation, wafting through the long hours of an undemanding vacation. And without my phone calls to Allie and Chase, the hours would be unbearable.

Recalling their conversations helps to steer her through the morning and onto the afternoon when she'll call them again. All the while, she's looking for things she can tell them or questions she can ask to keep the discourse interesting. She knows better than to bore them with the details of what she's really doing, paying Grandma's bills; submitting insurance forms, exploring places to stash her clothes. Instead, she decides to embellish a war she's waging with the squirrels in Earl's yard. The "tree rats" (as he calls them) are antagonizing two Southern Blue Birds who are trying to live in a birdhouse mounted on the fence. Although the squirrels are too large to enter the house, they anger the birds, so much so that Sheila fears they'll soon vacate the premises. When Mattie and Sheila's presence no longer deters them, Earl goes on the offensive. He arrives one evening with a gift, he says, she can really use.

"Here, darlin'," and he hands his lady a brand new BB gun. "This'll give the little shits something to think about."

Amazed, Sheila takes the gun, stroking the smooth, cool barrel with her fingers. "I don't know what to say."

"Don't mention it, blossom, I know how much those birds mean to you. Let me demonstrate," he takes the gun, loads and cocks it. "Just wait 'til your prey gets up on the fence, then." Ping! Startled and stinging, the "little shit" leaps from the fence in a single bound. After a few more pops, the squirrels do seem deterred. So Sheila spends the next few days gardening in the backyard with a BB gun nearby. It makes for great stories to tell the kids. *Ah yes, if my friends could see me now!* She has to admit, its fun popping the furry pests, and the behavior modification seems to be keeping her birds in residence.

Inevitably though, Sheila tires of the blue bird protection program. "I hereby delegate squirrel harassment to you, Mattie. I have to focus on other things, like improving my cooking, and, oh, my god, cleaning the house." Turning again to what she once perceived as a mindless task, she realizes there's dignity in doing it well. *And as I work, my thoughts can wander wherever they want. There's no need to rein them in to prepare for a meeting or write a proposal. My mind, not my job, is ruling my life...how novel!* But it soon is clear that there's still too much time for too many thoughts.

Sensing the danger in excessive introspection, Sheila looks for a job that might protect her from herself. When she's offered one marketing a new golf club, she embraces it as a blessed escape. The fact that it demands a fraction of her management ability matters not. The club's finances will depend on the membership base she attracts and she won't let them down.

Suddenly, it's May and her leave of absence from the college is ending. Although there's much of which she's unsure, Sheila heads north to be with her children, visit Mom, and resign from the position she'd worked so hard to attain. It hurts to learn her boss has been telling everyone she'd left the college in the lurch. Imagine, after eighteen years of giving it her all, her evenings, weekends and sleepless nights, after eighteen years of devoting way too much of her personal time to budgets, proposals, and personnel problems, after all that, she's left them in the lurch! *If I'd left for another position, I wouldn't have given them any more notice, but that would have been acceptable. This double standard world just keeps on spinning!*

Her thoughts turn to her current job. It is child's play compared to her previous position. It's also soaking in testosterone. The big burly men with whom she works are delightful, but they have no clue what she's capable of doing, nor do they care to know. From early on, the message has been she's there to do marketing, nothing more, so when she sees signs of systems running amuck, she keeps quiet. It kills her to be so ineffective, but in the interest of self-preservation, she chooses to don a "not-my-problem" philosophy.

Chapter 32
Bibliotherapy

By midsummer, Sheila's in really bad shape. Daily, she forces herself to manufacture a happy veneer for her public. The irony that her recent move was supposed to curtail such behavior eats away at her, still, it wouldn't do for others to see the quaking nothingness she is now. Allie and Chase play in her mind constantly. She misses them to the point of physically aching. They'd had a marvelous visit when she went home in May, and again, in early June. But a trip to see them in July is out of the question. The golf course folks — once so considerate in allowing her long weekends to see the kids — say this is a crunch month and her presence is mandatory. How she'll make it through July without seeing her children, she doesn't know, and how badly they must be missing her keeps her racked with guilt. But she made this commitment and she will see it through, even though the job, no longer new, has become tedious. By the end of a boring workday, she can't wait to go home to the man she loves. Once there, however, she finds herself in the throws of a romance too young to feel so old. Clearly, she and Earl have yet to calibrate their feelings. Since moving in with him, she's been frantic with unspent love. He, on the other hand, has settled into something resembling mid-marriage lethargy.

Who's right here? Who's wrong? Will we ever meet in the middle? Such worries thrash at her in the monotony of work. She's waited decades for someone to make her wild with passion. Now that she has him, she's in a constant state of arousal. After a boring eight-hour day, she races home like an addict in need of a fix. Earl, fatigued from a more stressful job, is content to just sit with his lady, sharing a drink while they watch dusk give way to night. Sheila loves the intimacy, but it makes her even hornier for what she hopes will follow. When, after another scotch and a late dinner, Earl finds sleep more irresistible than Sheila, she really starts to panic.

Oh god, please don't let it be I've traded one for another! What she's feeling is the threat of, again, being taken for granted. She won't stand for that. This time around, nothing less than perfection will do, especially when she so dearly misses Allie and Chase. If she's going to be away from them, even temporarily, it has to be for the best relationship of all time, nothing less.

Earl, on the other hand, seems to have put their relationship on cruise control. He tells her he loves her, but it's as if those words should suffice, no further romance is necessary. There's been no transition from point A, a place of passionate need and attention to point B, one of gentle complacency.

I would never have believed that, here in the flesh, I'd be pining for the long distance phone conversations and letters that first won my love! Did he deceive me? Is the warm attentive person, of before, the same one who now says, "I'll call you," then seldom does? Is the man who'd stop everything at the sound of my voice, the same one who answers in a harried, preoccupied tone when I call him at work? It comes to a head one morning when Earl gives her his "I'll call you later" line.

"No you won't!" she snaps. They're in the middle of a good-bye hug but Sheila's words push him away. Checking her eyes, Earl sees they're even colder than her response. "You won't call. You seldom do, so don't patronize me by saying you will."

Earl hasn't been privy to the smoldering beneath Sheila's crust. To him, everything has been going great. She's moved gracefully into his life. Not only has she blocked out memories of other women, she's fast become his best bud. Even his work is going better now that he has someone to achieve for. The fact that he's opened his life to her means everything, what more need to be said? He sputters something about not always being able to call, and she, of all people, should understand that. Then he backs his way to the car.

Sheila, still stewing in the juices of assault, continues, "It's demeaning to hear you say every day you'll call and then you don't." Underneath it all, she's silently pleading. *Don't you know talking to you is the only thing I look forward to in my stupid, boring day? When you don't phone I feel let down and forgotten. It hurts and frightens me. I'm so scared right now, if I had someplace else to go, I probably would. And I resent the fact that our sex is less frequent and that you never bring me little tokens of your love like you said you'd do. And, while I'm at it, I don't understand why, when I told you that night at the Cracker Barrel how fantastic it felt to hear you say I was pretty, you've never said so since. Did you think I told you not to say it? What gives, Earl? Why are you rationing such things at the very time I'm most insecure?*

This Sheila wants to know, but dares not ask. She knows how easily things can go tilt, and whatever role Earl has cast her in, it isn't one of nag. Instead, she waves and grins to assure him things are better than they seem. He returns a cautious smile, gets in his car, and backs down the drive. *Maybe I cast him in the wrong role. And maybe he's not the effusive, ever-verbal lover he seemed. If that's the case, can I adjust to this less demonstrative man? I'd better! My sanity dictates that I must.*

Little revelations like this help Sheila tiptoe through the unknowns of their relationship. Every day, she struggles to find reasons to continue their life together. That she loves him deeply, there's no doubt. He's a truly good man, a wonderful old soul, someone worth the fight. To assist in her efforts to understand her guy, she invests her spare time in bibliotherapy. *What Men Really Want* and *Women Are From Venus, Men Are From Mars* are titles that accompany her everywhere. She even renews her acquaintance with *Anna Karenina*. When she'd read Tolstoy's novel in college, she hadn't begun to understand Anna as she does now that they're soul mates in a common deed. Anna speaks volumes to her, teaching by example of what not to do.

Anna knew the anguish a love like this can reap as she faced life without her little boy. She was as needy as I am, craving Count Vronsky's constant attention. And when he was unable to be there for her every minute of every day, she started to doubt him as well. Maybe, what Anna and I see as neglect is really our lovers throwing themselves into their work to secure our futures. It's as if she's talking to me, saying pay attention, learn from my mistakes!

Yes, Anna, I know if I'm not careful, I could end up like you, jealous of Earl's work, and doubtful of his love. With no life of my own, and without my children, I may become so desperate I'd choose your way out. It could happen. Thanks, Anna, for telling me what I should do by sacrificing yourself at the altar of what not to do.*

With Anna's "don't-do-as-I-do" directive etched in her brain, Sheila struggles to be more tolerant of Earl's preoccupation with work. She tries not to miss the man in the letters by focusing on what's positive about the one in the here and now. She's determined to be less emotionally dependent on Earl and more reliant on herself. *I'm tough. I'll get through this. Not only will 1 survive, 1'll be better than before.* This attitude makeover succeeds to a point, but Charles's daily phone calls drag her back down. Every time she talks to him, her guilt is renewed and her already fragile psyche becomes more so. She endures each excruciating session hoping it will help move him through his pain. But for her, it only seems to suck the life from her body. At day's end, Earl's pleasant, but less-than-effusive companionship cannot revive it.

Anna, did you get this low? Sure, you did: that's why you put yourself in the way of a train. I'm afraid, like you, it's possible to get low then lower still, and finally, to descend so far into a hole that up no longer exists. And it scares me that I'm starting to feel it's no big deal to merge with the hole.

One night in particular, Sheila is almost there. She awakens, as she always does, with bones and muscles aching from the trauma of being without her children. She can feel the seductive presence of the hole. It longs to absorb her nothingness. *To do that would be saying Charles was right all along.* A weakened inner Sheila rallies enough to paint a picture of him smugly accepting the world's sympathy for having had such a crazy, self-destructive wife. *You're the sane one here, this is the most painful thing you've ever done, but it won't last forever. Think of it as natural childbirth, just when you think the pain will never stop, it does. And this time, you're not only doing the birthing, you're also the one being born.*

Sheila rises, and heads outside to address the stars so brilliant in the north Florida sky. "Lord, you up there? I think you'd agree, I don't give up easily, but right now, I'm in bad shape. If you've been letting me proceed in a laissez-faire sort of way, it's not working. I'm a mess and I could use some help climbing out of this hole."

She stretches out on the thick St. Augustine grass, and, as she searches the sky, the high-pitched love songs of hundreds of amorous tree frogs pierce her consciousness. *I love you, my little troubadours! I love you and all the natural glory so abundant in this place.* As it did with the Smoky Mountains, the natural beauty of this place surrounds her, saying it has always been thus, and unless the developers do away with it entirely, it will be here long after Sheila and her problems have left the earth. *Something far greater than you is at work here. Have faith everything will be fine.*

The peace in the message returns her to bed and to sleep. Three hours later she awakens feeling better, but she has no idea how the next twelve hours will challenge her newfound peace.

Chapter 33
The Double Whammy

The first blow comes as Sheila watches Earl shave. She's perched on the bathroom counter regaling him with a story about Mattie catching a skink. The huntress had actually gone next door to show the salamander-like lizard to the neighbors. Once everyone had made a fuss over the long tail hanging from her lips, she'd let it go without a scratch, proving just how gentle a Labrador's mouth can be. Sheila chuckles at the memory. Seeing his gal in such good spirits makes Earl decide this is the perfect time to venture into dangerous territory.

"Oh, guess what?" he asks, trying to sound spontaneous.

"You made the Senior Tour?" she teases.

"Next year," he winks, hoping to keep it light. "Ryan and Chloe are getting married in Daytona on the Fourth of July."

"Wow! That's in just two days!" Sheila's joy is genuine. She's extremely fond of Ryan, as well as the beautiful young woman with whom he's fallen madly in love. "What fun that'll be!" she exclaims, but noticing Earl's strain she doesn't continue.

"Darlin', they want a super private ceremony, Chloe's brothers aren't invited, nor is my ex's boyfriend, nor, I'm afraid, are you."

Sheila absorbs this information for a second. "That's fine." she lies as the fragile, blown glass figurine of Sheila Branford shatters in slow motion. First, the shards orbit around Earl. Then they spin out, smashing against the bathroom tile. Rationally, she knows the kids' wish for a tiny wedding isn't targeted at her. *And I'm not even married to the groom's father. My three-month tenure as his*

175

significant other, while still being married to someone else, relegates me to a less than familial position, one more like that of concubine or whore. What a nasty aura that would lend to a wedding! No, I'm not family. I have no family. I destroyed that entity to be down here with this same man who's allowing me to be recognized as nothing more than a girlfriend. The irony here is too, too rich.

Earl is watching her with nervous eyes. He's worried how she's taking this, and well he should be! Her anger isn't with Ryan or Chloe, it's with him. She could risk a fight and tell him how she feels; or she can pull down her protective shield and let it bounce off. Instinct tells her the latter choice is prudent, besides, she hasn't the spunk to risk a fight, not after the night she just had.

Take the high road, what they're doing makes sense. It's the timing that's bad. Sheila hugs Earl from behind to communicate all is better than it seems, then she invites Mattie for a romp in the back yard. Between ball chases, she kneels to hug her one true friend. *You can take it,* Mattie's licks seem to say, *remember he's only human.*

Sheila nuzzles the beloved dog's neck. Out of the corner of her eye, she sees Earl watching from inside. *As for you, my prince charming, my stalwart defender, I'll deal with you later. The jury's still out on you, buster!* Sheila blows a kiss and fakes a smile as she approaches the object of her wrath. Walking him to his car, she assures him everything will be fine. But as he pulls away, Earl has the distinct feeling this is the narrowest escape yet.

Later at work, Sheila, still seething, throws herself into the monotony of checking figures, copying, filing, checking figures, copying, and filing. The busy work is a blessing; she feels capable of little more. Just as she's wondering if her brain is starting to atrophy, the phone rings.

"Southern Pines Golf and Country Club!" she says with manufactured sparkle.

"How's the smartest, best-looking woman in Florida?"

Sheila searches the Rolodex of her brain, but she can't find a name to match the familiar baritone voice. "I'm sorry, I'm sure I know you, but..."

"Sheila!" it interrupts. "Don't you know who this is? Surely you knew I'd find you."

"Find me? Oh my God! Oh... my... God, Val!" Then, straining to sound nonchalant, "So what are you finding me for?" She asks this half hoping Val Arnsell, one of the richest, most attractive men she'd known up north, is calling with a great job offer.

"Ah yes, why ever would I be calling you?" His voice is flirty, not the least bit professional; no job offer is forthcoming.

Not in the mood for combative flirtation, she cuts to the chase. "Val, the last time we talked, I told you I wasn't interested in anything but a professional relationship. You went your way, and I went mine."

"Your way, my beautiful girl was an abrupt turn south, and I resent that you didn't even say good-bye. If you had let me know how unhappy you were, I would have renewed my proposal. I'm still certain we'd be sensational together, and now that you're on your way to being single..."

For years, Sheila had admired Val in the most professional way. She'd even found herself envying his lovely wife. But she'd never suspected he'd been secretly orchestrating a plan to bring them close and then closer still. Their appointments to serve on the same volunteer boards had seemed a mere coincidence. Only when he'd revealed his feelings had she seen the long path that brought her to the edge of his seduction. Although the protective shield of her marriage had saved her, Sheila had grieved a tiny bit for what might have been. Now, as she sits in the cellar of her emotions, she realizes hearing from Val feels pretty good. Before it starts to feel too good, she rallies to object, "Absolutely not! Besides, you're extremely married."

"I'd get an annulment."

"An annulment? With the family you have?"

"We're Catholic to the bone; no one gets divorced but an annulment is quite possible. It could happen, Sheila, although our relationship has yet to be romantic, you can't deny you've felt the pull. I could make you a happy woman."

"Val, I'm saving my life down here."

"Let me help with that. I can do it better than your Mr. Langley."

"What?"

"Sheila, I know more about that Don Juan than you do. Believe me; your future is not with him."

"How do you know about him?"

"With today's technology, it's easy. Now, when can I see you? How about spending the Fourth together?"

"I can't, Val."

"Ah, but you can — lover boy's leaving town and you're not."

Trying not to sound too spooked at his omnipotence, she lies, "Come down if you want; you won't find me! I have my own plans. Didn't your snooping tell you that?"

This throws him off, but he recovers, "Not as yet it hasn't. Sheila, this is ridiculous. You have to give me a chance."

"Val, you are so barking up the wrong tree! There wasn't a thing going on between us, and I'm deeply in love with someone else."

Still, he doesn't buy it. "All those meetings we cut eyes at each other, the innocent flirtations, the years — and I do mean years — I spent watching you, loving you from afar, all of that speaks volumes of what was and is meant to be."

"Years of loving me from afar? Come on, Val, you don't expect me to believe that."

"You felt my attraction; I know you did. I didn't press it, thinking you were committed to your marriage. With that no longer the case, I'm ready to go public with my feelings. You have to let me see you."

"That won't happen."

There's a silence as Val regroups. "I'm going too fast here. We'll continue this another time. Just know I love you and want you in my life." Click.

What was all that about? How weird that he knows Earl will be gone on the Fourth! Kind of sick, really, still as insecure as I am, it's nice to know someone cares so much.

Of one thing she's certain: she'll be far away from Earl's house on July fourth. Even if she has to hide out in a mall, or at an all day movie theater, she won't let Val find her. The phone rings again: This time it's Earl saying she's been invited to spend the Fourth with some of his river buddies. Sheila knows he's arranged this so she won't spend the day alone. Ordinarily, she'd be annoyed that he'd think she needs baby-sitting, but today she accepts it as a sweet gesture, one that will take her out of Val's reach.

Chapter 34
River Folk

Try to find me here, Val, Sheila chuckles silently as she jolts over the washboard ruts of a lime rock road. She's in the cab of Ronnie Stokes's shiny black truck. Ronnie's a good old boy who's seen plenty of life. His handsome face is weathered from the sun as well as the strain of a demanding welding business. In his early forties, Ronnie sports the physique of someone in the fifth decade of life. Hundreds of barbecues, washed down with beer and chased with Wild Turkey, have taken a toll.

As remote as Sheila's background is to Earl's, hers and Ronnie's are galaxies apart. Still, she enjoys the company of this simple, hardworking man as they rock and roll their way through miles of dense scrub. They've been talking steadily for an hour. Children, sick parents, and divorce are their common grounds. On these fronts, they are the same.

Ronnie steers the truck onto an overgrown lime rock road. As he does, Sheila smells water and involuntarily thinks of Lake Michigan. Beyond the scrub, she sees a narrow twisting ribbon of blue green current. They roll to a stop near a cabin that looks to be the survivor of many floods. About forty people are spread across the lawn. Some encircle a barbecue fabricated from one half of a steel drum, others playing horseshoes are cheered by a group of onlookers. Half of them look a little scary; they're the men. The other half is composed of the women folk and they bear no resemblance to Sheila's friends up North. Everyone, absolutely every single person, stops what he or she is doing to stare at Sheila as she jumps from the truck.

Melissa McDaniel

Embarrassed, she hoists up the top of her strapless swimsuit. *O.K. here I am, Ms. Yankee Doodle meeting the combined casts of* The Grapes of Wrath *and* The Dukes of Hazzard. She stands perfectly still, letting the eyes explore every inch of her as she waits for Ronnie to ease his frame down from his truck. *Where the hell is he?* When he does finally appear, he puts his arm around Sheila and pulls her forward for further inspection. "I know what y'all are thinkin', but she ain't mine. This here's T. Earl's gal, and she's a real lady. So y'all treat'er right, ya hear me?"

"Hey!" Sheila smiles, and waves as she pulls on the cut-offs and T-shirt she had the good sense to bring. By now, Ronnie has popped a beer, and joined the men watching a pig rotate on a spit. Sheila helps herself to a beer, more for something to do than any other reason. At first, she hangs around the edges of the male brood. She's never before heard true life yarns about fistfights and bar room brawls. One man is called Oak, short for Live Oak. It's a name his size and strength seem to have earned for him. He's tall, maybe 6'5, and thick, with a barrel chest that must be sixty inches around. When bar room fights are discussed, he just listens. Either he's a gentle giant or he's been there and done that too many times already.

"Say, did y'all hear Rona Dobbins got killed by a truck out on I-10?" he asks.

"Yeeup," the men shake their heads, grunting and groaning over the early demise of one who had been a "right fine lady, one of the good 'uns."

"I went to the funeral." Oak announces then gazes at the sky. "Yeeup, I was there...and I tell ya, that Rona sure had some hot friends!" He pauses to resurrect the beauty he'd beheld. "Ya know, funerals are great for meetin' chicks, cuz they all really fix up for a funeral. They get themselves all sophisticated lookin'." With this, he flicks his hand to suggest a fancy hairdo. "An they wear those sheer black stockins', those things drive me crazy!"

Oak's audience hoots and hollers. One says, "Well, maybe Oak, ya otta just hang out at funeral parlors. Be cheaper'n bars!"

"That's an idea!" Oak flashes a huge lumberjack grin.

"That's a terrible idea, Oakie!" A striking brunette with grass-green eyes gives the hulk a swat on his behind. She's almost as tall as he is, but she's a third his girth with a tiny waist, slim hips, and long, long legs. "You do that sugar, and it'll be your own funeral you go to!" Sheila watches the long, tall drink of water pull Oak's arms around her waist. Oak melts into the embrace, and Sheila knows Mr. Live Oak doesn't need to frequent funerals to find pretty women. He's already got the pick of the litter.

With a kiss on the cheek and an elbow to his gut, Long Legs leaves Oak to approach Sheila. "Hey! I'm Lou Ann, but you can call me Lou. I've been hoping to meet you. Oak and T. Earl are buds from way back. Here, let me rescue you from these rascals." Lou pulls Sheila over to the female side of the party.

There are mothers and children of all ages, shapes, and sizes. All are friendly and curious, but they don't pry. For this, Sheila's grateful. As yet she's unable to tell people she's twelve hundred miles away from her children. It's not good; staying so within herself must make her seem superficial, snobbish even. But to confess what she's done is asking for judgment of the worst kind. What mother would understand her actions? How long will her shame keep her from reaching out to people? Will she ever again be the exuberant extrovert she was when she was young?

Perhaps, the voice suggests, *in this foreign place, you can find that woman. Try taking baby steps in her direction.*

The first step, Sheila decides; is to get to know the tall brunette who is making her feel so welcomed. She learns that Lou and Live Oak became inextricably linked years ago. When Lou explains that Live Oak's real name is Earl Sheila asks in exasperation, "Is everyone in the South named Earl? For whom are they named?"

"Maybe there was a Civil War general named Earl, or a football player, who knows!" Lou laughs the hearty laugh of a happy woman.

"How did my Earl and your Earl meet?"

"They played ball together, then became hunting and fishing buds. Oakie has a degree in horticulture. He's a farm agent for the county."

The two women watch as Live Oak bastes the revolving pig as if he's painting a masterpiece. An army of men stands by to assist as spit turners, carvers, tasters, and hecklers. The female jobs are skinning and cutting potatoes, shucking corn, and shelling peas so Sheila and Lou decide to tackle the potatoes. They carry a bushel down to the river, and as they get situated on the bank with their toes in the water, Lou issues an order. "Sheila, you take off that hot shirt right now! I saw you cover up when you got out of the truck. Don't

Melissa McDaniel

worry about the other gals — Southern women are used to their men ogling anything with tits."

Sheila laughs as she peels off her shirt, "I don't think I'll ever adjust to this thing about breasts!"

"Breasts are the Southern male's yearning to get back close with his mama," As Lou philosophizes she pulls off her own tee to reveal an exquisite upper torso.

"Some mama your Oakie must have had!" Sheila chuckles.

One bushel of peeled potatoes and several beers later, Lou and Sheila have become fast buds. Lou's amazing. She's experienced the kind of hardship I've only read about. Neither an abusive father, nor a philandering first husband brought her down. There's so much I have to learn! And learn she does, throughout the day.

She surmises from the warmth of her reception that her own Earl is held in high regard. Ronnie's introduction — "She's T. Earl's gal" — has initiated a response not unlike being given the key to a city. The words get her all the "bubaque'd" pork and venison she can eat. Men constantly offer her their seats while others keep her supplied with beer. She's thoroughly enjoying these people and this place.

As dusk sets in, she sees the first burst of a Roman candle. In Florida, it's legal to sell and set off fireworks, so anyone with a few dollars can assemble an arsenal of firecrackers, silver fountains, and sliding galaxies. She's on her way to watch the display when something goes wrong. Dink, one of the younger men seems, to have pointed a Roman candle too close to the audience.

"Shit, Dink! Ya tryin' to kill our babies? Look how close ya come to my Tiffiny!" A fellow named Marty Ray is angry at Dink for nearly torching his own, sweet daughter. His short, muscular frame stalks the offender around the campfire until Dink whirls around to face him. "I ought'ta whoop your ass!" shouts Marty Ray, determined to leave an impression.

Dink stands firm, eyes wild and fists ready. A couple of women try to ease the strain, saying no harm was done. They're ignored. This is a man thing. More shouting accompanies pushing and shoving. They're seconds from a fist fight, something Sheila has never witnessed. She is positively riveted to the scene.

"All right! All right now!" A husky, tobacco-ravaged voice comes from the darkness. Dink and Marty Ray grow silent in deference to it. Stepping from the crowd is the voice's owner, Rud

Watson. With seventy-some years of experience, he surveys this conflagration of two buds out of sorts. The silliness of it all makes his salt and pepper beard scrunch up as a wonderful laugh comes from deep in his chest. "Ya don't s'pose liquor has anything to do with this, do ya, Dink? Marty Ray?" Both men are silent. "I thought so. Now, nothing more'll come from either of ya!" Rud grabs hold of the men's T-shirts and yanks them close enough to smell the Wild Turkey on each other's breath. With a smile, he talks down to them as though they're little children. "The show's over, boys. Now you two act like the buds you are, or I'll throw ya both in the river!"

By now, everyone's laughing, even Dink and Marty Ray. The foes shake hands as Dink explains it was an accident; the wick on the Roman candle had been way too short.

Marty Ray concedes that's probably true. Together, they walk to the truck where the Wild Turkey is stashed.

"Wow," Sheila whispers to Lou. "I thought they were really going to fight! Do you see that a lot down here?"

"Not so much anymore, it used to be a lot more often. Age has tamed them, but none of them will take shit from anyone, not even a bud."

Sheila draws close to the fire. *Good or bad, these people certainly are larger than life.* While Marty Ray's outrage is not to be applauded, she admires the integrity in his anger. His daughter had been put in danger and he'd wanted to get the son of a bitch who'd done it. Sheila edges closer to get a better look at Rud Watson, the godfather of the river. He sees her coming and with the full length of his arm, draws her close. *They touch a lot too. I like that.* Snuggling into Rud's sweaty warmth, she wonders what other roles he plays in the lives of the folks around the fire. He's as close as a father to Oak. Ronnie thinks the world of him too.

As if he's read her thoughts, Rud says, "These boys help me with my farmin'. White Acre peas are my favorite crop. And when the peas are in, they all get enough to last the winter. Do you like our peas, Miss Sheila?"

"Yes, I do, I never had them before I came down here."

"Don't surprise me none. They don't think much of 'em up North. That's cuz they fix 'em so plain. What they need is chow-chow to spice them up." Chow- chow, Sheila has learned, is a homemade relish that can be hurt-your-tongue hot. "You like our chow-chow, Miss Sheila?"

"Yes, sir," Sheila's pleased that this time she remembered to say sir, a Southern show of respect. At first, it had seemed strange to hear every single child addressing his or her elders as sir and ma'am, but now she likes it. She especially likes hearing Earl address his elders that way. The South has its problems but it also has virtues.

"Well now, you gotta come to my farm and get yourself some. My missus makes the best chow-chow around. She couldn't come today, on account of a sick headache. Where's your no 'count Earl anyway?"

For the umpteenth time, Sheila explains that Earl has gone to his son's private wedding and for the same number of times she's told he's dumb as a fence post to leave a "good lookin' thang" like her out on her own.

"That boy and I are gonna have a come ta Jesus over this."

"No, there's no need for that. This day has been perfect. I'm glad I could enjoy the river and meet everyone here just as myself and not as Earl's tag along." Sheila likes the person she is while interacting with these river folk. It's funny how she's come closer to her real self today than she has in years. Her lifetime affinity for the rural lifestyle is as strong as ever, and it's good to know she can be happy here, even without the great T. Earl by her side.

Chapter 35
Green Turtle

Toward summer's end Sheila, Earl, Murph, and three others embark on a weekend trip to Green Turtle Cay. Having never been to the Bahamas, she imagines Green Turtle, an island nestled in the Abacos, to be every bit as commercial as the ones portrayed in travel ads.

"No way, sweet pea," Earl protests, "Green Turtle's an untouched paradise."

When the day arrives, she and Earl drive to south Florida to join Murph, Hugh Chastain, Sandy Sanford, and Chelsey Cook on a direct flight to Treasure Cay, one of the larger islands in the Abaco chain. Not a soul can be seen as they land on a lonely airstrip and taxi to a tiny white clapboard house. The structure's only door opens to reveal a tall black woman in a short white skirt and official-looking blouse. She's the essence of grace as her long arm sweeps the air in a slow motion wave. She bends, from the waist down, to prop the door open with a rock, then, with the same grace, she backs slowly into the building.

Murph reads Sheila's mind. "That's the national speed here. No one moves out of low gear. There's no reason to."

She smiles, giving Murph a slow motion nod. "I'm going to like it here."

Having unloaded their bags and provisions, the pilot wishes them a happy stay. "You go through there," he whispers to Sheila, as if to say, "That's the way through the looking glass." They pass, single file, through the door.

"Welcome to Abaco." The woman's round tones sound like a commercial, but her smile is genuine. Throughout the passport process, her unhurried sense of humor plays into that of the group. First is Hugh, the only part-time resident. "Ah, Mr. Chastain, where you been? What kind scoundrels you bring us now?" She stamps the passport and hands it to Hugh. Then, noticing all the Bahamian stamps on Murph's, she quips, "Oh, oh, trouble! I tell you last time don't come back."

"I didn't do enough damage; I'm here to finish the job." Murph's deadpan tone gets a smirk from the woman.

Next, Sheila's passport prompts the observation, "Ah, you from Wisconsin. That's near Chicago. You a gangsta?"

"No, but I know a few," she lies.

When Chelsey presents her passport, the woman brightens, "Welcome cousin! She points to her nametag, "See, we both Cooks."

"I'm a conch, too!" Chelsey proclaims proudly. "My grandpap's from the Abacos."

"Their families could be related," Murph whispers, "Intermarriage is common here."

"How civilized! I'm not even out of the airport and already I like the Abacos!"

The six travelers pile into two taxis dating from the eighties. A short, bumpy ride on a narrow road takes them to a harbor on the other side of the island. Here, they board a boat the locals call a bolo. With everything loaded on the craft, they move out of the secluded harbor onto the rolling swells of God's great ocean. The up and down of it forces Sheila to sit, and as she does, she lets her eyes get acquainted with her fellow passengers.

The one she knows the least is Hugh. Evidently, he's a prosperous engineer. It's his house they'll be staying in. He seems a good guy, gentle, but always ready with a barb for his buddies. Hugh's married, but in the summer, his wife prefers the cool environs of their mountain home. *Must be nice!*

Next to Hugh is Sandy. He's made a killing in golf course construction. Sheila remembers him from Murph's New Year's party. He'd introduced Chelsey to her, saying they both were in the process of leaving their husbands. *Looks like she succeeded,* Sheila watches the happy couple. Sandy can't keep his hands off of her. Murph describes Chelsey as Sandy's "dream pussy." *That fits.*

Chelsey seems to have been the object of Sandy's lust for a long time. And why wouldn't she be? She's like an adorable foreign sports car, sleek and compact, a Ferrari maybe. She has tons of sex appeal, and look at that long, straight, black hair! There's also that perfect face and those coal-black eyes she uses to full advantage. Chelsey's good with men, and she knows it, but she won't come on to another woman's guy. I respect that.

The rakishly handsome Murph is very much at home in the pitching boat. An inveterate fisherman from Jupiter Sound, he wanders from one side of the craft to the other, asking the captain for updates on local stories. And there's Earl, the reason she's nutso these days, but also the reason she's here. *Here and now, here and now, dwell only on the here and now!*

What first resembled a giant green turtle floating in an ocean of blue is now an island of lush vegetation. The only spot that isn't green heralds a cluster of old whitewashed buildings and rainbow-painted houses. The bolo docks and Green Turtle's newest inhabitants unload their bags and three days worth of food. The two caretakers of Hugh's house meet them with a car for the folks and a truck for luggage and supplies. The car — an old Ford with no air conditioning — is fiery hot. All six crowd into it, raising the temperature even more.

"Everyone sweats down here," Hugh remarks as he throws the car into gear. Slowly, the Ford picks up speed until a breeze brings some relief. He points to a rusty skeleton of I-beams on a nearby hill. "That was going to be a resort, it was started years ago then they ran out of money or materials or both."

"Construction ruins!" Sheila observes. She's toured ancient ruins all over the world but these are the first of this kind she's ever seen. "In a way, I'm happy an attempt to commercialize this place was thwarted. But I guess I should also be sorry for what it says about the economy."

Everyone nods. All but Earl are native Floridians, and they're familiar with the yin and yang of the development versus no-growth dilemma. Having lived through real estate boons and recessions, Murph speaks up. "Nothing's worse than a construction gone bust." Still, Sheila wishes something would slow down "the whoring over" of her beloved Florida.

Melissa McDaniel

She wonders if Sandy, with Chelsey sitting on his lap, might possibly have an erection. He has the look of a man aroused. Chelsey, too, is melded into him, filling every curve of his body with one of her own. *She's more settled in the limbo of pre-divorce than I. That's because she took her kids with her. She didn't leave them to help her husband through the tough times. There's a virtue in not being so damned nice. How did I fall into the trap of always being the one to sacrifice? That's easy, I was the strongest, the brightest, the prettiest, and because of that, I was always supposed to put others first. I've lived my entire life by my mother's instructions, and now I'm paying for it.*

Not here, the voice warns *don't let your guilt find you here. This weekend is for you and Earl.* Sheila looks at Earl in the front seat. His entire being fills the car. As if he reads her mind, his eyes cut to her with heat enough to make her sizzle.

For another ten minutes, they bump along a forgotten road. Eventually, they come to a gigantic banyan tree shading a modest, flat-roofed house. Beyond it, a bluff of jungle vegetation leads to a white ribbon of beach. *That ribbon looks like it's holding the entire ocean in place.* Her breathing slows as she watches the aqua, turquoise, and teal blue waters churn in a vastness rivaled only by the sky.

"Wow!" She jumps from the car, and runs to the bluff so she can become one with the view. No longer aware of her companions, she again acknowledges that the guilt that keeps her paralyzed loses its power when it's confronted with the magnitude of nature. *If only I could take this perspective with me wherever I go! Maybe I can, but first, I've got to find a truth in it all, something that will lead me back to myself. Maybe Green Turtle is where I'll find it.*

After they unpack, the first order of business is snorkeling in the warm waters of the Atlantic. It's something Sheila's only read about, but having spent her life near water, she's at home in the submerged world that greets her. Hundreds — no, *thousands* — of fish don't care that she's entered their domain. Entire schools cruise within inches of her mask. Real live coral grows below. *That one really does look like a brain and over there's the largest fan I've ever seen! This is like swimming in an aquarium! No, it's better, far better. I love it!*

SLOW DANCE

Her breathing quickens when she recognizes a nurse shark gliding five feet below. Remembering Murph saying they're docile relaxes her some, but not completely. She surfaces to see Earl manning the boat while everyone else snorkels. Murph, holding onto the craft with one hand, raises a spear with a triggerfish impaled on it. Earl takes the spear, and with a knife, he pushes the quarry into the hold. Soon, Murph and Hugh will have speared enough mangrove snapper, hogg snapper, and triggerfish for them to have sushi and grilled filets for dinner.

Sheila fights the twinge of sadness she's always felt when any creature has to die. *Food chain, remember the food chain, Murph and Hugh are just getting to them before something else does.* Still, she swims in the other direction to avoid seeing the puff of red when a spear pierces its mark. Later, Sheila forgets her mourning when she feasts on the freshest seafood she's ever eaten, the best being conch, scorched with key lime and sour orange.

After dinner, the six walk to the tiny village of New Plymouth. The first stop is at Miss Emily's Blue Bee, a bar where hundreds of T-shirts and bras hang from the ceiling and business cards coat the walls. As Earl tries to locate son Ryan's T-shirt from an earlier escapade, Sheila sits, envisioning the women who'd felt compelled to offer up their bras to the cause. *I'm not there yet. There are still some things I will not do.*

After downing enough beers to send their spirits soaring, the group moves on to Bert's Sea Garden. As they enter the tiny drinking establishment, Sheila senses the cold, hard stare of an older woman. The platinum blonde's trendy clothes give a youthful impression, but her heavy pancake makeup makes her more than middle-aged cheeks resemble the cracking clay of a desert. Once beautiful, the eyes that stud the clay are framed with wrinkles and bags. An abundance of shadow and eyeliner cannot compensate for the ravages of sun and time. Sheila stares back, unable to pry her eyes from the caricature before her. *Will that be me in a decade or so? Will I fight age the same way, clothes too youthful, make up too thick, hair too blonde? Yuk! Please, God, give me more sense and less insecurity.*

Suddenly, the woman looks past Sheila. Eyes narrowing, she stretches to examine a new source of disdain. Sheila turns to see the raw beauty of an eighteen, maybe twenty-year-old woman who hasn't seen enough years to bear the slightest flaw. Her figure is perfect, post puberty, pre-motherhood. The young woman's sarong-style skirt draws attention to her slim hips, long waist, and flat, bronzed abdomen. To complete the picture, a single silk scarf is stretched and tied across the hard nipples of her perfect breasts.

Sheila checks back to the faded beauty. The old woman's eyes still scorch the younger version of herself. She hates what she's become and detests this girl for reminding her of what she's lost. Where am I in this? I think, maybe, somewhere in between the two for now. Will I be able to resurrect this scene fifteen years hence to show me what I don't want to be?

An arm reaches around her neck and the large, loving hand she knows so well, pulls her face close. "Where are you?" Earl asks, hoping Sheila hasn't gone inside herself again.

"I'm watching a slice of life being carved right in front of my eyes."

Earl winces, knowing such remarks often lead to unwelcome tears. She cries a lot these days. But why wouldn't she? She has a lot on her mind. He doesn't know if he could do what Sheila, thus far, has pulled off. He isn't even sure what brought her to him and, sometimes, he worries she might decide it isn't worth it after all. He pulls her face to his, their lips touch.

Sheila stays put, needing more. Throughout her entire life, she's wanted a man who could arouse her like this, with a look, a touch. Here he is. And she has him the same way he has her; she knows that.

He puts a frosty beer mug in her hand and clinks it to his. "To us?" his toast, mostly a question, reveals his own insecurity. Sheila winks and nods. Earl's obvious relief melts her heart. *I love this man!*

At one point, Bert, the owner and only bartender of this tiny establishment, asks Sheila if she'd like a conch shell. "I'd love one!" she beams, thinking the arthritic and aged Bahamian will pull one out from under the bar. Instead, he painfully eases down from his stool and, on stiff legs, lumbers out of the bar. Eyes wide with surprise, Sheila stares at the door, then at Earl. He's equally as mystified. For at least ten minutes, the customers of Bert's Sea Garden entertain themselves. No one asks where the owner has gone, and certainly, not a single one of them takes advantage of his

SLOW DANCE

absence by pouring another drink or opening the cash drawer. When Bert finally returns, he's cradling a magnificent conch shell in both arms. He allows Sheila to fuss over it a while before informing her that he has a ten-foot high pile of the shells at his house. They're the remnants of his son's conch dives.

Suddenly, Hugh breaks in, "Forgive me Bert, I have to kidnap your lady. Come Sheila, The Rooster's Rest awaits!" Sheila leans across the bar to give her new friend a kiss, and with the shell in her arms, she makes her way to the door. Before leaving, a prickly sensation makes her turn to see her aged counterpart studying her again.

It's not your fault, that's what you were raised to be. Maybe I was raised to that end as well. A frosty smile curls the old beauty queen's lips as she raises her glass to Sheila. Sheila nods to the woman and pivots out the door, but chilly ripples of the encounter cling to her all the way to The Rooster's Rest.

Whether she knew it or not, that old gal was telling me I've got to deepen myself so there'll be more to me in old age than a peeling coat of paint. For too long, I ignored my soul, and now that I have a second chance, I'll give it the attention it deserves. I jettisoned my identity when I left Wisconsin. Out went the career me, the wife me, the daughter, and mother me, I have none of those now. I'm an empty slate so I might as well go for it.

For the next three hours, Sheila does go for something. It's not the meaningful search she'd envisioned, but it does feed the "gotta live!" child within. The music is created by the Gully Roosters, six well-built Bahamian men whose music is as sexy as they are. Within seconds, she's ablaze with sexual energy. Her turn on grows as she watches the other dancers. Bahamian women with exquisitely subtle rhythm ease themselves suggestively around their partners. Their arousal is evident as they tease their men with moves that promise everything. A set of slow dances brings the white tourist girls and island men together. A term Sheila's sheltered ears had to go south to hear is being demonstrated on the dance floor. *This is it! This is what they call the dry fuck.* Sheila sees it all around her.

On this topic, one couple commands center stage. A tall, stick-figured man in a stark white suit is wrapped around a short, wide woman sporting a spandex jumpsuit of the same color. Their skin is black velvet against shiny white. The man's arms stretch long, to

Melissa McDaniel

enfold the breadth of his lady. In turn, her short round ones place a hand on each of her lover's buns. Their dance is one of no movement as they stand completely still, each body sucking in the other. Once, they shift an inch to the left then suck in again, this time, even closer. Earl stares at the couple, as do Murph and Hugh. Chelsey and Sandy are riveted. Sheila is capable of only one thought, *in a world where pulsing rhythm is a turn on; this absolute stillness beats all.* Apparently, the couple agrees. When the music speeds up, they pry themselves apart long enough to move to a corner where they resume contact.

Unable to resist the beat, Sheila starts to dance expecting Earl to follow, but hours on a rocking boat have taken a toll on his knees. Sensing his friend's discomfort, Murph leaves his harem of Bahamian girls to dance with Sheila who, well into her zone, is not going to stop.

They dance well together. Earl, sitting three feet away, smiles serenely as he watches their moves. Murph dances close enough to whisper; "You know, don't you, he's seething with jealousy right now."

"Wrong!" Sheila guffaws, "He's never jealous."

"You haven't caught on?"

"The great T. Earl doesn't do jealousy."

"No, I mean it, he's raging inside. Now, if we dance close like we're coming onto each other, he'll look even more serene. It's his m.o."

Sheila sees Murph is earnest. "You mean he's vulnerable after all?" Murph nods in time to the music.

It's an act? Murph does know him better than anyone. Sheila, miles away in her revelation, hugs her partner as the dance concludes.

That was the last set, and the band is packing up. "Now's when reality sets in," Murph observes. "These little tourist bitches will have to ease themselves away from the island boys they've teased all night, 'Oh, I was just pretending I'd like to go to bed with you, I didn't really mean it.' I like watching them try to squirm away. Some succeed, some don't."

The party of six is now four. Chelsey and Sandy cut out earlier to take advantage of the empty house. Hugh, Murph, Earl, and Sheila exit the bar like blurry-eyed teenagers leaving a dance.

Having experienced Green Turtle before, the three men walk into the night without trepidation. Sheila doesn't share their trust. She feels like a tourist, naive and vulnerable in a foreign place. Every one of the stars blazing above hears her prayer to keep this merry band of drunkards safe. Murph and Earl are singing their own renditions of the Gully Roosters' songs, and Hugh mimics a howling dog as all three men stagger a slalom course down the dirt road. Actually, it's pretty great seeing these middle-aged men, these grown-up boys, having such a silly time with each other. Never before has Sheila seen anything close to it. And, though she knows her presence is superfluous, she doesn't care. If there is such a thing as male bonding, this is it. Men secure enough to be silly and silly enough to be secure. These are rare individuals, caught in a moment when nothing matters but their sheer enjoyment of each other. *File this away and pull it out when you need to see the little boy inside the man you love.*

Another fifteen minutes brings them to the doorstep of Hugh's house. The men linger outside to use nature's plumbing while Sheila runs in to the only bathroom. The four meet again in the kitchen, where they opt for milk and cookies. Sheila dunks her cookie in sheer contentment as the guys kibitz about a mutual acquaintance that has finally gotten married.

"Yep," Murph says, "Ol' Hank told me he's afraid Constance may be the last pussy he'll ever have, says he can't imagine never, ever having another."

Sheila dunks more slowly now, absorbing every shocking detail. She starts to give the woman's side, but checks herself. She'll learn more if she keeps quiet. Earl's response impresses her. "He needs to see it as an athlete whose career has ended. It was great, but it's over and it's time to move onto other things." Sheila's certain his perspective is autobiographical. She decides it shows class and hopes it will be enough to keep him faithful to her.

What about Constance? Maybe she's not so thrilled she'll never, again, have the pleasure of anyone other than Hank. Has that even occurred to him? Such speculation accompanies Sheila to bed. And, since Earl goes to sleep the instant his head hits the pillow, she tosses about pondering the dichotomy of "sexpectations" between men and women. When she finally does go to sleep, it seems she's awakened moments later by an explosion of light.

It's morning and morning on Green Turtle is something to behold. Light is everywhere! Earl's absence tells her he's already busy in the kitchen. She staggers to the door and peeks around to see Murph reading a newspaper at the table where the pussy debate was held a few hours prior. She watches him, realizing that for all his bravado the night before, he really misses Janice. He'd been so looking forward to having her with him. But when her father had a bad fall, he'd understood her decision to stay home. Janice has her plate full with an ailing parent on one side, her toddler on the other, and a full-time job devouring every other available moment. Memories of Sheila's own sandwich situation come to mind. To shake them off, she focuses on the blazing venue outside. An almost abnormal brilliance dances before her eyes. *Brighter than bright, no, even that can't do it justice.*

She hugs Earl from behind, "Hello darlin', mmmm, good." Earl turns and pulls her to him. He's a superb kisser, and, like most good kissers, he enjoys his craft. God, she loves him!

"Hey you two, show some mercy, I'm horny enough already," Murph whines.

Still in Earl's embrace, Sheila reaches around his back to steal a pork sausage link. Earl lets go and she ceremoniously takes a bite.

Snap! The end of a twisted dishtowel hits its mark as Earl defends his food.

"Ouch, that hurts!"

"You'll get it again if you don't behave. How dare you seduce me to get at my sausage?"

"What sausage? You mean this?" Sheila, lunges for the real thing, and gets snapped again.

"If you don't stop, you're gonna pay big time!" Earl warns.

"Promise?" Sheila asks, snapping her own dishtowel.

"Children!" Murph interrupts, "If you don't behave, there'll be no snorkeling this afternoon." Earl shakes a finger at Sheila and she laughs, wondering when it was she last acted like a child.

Despite Murph's warning, there's snorkeling, boating, eating, drinking, and dancing all afternoon and most of the night. Adding to the day's perfection is a heart-to-heart Sheila and Chelsey share on the beach. Sheila has kept almost everything about herself from the people in Pine Springs. Few know what she's done or who she's been, and the less they know about her, the more intact she'll be.

Breezy, superficial small talk has become her forte. It's different with Chelsey though; ever since their New Year's encounter, she has wanted to pour her heart out to this woman, so like her own self. When Chelsey asks her how she really is, Sheila confides that although her bouts with the black hole seem to be getting less, she still has a long way to go.

"All I can do is free fall into this life I've chosen. And I did choose it; no one forced it on me or seduced me into it. The problem is I worry about positively everything, about Earl and me, my divorce, my mother, and most of all, my children. I even worry that all this worrying will make me sick. And that's pretty ironic, because I used to have the same concern about my life up North."

"Well," Chelsey slowly responds, "I like what you said about free falling. Maybe it's time to let go of the worry and just enjoy the ride. Don't worry 'bout a ting," she starts to sing, "every little ting gonna be alright!" Sheila joins in; she really likes Chelsey. Not only is she fun, she's also wise.

"I wish I could take a pill that would help me focus on the good parts of this second chance, not the bad," Sheila confesses.

"Do it! Imagine yourself taking a pill each morning; and it has just that effect. You know, Sheila, everyone who meets you thinks you don't have a care in the world. You're quite the actress, aren't you?"

"Takes one to know one!" Sheila winks, giving Chelsey's sleek hair a tug. "And while we're on the subject of role playing, let's not let any of this get back to the guys, O.K.?"

"Deal! Sandy doesn't need any more of a guilt trip than I've already given him."

Later, on the plane, Sheila turns sleepy eyes toward Earl's perfect profile. She's had more fun with him this weekend than she's ever had with any man, ever. As carefree refugees from the real world, they've come even closer. *This weekend is the imaginary pill Chelsey was talking about. I'll resurrect my Bahamian adventure every morning to help get me through the weirdness of each day. Thank you, Green Turtle!*

Chapter 36
Val

"Green Turtle, where are you?" Sheila moans this as she enters her office after the Bahamas respite.

Jenna, the receptionist, laughs and hands her a stack of messages. "Did that dreamboat ever find you?"

"Which dreamboat, there are so many!" Sheila jokes, certain it's someone interested in a golf club membership.

"Just the most handsome man I've seen in a long time, maybe ever!"

Fingering through the memos, she reads aloud, "*Val Arnsell phoned Friday, 9:15 AM, 10:30 AM, and 1:33 PM. Val Arnsell stopped by Friday, 4:15 PM.* He was here?"

"Yes, he told me he'd flown down from Milwaukee just to see you. He was more than a little chagrined to learn you were in the Bahamas and he demanded to know when you'd return. Not liking his attitude, I wouldn't oblige."

"Thanks, Jenna, he's only an acquaintance and I really don't care to see him." Sheila can't believe she saying this about a man she'd always put on a pedestal.

"Well, I don't know that much about your personal life, but I do remember seeing you with a hunk, and he and Mr. Arnsell are not the same."

"Right again!" Sheila points to the memos, "I don't know what this is about, but I'm glad I wasn't here."

"Well, I have to tell you, his persistence bothered me some. And I don't think this is the end of it. He's the type that won't take no for an answer."

"Thanks friend, but I'm not worried," Sheila closes the door to her office, and studies the memo. *Best confront this head on,* she thinks, dialing the number on the memo.

"Arnsell Enterprises," a familiar, almost motherly voice answers. "Hello, Ann, I'm not sure you'd remember me...this is Sheila Branford, I'm returning Mr. Arnsell's call."

"Why Sheila, we haven't talked in such a long time! Mr. Arnsell will be sorry he missed you, but he's away for the day."

"Is he? Well, would you please tell him I called?"

"Does he know where to reach you?"

"Yes. Thanks, Ann!"

He's still here, isn't he? Sheila feels she's asking fate that question. Every time the phone rings, she expects it to be Val, but it's not. When someone stands in the doorway, she looks up, expecting to see him, but she doesn't. By noon, her fretting has calmed; surely, he'd have surfaced by now.

For lunch, she and her office mates order in Chinese food. Gathered around a conference table is an assortment of people of many ages, races, and educational backgrounds. They dig into their cardboard cartons with locust-like gusto. Sheila relaxes, feeling she's among old friends. Her affection for these people was ignited when they were so welcoming and friendly despite her overly professional wardrobe and formal ways. She'd arrived the first day, looking, as the regional dialect might describe, like "a tight-assed Yankee." Despite that, each of them reached out to her with genuine warmth. And because she doesn't supervise a single one of them, she's able to relate to her colleagues as themselves, not as employees.

As a Northern transplant herself, Jenna had been the first to offer her friendship. Sheila pictures Jenna to have been an accomplished charity volunteer in her earlier life as corporate wife. Now, retired to Florida, she chooses work as a pastime. Miranda, Jenna's best bud, blends the looks of a model with the warmth of an old school chum. She's tops in sales for the homes that will soon surround the golf course, but her friendliness hasn't a trace of insincerity. Every other person around the table is equally as genuine. Sheila's telling them about Green Turtle when Jenna gives her a nudge, and cocks her head toward the window. Val is crossing the street. Upon seeing him, her first thought is to wish he weren't so incredibly handsome. He's tall, fit as ever, and even younger looking than she remembers.

Sheila excuses herself. *Tired and unkempt after the Bahamas trip, I'm certainly not at my best, but then, nothing short of a makeover would bring me near the person he's expecting to see. Maybe I'll fall so short of his fantasy he'll decide I'm not in his league.* Sure of this, she approaches Val with an "I-told-you-so" swagger. He watches her move toward him. Except for a brief second when he scans her firmer, thinner body, Val's eyes never leave hers. She stops dead in front of him.

"Hello, gorgeous." Blue eyes, every bit as electric as she remembers, reach for her. Despite her convictions, she realizes how natural it'd feel to flow into his arms this very second. *Why, oh why, is this happening now?*

"You shouldn't be here."

"You're right about that! And I shouldn't have been in this one-horse town all weekend. I'm furious with my sources for letting you sneak off to the Bahamas without my knowledge."

He gets no response. Sheila's too busy appreciating the face she'd so often admired. In her wildest dreams, she'd never have cast him in the role of unrequited lover. His hand reaches to touch her cheek. She swats at it as she did a dusk moth that buzzed her yesterday evening, "Val, I already told you, I came down here to be with someone."

He sounds weary of the topic. "Yes, yes, I'm aware of Thomas Earl Langley, born and raised in Flowery Branch, Georgia, attended high school in Atlanta, recruited to play for... "

"If you're so aware of him, why are you here?"

"Because this isn't you." Val gestures around. "You don't match these surroundings. I think you did the right thing in leaving your marriage, and if Earl helped make that happen, I owe him a debt of gratitude. But he's not the only one who wants you, Sheila. Don't you remember the synergy we created serving on all those boards together? We were a force to be dealt with, better, more powerful than either of us alone. And didn't we have fun? We could have that again, only this time you'd be by my side, helping me run my companies. In time, I'll turn the reins over to my kids so we can fill our lives with the adventure you crave. You do still crave adventure, don't you?"

Val pauses to let this sink in then he's off on another tack. "You never thought of me in romantic terms because I seemed as married as you did. But I say to you, here and now, I will leave my marriage for you. Sydney and I have only a congenial partnership, something like you and Charles had. If I'd known where you were in your marriage, there'd be no Earl now, only you and me."

Sheila shakes her head no, and without looking into the electric blues, she commands, "Go away, Val, I don't want you here."

"I'm sorry to be adding to an already stressful situation, but you must know you have another choice."

"I told you when you called, I'm not interested!"

"Not in me as a married man, but like I said, that would change."

For an instant, Sheila's heart aches for Val's wife. *Does she have a clue what her hubby's up to?*

Thinking her silence means she's actually considering what he's said, Val decides to close his argument. "Give me a chance, Sheila. If you don't, you'll always wonder what might have been."

Explosions rock her brain. Her children, how she wants them! If she'd stayed up there, they'd be together right now. If it'd been Val she'd gotten involved with all those months ago, she'd have them with her; she might even have her job! Another explosion ignites thoughts of Earl's complacency. Where did that man in the letters go? Her thoughts fly again to Allie and Chase. *They're so little! Oh Lord, I'm way too vulnerable right now. Don't let me do anything stupid here.* Harnessing some internal force, she looks straight into her suitor's eyes, "Go home, Val. There's nothing for you here."

Not believing her for a second, he smiles, "All right, I'll leave, but this isn't over. Time is Earl's enemy and my friend."

Ever conciliatory, Sheila decides to end things on a positive note. "I'm honored you think we're right for each other, but I'm more the country girl than you know. My life is here, in these wide open spaces, and Earl Langley is perfect for me."

"How about I meet this Casanova?"

"That won't happen."

"Well, if you won't help me know my competition, I'll do it on my own."

"Doing that will change nothing. Now go!" She glares at Val, doing her best to boss a man she's always considered her superior.

Unfortunately, he finds her behavior endearing. "I love you, sweet little Sheila. Don't make a mistake here, we'd be great together!"

"Go!" Sheila points to the street.

"Yes, madam," he turns, then, as he's leaving, "Everything I've just told you, you'll want to hear again someday."

Exasperated, she pivots toward the door, steps inside and slams it shut. To take one last look at Val crossing the street is something she'd like to do, but he'd see it as too encouraging. She stalks past a concerned Jenna, and heads straight to the washroom.

Behind the locked door, she confronts the face in the mirror. "What's going on? As weird as it has been, it's just gotten more so!" Now, addressing the ceiling, "Are you behind this, Lord? With all the praying I've been doing, I have to scrutinize everything as a possible response from you. It makes sense you'd see Val as a good partner for me, but isn't that what Earl's supposed to be, and what about Val's wife? How many marriages must be wasted before things are set straight?"

The face in the mirror still looks disappointed that the little girl with so much potential is now a middle-aged disaster. *Really, it's kind of funny,* it seems to be saying, *a man you never dreamed could fall in love with you seems to have done so hook, line, and sinker. What would be perceived by some as the catch of all time is the easiest, most unwanted one you've ever made, go figure.*

So what? It doesn't matter, does it? I'm here, working on a new life with a man I truly love. Nothing will deter me. Still, it's comforting to know someone desires me so. Since moving in with Earl, I'm not sure where I rank in his life. I probably place somewhere behind his work, even with Mattie, ahead of his vegetable garden, and maybe his boat.

Of one thing she's certain: she's an intruder. He's had to adjust to the constant presence of someone else, and a female at that. After fifteen years of bachelorhood, that's sure to be a challenge. Sheila can buy that, but what about the sex? She's still running red hot for the torrid sex she's recently come to know. It wounds her pride he doesn't seem as crazed for her as she is for him.

There are other things, too. One of the reasons she'd fallen so deeply in love with Earl was what she'd perceived to be his strong code of ethics. Loyalty to the one he loves had seemed to be a value embedded in his character. He's never given her reason to distrust him, but the entourage of women who fuss over him still makes her nervous. Satin, especially, is driving her crazy with her phone calls. She never even says hello to Sheila, just asks to speak to Earl. Then they talk on and on about Earl's son or Satin's job. Sheila's certain Satin's calling to see if her guy is unhappy or, better yet, available. To his credit, Earl always tells her he's never been happier.

Maybe it's guilt by association. Earl's friends, a wild, crazy, and fun-loving lot, seem to pass that aura onto him. *Perhaps I expect too much, but who can blame me for wanting perfection in light of all I've given up?* On and on go her arguments. First, she serves up proof of the vulnerability of their relationship then she fights back in defense of it. At least, Val's visit didn't leave a mark on her heart. Her love for Earl is not under attack. In fact, his appearance strengthened her conviction to protect what they have.

Chapter 37
New Orleans

With fall comes football, and as the only game in town, the College of Pine Springs renders every Saturday to be one of pre- and post-game celebration. Home games bring weekend guests and away games take the fans on road trips to places that seem to step from Civil War novels. The best away game venue is New Orleans. Football may be the reason; but a weekend in the Big Easy is the real incentive for this trip. Earl and George Church, a popular state senator, are already there on college business.

Sheila and Cassandra, the senator's wife, are to drive to the Jacksonville airport where they'll hop a plane to meet their husbands. Cass, as she likes to be called, reminds Sheila of friends back home. She's smart, funny, trustworthy, and she's seen too much of life to believe the gossip she's heard about Earl's new lady. This makes Sheila unfold like a flower, telling Cass everything about Allie and Chase, and the misery of being without them.

"Up there, people see me as a middle-aged crisis spinning out of control. They didn't know what an emotional disaster I was. I didn't care about my marriage, my job had lost meaning, my mother was draining what little spirit I had left, and I detested how crowded the suburbs had become. The only light in my life radiated from my children."

Sheila careens on, describing the iron fist within her mother's velvet glove and the long-range devastation it caused. "Now I have my soul mate in a place I love, but I'm without the two most important things in my life!"

SLOW DANCE

"Whew! I never guessed you were lugging all that around!" Cass observes in complete amazement. "I wonder, if she had foreseen these consequences, would your mom have been so selfish?"

"Cass, I think about that all the time. I hope she wouldn't have intentionally done it, but I'm not so sure." As the cab pulls up to the Royal Orleans Hotel, Sheila apologizes for the hours of catharsis.

"Are you kidding?" Cass hugs Sheila good-bye, "I can't wait to hear how it all turns out!" The new friends hug and head to their respective rooms. On the way to hers, Sheila feels the usual rush she gets at the mere thought of seeing her guy. Rather than use the key, she knocks.

"Yo!" The door opens to reveal the big, handsome lug. "I don't want any," he says in a monotone before slamming the door in her face. *So, what else is new?* Still cringing at her aside, she sees it open enough for one eye to peek out. "How do I know it's you?" Earlier in their romance, Sheila would have said something enticing, but she's tired of being the sex-craved aggressor. Her silence prompts, "Do you have any identifying marks?" Encouraged, she winks and raises her skirt to reveal a well tanned thigh. "Nice, but it could be anybody's."

"How about these?" Moving closer to the crack in the door, Sheila unzips her top to reveal two mounds, looking rather huge in her new Wonder Bra.

The door opens and Earl pulls her inside.

"I'd know those tits anywhere!" What follows is the lovemaking they'd known in the early days of their romance. It's the pent-up, unfulfilled lust of what once had been a secret love. *Was that the root of our passion those many months ago? Were clandestine meetings in hotel rooms our aphrodisiacs?*

As she considers this, an odor that hit her when she'd first entered the room becomes almost unbearable. "Wow! This hotel uses strong disinfectant. It makes my eyes burn."

"Uh, that would be me, sweet pea."

"You?"

"I smell like a hospital because I'm putting something on my old, sports ravaged knees to help me get around better."

Suddenly, it comes clear. Having never experienced the throb of constant physical pain, and because Earl never complains, Sheila has been blind to the degree of his discomfort. Not discomfort — agony

— best describes the torment of bone scraping on bone. It took the pungent odor of eucalyptus to finally get her attention.

Later, strolling through the French Quarter, it's clear the ointment barely touches the pain. A souvenir pirate hat is perched on his head in an attempt to create a devil may care impression, but it can't disguise his suffering. And the walking stick, he brought "for fun" is seeing serious use. Even several milk punches at Cafe Pontalba cannot soften the agony in his eyes.

How long has this man been suffering so? Sheila feels small when she realizes this is the reason their sex life has slowed. Earl isn't tired of her, he's hurting, and it's an enervating force that robs him of desire.

Throughout the weekend, Sheila watches his gallant attempts to be fun. She sees his discomfort on the bus ride to and from the football game, and she can almost feel his pain during a slow, tedious climb to their stadium seats. The torture of the two-hour plane ride home is evident on his handsome face, as is the ordeal of a long car ride from the airport. Besides being great fun, the weekend has served another purpose. It has finally pushed Earl to the conclusion that knee surgery can no longer be postponed. November, he decides, is the month he'll go under the knife.

Chapter 38
Water Haven Revisited

It's October. Allie and Chase are back in school and Sheila should be there. Her body aches so much with missing them it almost feels like the flu. *They're the tonic I need, and they need me too, damn it!* With the grand opening of the country club just six weeks away, her only chance to see them is over the Columbus Day weekend so she flies north to spirit Allie and Chase, her Mom, Louada and Wookie away for a weekend in Water Haven.

"Oooooh, Sissy, your ma's excited to see you!" The loving nurse greets Sheila at the door.

"Me too, Louada," rushing to her mother, "Mom, you look lovely!" It's a lie, but she knows Dora Ronson has taken pains to look her best. Bending down, she feels she could wrap her arms twice around the tiny form. This is her fourth trip home since March. On each occasion, she's been shaken by the reality that is her Parkinson's-riddled mother. The deterioration seems to be more shocking when it's witnessed in intervals. *This time, she looks smaller; last time, she was listing more,* "Ready for Water Haven Mom?"

"Mm-huh!" is the weak, but enthusiastic reply.

As Sheila packs the car, Louada gets Wookie and her mistress situated in the front seat. Soon, they're off to pick up Allie and Chase. As she steers the car down the long drive, she feels dizzy with anticipation. *Where are they? There they are, peeking out the window.* The joy on their faces matches hers. The front door opens and the two most precious beings in the world run into her arms.

Melissa McDaniel

"My own sweet babies!" Enfolding them, she says the words they've all been missing. "Both kids, I've got both kids!" All three revel in that time-worn phrase.

"Mara, how are you?"

"Good! You?"

"I'm fine now!"

The sitter smiles at Sheila with a hundred questions in her wet eyes.

"I know you don't understand. You work thousands of miles away from your family so you can support them. And you see me leave, for what? Mara, I never dreamed it would come to this."

"Tak. Tak." Understanding nothing, Mara feels she should say something.

"Anyway, we'll be back Monday night," Sheila says as they pull away.

Toward the end of their long drive, she's hit with the full rapture of Wisconsin autumn. *My eyes have missed this so!* Everywhere, grand old maples show off their brilliance.

The next morning, they set out to pick apples at a century-old farm that markets itself as the Halloween Mecca of the dairy state. Her mother loves the outing, as does Louada. They spend time in the huge red barn where historic displays remind them of their childhoods. While they're doing that, Sheila, Allie, and Chase take a hayride, first to a field to choose their pumpkins, then to the orchard to pick apples. As they're paying for the apples they just picked, someone hugs Sheila from behind. It's Barb, the summer buddy, who'd paid her a visit last February. They'd been coconspirators, each one in the process of exiting her marriage.

Barb updates Sheila, saying although she's officially separated, she hasn't entered divorce proceedings. "I don't know what I'll do; the timing is just so bad with my daughters and all. They're taking it hard, blaming themselves and fighting with each other about who caused what. Of course, none of it is their fault but they don't believe it."

Sheila recalls her own counselor's opinion that ending a marriage when children are very young seemed not as hard on them as when they're older. Barb's daughters are thirteen, eleven, and eight — that very well could be the problem. "I'll bet it's hard, too, being in such a small town with everyone knowing your business."

Barb nods, "Hardest of all is putting an end to the family we've always been, I don't think I can do it."

"That's it! That's what's so difficult!" Sheila exclaims, "It's that awesome, powerful animal to which we all commit, and maybe even, subjugate our spirits. 'The family' is what's slowing your momentum. It would have broken mine if I hadn't moved out of its reach."

Sheila hugs Barb good-bye, remembering the night they'd soared together, two high flyers riding the currents above the realities of lives gone wrong. Now, a crosscurrent is causing her kindred spirit to flounder, and Sheila wonders if she'll soon be alone in her efforts to spin into control.

On Monday, she and the kids venture out to see the cottage she and Charles had owned. It has been sold, so she doesn't feel comfortable getting too close. For a place that once held such joy, it stands cold and argumentative before her.

"Let's go in," an innocent Chase suggests.

"Why don't we stay here, Mommy?" Allie asks.

"Remember me telling you Daddy and I sold it? Now it belongs to someone else. Like your toys belong to you, and when you don't want them anymore, we take them to the resale shop? Well, this was something Daddy and Mommy didn't want anymore."

The kids are trying to fathom why their precious cottage is no longer an object of desire. Before they can ask, Sheila says, "Bye, bye house. Thank you for all the fun we had in you!"

"Bye, house!" Chase chimes in, and Allie blows it a kiss.

Back at her Mom's, Sheila loads the car. Already, she's feeling low. In six hours, she'll again be gone. She's cried often during the weekend, especially when she had to explain to Allie and Chase that they'll continue to be with their daddy, "for the time being."

"Don't cry, Mommy," tenderhearted Chase had implored.

"Crying is healthy. Always remember strong people aren't afraid to cry." Sheila had tried to sound reassuring but inside, she was lower than low.

Back in Richmond Heights, Mom, Louada, and Wookie are her first stop. Then Sheila must return her precious children to their father. On the front porch, the estranged husband and wife embrace with awkward courtesy. They even pull Allie and Chase into a traditional sandwich hug with Mommy and Daddy as the bread, and

Melissa McDaniel

the kids as peanut butter and jelly. After a moment, Sheila breaks away to kneel by her son and daughter. Hugging them, she feels the tears in her eyes, in her throat, and splashing hard upon the fist in her chest. She mustn't make a scene; it'd be too tough on the kids. *But maybe it'd be good for Charles to see how hard it is for them to part with me. No, it would only validate his contempt!*

Holding it together, she keeps things light so Allie and Chase won't sense the finality of the good-bye. Smiling the best she can; she pulls almost recklessly into busy traffic. All the way to her mother's she curses herself. *So, I didn't love Charles, as I should have. So, my mother kept me from marrying the men I really loved! So, so, so!* At this moment, she hates herself for what she's done. *Was it worth it? Not if it means being away from my children! Funny, they seem to be weathering it better than I am. Am I not as critical to their lives as I'd thought? That can't be!* Vowing to think on that later, she goes in to say good-bye to Mom and check the cabinets for assurance that the food delivery service is going well. Everything seems to be in good order. Next, she gives Louada eight weeks of payroll checks for the nurses. Each is in its own envelope with the respective date and the nurse's name on it. Now they're set for two more months.

By now her cab has arrived so the good-bye is quick. She hugs Louada and kisses her mother, "I love you, Mom. Remember to drink plenty of water!"

On the way to the airport, she prays for her mom, her kids, and herself. She's still praying as she pays the cab driver and pulls her bag from the back seat. Behind her, there's a familiar voice, "Here, gorgeous, let me help with that."

Chapter 39
Airport Ambush

"Val! What are you doing here?" Sheila demands.

"Oh, I'm Atlanta-bound. I like to get in the night before a meeting." It sounds logical but his destination is the same city as her connection.

"Atlanta's my first stop," she announces with a suspicious look in his direction.

"No kidding? What flight?" The question seems innocent. When she tells him Val exclaims, "We have a match!"

Eyeing her suitor; "What a coincidence!"

Ignoring her sarcasm, Val carries her bag to curbside check in. Sheila trudges behind like a little girl being attended to by an adoring father. After tipping the man more generously than she could have, he grabs her hand, "Let's go, we can relax in the lounge."

Inner Sheila floats above observing the couple below. There is an incredible specimen of a man, confident, powerful, well-groomed, and there's a woman, grubby, vulnerable, and unsure of everything. What can he possibly see in her?

"Wait, Val," pulling her hand from his, "I'm not going to the lounge with you."

"Why not? It's more comfortable."

She shakes her head no and keeps walking.

"O.K. then, we'll go to the gate."

People stare at them as they pass. *They wonder what he's doing with me!*

Melissa McDaniel

Val interrupts the thought, "Did you see that man look at you, then at me? He's thinking how lucky I am." Sheila scoffs at this. "Oh yes," he confirms, "I know, because I did the same when I'd see you with Charles."

She's been courted and she's been stalked. This seems like a little of both. What Sheila doesn't like is it's starting to feel good. At the gate, Val hands their tickets to the pretty young woman behind the counter. The woman's eyes widen in obvious appreciation of Val's good looks. She smiles and bats her lashes but he seems not to notice. Instead, he pinches hold of Sheila's sweatshirt and pulls her close to his side. With an arm around her waist, he asks if there's an opening in first class. If there is, he wants his companion's ticket upgraded, and assigned to the seat next to his. Sheila's mouth falls open. Her eyes meet the young woman's, and she's certain a less-than-favorable assessment is being done on her.

Without a hint of sympathy, the woman responds, "Sorry, there's a waiting list for upgrades."

Relieved not to have to refuse, Sheila reflects again on the woman's reaction to Val. He hadn't seemed to notice her gush. *Is he so used to it he doesn't see it anymore?* Still, most men would respond favorably to the flirtation of a beautiful woman. Earl probably would, she thinks then stops. Comparing the two is the last thing she should be doing.

The first class passengers board, all but Val. He sticks with Sheila and when they call her row, he follows her to her seat.

"What?" She's running out of patience. "You think I can't find it?"

"No love, you could find your way anywhere," then he whispers, "Maybe that's why I'm so crazy about you." Sheila won't look at him; she's busying herself with locating her window seat. She finds it and is about to sit by a teenage boy when she hears Val say, "Son, would you be kind enough to trade seats with me so I can sit by my friend?"

"Uh, I better not, that's my mom and little sister." He points to the two across the aisle.

"It's in first class; do you think they'd mind that?"

The young man brightens and looks like he's about to ask his mom when Sheila interrupts. "No, Val, I don't want this, go back to first class!" Her demand is loud and embarrassing.

"All right then, I'll see you in Atlanta!" Obviously annoyed, he turns and squeezes up the aisle toward his usual class of comfort. The teenager, meanwhile, is telling his disbelieving mom what he's just given up to be near them.

Ignoring them all, Sheila stares out the window. God, you're not making this happen, are you? How can you want Val to mess things up further? Or is this some kind of test to prove my love for Earl? Whatever it is, don't you dare let me succumb!

For the next two and a half hours, Sheila attacks the why of it all. *Why is Val so committed to this chase? Why do I almost like it? Why, oh why, is Earl so passive about our relationship? Passive, that's a word I used to use in context with Charles. Is Earl becoming Charles and Val becoming Earl? No, for my own sanity, I can't let that happen!*

She's still stewing when the plane lands. As she files closer to first class, she wonders if he'll be waiting. He is not. Continuing out, she sees he isn't in the waiting area. It's not a good sign that she's just a little disappointed he's not there. Heading for a flight monitor she hears, "Ms. Branford?" Val, the successful businessman, is peeking out from behind a pillar. This time Sheila knows she's glad to see him. She laughs and he joins her; pleased to see her warmth returning.

"How much time do you have?"

"None, it's a close connection and a long hike."

He marches along beside her, down a corridor to a long escalator that leads to a monorail. After a short ride, they go back up an escalator to another corridor.

"This is it," Sheila says as they finally arrive at her gate.

"Have you ever thought of walking to Pine Springs?"

"I know what you mean; it's not the easiest destination."

"So why try?" Becoming serious, he pulls her close. "Why, oh why, are you doing this, Sheila?" She doesn't answer, "Tell me then, do I have a chance?"

This deserves a response. "Val, what I did last spring was a major, mental health threatening thing. To step over that line another time would kill me."

"You mean you can't start a new relationship until you deal with the one you've got?"

"Yes," it's not really what she meant but it's close enough for her tenderhearted nature.

Val looks at her with eyes that simmer, "I can wait. I'm not going anywhere. The time it'll take for you to get past this guy is just seconds compared to the eternity I'll wait." Finally, Sheila is coming to understand the intensity of his love. As the last call for boarding is announced, he escorts her to the door. "May I call you from time to time?"

"Only as a friend."

"As a very good friend! Have a good flight kiddo, I love you."

Ignoring the last three words, she says, "And you have a good meeting tomorrow."

"Oh, I don't really have business here, I'm heading back tonight. I just wanted to spend some time with you."

Sheila smiles, shakes her head and turns toward the walkway, wondering why she feels so elated. Well, who wouldn't be moved by such a grand gesture? But wait. Who told him I was in Milwaukee and leaving on that flight? Wherever does he get his information? Sheila is still pondering this when she lands in Pine Springs.

Earl's the tanned, handsome one in golf clothes. "Hey darlin'!" he whispers as he pulls her to him. "We missed you so much! All weekend the dogs and I have been bumping into each other, looking for you and wondering what we'd ever do without you." He tightens his hold, rocking her in his embrace. Sheila remembers similar hugs in other airports and it pleases her to know the feeling is still there. *Here, in this one man is all the love I'll ever require. I need go no further.*

At home, their lovemaking flows from a mixture of arousal and jealousy. And it's not only Sheila who's feeling jealous. Earl worries, too, about the guys who may be pursuing his Sheila up north. He's been haunted by such thoughts all weekend. Now, he hopes he's obliterating whoever they are in the best way he knows, with his body in hers.

Sheila, also, is eager to wipe out whatever female predator mothered Earl through these past three days. She has to pull him back into her reality and make him hers. When she sees his face scrunch into that final ecstasy of his, she knows she's been successful.

As they lie in bed, she notices the crisp, fresh smell of clean sheets. Warning lights flash in her brain. To her way of thinking, there's only one reason a man would change the sheets before his lady comes home. "Clean sheets?" she tries to sound casual.

"Yes, aren't you impressed?"

"Did you want to get rid of some evidence?" Sheila hopes it's genuine shock that crosses Earl's face before he gives her one of his "are you crazy" looks.

"Blossom, I love you more than I've ever loved any woman, cross my heart. Don't ever think such a thing." With this, he closes his eyes and starts to snore.

Listening to the roar, Sheila wonders why it is she feels less secure now than she had a year ago when they could only be together through the mail, the phone, and an occasional weekend. *Well, for one thing, my diminished self-esteem needs more reinforcement than this man's inclined to give. The true source of my insecurity though, is my deepening love for him. I couldn't bear it if Earl were unfaithful, not with the sacrifice I've put forth. So, please, if he is a bad sort, tell me now, Lord, before I dig in any deeper.*

For a nanosecond, her mind flashes on Val's loving words. How typical, how pathetic that I'd seek a back-up plan to feel good about myself! Still, it is kind of nice to know someone cares so much about me.

To ease her anger, Sheila raises snapshots of the weekend in her mind's eye. The time with Allie and Chase was idyllic. They were the trio they'd always been, united in perfect love. The distance that separates them is kind in the fact that when they do come together they cherish every second. Finally easing toward sleep, she whispers her classic prayer. *Give Allie and Chase safe, healthy, and happy lives; make them always feel my presence, and please, Lord, please save me!*

Chapter 40
Flirt

By November, the pain in Earl's knees is so severe he can't wait to have them scoped. Early on a Friday morning, he checks into Pine Springs Hospital for 10:00 AM surgery. Sheila had wanted to be with him, but the deadline for charter membership in the Southern Pines Country Club is near and her presence is required. As instructed, she calls the hospital after 3:00 PM. Still groggy, Earl answers; assuring her he'll be running wind sprints by morning. Right now, though, sleep is calling, so he'll see her when she gets off work. Several cold calls and one presentation later, she leaves work to visit her honey.

When she locates his room, she finds the great T. Earl looking, as the river folks would say, "kinda puny." Pale under suntanned skin, he reclines against a pillow, too zonked to lift his head. Both legs are strapped into torture devices that are slowly, continuously, bending and straightening his knees.

"Hey, sweet pea," he manages, "could you scrounge me up a blanket? I'm freezing."

"Sure," she says, kissing cold lips and smelling post-operative breath. "Be back in a jif!" At the nurses' station, heads bow low in paper work. Sheila doesn't even try to interrupt; instead, she follows her instincts around a corner and into the first door that looks like a storeroom. Sheets…towels and blankets, yes! She takes one, (no, make that two) cotton blankets and marches, with her prize, back to her patient. As she tiptoes in, she's struck by how helpless Earl looks. Eyes closed, he resembles the old man he'll become in the hopefully distant future. How pathetic he looks, not at all like the dazzling man who sat across from her at that conference breakfast two years ago.

She's seen three decades of old age and disease, first, her grandmother in the bed next to her in her little girl's room, next, her father, and now, her mom's slow demise. Each haunts Sheila as she stares down at Earl. *When the time comes, will I see you through the ravages that will wither your body and sap your spirit? Do I love you enough to add you to the list?* Sensing her presence, Earl reaches for Sheila's hand and squeezes it. *Yes, my love, when the time comes I'll never leave your side.*

Mullet stops by to check on Earl. He's on his way to Alvira's Medicine Shoppe for happy hour and beyond. "Why don't ya come along Sheila? It's the usual gang; we'll keep you out of trouble."

It would be fun but Sheila declines. Mattie and Dakota, a new yellow lab puppy, are expecting her at home. Her real reason for declining is that she feels partying in a bar wouldn't be appropriate when her honey's laid up in the hospital.

Later, while cuddling with Mattie and Dakota, she prays for Earl, all alone in his hospital room with machines bending and straightening his knees all night. *Lord: watch over that precious man tonight, let him get some rest. And keep Allie and Chase safe, healthy, and happy all their lives long. Help them, someday, to understand what I've done.*

The next morning she rises, wondering how her honey has endured the night. When she phones, his stronger, more cheerful voice informs her that he'd been given a sleeping pill which put him so far under he never knew his legs were in motion all night. Now, he's doing so well he's just walked the entire perimeter of the fourth floor with the help of a nurse. Sheila, glad he's better, says she'll be right over.

When she walks into his room, Earl's eyes fix on her hips. "Woman, where you goin' in those tight-fittin' jeans?"

"To the office, in case the charter membership deadline attracts any takers."

"Well, blossom, I reckon they'll buy a dozen with you looking that good." His voice is kidding, but accusatory.

"Thanks! I'll take that as a compliment. Is there anything I can do for you?"

"That's a terrible thing for a foxy lady to ask a man who can't move!" Glad her honey's got his spunk back, she goes to the window and is admiring the view when she hears a woman's voice.

"How's my superstar?" A nurse with a beautiful smile is zeroing in on Earl like a heat-seeking missile. So intent she is on her "superstar," she doesn't notice Sheila seating herself in the corner.

"Just fine, hon," Earl answers warmly.

The nurse takes his pulse and places his wrist on the bed with both hands, then she smiles and cocks her head. "How are the knees? Ready to take me dancing?"

"What knees?" Earl gives Florence Nightingale a wink, and she giggles at the obvious reference to the pain medication.

It's like I'm invisible! An amazed Sheila stares at the scene unfolding in front of her. Earl twinkles on having forgotten the love of his life is even present. It's when Florence leans in to put the computerized thermometer in Earl's mouth that Sheila makes her presence known. "When can your superstar come home?"

"Oh!" the nurse starts in honest surprise. "I didn't see you."

"I know," Sheila smirks coming forward, "I'm Sheila, and you're...?" It's meant to magnify Earl's oversight in introducing them.

"Oh, I'm so sorry," he smiles, mustering his charms, "Sheila, this is Mia, right?"

"Pleased to meet you," the nurse says with a decided edge in her voice. Instantly, she's become the cool professional. Stepping away from Earl, she addresses Sheila, "When his doctor comes by, he'll tell you."

"Great!" Sheila beams.

Mia picks up the blood pressure sleeve and wraps it around Earl's arm without looking at him. His eyes search her face. He's genuinely surprised at the cold front.

I get what's going on here. This is a decent woman, a good nurse who happens to be single. Earl is a handsome and charming patient who, according to his medical record, is not married. What's more, that warm demeanor of his has led her to believe he's eligible. But here, in his room, is a woman acting as though she's a significant part of his life. It's obvious from her reaction Mia feels she was led on.

SLOW DANCE

Earl's bewilderment continues as he watches the nurse complete his chart. He resembles a child, afraid to move for fear of retribution. From both sides of the bed, he's being silently chewed out.

Do you really not know what just came down? Oh, you Southern men with your casual flirting! Are you really clueless as to the trouble you reap? Is that why so many of you are on your second or third marriages?

Nurse Mia leaves, but Sheila seethes on, wondering what Earl's earlier encounters with Ms. Nightingale were like. What did you do or say to make her respond to you so? And all the while, I was home, alone with the dogs, praying for you! You bastard!

Sheila wants to believe this was an isolated incident, but she knows what she's just witnessed could happen any time, any day. With no desire to fuss over her patient, she escapes into the college pre-game shows on television. She sees, but she doesn't listen. Her brain is visiting other places and times when she'd witnessed Earl's aptitude for flirting. *What does it mean? Is it the tip of the iceberg? Does a philandering womanizer lurk inside the charming flirt? This is too foreign to me. The men I knew up North didn't do this to their women.* Suddenly, she misses every one of those steady gents.

But you don't love them, inner Sheila counters, *it's Earl you love and, to him, flirting is the spice of life. Just as you enjoy being the center of attention; so does Earl. You're acting like a prude. After all, Charles didn't flirt like Earl, but he went and had an affair anyway. Flirting is an inaccurate measure of a man's fidelity, or lack of it.*

Later, at her office, Sheila searches her brain for ways to forestall what she fears may be inevitable. To her, the sexiest men alive are ones who *don't* come on to other women; they're the ultimate in masculinity. Unfaithful men hold no attraction for her. She finds them repulsive. Earl's apparent desire to flirt and win over women is the very thing that could erode her feelings for him. When he's like that, she isn't attracted to him, physically or otherwise.

Does he think making me jealous is good for our relationship? It only makes me worry that I came down here for one kind of man and I'm finding out he's another. She pulls into the drive of Earl's home where Dakota and Mattie are waiting with licks and nuzzles. Oh Lord! Won't you please make Earl as loyal as these two are?

Chapter 41
Taking Earl North

With the country club's grand opening under her belt, Sheila decides it's time for Dora Ronson to meet Julius Caesar. In the second week of December, they head to Milwaukee for a long weekend with her mother and the kids. As their plane taxis toward the runway, Earl takes her hand. She beams at him, thinking how great she feels. *Not only will I see Allie and Chase, but my mother will meet the man I, alone, have chosen — and for the first time in my life, I don't care what her reaction will be. She can disapprove, withdraw her love even tell me she never wants to see me again, it matters not!*

Earl kisses the center of her palm and gets whisper close. "I love you," he mouths. She's the one for him; he knows that for sure. The past nine months have been great. Of course, there's been stress. He'd been single for fifteen years, then boom! There she was with her things all over the house, overflowing the closets and drawers, files, and papers everywhere. The upside is they're true buds, and they're growing closer all the time. In fact, he can't imagine life without her. She likes sports and he loves her sense of humor. Getting along with her is easy. What does she call them? Soul mates, split-a-parts even, there may be something to that. Never has he felt so complete. How had she managed to pull up the stakes of a lifelong home to begin again in a different place? It makes Earl nervous just thinking about it, but Sheila's a risk-taker and she's brave. If anyone can get through this, she can. Still, she's seemed unsettled lately. She's not crazy about her job, small wonder,

SLOW DANCE

considering what she left up North. And, of course, she misses the kids. That's got to be hardest of all, it must have been like having them ripped away. All he can do is watch her hurt and pray her turmoil won't grow so large it pushes him away.

The pilot comes on to announce that a storm will cause a delay in their arrival in Atlanta. "No! We have a tight connection, and it's the last flight to Milwaukee!" The thought of even the slightest delay in seeing her children makes Sheila panic.

"We'll make it, darlin'; these guys always come through." Earl says, exuding his philosophy that things always work out. And they do. Having landed nearly ten minutes after their connection should have departed, Sheila, Earl, and four other Milwaukee passengers are corralled by a Delta representative. Mission burns in the young man's eyes. "Come with me," he commands. Obediently, all six follow.

"Is it because he looks official we're so trusting?" Sheila asks. As if he'd heard that, their leader announces, "Your plane's being held for you, walk this way!" Earl and Sheila exchange conspiring looks and slouch into Marty Feldman's hunchback walk. Soon, the other passengers join in with their own impersonations.

"Down here," he orders. They trudge downstairs, through a "crew only" door, and onto the tarmac, where an old van is waiting. No questions asked, they pile into the car.

"Did your mom let you borrow her van tonight?" Sheila quips. The driver laughs, and lays rubber across the tarmac to a waiting plane. Screeching to a halt, he shoos them toward the plane. "This is it, go, go, go!"

The cabin of impatient travelers frowns at the latecomers as they file in. "Sorry!" Sheila smiles an apology.

"No, we're not," Earl whispers into her ear. Then he lightens the mood with his fetching smile, "I told her she looked fine but she just kept on fussin'!" Even the most disgruntled passengers laugh, Sheila most of all. *He has such an ability to make any situation fun!*

When they arrive in Milwaukee, they learn their luggage is still in Atlanta. Sheila doesn't care; she's made it home and tomorrow she'll see her kids. In great moods, they jump in a cab and laugh all the way to her mother's house.

Louada meets them at the door. "I waited up for you," she says, hugging Sheila like long lost family. "Hey Earl! How'r ya doin'?"

"Louada, I'm so glad to meet you! Sheila's tells me every day how wonderful you are."

"Aw, go on now."

"He's right, you know! Is Mom awake?"

"She's sound asleep and, I'm afraid, if you rouse her, she'll be up all night."

"That's true." Secretly, Sheila's glad. This affords her the opportunity to take Earl to a favorite place. "We're starved," she says, steering Earl toward the garage, "So we'll pop over to O'Hara's for a bite to eat. We'll see Mom in the morning."

"All right, be careful," Louada warns, and Sheila wonders how many times she's heard the dear woman say that.

They climb in her mother's old Lincoln, and as they back down the drive, Sheila realizes how excited she is to show Earl her childhood stomping ground. Over the next four days, she'll show him everything that had to do with her childhood. The photos he's seen of her in the last house she occupied portray her as more sophisticated than she truly is. The little girl who spent her time ranging around in cornfields and forests is the woman she is now.

"This was my backyard," she explains, weaving the car through the crowded subdivision that once had been her cornfield. "When they first started building these homes, we kids called them ugh-houses because we hated what they were doing to our domain. When the ugh-houses took over the field, we had a funeral to commemorate the passing." Sheila points to a crowded cul-de-sac. "I caught a rabbit somewhere around here."

"You're kidding, right?"

"God's truth, I ran him down. Maybe he was old and I was young, anyway, I walked home with him in my arms. Mom let me put him in the basement in a huge appliance carton I'd found behind one of the newly built ugh-houses. I cut a little door in the side so I could give him food. It never occurred to me how cruel I was being. But the next day, he was gone."

"Where'd he go?"

"I figured he'd jumped out of the carton so I searched the basement calling, 'Rupert!' That was his name, Rupert Rabbit. Years later it occurred to me my parents probably aided his escape after I'd gone to bed."

"So, you're a cornstalk-hugging rabbit-trapper. Anything else I should know?"

"I'll let it unfold as we go. Right now, you're about to dine at my all-time favorite hamburger joint, O'Hara's Bar and Grill. It's been said this establishment was once a secret hideaway in the woods, better known as a speakeasy." They enter, and though it's near closing time, the "tourists from Florida" are graciously served the legendary burgers accompanied by the best onion rings in the world. Laughing and talking, really talking, for the first time in ages, Sheila realizes they still have it. *My missing the kids, and fighting the divorce war, plus Earl's hurting knees have worn us down, but it's good to know the love's still here.*

Having devoured their midnight supper, the middle-aged lovers return home. There, parked in her mother's old car Earl makes her feel like the high-spirited woman she'd once been. Later, in her little girl's room, he makes her feel like the woman she's yet to become.

They awaken early to be in the kitchen when Mom comes in. "Mz. Ronson, looky who's here!" Her mother looks past Sheila to lock eyes with Earl. She continues to stare as he rises and goes to her side. Squatting with knees still sore from being scoped, he places a large hand on her shoulder.

"Mrs. Ronson, ma'am, I'm so pleased to meet you," Earl is using his "Yankee Speak," clearly articulating each word so he can be understood.

What's she thinking? Does she think he's the actor who played Julius Caesar? Does she know, this time, her reaction doesn't matter? As if her mother is reading her thoughts, she turns, and looks at her daughter. Then she turns back to Earl, and extends a shaky hand, "I'm pleased to meet you, too." Slowly, her lips tremble into a smile.

It's hard to tell what's going on behind the smile. Sheila learned long ago not to trust her mother's polite reactions. Too often they'd be negated when Mom could get her in private. Earl takes her jerking hand in both of his. Now, all three pump up and down.

"Mrs. Ronson, may I serve you some breakfast?"

"That would be nice," Mom consents, eyes still glued to the handsome face.

The airport escapade of the previous night dominates the conversation. Throughout it, Sheila's amazed at the way her mother is staring at Earl. Louada notices it, too

"Bet she sees your daddy in that face."

"Noooo! Well, maybe," Sheila says, remembering her father's good looks and chestnut hair.

"It's so; she's seeing her own man, I swear."

Sheila eats her breakfast, wondering what faults her mother would have found in Earl thirty years prior — *too Baptist, too provincial, too much like Daddy?*

The meal completed, they wheel Mom to her living room chair where they visit until the exhaustion of breakfast makes her nod off. Knowing she'll sleep for some time, they leave to call on some of Sheila's friends and colleagues. She owes them this opportunity to meet the reason for her sudden departure.

Each encounter is filled to the brim with Earl's personality. Sheila loves watching him win over every one of her friends. *And all this charm is genuine. There's not a false bone in his body. I wish I could be as real. When I was here, my identity was the product of the roles I filled. Now, all but one is gone. It's the one role I truly loved, but sadly, I must do it at a distance, at least, until I have Allie and Chase with me in Florida. So here I stand, with none of the identity and a million times more guilt. Not a pretty picture.*

Puh-leeze! Inner Sheila can't stand it. *This roundabout is getting old. Besides, it's time to go get the kids!* Apologizing to Samantha and Laura, she pulls her big beguiling bear away so they can head to school.

Once they're in the pick-up line, Sheila's get out of the car to better scrutinize every bundled little body that exits the school. "There's Chase! No, but close. There he is! And Allie! No, not them either." Finally a white-headed munchkin runs to the street corner. He's jumping up and down impatient for the crossing guard to let him go. Then, lickety-split, across the street and into Sheila's arms, Chase runs. The rapture! "This is better than anything," Sheila tells Earl, kneeling to her son's level. Then another little body slams her from behind. "Allie behind, Chase in front, this is the ultimate sandwich hug!" Sheila looks up, surprised to see Earl's wet eyes.

"Why don't I chauffeur? You get in the back with your little ones."

"Sometimes you read my mind."

"No, I just understand." After bear-hugging the kids, he opens the back door so they can pile inside.

The car's windows have steamed up, so Allie and Chase draw pictures on the frosty white. "Here's a smiley face," Allie proclaims, "and Wookie!"

"I'm doing Mommy and me," Chase draws one big circle and a little one. The little face is smiling but the big one is frowning with dots on its cheeks. "Mommy's crying 'cuz she's always sad."

"No," a startled Earl objects from the front seat, "your mommy likes to laugh. She's a happy person."

"She cries a lot, too," the little boy counters.

Is that the image I give my son? Probably so, he and Allie have seen me cry a lot these past nine months. "Yes Chase, you see me cry because I miss you so much. But remember when I told you it's healthy to cry?" Chase nods but he doesn't change the drawing, his mommy is best portrayed as a crying fat head. *See Lord? If you'd just answer my prayers to have them with me, I could be a happy fat head!*

The weekend rolls out in joyous revelry, as Allie and Chase help their mom get Grandma's house ready for Christmas. Earl, sensitive to intruding, participates on the periphery. Whenever he feels Sheila wants to be alone with the kids, he takes Wookie for a walk. By their third outing, he's her new best friend.

On Sunday, Louada announces she'll make dinner. "I want to do some Southern cookin' for Earl." *Even she has bonded with the guy!* Having originally hailed from Mississippi, Louada tells him to go to the store and, "Buy a big mess of wings and legs, and some sweet taters, cabbage, and cornmeal."

"Yes ma'am," he agrees, licking his lips in anticipation of the Southern fare.

That afternoon while Louada and Sheila are in the kitchen, Earl keeps company with her mother.

"I want a kiss," Mom tells him.

"Ma'am?"

"I want a kiss." A shaking finger points to her cheek. "Right here."

Earl rises. "I'd be honored, Ms. Ronson, ma'am." Leaning toward her, he plants a long, sweet kiss on the withered cheek.

Sheila rounds the corner in time to witness the kiss followed by a gentle hug. Mom's face, with eyes closed, is buried in Earl's shoulder as each of her arms reach to hold him. *Is she remembering Daddy or is she as sold on him as I am? For two days, she's said nothing about Earl and I haven't asked. Maybe she does care for him or perhaps she knows, this time, she'd lose.*

Louada's Southern fried chicken is an all-around hit. Allie and Chase down three drumsticks each, and Earl makes her proud by taking seconds of everything. After dinner, the children and Sheila exchange early Christmas presents with Grandma. This will be a drastically different Christmas for everyone concerned. But she's done the best she can. Mom's house is decorated and checks are written to serve as presents for the relatives for whom Sheila ordinarily would have spent days shopping. The rest will fall to her brother to fill the void during the Christmas holiday. She knows he will, and hopes he'll understand her absence.

Suddenly, the long weekend snaps closed; first, are the tear-filled hugs, kisses, and "see-you-soons" with Allie and Chase, then more good-byes with Mom. Going to the airport, Sheila gives the weekend high marks. Besides having four blissful days with Allie and Chase, she's shown her mother the respect of having her meet Earl, and she's introduced him to her Midwestern roots.

Chapter 42
New Traditions

For months, Sheila has worried about the holidays, grappling with ways to assure her children the healthiest, happiest Christmas possible. To this end, she's decided they should be with her the week before Christmas, then they'll go to their daddy on the twenty-fourth so they can wake up in their own beds on Christmas morning. It'll be awful for her, but it'd be wrong to shuttle them back and forth between a hostile mom and dad. *I'm the one who should bow out so they can have their daddy, their grandparents, and their family traditions. Traditions! Those were my traditions! I was the one who put them in place and so lovingly observed them each year.*

The voice interrupts. *You're here, and those traditions are up there so there's no point in missing them or the Christmases to which they belong. From now on, your Christmases are with Earl, and someday, your children will cherish the new traditions the four of you make.*

Following the voice's advice, Sheila plans a holiday packed with wonderful new traditions that she, Earl, Allie, and Chase will observe for many years to come.

"This will be a day of adventure!" she announces, as she and Earl meet the kids at the airport. "The first thing we're going to do is cut down our very own Christmas tree! Then we'll watch Earl shoot mistletoe down from another tree. "

"He's going to shoot something?" Chase seems thrilled.

"Oh no, honey pie! Mistletoe is a parasite that lives in trees. It's a plant that gets its food from the air, and at Christmas time, people make a tradition of kissing anyone who stands beneath it." The six-year-old looks totally confused. "I'm digging a hole here. Earl, would you please explain? I was clueless, too, until a short while ago!"

"Here's the deal, little pal, I'm going to aim my .22 at a bushy plant that likes to cling to the branches of trees. If I'm lucky, I'll break off a piece and it'll fall to the ground."

"What do we do then?" Allie asks.

Earl laughs and yields this question to Sheila. She thinks a moment, then responds, "How about we separate the mistletoe into bunches then tie them with ribbons, and give them to our neighbors for Christmas?" Allie nods, wondering if the mistletoe people buy in stores up North is always shot out of trees.

They turn off the highway by a sign that says Avery's U-Cut Xmas Trees. Sheila met Ramona Avery through a group of women who meet at Alvira's Medicine Shoppe for Wednesday night happy hour. "The Stitch and Bitches" (as they call themselves) are bound together in the mutual experiences of marriage, divorce, dating, and the desire to laugh. Ramona and Starling Wright, the group's catalyst, introduced themselves one night, when Sheila and Earl had stopped in for a drink. She'd lapped up their warmth, and soon became a regular at the Wednesday night Stitch and Bitch. When she heard about Ramona's Christmas tree farm Sheila decided it'd be fun to chop down a tree of their own. A gravel road surrounded by hundreds of cedar trees leads the way to Ramona's cracker house. The cedars concern Sheila some. Although they are traditional Christmas trees in the South, they bear no resemblance to the Douglas Firs her children are used to decorating. But the kids don't seem to care; they scamper up and down the rows, gleefully arguing back and forth, "This one! No, this one!" Chase settles on one that towers above the rest.

"Big thinker!" Earl chuckles to Sheila. Allie, approves her brother's choice and runs ahead to find the dogs she hears barking.

"Hey!" Ramona calls the greeting Sheila's heard constantly since coming south. A well-built brunette strides toward them with the confidence of a woman who knows exactly who she is.

"Hey to you too!" Sheila hails as she admires the most authentic cracker cabin she's ever seen. "You've got my dream house!" She scans the architecture named for the Florida cowboys who cracked their whips to herd the cattle that used to roam the Florida plains. It's a simple design with an open-air porch and shiny tin roof.

"Mommy, it's the house in *Cajun Night Before Christmas*!" Allie's amazed at the resemblance between Ramona's cabin and the one in a storybook Earl had given to her.

"It sure does! It's got everything but the alligators."

"You like?" Ramona asks, hugging Sheila.

"This is the place I've always wanted," Sheila says, realizing how near she's coming to the person she once was. "Someday, I'll have a cottage like this!"

Spirits soaring, she and the kids frolic with the dogs as Earl cuts down the chosen tree with the swipe of an electric saw. Suddenly, they grow quiet, sorry to be the reason for its death. Understanding this, he distracts them by pointing toward an oak tree in a nearby pasture. Near its top, several round tangles of green are clearly visible. "Behold your mistletoe!" He instructs them to stay put, then walks fifty yards into the pasture and takes aim, "Ya'll stay way back now." Sheila pulls her children close. Earl pulls the trigger, and when he does, his torso is thrust backwards by the recoil. This makes Allie and Chase laugh. They've seen thousands of guns fired on television, but this is the first they've witnessed in person.

"You missed," Chase informs Earl after a scrawny branch falls to earth. Moving to another position, the hunter fires again. Still, his prey won't fall.

"Get closer!" Allie instructs.

"Like this, darlin'?" He steps two feet closer, the .22 fires, and a huge clump falls to the ground. "Yeah! Earl, you got it!" Both kids cheer the achievement, proud to know this nice man.

The mistletoe hunter picks up his trophy and strides over to his audience. He bows, and with great aplomb, presents it to Sheila. "For my lady."

"Thank you, kind sir." Sheila curtsies and takes the tangled mass of leaves and white berries. "All this would cost a fortune in a store up north, but here, like so many of the good things in life, it's free!"

Once the tree is tied on the car, and the mistletoe is stashed in the trunk, everyone goes inside for a tour of Sheila's dream house. Earl marvels at her delight in all things rustic. Most of the women he's known have wanted to escape their country roots. Now here's this city gal who can't get enough of it. Go figure!

Melissa McDaniel

"Someday, we will have a place like this." He whispers with emphasis on *will*. Desperately wanting to make Sheila happy, he decides if that is what it will take, by God, that's what they'll do. Several hot ciders later, they leave the warmth of the cracker house to return to Earl's for the first of many new traditions. Allie and Chase proceed to decorate a new kind of Christmas tree, in the home of this new person, who makes their mommy happy in a new sort of way.

Sheila's worry that kids might get homesick never comes to fruition. With each hour that passes their emotions range from ecstasy to happy contentment. Throughout it all, love is rampant, flowing from mother to child and back again. As December 24 draws near, Sheila lives each remaining day as if it's a lifetime in miniature. Never has she been so completely in each moment. No longer is she half there, as she'd often been, when pondering a problem at work, or with her mother. For the first time ever, Allie and Chase have all of her. *Is this part of a grand plan? Is this God's scheme to bring me back to myself, and to them? Maybe these few snatches of joy are the true times of our lives.*

Chapter 43
Dixie's Gift

They're so little! They shouldn't be going anywhere without me! Sheila is waiting for the flight attendant to escort Allie and Chase on to the plane. She uses the time for kisses and hugs, trying to pour as much love into their little beings as she possibly can. When Allie sees her mother's eyes are getting glassy, she pleads, "No tears, Mommy! Please don't cry. If you cry, I will too, then Chase will, and people will stare."

At her daughter's command, Sheila stuffs the tears back down her throat. *Lord, this can't go on. Please, won't you please, make Charles see they should be with their mommy?* Like brave little soldiers, the kids kiss her good-bye and march off with the nice flight attendant. All the while, Sheila is lecturing herself on how important it is for them to wake up with their father on Christmas morning. *They don't need big changes right now, and neither does their daddy.*

Their daddy this, their daddy that! Inner Sheila is sick of all the Charles-pity. *You're the one who's had constant change since last March. You've been the one off balance every second. From the child's play of your job, to Earl's passive affection, to the macho weirdness of his friends, onto the total change of food, scenery, and lifestyle, there's been no stability anywhere. Even you have changed. The executive you once were is gone, and the Mommy in you can only operate at 10% capacity. Without those defining structures of your identity, you're an empty shell.*

The voice is right. There's such a gaping hole in her identity, she feels she could fall into it at any moment. The smart thing to do would be to replace the void with something of value. *But my children are the only things of value. If I can't have them with me, what's the point?*

The point is you don't have the Mommy role anymore. It's gone and it may never come back so you'd better find something to grab on to, cuz darlin', if you don't figure this out quick, it will be one hell of a Christmas!

I've got Earl.

Not for long, the voice warns. Not if this pining for your kids gets away from you. You need to get back in touch with that "glass-half-full" woman who first came down here. Find the leak and repair it before you run completely dry. Even a temporary fix will be better than the self-pitying creature you're about to show Earl.

A temporary fix is something she can do, so she resolves to have a great Christmas with Earl and his Atlanta relatives. By the time she reaches him in the parking lot, she's managed to assume a convincingly happy persona. "O.K., darlin'," she says in her best go get 'em voice, "Show me a Southern Christmas!"

What a pleasant surprise! Earl had been anticipating a dreary ride to Atlanta. Instead, his lady seems to have willed herself to be cheerful. Throughout the drive, she steers the conversation to relive every detail of the past week. It's as if she's depositing her memories into a bank for future withdrawals.

On the outskirts of Atlanta, they merge with what seems to be the city's entire population. The herd of cars thunders through the downtown then north, through miles of urban sprawl. As they take the Woodstock exit, Earl explains, "This once was a pretty little town, considered to be too far north for real development. Well, guess what? Progress found it in a big way."

Sheila surveys the rooftops. "I feel sorry for all the little towns that have been forced to surrender their landscapes to subdivisions and strip malls. It doesn't matter where they are; they all get swallowed up eventually!"

"Amen, blossom! Even Pine Springs, the perfect little city, is a boom-town of growth."

"It seems wherever I go, thousands of people are sure to follow."

Although Atlanta has impacted Woodstock, it hasn't changed Earl's relatives. The Langleys have maintained their integrity as simple country folk. They are who they are, and they welcome Sheila wholeheartedly, even though they don't know what to make of a woman who chooses to be without her children on Christmas.

Effie, Earl's sister-in-law, immediately reaches out to this gal who loved her brother-in-law enough to leave her own home. Sheila responds to her warmth with misty disclosures about the place she's from. As one who's never ventured outside the state of Georgia, and has no real desire to travel over forty miles in any direction, Effie can only listen. One thing she knows for certain is she's never seen her brother-in-law so happy and that's got to mean something.

Effie's husband, Johnny B., their son, Mac, and daughter, May, all possess the Langley genes for good looks and high spirits. They agree Sheila's a fine addition to their family, and she, in turn, enjoys being with these nice strangers. But it doesn't feel like Christmas Eve. She's too much of another life to be able to relate to the traditions of these good folks. Here, she stands alone. Even Earl seems less hers.

When she calls her mom, she interrupts a visit between her mother, Charles, and the grandkids. "I'm in the Christmas dress Grandma gave me." Allie informs her.

"Wonderful punkie-pie!" She says this realizing how thoughtful it was of Charles to have her wear it for Grandma, and it was especially nice of him to take the children to see her.

"I'm in my Packers shirt!" Chase announces. It, too, was a Christmas gift from Grandma. *They're there and I'm not. Why, oh why am I doing this?*

Christmas morning, she awakens to the sounds of a family in the midst of its own gift giving traditions. It's as though a curtain has risen on a theatrical production. The actors are intimate with each other, and comfortable in their roles. Year after year, this story has been winding around itself. Age, death, and divorce have changed the players some, but the core remains the same. After a relaxing morning, the production moves to the home of Effie's sister, Margie, for an early Christmas dinner.

The house is a sprawling estate, but for all its beauty, there is a profound sadness within. Margie is its mistress, but her ex-mother-in-law is the owner. Margie's husband exited their marriage long

Melissa McDaniel

ago, leaving her behind to care for his mother, and maintain her home, while raising their five sons. *She's put her own life on hold, and her tears are as close to the surface as mine.*

"I'm here for the sake of my boys. It's the only way they can have this." Margie sweeps her arm to include the house, expansive grounds, and swimming pool. "But we're trapped — she has us right where she wants us." As she says this her eyes settle on her short-tempered and senile ex-mother-in-law.

And I thought I had the mother from hell! Not being able to act can be as costly as acting too radically. Sheila pulls the woman close. "This too shall pass," is all she can think to say. Margie hugs her back; she likes this Yankee gal. While most people think she's lucky to live in a fine house, this one understands what a prison it is.

"Hey y'all! Guess what's happening!" Dale, one of Margie's ex-brothers-in-law, is hollering through the sliding glass doors that open on to the pool. "Dixie's having her pups!"

Dixie is a stray black lab that Dale recently rescued from traffic. When no one claimed her, he took her in, and soon realized she was in a mothering way. As to when the delivery would occur, he had no clue, so he built her a doghouse and pen in his mother's backyard. Dixie welcomed her pen, making it hers with all the appropriate digs and wallows. Steady meals and her rescuer's good-natured visits have convinced her it's the best home in the world. Now, her timing is perfect. Here, at the close of Christmas day, she's presenting her savior with the best gift of all.

Everyone follows Dale to the pen. In awed silence, they peer into the doghouse to see Dixie bumping two black rat-like creatures with her nose. She bites and gnaws at something, maybe an umbilical cord; then eats the gooey sack that had encased a pup.

"Yuk, what's she doing?" Squeals and shrieks come from the youngsters in the group as their elders look on in reverence.

Not wanting to seem a know-it-all, Sheila whispers to Earl, "It's starting to sleet. Do you think we could take them inside?"

"Good idea, sweet pea," then to Dale, "Let's move Mama and the pups in where it's warm. How about the laundry room?" With that, Dixie's relocation becomes a group project. It's pretty much everyone's first time having puppies so they don't know how territorial the mother might be. Maybe she doesn't want to be moved. Should they let her call the shots? Well, no, they have to think of the puppies. It's getting colder by the minute; they couldn't survive. Or could they?

Dale solves the problem. Cashing in on the trust he's earned, he extricates the pups from Dixie's domain. Once they're gone, Mama follows, waddling slowly to the house. The humans file though the garage, and into the crowded laundry room. Papers are laid on the floor. Old towels and blankets form a makeshift bed onto which the laboring mother is lured. And just in time! Squatting as if to pee, Dixie grows still, waiting for something to happen. A long, slow surge heaves from within and a gooey sack appears; sliding out as gravity takes over. This time, a yellow pup is the occupant. Dixie performs the same ritual as before, chewing open the sack, then nudging and gently massaging her offspring with the tiniest of bites and licks to stimulate circulation. Sheila remembers how important this is from her an experience, long ago, when she'd assisted a veterinarian friend. What a great profession her buddy had chosen. Now there was a woman who knew how to follow her dream!

Two hours pass. Spectators come and go. Some are skittish about the gore. Others join Dale, Earl, and Sheila in riveted fascination. They're witnessing a miracle, on Christmas yet!

The puppies come more slowly now. Dixie seems exhausted, but she still tends to each as if it's the first. Eight, nine, ten pups, six resemble Labrador retrievers, and four others are smaller and multicolored. "Dixie-darlin! What'd I tell you about sleeping around? Looks like your pups got two daddies!" Four blacks, two yellows, and four calico puppies struggle to belly up to their mama's tits.

Dale, who'd assumed Sheila wouldn't be much help, gratefully thanks her for sticking with him through the process. "I'm the one to thank you, Dale, for sharing this once-in-a-lifetime experience."

Looking around the laundry room, Sheila realizes it's now full of dear friends, family really. If they'd merely finished dinner, had presents, and gone home, it would have been a family get-together with Sheila there in the third person. But Dixie, the stray sent from heaven, has changed all that. Her gift of life has brought them close. Sometimes the simplest thing can work the greatest wonder.

Later that night, Earl and Sheila review the blessed event in as much detail as they can remember. Both want to hold tight to the glory they've witnessed: Dixie in pain, yet performing her motherly obligation. And the puppies! Eyes closed, yet driven to find their mother's warmth and nourishment.

Earl's long arms scoop Sheila close. "Thank you," he pauses to hide the catch in his throat, "Thank you for being here."

His words mean a lot. The past two days have been worse than Sheila had anticipated. Just this afternoon, she'd ached so from being without her children, she'd wanted to do nothing but sit in a hot bath and cry. The miracle of the puppies helped pull her through, and now, with Earl's appreciation, Sheila sleeps better than usual on this Christmas night.

Chapter 44
Avoidance

The new-year kicks off in a positive way when Sheila learns she's been appointed to the Pine Springs Volunteer Alliance. Through its activities, she hopes to find some of the meaning that's missing in her life. For their first meeting, each participant is assigned someone else to introduce. When a woman phones to ask Sheila what she should say about her, Sheila says, "I can't talk now, but I'll fax you my bio." The caller says fine, and Sheila has, again, avoided answering questions about herself and her absent children.

Avoidance behavior, like the bio side step, continues all spring. Through a myriad of Alliance activities, Sheila manages to always steer the focus away from herself, and onto the other person. On one occasion, she does this with Tina Easton, the unpaid leader of the program. It is Tina's coaching, and summarizing that gives continuity to the course's six-month format. *What does she get for her time and effort? Probably a job well done will get her appointed to the Alliance's board of directors.* With no husband or children to care for, one would assume she has plenty of time to herself, but Tina's career and charity work are her family, and to that end, she has overloaded her plate. If she's unhappy or frazzled to the core, it doesn't show through her positive façade. *I see so much of me in Tina it makes me anxious for her. While she's taking care of everyone else, who is taking care of her?*

"You know, Tina, you're the same overachiever I once was. My biggest regret is that for years I piled it on, thinking the busier I was, the happier I'd be. But it worked in reverse. When I finally heard my soul screaming for attention, it was almost too late."

"How so?" Tina's interest is encouraging.

"Well, a couple of years ago, I realized I hated the life I was living. It had been true for a long time but I'd ignored it. Finally, when I realized change was a better alternative than cracking up, I started to plan my way out. Exiting, however, has been the most traumatic thing I've ever done. One year later, I'm still in the throes of it. It's as though I'm having a slow motion breakdown. There's hope though; I'm inching closer to the real me, and she's someone I haven't seen for decades."

"I have no clue who the real me is," Tina laughs. "Is she the workaholic or the volunteer's volunteer?"

"Maybe the real you is hidden in your personal life?" This gets no response. "Is there too much work and volunteerism to allow a personal life?"

"Bingo!" Tina confirms with a mean laugh. "Anyway," she says much too brightly, "let me tell you about a literacy meeting I attended in Tallahassee!"

No one could have warned me either.

In the course of her activities with the Volunteers' Alliance, Sheila gets further proof that her adopted town is a gem of a little city. But like any rapidly growing burg, it has its share of problems, too. The greatest eye opener comes the night she rides in a squad car with Sheriff's Deputy Sally Castle. The deputy looks like a pretty linebacker in her uniform and bulletproof vest. She's twenty-six years old and has just broken up with her boyfriend because he couldn't take her working nights. Sally has a mother who worries for her safety, and a condo that's decorated in French provincial. She loves caring for her plants, and has no time for anyone who thinks because of her gender, she's not as much a deputy as her male counterparts.

The young woman's confidence is impressive. Every call she answers is a confrontation with danger. First, there's a stolen car that's been ditched and set on fire. Next, they pick up and jail a reckless driver who already has a suspended license. Duke, a police dog, is brought in to search the woods for someone who fled the scene of an accident, and finally, there's a violent marital dispute at what's supposed to be a romantic bed and breakfast.

It's almost dawn when Sheila gets home. A review of the night confirms to her that, when in trouble, people lie. Everyone they'd encountered had tried to squirm out of his or her predicament with whatever fabrication they thought might work.

"When in trouble, lie." *That's what Earl once said and I've wondered ever since if he was joking or if it really is his credo. Damn this place, so seductively beautiful in its pristine disguise! How can its people seem so innocent, so close to nature, and yet, be such lying bastards? And compared to the capable Deputy Castle, I am a self-centered whiner.*

Other activities of the Alliance continue to confirm her pathetic, self-pitying existence. The crack babies in the hospital, the battered wives, the rural family with a mother dying of cancer (yet too proud to take assistance) all speak volumes, giving Sheila hours of material with which to search her own shallow soul for answers.

Chapter 45
Change

It has been a year since Sheila left. Would she do it again? It hurts too much to consider that question, let alone answer it. Still, the children seem to be thriving, and she and Earl are more committed to each other than ever. But just as she's thinking things may actually work themselves out, some major changes occur to keep her off balance. The first happens when Sheila leaves her full-time job to represent a group of local artists. Financially, this move will cost her dearly, but it's necessary if she ever is to have enough time to visit with her children.

Close on the heels of that change is a far more devastating change. Louada, her mother's beloved nurse has died. *No! Not Louada, please God, not her!* The dear woman has worked for Dora Ronson some thirty years, as a cleaning woman, then as a caregiver, but their relationship really has been one of deep friendship. Her absence, Sheila knows, will take a toll on her mother.

Hoping to fill the emptiness, she drives home to be with her mother for her eighty-fourth birthday. At first glance, it's evident to Sheila that Dora Ronson's battle with Parkinson's has united with the trauma of Louada's death to make her decidedly worse. *At what point does the spirit decide to team up with the disease and end it all? What words, if any, will give her the will to go on?*

"You know, Mom, I can still feel Louada with us. She's in heaven right now looking down on us, I can almost hear her deep, rumbling chuckle."

"Yes, she went ahead to show me it's O.K."

Sheila considers this, then says, "That sounds like the thoughtful kind of thing Louada would do. She wants you to know there are good things yet to come."

Throughout her life, Sheila has witnessed her mother's ambivalence toward God. It's as though she thought God had let her down at some point. Whatever it was, she's never seemed open to the Almighty; and because of this death is also her adversary. Since she's never had much to do with God, death must be the end of everything.

"Let's pray to Louada!"

"Pray *to* Louada?"

"Yes, if we'll pray to her spirit, I think she'll hear us." Taking her mother's hand in hers, she begins, "Louada, this is Mz R and Sissy. We miss you terribly but we know you're at peace, and you've gone ahead to show us we have nothing to fear." Sheila peeks. Mom, eyes closed, seems intent on every word. "We know you're happy because you're sending us good feelings. You're up there with your loved ones. I bet you've even shared some laughs with my dad! We'll see you when our times come, but for now, we hope your spirit will feel free to visit us whenever you like. Bye, Louada, we'll think of you often."

"Good-bye," Mom says, believing. She opens her eyes, "That was nice." The frightened animal mask of Parkinson's has subsided some. "I think I'll lie down." Sheila wheels her mother to the couch. Bracing herself with the Parkinson's grip she learned in the hospital, she lifts, pivots, and gently guides the rigid form onto the cushions. *You're not going to die now, are you?* She removes her mother's shoes, and covers her with a blanket, things she's done hundreds of times. Now, each one is done with reverent foreboding. Will their prayer to Louada help ease her mother toward death? If it makes her passing more peaceful, so be it. But right now, Sheila feels, as all daughters must, no matter how old they are, *not yet, it's too soon!* She kneels by her mother and kisses the thin, cold lips. "I love you, Mom. I love you so, so much."

"I love you, too, honey. You're my precious little girl." This transports Sheila to a time when she really was Mom's precious little girl, not the damaged goods she is today. Nestling into her mom's shoulder, she wishes she could start over and do things right this time. *What a mess I've made of things! No one said life was easy but*

I've made it impossible. She pulls back to look at the old woman and fear grips her by the throat. *Is she breathing? Mom!* She holds a finger under her mother's nose. *There's no breath!* Wild eyes search the pale face. "Mom!" she shouts, shaking the torso. "Mom! Don't go!"

The eyes flutter open. "I'm not. I'm trying to go to sleep."

"Ah! Sorry! I was afraid you weren't breathing. Have a good rest, Mom, I love you." Sheila kisses her mother and rises to see Prudie, Louada's replacement, standing in the doorway.

"Did you see me panic? I thought she'd stopped breathing."

"I know," Prudie whispers. "She breathes so light it's like there's no breath at all. That was nice, what you said about Louada."

"Thanks, Prudie, I believe every word."

"I know you do, and so does she."

Two days later, Sheila prepares an eighty-fourth birthday lunch for her mother and two old school chums. The first to arrive is Miss Worthy, the robust octogenarian who'd (two years earlier) lunched with Sheila and her mom in the new house. She's been one of very few to support Sheila's decision to do what she's done. An avid Christian Scientist, Miss W says she prays daily for Sissy and the children. This comforts Sheila for she's certain, aside from herself and Earl, Miss W is the only person who finds her worth praying for.

"Hello!" another hearty voice calls. *That can't be Eleanor.* The statuesque Eleanor of Sheila's little girl memories has been ravaged by a stroke. Although she survived her ordeal, it left her partially paralyzed. With her is the owner of the voice, her part-time caregiver and niece, Lara. To the childless Eleanor, Lara has been like a daughter.

"I'm glad to meet the Lara I've heard about all these years," Sheila beams.

"You, the Lara, and I, the Sissy!"

They both cringe, remembering the countless times they'd had to sit and endure the tales of each other's accomplishments as told by a proud mother or aunt. "Guess they were pretty proud of us," Sheila remarks, wondering if her mom is at all proud of her now.

Her mother interrupts these thoughts with a weak, "Oh! Eleanor!" Wheelchair meets wheelchair. Two frail and damaged skeletons reach for each other in awkward embrace. They pull back and look at each other surveying the ruins of age and ill health, then the tears come. Sheila senses immediately, they're not crying for the damage they see, they're crying for their youth. *They want to be young again, to start over in the beautiful and healthy thirteen-year-old bodies they had when they met.* She and Lara pull the two as close as the chairs will allow. Then, on the same wavelength, they engage Miss W in conversation so she won't interrupt them. For several minutes, Eleanor and Mom sit holding hands, content just being together. Sheila distributes a punch made from Allie and Chase's favorite Five Alive recipe. All three school chums have firsts and then seconds. The hors d'oeuvres crackers fail, however, causing both Mom and Eleanor to choke.

"That wasn't so smart; maybe chicken salad and soft rolls will go down easier." Miss W takes her seat as Sheila and Lara wheel their charges into the dining room for the main course. The luncheon is perfect. Everyone loves the finely chopped, slippery-down-the-throat chicken salad. Sheila sits next to her mother, and, at inconspicuous moments, she sends a spoonful her way. Mom, used to the routine, opens her mouth, like a bird, at just the right times. Lara assists her aunt. Only Miss W, the indomitable apex of the threesome, is feeding herself, asking for seconds, and leading the conversation wherever she wants it to go. She steers it to their teachers, school trips, and old Chicago neighborhoods. No one speaks of the present. All three are happy to dwell in memories of their youth.

The younger women listen and learn. Sheila hadn't known her mother made the dean's list every single semester of high school. Nor had she known that the school newspaper named Dora the smartest and prettiest girl in the senior class. From Miss W's comments, she also learns it was her mother's German immigrant father who saw no need for his "girl" to go to college.

Mom would have loved college! For the first time, Sheila sees the sacrifice her own mother made in yielding to her father. *That wheel just keeps going around. Lord, don't ever let me do that to Allie and Chase!*

Lara learns similar things about her aunt. "Aunt Eleanor had such high expectations of me; now I see where she got them." She and Sheila had excused themselves to clear the table, making way for strawberry shortcake. In the kitchen, the two commiserate about the strict guidance they'd both received.

"That's why I didn't marry for so long," Lara begins, "My boyfriends were never good enough. They weren't smart enough or rich enough or they weren't 'university' men! I let her influence me even though she, herself, was never married. And when I married a cabinetmaker at the age of thirty-six, she was very cool about it. I guess he was too 'old country,' too much like what she'd tried to leave behind. But you know what? My artistic husband makes me happier than I've ever been."

"I guess they did what they thought was best. The place and time in which they grew up gave them a different definition of success," Sheila observes.

"And most of that success was supposed to be achieved by the man one married, not by the woman herself," Lara chimes in.

"How many are like us?" Sheila wonders aloud. "Are other middle-aged women living scripts written for a time when fathers thought their smart daughters didn't need college, and little girls were raised to marry 'university' men — or not marry at all?"

"At least we figured it out!" Lara says with some triumph.

"You caught yours in time. I didn't; I gave in too soon and I'll pay for it for the rest of my life." Sheila's thoughts fly to Allie and Chase. *No, don't go there. Take this out on a happy note.* "But," she says with artificial brightness, "that water's already flowed under the bridge."

By now, the dessert is assembled and the new friends present the old friends with towering strawberry shortcakes under mounds of whipped cream. The classic confection makes their elders as giddy as schoolgirls. All three chatter and giggle more energized than they've been in ages. They stay in this suspended state for another twenty minutes. Then, like helium balloons that have lost their pep, they float back down. Mom's body seems to compress as exhaustion sets in. Eleanor is weary, also. Only Miss W — the Christian Science practitioner, without a trace of caffeine, medicine, or vitamins in her system — is still going strong. She offers to help Lara take her aunt to the car, but no, before separating, Eleanor and Mom have another good cry. Sheila feels certain these are the tears of final good-bye.

Miss Worthy, on the other hand, is not tearful. Death isn't in her realm of thinking. She gives her pals bear hugs and kisses, telling each she'll pray for her, then out the door the eighty-four-year-old bounds with more life to be lived.

Chapter 46
Unexpected

Only three weeks have passed since Sheila drove home for Mom's birthday. Still, an eerie "all-is-not-well" impulse has her again driving north. This time, thanks to her flexible new business, she and the kids will be able to spend time with her mom in Water Haven before driving down to Florida for two marvelous weeks. Tonight, she'll stay in Nashville with Sara Boudreau. The two friends haven't visited for over a year.

Before leaving, she phones Water Haven. Prudie answers, "Your ma's feelin' pretty punk, she's asleep now. I'll tell her you called."

"Good, rest is the best thing for her. The drive will take a couple of days, so I'll see you the day after tomorrow. Take care, Pru."

Sheila jumps in her car and for the next nine hours, she drives through some of the best rural scenery she's ever seen. It is early evening when she rings her friend's doorbell. Sara greets her, saying her husband and son are out so the two have all the privacy they need for a good heart-to-heart.

First, they focus on Sara's mother. "It's never enough!" She sounds almost frantic. "I work constantly when I'm there, doing everything, taking her everywhere, then the day after I leave, she starts in again on how I never help."

Sheila's neck tightens in empathy. She sees Sara harrying herself, trying to prove over and over again that she's a good daughter, and all the while, her own family must cope with a distracted, frazzled mom. "Call me when it gets bad, Sara. Let me be your dumping ground. The most destructive thing you can do is to keep a lid on what's boiling inside. I did that until I blew. No one knew what a cauldron was churning inside me. They didn't know it then, and few believe it now."

"I do! I believe it," Sara interrupts. "But that's history, now you're with Mr. T. Earl Wonderful."

"He is pretty fabulous, isn't he? I still find myself marveling, 'So this is what it's like to truly love a man!' It makes me sad for Charles, though. I'm sure, if my mother hadn't gotten in the way, he would have found a woman who'd feel about him the way I do about Earl. I hope before too long he will find someone better suited to him. That may help him to see Allie and Chase should be with me." Sheila's eyes are suddenly tearing up, "My children, Sara! I never dreamed I'd be without them this long!"

This makes Sara shiver. All along, she's worried that Sheila's been deluding herself.

"I'm scared, really scared that I may not get them after all!"

"Well…what's your plan?"

Instantly, Sheila regrets her outburst. With Sara fresh out of law school, she's all about taking Charles to court.

"No, Sara, a court fight is not an option. It'd destroy Charles and me and jeopardize the kids' well-being."

"Sheila! You're their mother. Little children should be with their mothers. Stop looking out for Charles and think of them!"

"I am thinking of them! How can I drag them through the Armageddon of court battles? It'd take years, and the kids would hear horrible things about their father and me. They might even have to testify. I've seen kids do that and it scars them for life."

"What about the scar of not being with their mother?"

Sheila winces, "I've thought of that, Lord how I've thought of that! But it's more than likely I'd go through a horrendous fight, and still not get the kids. The Branford name is so influential within the Milwaukee court system I'm not sure any judge could be completely objective when it comes to Charles Branford's children."

"Hmmmm." Sara seems stumped.

"The way I see it, my best weapons are the passage of time, and lots of praying for their daddy to see they should be with me."

"Why would he do that?"

"Because, in his heart, he knows it's the right thing! He may be a 'hands-on' Daddy now, but in time, I think he'll assume a more passive role. Or," Sheila brightens, "maybe he'll remarry and his new wife will already have kids. That'd be a good time for them to come to me."

"Sheila, that's the weirdest back-door approach I've ever heard."

"I know. That's why I'm so scared. Leaving the kids with Charles was the most gut-wrenching thing I've ever done. The only reason I could do it was because I was so sure he'd be in trouble without them, and I saw it as my responsibility to help him through the ordeal. I spent hours figuring out a timeline that would ease him into an existence without me. And stupidly, I believed Allie and Chase's presence was an essential part of it." Sheila takes a jagged breath. "You can't imagine what it's like to, one day, be hugging your kids and the next, be hundreds of miles away. I exist, down there, in a state of suspended animation waiting always for the next time I can be with them. I see a school bus, playground, anything that reminds me of them, and I start to cry. Only Earl, with his positive 'You didn't leave them, you're always with them' philosophy is able to lift my spirits."

On and on they talk; even after Sara's husband and son return, they continue the emotional give and take. It's after 2:00 AM when they finally go to bed. In the morning, Sheila dials the Water Haven number. After eleven rings, she's worried. "Sara, I have to leave this instant. No one's answering the phone at Mom's and that's a bad sign." Quick to understand, her friend moves out of the way so Sheila can bound upstairs to reappear in seconds, with her carryall.

"Hopefully, it's a false alarm, but just in case," Sara, palms together, looks heavenward.

"Thanks, all prayers are welcomed."

"Any time! Now, promise you'll be gentle with yourself." Sara commands.

"And don't you allow your mom to make you miss out on your own family!" Sheila admonishes while giving her chum a big hug.

We're so alike, she thinks, as she backs down the drive. *Will we be as hard on our kids as our moms can be on us? Please Lord! Give us keen memories to remind us what not to do in our old age!* As she drives away, panicky thoughts of her mom's condition take hold. *I know! I'll check the answering machine at Earl's.* Pulling up to a payphone, she dials the Pine Springs number. Sure enough, Prudie has left a message.

"Sissy, I hope you get this. I took your ma to the hospital. The doc says they'll check her out; then maybe keep her overnight. I called your brother, too. Talk to you later, bye." *That's what I thought, she's probably dehydrated or her meds are off kilter. The hospital will fix that.* Prudie's voice had not sounded urgent so Sheila decides to drive as far as her sleep-deprived body will allow. Then, for safety's sake, she'll pull off for a good night's rest.

She makes it through Louisville, Kentucky, with what Chase calls 'its cobweb bridges,' then on to Indianapolis. Outside Indy, a fuzzy feeling in her head signals severe fatigue. When a can of Mountain Dew fails to revive her, Sheila pulls off at an economy motel. In her low-budget room, she lies down on the surprisingly comfortable mattress and calls the cottage; no answer. *O.K., call the hospital.* She punches in long-distance information, gets the number for Water Haven Hospital, and asks to be connected. "Hi, I'd like to speak to Dora Ronson, she's a patient."

"One moment." More than a moment elapses. *Come on! Any longer and I'll be asleep.*

"Hello?" it's Prudie.

"Hi, Pru, this is Sheila. How's Mom?"

"She's the same, her breathin's real soft." There's a concern in her voice that wasn't there before.

"Can I speak to a nurse?" Moments pass, then one comes on. "Your mother's having difficulty breathing. I see her blood pressure dropped dramatically but it's better now. We're awaiting test results. Here, she'd like to talk to you."

"Hello?" The voice is faint.

"Hi, Mom! How ya doin'?" No answer. "The kids and I will be there tomorrow. O.K.?" Still, no response, "I'm bringing you a jar of Key Lime jelly, and bag of the Honey Bell oranges you like. I love you, Mom, so, so much!"

Sheila thinks she hears, "I love you, too," but the voice is too soft to tell.

Prudie again, still worried: "Come real soon, now."

"I will, Pru. I'll arrive tomorrow afternoon. It wouldn't be safe for me to drive anymore today. Bye now." She puts down the receiver, and for a moment, curses her heart-to-heart with Sara. As therapeutic as it had been, it's the cause of her fatigue and the reason she can't get to her mother sooner, but the bed is unbelievably comfortable and, despite her anxiety, she falls sound asleep.

When she awakens around nine the next morning, her first thought is to call the hospital. "Yes, would you please connect me to Dora Ronson's room?"

"One moment please." A voice puts her on hold.

Finally someone answers. Hello? We've been instructed to tell you to call the following number."

Sheila recognizes the number of her mother's cottage. With a whirring sensation in her head, she feels herself leave her body to float above. From up there, she watches the figure below ask the inevitable. "Did she die?"

Taken aback, the nurse stammers something about being "instructed to."

"Please tell me, I'm her daughter!"

"I'm so sorry; she passed away early this morning." Instantly, Sheila's back in her body, feeling full force the words she hadn't expected to hear. "I truly am sorry; someone else should have told you. Her son and caregiver were with her, but they've gone home."

"Thanks, I'll call there." Sheila clicks off, lying back down in the position she was in when she'd last talked to her mother.

"Mom!" she calls to the ceiling. "Don't be dead! We were going to have such a great week together!" She pulls into a ball as her mother — her pretty, young mother — plays in her mind. Mom holding a basket of award-winning flowers, cradling a puppy in her arms, or coming in to tuck tiny Sheila into bed on any one of thousands of nights. "Mom, you know how much I love you. I'm sorry I wasn't there." Amid tears, Sheila recalls something she'd read in a book on death. *Has your spirit flown by to check on me? Are you here now?* She scans the ceiling. "Are you here Mom? If you are, I love you soooo much and I'll miss you!" In her heart, she knows, she'll miss the mother of her youth more than the one of recent times but that seems natural. "Go safely, Mom. Enjoy it wherever you are. I hope you're the young, vibrant beauty of your youth. Are you with Dad? If so could both of your spirits do a fly-by from time to time?" These thoughts interrupt Sheila's crying enough for her to sit up. Swinging her legs to the floor, she feels an urge to vacate this place where death has found her. *Got to get going. No. I need to call the cottage, talk to Dan.*

She stares at the phone and wonders if big brother will be mad she didn't get there in time. *No, he's not like that.* But her own guilt reminds her that, like the townsfolk in the story of the little boy who cried wolf, she hadn't believed this was the time. *But I was there every other time, every single one!*

She dials the cottage. The second Dan hears her voice; he assumes his characteristically kind, big brother role. "She went quietly, Sis. I was with her and we talked, well, I talked mostly about the good life she'd had. I think she was ready, honey. It was for the best." Dan describes the preparations he's making for their mother to have two funerals, one in Water Haven and one in Richmond Heights, where the interment will be.

"Mom would like that," Sheila says with certainty. "I guess I'll arrange for Allie and Chase to stay with Charles this weekend. They don't need to endure two funerals. See you this evening, Dan."

Her next call is to Charles. "I'm sorry," he says "she was a nice lady."

Sure, she was nice to you. You posed no threat to her dominion over me! Sheila thinks this, but says instead, "You were good to her too, Charles. Listen, I think it'll be easier on the kids to attend just the Richmond Heights service. Can they stay with you until Monday?" Charles agrees and Sheila gets underway.

The flatlands of Indiana provide hours of easy driving, plenty of time for Sheila to work through a maze of feelings. For the moment, the resentment she felt toward her mom is non-existent. Also absent is any fear of being without her. What is present is a kind of "what now?" anticipation. There's much to be arranged and settled. It's documenting what's left of Mom's finances, tracking down insurance and death benefits, working with an attorney to take the estate through probate, selling her house, and distributing her things to the appropriate people. *Eventually, though, life will simplify. No longer will I be a personnel office for Mom's nurses. The red tape of insurance forms and bill payments will slow to a halt. So, with Mom's death comes the responsibility of managing my newfound freedom. And, it's not just the freedom from the details of managing her care; it's the absence of a force that has constantly driven my life. What will I do without it? Mom! You can't be dead, you just can't be!*

SLOW DANCE

Sheila drives the last two hours with the solitary feeling of being an orphan. When she arrives, she finds it painful to pull down the cottage drive. *Mom's not home; she'll never be here again!* Dan sticks his head out the door and, in an almost fatherly way, watches little sister emerge from the car and tentatively navigate the path. They embrace longer than they ever have, each one thinking, *you're all that's left.* It's dusk and the lake, always a source of solace, beckons to them. They sit on the dock, downing beers, and watching the lights come on around the shore. When mosquitoes chase them into the cottage, Sheila, relaxed by the beer, starts to sob. Dan lets her cry into his shoulder.

"We had great parents," she tells him.

"Yes, we did, honey, and Mom loved you very much. You were her precious little girl."

That came from Mom. Sheila thinks this realizing an image of her as a child, not the jagged middle-aged daughter of late, had been with her mother in death. *That's fine; my best memories of her are also from the early years.* Little sister gives big brother a squeeze, then pulls away to gaze into his red, wet eyes. "I loved her, too, Dan." The child inside adds, *she was my own beautiful mommy and I loved her more than anyone or anything.*

"I know, Sis, I know." Dan has read her mind.

They sit a while longer, wrapped in each other's grief. Then, heavy with beer-drenched fatigue, they go to their rooms. In the trundle bed of the tiny room she'd shared with her grandmother, Sheila closes her eyes and becomes that little girl drifting by snapshots of her mother. She loved her so! She'd do anything for her mommy, anything.

And that, little girl, is exactly what you did, the bruised adult in her interrupts. Whatever she wanted, you did in order to retain her possessive love.

Not now...let me grieve, the little girl fights back.

Don't tell me all's forgotten, all's forgiven.

No, but I'll deal with those feelings later. Now I just want to remember the good times, and there were many!

Chapter 47
Funeral # 1

Funeral number one is underway. Dan is delivering a eulogy on their mother's behalf. Sheila had considered saying something, but nixed the idea when it occurred to her that the audience would certainly detect an edgy undertow in whatever remarks she'd make. As big brother does the honors, she silently addresses the body in the open casket. *I never did have it out with you, Mom. I thought about it, but you were so ill, I felt I'd be bullying you. I hope along the way, you realized the role you played in the demise of Charles's and my lives. I thought my anger would die with you, but I'm still mad. You may be gone but the consequences of always having to do things your way live on. Charles is a victim. I'm without my son and daughter and they are little ones without their mommy.* Sheila looks around at the women in the room. *Mothers everywhere, please recognize the power you have to misshape the lives of your children. Don't tweak at their devotion until they have no choice but to surrender to your will. Let them script their own lives otherwise, when you die, an ugly part of you will live on as they face the mistakes they made to keep your love.*

As the service ends, Sheila wonders, what was it about my own makeup that made me so blind to your ploys? Why couldn't I see your manipulation for what it was? Would a sister have seen it, and clued me in, or would she have been under the same spell? Oh Mom, what a powerful, awesome thing your love was for me, and for Dan, too. It was the most fabulous, yet dangerous attachment either of us will ever know.

SLOW DANCE

The service concludes and friends come forward to extend condolences. Warmed by the love in the room, Sheila and Dan begin to smile. The first leg of Mom's two-state funeral is over. This is Friday; her Richmond Heights wake is Monday, and the service is Tuesday. They have the weekend to relax before facing the finale.

Saturday morning is filled with calls to her mother's relatives and neighbors to convey the sad news. Acceptance, not shock, is the response. "It's for the best. Her suffering is over." Such is the chorus of sentiment Sheila hears as she plods through the calls. Her carrot for completing the chore is going to a Harvest Festival parade with Barb Considine and her girls. So sorely is she missing Allie and Chase, their company will be like a tonic. On a whim, she invites Dan to go along too.

"Sounds like fun, I'll drive," he says agreeably. Sheila stares at her brother, amazed at his sudden enthusiasm. She'd forgotten this go get'em spirit was in his nature. *Has Mom's death lifted something from his shoulders as well?*

They pick up Barb and her kids, and head to town, where they park on the lawn of a church raising money for its mission. Next, they scout Main Street for the perfect parade venue. All agree the curb in front of Byrd's Drug Store is excellent. Dan buys cotton candy for the girls, and teases them about getting it stuck in each other's hair. Sheila's still intrigued by her brother's ebullience. She's even starting to speculate on what a nice couple he and Barb would make, when Ron, Barb's estranged husband, appears from nowhere.

"Sorry I'm late." He kisses Barb on the lips and hugs his daughters. "I had to drop papers off to a client." Barb smiles at him then throws her friend a look that seems to say "I should have told you."

Told me what? Sheila's own eyes fire back. *That you're leaving me to mush through the humiliation and depression by myself?* She stares at Ron, a man she's known and liked for fifteen years, but in this instant, he is not to be trusted. As the parade starts, he sits on the curb next to Barb. His body leans into hers and an arm drapes over her shoulder. *Wait just one minute, Ron, I don't recall you ever being so loving, and Barb, why are you sitting there letting him do that? Have the scales tipped completely in his favor?* In the midst of this surreal scene, Sheila tries to watch the parade, but its homespun charm can't hold her attention. She's afraid for her friend. Twenty minutes pass and when the final float rolls by, the girls ask their dad to take them on some rides. Dan goes too, leaving Sheila to confront Barb with questioning eyes.

"We're dating," Barb explains, "sort of feeling our way. Things are actually pretty good. But I'm paralyzed with indecision. How can I be sure it will be different this time?"

"You can't! Don't you remember the neglect and apathy we talked about?" Barb nods, but her mind seems far away. Sheila tries again. "Last fall, we agreed momentum was the key. Is that it? Has your momentum slowed?"

"It hasn't just slowed — it's come to a halt. We're going to a counselor and Ron is trying to change. He never knew all the things about our relationship that bothered me. He says if he'd known, he would have corrected them sooner. And you know what, Sheila? He's right. I suffered in silence until my list of grudges became so long I felt only divorce could bring relief. Now that I've learned how excruciating it is to dismantle a family, I'm thinking maybe it'd be better to save the marriage."

"I know what you're saying. I feel 'the family' pull at me all the time. It's a sweet, seductive force that can suck you in and before you know it you're right back where you started." The tears in Barb's eyes tell Sheila she's hitting home. "It's awful being away from Allie and Chase, but I know I could never have done what I had to do if I were back there, in the midst of home and family." They stroll, arm in arm, along the sidewalk, two women in similar situations, going in opposite directions. After a while, Dan appears with a message from Ron. "He says he's taking the girls home since it's their night with him, and he wants you to join them for dinner."

"Super," Barb's delight is genuine, "you can drop me off on the way home." Then, as Dan pulls up to Ron's condo, she whispers to Sheila, "Good luck to us both!"

Sheila nods, "If it's what you want, I hope you do get back together."

The next day, she and Dan close up the cottage and drive to Richmond Heights in their respective cars. Sheila feels fortunate to have Wookie's company on the trip. The adorable mutt's fate is still in question. Allie and Chase would love to have her for a pet, their counselor is in favor of it, and Wookie deserves their company after years of service to an invalid. Of course, it all depends on their father.

Thinking about Charles somehow leads her thoughts to Barb and Ron Considine. Barb had seemed so sure their marriage was over. *What happened? Momentum is key, that plus not thinking or feeling too much when inside the family "unit". I knew from early on that it would be impossible to leave Charles and stick around. Even now when I visit Allie and Chase, it's excruciating to be around him or anyone who knew me "when." And the shame! It hurts to know people whom I thought were my friends have judged me without once asking why.*

"That took great courage" is the single-most favorable remark anyone has made on my behalf. And the woman who said that is someone I deeply respect. She'd never do what I did, yet she looked beyond the deed to find some redemption. Ah, but she's an enlightened human being, few others share her depth. The reality is that I will always live with an element of shame about me.

With this last thought, Sheila pulls into her mother's drive. There's the blue spruce her mom planted forty years ago. It was less than three feet tall; now it towers over the house. Around the corner is a trellis of spectacular roses she'd planted before the Parkinson's set in, and over there, a robin is enjoying the birdbath she'd purchased at a garage sale. Sheila braces herself as she opens the door to the warm and cozy kitchen, decorated with her mother's favorite knick-knacks. Wookie runs ahead, tail wagging in anticipation of seeing her mistress. Sheila follows the dog, beating back the impulse to call, "Mom, where are you?" She can't bear to say the words to which a reply will never come. From room to room, she senses a presence. It's not the frail octogenarian of late, but the fun-loving Mommy of decades past. "Mom, I loved you so. Never doubt how much I loved you!"

Chapter 48
Funeral # 2

It's Monday afternoon and despite the sad venue of the funeral home, Sheila's ecstatic at the prospect of seeing her children. When they arrive, she runs outside to sweep them into her arms. Caught in the rapture, she doesn't notice Charles standing by. When he steps forward, she pulls him into the embrace, and for a nanosecond, she wishes they could be the family they once were. *Here it is again: the family!* Allie and Chase snuggle into both parents for a classic sandwich hug. They're now six and eight; Sheila has been gone for a year and a quarter.

"You both look fantastic!" she tells them. Allie is precious in a navy and white sailor dress her mommy found in a Pine Springs thrift shop. And Chase is adorable in his blue sport coat, also a resale treasure. "You look good, too," Sheila lies to their daddy, trying not to stare at the grid of lines etched around his eyes.

The foursome enters the funeral home. Dan says hello, then leaves them to their privacy. "Do you want to see Grandma?" Sheila asks, seeing nothing wrong with her children looking upon their granny one last time. Allie and Chase nod soberly. "Now you know, honey-pies, Grandma's soul has flown to heaven. This is her body, where her spirit lived when she was alive, but she doesn't need it anymore." Their eyes answer hers with, what seems to be the wisdom of the ages. Holding each of their hands, Sheila walks with them toward the coffin. About six feet away, Chase pulls back. "Is she going to sit up and scare me?"

"What?" Sheila gasps.

"You know. Will she sit up like the guy on *Tales from the Crypt*?" Chase's brow is furrowed, his question sincere.

"Sweetheart!" Sheila gasps then kneels to be eye level with her son. "Grandma's not going to move. What you see on *Tales from the Crypt* is all pretend, like Halloween."

Once they've absorbed this welcome information, both kids proceed, more curious than afraid. This is the first corpse they've ever seen. Chase is just about eye level with the body. He inches along its length from head to toe and back again.

Allie's eyes study the face, and move on, but always, they come back to the face. "She looks like Grandma...yep, she's Grandma!" she finally pronounces with certainty.

Sheila remembers thinking the exact same thing when she first saw her mother laid out in the Michigan funeral home. She reaches for the hand she's held so often. It's cold, stiff, and waxy: life has moved on. "Grandma doesn't need this body anymore. She's happy and healthy in heaven."

"Is she an angel?" Allie asks.

"Maybe, and if she is, I'm sure she'll watch over you both, she loved you so!"

Chase, still inspecting every inch of the corpse, asks, "Can she see us now?"

"I'll bet she can, and she's thinking how grown up you look in your sport coat." Chase smiles at the thought. He looks from his grandma's body, toward the ceiling. Sheila's heart melts as she watches her son's speculation.

To be with Allie and Chase is Sheila's own kind of heaven. She could stand here forever, watching them figure out their own versions of death and the hereafter, but other visitors are arriving and she has to do her part. Charles takes the children to a couch by a window where they continue to sneak peaks at their granny.

Miss Worthy bounds up. "Oh, Miss W!" Sheila wails, recalling the birthday luncheon of not so long ago.

"Shhhh — don't let your mother see you so sad. Her spirit is in transition now and if she sees you doing poorly, it will be hard for her to move on." Sheila pulls back to study Miss W's eyes. "Show her you're doing fine. You miss her, but you'll be fine."

They approach the body. "Can you believe less than a month ago, we were celebrating her birthday?"

"I knew then she was preparing to leave."

"Really?" Sheila's asks.

"Of course, you could tell, couldn't you? Well, maybe you didn't want to."

"I do remember how final her goodbyes to you and Eleanor had seemed."

Miss W nods, pulling Sheila to her huge breast as if she's the daughter she never had. Then she spots Allie and Chase. "Oh, would you look at those two!" she exclaims, making a beeline for the children. There's no reason for her to linger by Sheila's mom. She's already said her farewell.

With Miss W on the couch with the kids and Charles, Sheila's free to focus on other people arriving to pay their respects. There are Mom's nurses, and neighbors, an old teacher of Sheila's, her divorce attorney, and Phoebe, a grade school pal who has agreed to take her mother's estate through probate. Many relatives are here and, as usual, everyone bemoans the fact that it takes a funeral to get people together. The most meaningful, albeit uncomfortable, appearance is that of Charles's parents, Sheila's soon to be former in-laws. *These are two of the best people I'll ever know.* She thinks this as she laces the air with awkward conversation.

Later, as she relaxes with Bootsie, her Oregon cousin, Sheila reflects on the Branford's visit. "Think what it took for them to be there, to face the she-devil that caused their son such pain! I don't know how they could look at me."

Bootsie frowns. "Wait a sec, hon, your exit doesn't negate the two decades you spent being a good daughter-in-law and wife. On top of that, they should be deeply appreciative that you are allowing your children to stay with Charles. Certainly they know what a toll it's taking on you."

"I doubt it, and the irony is they're one of the reasons I thought it'd be better for Allie and Chase to start out with Charles. Not only was their presence good for their daddy, they could also be in their own house, go to their own school and have their grandparents nearby."

"That's right, honey, knowing you as I do, it's not hard to see you put Charles and the children first in that decision. I'll wrestle to the ground anyone who says differently."

SLOW DANCE

"Boots, you know that, but few others see it that way. To them, Charles is the good guy and I'm the baddest of the bad."

"Honey, are you aware you're your very own whipping boy? You need to be gentle with yourself, especially in emotional times like this."

Over the decades, her relationship with Bootsie has evolved from one of a little girl's crush on her pretty older cousin to the more equal, peer-like relationship of recent years. Now Bootsie's unconditional love is as soothing as a salve for Sheila's self-inflicted wounds. *Family is everything, and I have so little left!*

The next morning is a bustle of activity as everyone prepares to leave for the funeral. Sheila, Dan, Bootsie, and the children are in good moods. Maybe it's relief that the strain will soon be over. Dan and she have been on this funeral circuit for five days. It's brought them closer than they've been in a long time. Adjusted to their mom's absence and buoyed by their love for each other, they've clicked into a "let's-get-this-done" mode. High spirits accompany them as they head out the door to the limousine that will take them to the funeral home. Sheila does a last check in the hall mirror. Her colorful Key West print dress isn't the least bit funereal, but her mother always liked it. And recalling Miss Worthy's advice about the spirit being in transition, she feels her Mom's spirit would see it as a good sign. With a smile, she beckons toward her mother's favorite chair, "Come on, Mom — if you liked Friday's ceremony, you're going to love today's!"

The chapel is already overflowing with people. *Look, Mom. See how many people have come to show you they care?* Several times during the service, Sheila's eyes threaten to cry, but with five days' practice, she knows how to keep them under control. Later, a feeling of closure sets in when she greets the relatives who have returned to her mom's house for coffee and cake. From this point on, she'll write her own story, and she'll own one hundred percent of her mistakes. First, she needs to write her way out of this one. She looks at Charles from across the room. He's over there, nicely mixing with her relatives as he's always done. Despite all the hateful things they've said to each other over the past year and a half, she still cares deeply for him. *He's the father of my children. He's been family for almost two decades.*

The family! How she misses it: that living breathing, laughing, loving, entity she's torn apart. Deep down in her soul, she longs for it. For a year and a half, she's mourned its demise. *I miss it far more than I'll ever miss my mother. That's how much I yearn for the animal that was my family!* But returning won't reconstruct it. Her piece of the puzzle has changed its shape and texture and it no longer fits. It would be disastrous to even try to be the woman she was before. Sheila, herself, is in a transition of sorts, and it's taking her far from the life she once knew. This evolution will be happier once her children are with her. But there's no way she'll be allowed to have them in her current state of limbo, so, although she hurts terribly for Charles, she must continue to murder their marriage.

The afternoon moves on as relatives and friends drop by. They want to linger in the comfortable surroundings they'll never see again. Sheila spends time with Lillian, the widow of one of her cousins. The tall, graceful woman represents a part of the family her mother had manipulated to the hilt. *She's good to be here after all the years of Mom arranging things behind her back.* Such thoughts and feelings inspire Sheila to invite Lillian and her daughters to each choose one of her mother's fine porcelain figurines to take home and enjoy. Annette also deserves one, and of course, Bootsie, and the nurses. Soon her mom's cherished figurines have found new homes. What began as a spontaneous expression of gratitude to those who had known her mother has become a way for the best part of Mom's spirit to live on.

As five days of funeral pageantry draw to a close, Sheila and Dan turn their focus on getting the house ready to sell. When they have accomplished all they can, Sheila loads her old Seville with as many girlhood memories as it can hold. The only available space is reserved for Allie, Chase, and the homeless Wookie. Instead of spending time in Water Haven, as had been the original plan, they will drive straight to Florida for two glorious weeks.

Chapter 49
Driving South

Sheila feels free — dauntless even — all because Allie and Chase are with her. She's in her most complete state when they're together, and they, too, are thrilled to be on a road trip with Mommy. They talk and laugh their way from Wisconsin to Indiana, breaking up the tedium with a picnic at a rest stop and two pullovers to play and exercise with Wookie. At dusk, they check into a Holiday Inn just over the Kentucky border. It's the perfect backdrop for the slumber party that ensues. Sheila, Allie, Chase, and Wookie pile into the king-size bed to watch TV. The terrier is ecstatic; she has never in her doggie life had so much attention. For this, she repays her charges by staying awake all night to protect them. Every sound, she's certain, deserves a ferocious retort. Unlike Allie and Chase (who sleep too deeply to be awakened), Sheila endures an almost sleepless night. Around 5:00 AM, she decides she might as well make things ready for an early start. At the first hint of dawn, she carries her sleeping children to the car. "Do you want me to wake you if there's a pretty sunrise?"

"O.K.," Chase says woozily.

"Uh-huh..." Allie yawns.

Sheila frowns at Wookie, the reason for this early exit, now sound asleep on the passenger seat. But her sleepless night is, indeed, rewarded with an amazing sunrise. "Hey, you sweet things!" she sings, "Here comes the sun!"

Groggy eyes fix on the horizon. " It's on fire!" Allie proclaims.

Melissa McDaniel

"It's one big glow! I can't look at it!" adds Chase. As the glow levitates above the horizon, neon clouds splinter the light, casting shards of gold across the land.

The little girl and boy watch in amazed, almost reverent, silence. Finally, Allie says, "That was good, Mommy, thank you!"

"Yeah, that was awesome!" Chase observes.

"You don't have to thank me, punkie-pies; that was God's work. Maybe you could say a prayer to Him." The car gets quiet, and Sheila knows that's exactly what they're doing. By now, both children are wide awake, and intrigued by the foreign-looking landscape.

"What was that?" Chase asks startled by a loud bang that sounded like a shot from Earl's .22.

"Probably a backfire," Sheila answers.

"A what?" Allie asks.

"It's when a car has a poofer." Sheila chuckles at her description.

"Cars have poofers?" Both kids think this is hilarious.

"Sure," she starts to explain, but suddenly there's a loud hissing sound, and the rear right wheel seems, almost, to fall off; next, is the kalump, kalump, kalump of a blown tire. She flicks on the warning lights and the old Seville limps to the right shoulder of the highway. Struggling to sound calm, "We're fine; it's just a flat tire."

Oh, my God! The spare tire and jack are buried under layers of Mom's stuff. How can I empty that trunk on the side of the highway? "O.K. kids, we'll get out of the car and climb up that hill over there. Chase, will you please put the leash on Wookie?" Eyes wide with fear, he obeys. "Now, open the door and scurry up the hill." Allie and Chase run as if their lives depend on it. Wookie scampers along, thrilled with the chase. Next, Sheila moves the books, tapes, and coffee thermos blocking her exit from the right. As she scoots across the seat, she starts to pray. *Please Lord, be with us now; make this turn out all right.* Freak accidents and serial killings flash in her brain. *Well, Ms. Superwoman, you've done it now — putting your children in such danger. How could you?* Sheila grabs a blanket and a box of Wheat Thins from the back seat and runs up the hill.

"Here! We'll sit on this like we're having a picnic!" Chase and Allie sit down immediately. Frightened, they check Mommy for cues on how to behave; she looks worried. Only Wookie is relaxed and happy as she stretches out on the cool grass for maximum tummy satisfaction. Sheila kneels on the blanket, one arm around Chase, the other around Allie. Behind them is a barbed-wire fence, and well beyond it, is a herd of black and white cows. Their pasture stretches forever in all directions. In front of Sheila and her children is a racetrack of thundering cars and trucks. With her best fake smile, she says, "We'll be safe here until a nice person stops to help us." *Nice person? Feeling like someone's potential prey, she flashes on the horrors that have beset occupants of stranded cars. Now is when I need a cell phone! So do I have one? Of course not! I decided I wouldn't use it enough to make it pay. Well, it would pay plenty now, Ms. Thrifty-pants!*

Allie and Chase sense trouble. Their mommy is tense and angry-looking. Chase, especially, feels his mother's fear and is on the verge of tears. A good ten minutes have passed and not a single truck or car has noticed their plight.

"I'll bet they think we pulled over to have a picnic!" With this revelation, Sheila jumps up, and with huge gestures, starts to pantomime to every passing truck that it should use its radio to call for help. Soon, she's created a string of movements that take on a dance-like quality. When she explains to Allie and Chase what she's doing, they join in with their own renditions. *What a sight we are! Oh, please, Lord, let this strange ballet work!*

Still, cars and trucks charge past the threesome as if they're invisible. *Come on, all you truckers, you were always so polite to me at truck stops when I'd drive back and forth to see Mom and the kids. Won't you please help me now? Wild and reckless! Wild and reckless! That's how Charles describes me. This proves how right he is! I think I'm such a wonder woman, there's nothing I can't do. Well, here's a news flash, wonder woman I'm not. I'm stranded in the hills of Kentucky with my six, and eight-year-old, and not a soul is stopping to help. But if someone does stop, we'll be forced to depend on the kindness of a stranger and that can be even more dangerous!*

With this, the turn signal of a shiny black eighteen-wheeler signals it's pulling off the highway. It lumbers to a halt far beyond Sheila's crippled Seville. She stands frozen, gazing at the rig. *His intentions are good. I've always been treated well by truckers.* She looks from one child to the other. The trusting little things are ready to put all their faith in the trucker. "Mommy, hurry," Allie prompts, starting to run. "Don't let him leave!"

Sheila catches her daughter's jacket and pulls her back. "No, you both stay on the blanket."

"I want to go!" Chase begs.

"No, I need you to stay with Wookie."

"Please!" Huge tears are forming fast.

Sheila waves to the truck, then runs to the car to get a box of Milk Bones. "Here!" she tosses it up to Chase, who forgets all fear as he tells the terrier to sit.

"We'll take turns. First, she does a trick for you, then for me." Allie says, taking charge.

"Thanks, kids, I'll be right back." Sheila runs full speed to the truck. The door on the right side opens slowly as she approaches. To look inside, she must stand on her tiptoes. *This thing is huge!* "Thank you, sir, for stopping! I have a flat and my jack is buried under tons of stuff." The man is sitting on what looks like a leather throne. He's young, well-groomed, and adorable, one of the best-looking men she's seen in a long time, maybe ever. She stops talking and just looks. Gorgeous brown eyes, so light they look yellow, a perfect nose and dimpled smile all seem to accentuate her next thought. *Whoever thinks truckers aren't good looking has got to see this.*

A slow, Georgia drawl seeps into her consciousness, "Yes'm, I reckon y'all could use some help."

"I sure could!" Sheila starts again, "I can't get my jack out without unloading half of my life on the side of the road!"

The yellow eyes seem to chuckle at the image. "Want me to call a state trooper?"

"Great idea!" With this, the trucker extends his hand to help her climb into the cab to use a phone mounted on the floor. To do so, would take Sheila out of sight of her kids. She'd also be at the mercy of this incredibly good-looking, well-groomed hunk of a truck driver.

He waits as she stands, paralyzed by her dilemma. *Will I offend him if I say I don't want to get in the cab? He looks like a gentleman. It's probably fine.* But she knows what must be done.

"Would you please make the call? I, uh, don't want to be out of the sight of my children." Complete understanding flashes in the awesome eyes. He dials the Kentucky State Troopers, and she waves assurance to Allie and Chase.

"Help will be here right quick; they'll get a tow truck and take y'all to a service station."

"Oh, thank you!" Sheila gushes from her place below the cab. She'd like to reward her hero. Would money offend him? How about an antique from her trunk, or Wookie, the homeless dog?

"Sir, you've done your good deed for the month, the year even! How can I repay you?"

The trucker's smile is fetching. "Just seeing y'all are safe is my reward."

"We will be, thanks to you. I'll never forget you."

The eyes flicker warmly, "Thank y' ma'am." The cab door swings shut, and Sheila watches the rig ease forward until there's an opportunity to pull onto the highway. She gives it one last wave, then pivots, and does a joyful victory leap for her children to see. Allie and Chase, familiar with their mom's non-verbal antics, jump up and down in celebration. Back with her little ones, she's telling them about the state trooper when an old beater pulls up. A pretty black lady with yellow hair leans across the passenger's seat. "Anything I can do?"

"A state trooper is on the way." Sheila approaches the car to speak directly to the lady. "But thank you for stopping."

"I stopped 'cuz last week I had car trouble and not a soul would help."

"That's awful!"

"Not a soul!" the woman repeats.

"That's terrible, I'm really sorry." Sheila wants to apologize for motorists everywhere. "You're better than all of them! God bless you."

A smile replaces the woman's frown. She tootle-loos and pulls back on the highway. *Man, that's a lesson to remember. I've got to pay more attention to stranded motorists, female ones anyway!*

Throughout all this, Allie and Chase have stayed on the blanket. Wookie sprawls between them, stuffed with Milk Bones. With glorious relief, Sheila explains, "Not only have we survived a blow out on a Kentucky highway, we're also going to ride in a police car!" The sparkle returns to their eyes as Allie and Chase cheer their mommy for making everything better.

As if on cue, an impressive squad car pulls up. A tall, fit state trooper emerges to stride over to Sheila and her children. "Morning, ma'am, I'm Trooper Moffit." He tips the brim of a Smokey the Bear hat and removes the sunglasses that have been hiding the kindest eyes she's ever seen.

"Officer, we're sure glad to see you! I'm Sheila Branford and this is Chase and Allie."

"Hey!" he bends down to their level, "You two O.K.?"

"Mmmm-huh," they nod, completely in awe of the uniform.

"I'll call a tow truck to take your car to a repair station. You and the kiddies can ride with me." Trooper Moffit strides back to his car. Leaning against the door, he says something into the radio receiver, then looks up to see Sheila and the children staring at him. "Everything's going to be fine!" he smiles. As he lopes back to Sheila, she sees him focus, for an instant, on her left hand.

Self-conscious in her seemingly unmarried state, she sputters, "You must have more pressing things to do than taking care of flat tires."

"Ma'am, a lady with a big car an' two itty bitties by the side of the road's an invitation to trouble. All kinds of things can happen. My job's to make sure nothing does." His smile is long and luxurious. Sheila inhales deeply and looks away. This man reminds her of Earl. Both men possess a power that's enhanced by their size and good looks. Their smiles and the way they talk just naturally draw people to them.

Men like this are dangerous; women fall for them too easily. Or does one lucky woman get all of this man? I hope so; I really, really hope so. But the trooper's steamy aura makes her think otherwise.

"Will Wookie ride in the police car, too?" Allie inquires.

The trooper shakes his head no. "She'll ride like a queen in yours."

Sheila wonders what's regal about being dragged at a forty-five degree angle. But when the mother ship of all tow trucks pulls up, she understands. It has a hydraulic lift that raises the entire car off the ground. Wookie will be more than fine.

"Here you go, Wook!" Happily, the terrier jumps in expecting her little charges to follow. Instead the door slams, and in a few minutes, up goes the Seville. Wookie's eyes never leave the children.

"Look how cute!" Allie shouts.

"She loves it!" Chase chimes in.

Sheila isn't so sure, but she doesn't let on. Trooper Moffit leads the threesome to his car. He opens the right rear door. "Allie? Chase?" His eyes meet hers. Sheila smiles nervously and gets in.

"Mommy sits in the middle!" Even in a squad car there must be equity.

"So, y'all going back to Florida after a trip?" the trooper asks.

"My mother died and we're bringing some of her things back from Wisconsin."

"Condolences," he mutters, then, "You kids ready to start school?" "No!" is Allie's scornful reply. "I don't want vacation to end."

"I want to stay with Mommy!" Chase whines.

To Sheila's relief, the trooper doesn't pursue her son's peculiar response. Instead, he commiserates with the little boy. "I know what you mean, sonny. When I was your age, they had to pry me from my mama; she was something special, like yours. But you know what? School turned out to be cool. I got to see my friends and play games at recess. I ended up liking it just fine." His voice is deep, authoritative, and ever-so warm. Chase sits transfixed, considering every word the God-like officer is saying. Slowly, he nods his head.

Dangerous hormones course through Sheila as she sees her son relating so well to this male role model. *This is a classic case of a mother desiring a protective, nurturing male for her offspring. These days, I react positively to any male who treats my children well!* As they pull into the service station, Sheila prompts her little ones to thank Trooper Moffit for the ride. Next, she extends her hand, thanking him only with a darting glance to his eyes. When he offers to help unload her trunk, she is too uncomfortable to accept. "You really must go; we've monopolized you long enough."

"That'd be true if I were working, but I'm off duty now and Sally's the best cook around." He points to a sign, *Sally's World's Best Omelets*. "You and the kids hungry?"

Oh cruel fate! Of course, we're starving. It's midmorning, we haven't eaten anything but crackers and we love omelets! With a 'don't-hate-me' look, she declines, "Thanks, but we better not. Besides, I should stay here by all this stuff."

The trooper gives her a knowing smile. "I was going to suggest I'd put your order in so the food will be ready when you're done."

Melissa McDaniel

Feeling stupid, Sheila thanks him and requests three bacon-and-cheese omelets.

Allie and Chase, she notices, are racing around with Wookie. The adrenaline that surged through them by the side of the road now has them soaring in the joy of feeling safe. Twenty minutes pass and the state trooper emerges with a toothpick in his mouth. He does a double take at the assortment of things surrounding Sheila's car. Boxes, lamps, framed photographs, scrapbooks, and an old radio guard the car.

"I know," Sheila chuckles. "It looks like a flea market!"

The trooper laughs. "Food's ready." He tips his hat, gives her one last luxurious smile, and leaves.

Soon, the Seville sports a new tire, and the jack is, again, buried under Sheila's treasures. Wookie gets tied to a shade tree and all three can go inside for the world's best omelets. Feeling festive, Sheila tells the kids to choose a souvenir from the diner's makeshift gift shop. Allie picks a black plastic change purse with Kentucky painted across it. Chase finds a pseudo Swiss army knife, also bearing the state's name. Then, to personally commemorate her adventure, Sheila purchases a cookbook of old Kentucky recipes. Soon they're off, happy campers once again, as the rest of the journey unfolds without a hitch.

Chapter 50
Wookie

Fourteen days of feeling like a mom! How Sheila's looked forward to this time with Allie and Chase! Earl's welcome, too, is warm and wonderful. Sympathy for Sheila's loss is one reason. The other is the death of Mattie, the chocolate lab who'd been his love and confidant for thirteen years. Mattie had nurtured Earl's son from puberty to adulthood, and she'd done much the same for the father. Then, too suddenly, it was over. Not until the very end, did Earl know his beloved dog was full of cancer. When the vet asked if he wanted them to cremate her, Earl had refused. He'd retrieved his girl from the vet and placed her in a heavy cardboard carton. Eighty-some pounds of dead weight in a carton had been nearly impossible to carry but he'd managed to transport the makeshift coffin to a piece of property he and Sheila had recently purchased. There, he'd prepared a proper resting place for his girl.

"She's there now," he'd told Sheila over the phone, "in the woods she loved." From twelve hundred miles away, she'd sensed the soul within the man. Now, with Sheila and the children home, Earl and Dakota are less lonely. Wookie helps, too. A Labrador she's not, but Dakota loves her spunky terrier ways and feminine smells. Earl's heart she'd won eight months earlier when he'd met Sheila's mom.

He's sorry about Dora Ronson's death, but in a bizarre way he's isn't really. Long ago, that woman maneuvered Sheila into a decision that, fifteen years later, led her into his arms. Now he has Sheila, and she's finally free of her mother. (Funny, how things work out.) Now, if only she can escape whatever haunts her nights! Whether it's the ache of missing her kids or the frustration of having lost so much of her identity, he doesn't know. All he can do is put faith in Dr. Time, the healer of all things. With time, she'll conquer her demons. In the meanwhile, he's here for her. He wants always to be here for her. That's why he wants to marry her. And seeing her with her children makes him realize, too, how easily they could become a family.

Too quickly, however, the time has passed, and in one swift jolt, Sheila and the children are back in the Seville, heading north. As they near Milwaukee, she glances at Wookie, asleep in the back seat. Her head rests on Allie's lap while Chase uses her haunches as a pillow. The dog is adorable in her buzz cut. Her new look is Sheila's attempt to make the pooch more desirable to Charles. Earl and Dakota loved having her in their home but Wookie should be with Allie and Chase. They need her. And Wookie deserves the joy of a life with children. As the companion to an invalid for six years, she'd provided her mistress with affection, comic relief, and noisy protection. Now all that loyalty will be rewarded with a home on Lake Michigan. Wookie, an avid swimmer, will love the beach. Sheila smiles as she pictures the kids and their new dog splashing in the water. Yes, Wookie belongs with them, and when they come to Florida, she will too.

Charles has consented to the terrier entering his home, although, while they were in Florida, he'd called to suggest that Sheila could pay some of Wookie's expenses. Sheila had laughed, thinking he was joking.

"No, I mean it," he'd persisted, "if we go out of town and need to board her. Would you help with that?"

"Noooooooo," Sheila had drawn out the word to savor the lunacy of the request. "I'm not going to pay puppy support." *If I ever question why I left this man, all I need do is revisit this conversation!*

"We're talking about a dog your son and daughter adore, one the counselor says they should have," she'd responded. "It's not for me you're taking her, it's for them!"

"All right!" he'd interrupted in a 'don't-start-with-me' tone. "Bring it back."

All three of her passengers are asleep when she pulls into the driveway of the house she no longer calls home. Sheila parks the car and looks over the seat to survey the sleepy scene. *They're so little! Why, oh why, is it taking so long for Charles to see they should be with me?* Deep within, the grief is building again, threatening to bury her as it does every time she and the children must part.

She reaches back to stroke the platinum locks of her six-year-old son. Loving his mother's touch, Chase grabs her hand and holds it to his cheek. Sheila starts to whisper, "we're home." But it's not true, and she can't bring herself to say, "you're home" because she hates that it's a place without her. Allie moans, and looks at her mother. Seeing the pain in her little girl's eyes, Sheila knows she's thinking that soon she'll be without her Mommy. Every time this happens, another layer of self-loathing encrusts itself on Sheila. This whole business of leaving Charles has taken on a life of its own. Here she is, entrusting her children to live the very life she was so desperate to leave. She'd thought she'd been fair to Charles in not disappearing with the children. But was it fair to them? It certainly wasn't to her.

The familiar click of the front door opening stops her thoughts. Charles steps onto the porch. "Hi, guys!"

"Daddy!" Chase runs into his father's arms. Allie, still woozy, also approaches her daddy. The three exchange loving hugs and kisses. *They really do love him; maybe it's best they're with him for the time being. They have this fabulous house on this awesome lake, they go to a great school, and they have their friends and grandparents nearby. How can I give them this kind of stability with my own situation so unresolved?*

During these thoughts, Charles's eyes have met hers. The days of trying to win her back are over. He now regards his estranged wife with an angry "don't-mess-with-me-and-my-kids" defiance. "Your attorney called," he says with a voice as cold as his eyes. "She wants a conference call to go over some revisions to the agreement."

"Great, let's call her right now." Sheila's trying to sound upbeat.

"The sooner the better," he scowls.

To lighten the mood, she offers him the leash. "Look! Wookie had a makeover just for you!"

Charles doesn't take the leash and without even a glance at the pooch, he steers Allie and Chase toward the house. "Put her in the back."

"Sure thing!" Not wanting to incite Charles further, Sheila trots Wookie around to the backyard. "Look girl, this is your new home,

Melissa McDaniel

complete with a view of Lake Michigan!" She makes sure both gates are closed then enters the house through a glass-enclosed porch. Charles hands her the kitchen remote. "You stay here; I'll take the call in the study."

He's talking to a stranger; maybe it's for the best. She goes inside to find Allie and Chase, searching for snacks in the kitchen.

"Want anything, Mommy?" Allie asks.

"No thanks, honey-pie, I'll be on the porch, doing a business call." Sheila sits down at the wrought iron and glass table she's always loved. With the stack of dog-eared papers in front of her, she takes a moment to gaze out at the lake. It's a postcard-perfect view, framed by the feathery green of mammoth willows. Water is the thing she misses most in land-locked Pine Springs. *They may have ocean to the east and gulf to the west, but Pine Springs is wet only in its swimming pools and golf course hazards. And the wind! This wonderful lake breeze doesn't exist down there.* Pushing that thought away, Sheila presses the talk button on the receiver. The phone rings. The attorney answers and, after a few seconds of pleasantries, the three are focusing on the revisions. Line by tedious line, they inch their way down one page and then another. Sheila's considering a particular point when her peripheral vision sees something streak by the window. *What? Oh no!* It's Wookie in hot pursuit of a chipmunk. Fortunately, the little fellow escapes down his hole. Undaunted, the terrier starts to dig after it. Power driven paws spin dirt in a 180-degree arc. Frozen, Sheila watches the huntress thrust her nose into the hole, then dig some more. *Wookie!* Her brain screams, as her ears hear her attorney's voice saying what? She doesn't know. *Stop, Wook! Don't blow your chances here!*

Sheila breaks into the droning, "Excuse me, I'll be back in a sec." Pressing the mute button, she runs to the kitchen. "You guys, can you keep Wookie from digging for chipmunks?"

The kids look up from their snacks. Wookie? Chipmunks? What's Mommy saying? "You mean like Chip and Dale?" Chase asks.

"Yes! Go!" she points out the window. The kids scream with laughter as they see the crazy pooch excavate another hole. The only thing that moves as fast as her paws is her wagging tail when she stops to sniff. When they call her, she looks up long enough to reveal a muzzle encrusted with mud; then she resumes her search. *This couldn't be worse!*

Charles, impatient with the delay, might soon appear, so Sheila tries to get back into the call. But her mind's outside with the huntress. She watches Chase distract Wookie with the remainder of his potato chips. Then Allie has the good sense to put her on a leash. It takes the strength of both children to pull the terrier away from her last hole. Barking, she strains toward it, out of her doggie mind by the unfulfilled hunt. Before the conference call is concluded, she's able to toss a towel to the kids. Gleeful laughter accompanies their attempts to clean the frustrated pooch.

Charles appears. He throws a hostile look at Sheila and heads for the kitchen. She follows, searching her brain for the best way to tell him his new ward has just dug up the yard. "Wookie got a little dirty going after a chipmunk. But that won't be a recurring problem. Once they figure out she's in residence, they'll pack up and leave!" Sheila chuckles as she imagines Chip and Dale packing their bags. "I'll make sure she's clean before I go." She says this, looking at the white carpet she, herself, had selected. *Whatever was I thinking?* "In fact, I'll do it right now," she tells Charles, eager to be outside with the kids. They pull the hose onto the lawn to give the filthy dog a wash down. All the while, Sheila lectures, "Don't blow this, Wook. Allie and Chase love you, and as you can see, this place is doggie heaven." The mutt grunts back, not in agreement, but with disgust at being restrained.

"Better put her on a leash when you take her outside." she whispers to Allie. The precious eight-year-old, so wise for her years, gives Sheila a knowing nod.

Back inside, Charles's frosty demeanor tells Sheila she's not welcome to stick around. How can I blame him? I'd be the same way. Besides, this good-bye needn't be too sad. I'll see them lots over the next few days as I prepare Mom's house to be sold. And see them she does. Every chance she can, she takes them to her mother's where they have a marvelous time sorting through Sheila's history. When school starts, she takes them on the first day to assure their teachers that, although she lives far away, she will do everything she can to be with her children in spirit.

Chapter 51
Divorce

It's early October and Sheila is in Earl's backyard taking a break from the red tape of her mother's death. *What I love about this place is it's far enough North to make the change of seasons apparent, yet so southern the winters seem like Indian summer back home. Home, there's that word again. Thoughts of it keep taunting me. Mom's absence makes the North seem less like home and more like hostile territory. When her house is sold, it will be even more so. No, home's not there, but neither is it here. I love this place, the people, the natural beauty, the weather, even the cost of living is friendlier, but I have no roots. Here, I'm T. Earl's live-in, his squeeze. And no place can be home without Allie and Chase.*

Dakota crawls out from under Earl's boat trailer. He wags a hello and proceeds to scout the yard. It's a ritual he and Mattie had shared. They'd track the perimeter of the fence, stopping often, to share the thrill of an exciting scent. Now, Dakota does this solo, without the joy of sharing his finds with his beloved Mattie. It's sad to see him without his surrogate mother.

How badly do you miss her? How much do Allie and Chase miss me? The obvious answer makes tears swell in her eyes. Oh Lord, how is this all going to turn out? Day by day, it's almost bearable, but over the long haul, I'm not sure I'll make it. And what is it doing to Allie and Chase?

Such thoughts will bury you. Stop them before —.

Oh, shut up! The last thing she needs is a pep talk from that pushy inner voice! She swipes a red Confederate Rose blossom from its bush. Next, she grabs a pink, and then a white, all from the same plant. Every single bloom moves through each shade. Admiring the tricolor splendor calms her enough to let the voice, within, surface again.

I only meant you should keep moving forward. Momentum is everything. Make it your goal to be single by Thanksgiving, maybe then you'll be closer to getting the kids. Sheila does see the sense of adopting such a goal, and in November, she finally achieves it.

It's November 19, and she's on the phone with her lawyer who is about to appear in court with Charles and his attorney. "It's so sad! I feel like I'm murdering a living, breathing thing!" Knowing how emotional Sheila can be, she'd long ago ordered her client to stay in Pine Springs on this date. "Can I talk to Charles?" she asks.

Her attorney gasps, "I don't think that's wise! We're going in now, wish us luck."

"Luck to us!" Struggling to be positive, Sheila clicks off. She's achy all over and her breathing is faint with skittish anticipation. An execution is underway. A marriage is about to die. She tries to busy herself with paperwork but that gives way to pacing, first around the living room, and then around the yard. Outside, she fills the sky with prayer. "Lord, be with Charles; assure him everything will be all right. And please don't let him hate me too much." How quickly the last couple of months have gone, yet how painfully tedious the day-by-day negotiations have seemed! Now it's almost over; a phone call will soon proclaim her a single woman.

Wow! Who'd have thought Sheila Branford would do something like this? Am I really that over-achieving, goodie good who never did anything wrong from kindergarten through graduate school and a couple decades there after?

The phone rings. "Congratulations," her attorney says, "you are officially divorced, or at least you will be when you sign the papers I'm expressing to you."

Sheila is in no mood to cheer, "Did it go O.K."?

"Everything went fine. But then, you weren't asking for anything more than your fair share, not even that. You're one of the most conciliatory clients I've ever had."

"You think?" Sheila asks, dismissing the comment.

"All right then." The attorney's ready to put this baby to bed. "When you get the decree, sign it, return the original to me, and keep your copy in a safe place. Good luck, Sheila!"

They click off. A courtroom, twelve hundred miles away, has just made her a single woman. Her marriage is over. There's relief, yes, but the overwhelming feeling is sadness.

"Dakota! Come here, fella!" Kneeling down to receive the lab's eager kisses, she starts to cry, "Dakota-dog, I just did the one thing I never dreamed I'd do. I murdered my marriage!"

Smelling tears on his mistress's face is nothing new. When this happens, he knows she needs him. With loving concern, Dakota nuzzles her with every part of his being. He licks the tears from her cheeks and leans his torso against her so Sheila can hug back. When her tears flow harder, he licks faster, he is the dogification of unconditional love.

The phone rings, and Sheila answers it, hoping it's not Charles accusing her of murder. "Hey, blossom!" Earl's baritone greeting is soothing, but a choked "hi" is all she can manage.

"What's wrong?"

"My divorce is final. I know I should be happy, but it's hard right now."

Remembering what was to happen this afternoon transforms Earl's voice into a sympathetic coo. "Sweet Pea, I'm so sorry, of course you're hurtin'. You poor thing, you've been through so much. Would you rather not go to Alvira's tonight? We could stay home, put steaks on the grill."

"No." Sheila's adamant. "I need to surround myself with people." By people, Sheila means the Stitch and Bitches. In the seventeen months since her arrival, Sheila has bonded with these women so completely that she needs to be with them now. As she's done on most Wednesdays for the past year and a half, she dries her tears, drags herself into a hot shower, and proceeds with the ritual of attempting to look as terrific as she can. Then she goes to see her buds, hoping their good humor will coax the sadness from her heart.

She arrives at Alvira's Medicine Shoppe to find the Bitches at their usual table. After the initial greetings, she announces the next round of drinks is on her. "Tonight, I celebrate my freedom. My divorce became final today!"

The gals know Sheila's been struggling to end what seemed to be a marriage that wouldn't die, but they also understand she's putting up a good front. All but one of them has been divorced and they know it's not truly a cause for celebration.

"The celebration comes later," commiserates Starling, a petite bombshell with an infectious personality.

"It takes time, but soon you'll feel 100 percent better," confides Genevieve, another knockout.

Ramona, her friend with the Christmas tree farm, adds, "In a way, it's empowering."

"And soon, you'll experience an almost euphoric relief. It happens to me every time I get divorced!" That's Wanda; she's been to and from the altar three times.

Sheila sees truth in their remarks. She also knows her own tendency to over-sentimentalize just about everything. *In no time,* she tells herself, *I'll be that go-for-the-gusto gal I once was.*

Earl is sweet and attentive the entire evening. After sharing a quiet meal at a family-owned Tex-Mex café, they go home and to bed. Sheila initiates their lovemaking, hoping it will fill the emptiness inside. It does not.

Chapter 52
Plans

For too long, Sheila has been mired in the muck of death and divorce. It's time to make plans, and plans require decisions, such as, does she really want to stay with Earl? Of course she does, but if she continues to live with him, they must be married or Charles will never allow Allie and Chase to be with her.

Earl says he's looking forward to marriage. *So why, after all I've gone through to be with him, am I afraid?*

Why? Have you forgotten the hours of worry you spent last year wondering if Earl's love was cooling? Remember how he went into his old married couple routine and you about died from benign neglect? Beyond that, aren't you just a little threatened by all the gals who find him so adorable? Satin's waiting in the wings, and what about Carlene? Then there's the small issue of protecting your money. Does he love you, or the security you offer? Think of the marriages that go tilt when the guy starts acting like his wife is a ball and chain. And if the marriage does collapse, he'll be entitled to half of your holdings because you'd never ask for a pre-nup. Think how happy that'd make Carlene!

Sheila takes everything the voice says under advisement, and, after a week of excruciating soul searching, she concludes life with Earl is still too good to miss. The calendar provides the framework for her next big step. At Christmas, if he wants, Earl can give her an engagement ring. That's how they'll introduce the kids to the idea of their getting married. When they visit in February, they'll be included in some of the preparations, and finally, in March, she and

Earl will be married in a tiny ceremony. It will be during the kids' spring vacation, so there will be no honeymoon. Instead, they'll all settle in together, like a real family.

"Let's do it," Earl says, delighted with the plan.

Outwardly, Sheila seems happy about the impending marriage, yet inside, she's a mess, and deep down, she knows why. The voice's concerns were legitimate. Added to this is the fact that she has become extremely independent. The past two years have been a huge learning curve as she's assumed all of the financial and bureaucratic responsibilities that once had been done by Charles. She doesn't want or need a man to perform such tasks. So, why would she risk allying herself with or worse yet, subjugating herself to any man in the name of marriage? The turmoil this question inspires is apparent in her wedding plans.

"It's an anti-wedding," she explains to the Bitches. "I don't want it to look anything like a traditional wedding. It'll be a tiny ceremony with a huge party."

"So, who's going to marry you?" Wanda asks as she sips a Cosmopolitan.

"Earl, I hope!"

"No, darlin,' I mean who'll perform this anti-wedding?"

"I've thought about that. My first time around, I did everything on the up and up with a minister, church, the works. This time, I want Sean Murphy to marry us."

"You mean just anyone can perform a wedding?" Genevieve asks.

"No, Murph's an attorney, so he'll act as a justice of the peace," Sheila explains.

"Wouldn't it be more fun to drive up to his house in the middle of the night and have him marry ya'll right there, like in the movies?" Genevieve loves drama.

"For God's sake, Gen!" Ramona cuts in, "This isn't a shotgun wedding. They're not escaping pissed-off parents."

"Actually, I did consider eloping like that once, but I was too young and too scared of losing my mother's love. That's how I ended up down here." Sheila pauses, she's never told that to anyone. The Stitch and Bitches are opening channels she'd thought she'd always keep sealed. "Anyway, Murph will be our J.P. and I've told him to say whatever comes into his mind."

"That renegade?" Ramona laughs. "I'm getting real close so I can hear every word. Are you going to be *given* away?"

"Originally, Mullet was a candidate to hand me over. The way he and Earl bicker like an old married couple, I figured everyone would get a kick out of the changing of the guard."

"That's perfect! Mullet'll love it!" Starling, Mullet's gal pal, heartily approves.

"Really, though, it's important for no one to give me away. I've worked too hard taking myself back to let that happen. I've decided the ceremony will begin with us standing side by side."

"Baby, are you sure you know what you're doing?" As a three-time divorcee, Wanda is genuinely concerned.

The question jolts Sheila to absolute frankness. "Yes, Wanda, I am. I love Earl beyond belief. Besides, if I don't marry him, I'll never get my kids!"

With this, the women grow quiet. All they really know about this Yankee is she appeared from nowhere, so deeply in love with Earl they'd all been a little envious. It seems she's given up everything to be with him in this town, a place each of them at one time or another has dreamed of escaping. Over the months, they've seen her scratching out an identity, but still they don't know who she is, not really. Always on the surface, she seems to glow with happiness, but underneath, something's raging in major proportions. Will the "anti-marriage" created by this "anti-wedding" call a truce between what she once was and who she is now? On the side they're making bets the marriage will be rocky. It's too crazy. And look at the guy she's marrying: one of the roughest riders in Pine Springs! Sheila doesn't know her friends are betting against the success of her marriage. She only sees their support and loves them for it. It will be good to have them at the private ceremony preceding the celebration party.

Chapter 53
The Anti-Wedding

For Sheila, the weeks leading up to her wedding are every bit as surreal as the ones that preceded her departure from Wisconsin. With trancelike detachment, she defies tradition in every preparation she makes. Her wedding ring is purchased at Pine Springs Pawn and Gun. Her anti-wedding dress is a real find at Colette's Designer Resale, and the Junior League Thrift Store provides darling outfits for the kids. The private ceremony will take place on a small balcony overlooking the Pine Springs Golf Course, and even the invitations are worded so obscurely, few people realize the T.G.W.M. ("Thank God We're Married") bash is really a wedding reception. Wanda and Genevieve add to the confusion by telling everyone T.G.W.M. stands for "two good white males," and they have first dibs.

This isn't the behavior of someone looking forward to marriage, but it's the best I can do. The less I invest both financially and emotionally, the less disappointed I'll be if things go tilt.

Few people from her past know she's about to remarry. Allie and Chase, Dan, his ex-wife, Annette, and Samantha are the only ones coming from Wisconsin. In her fragile state, she couldn't bear to have others there who would remind her of what she had to do to get to this point in her life. *Besides,* she thinks as she ticks off the RSVPs to her wedding bash, *from the river folk to the Bitches, and on to Earl's friends at the college, these people constitute my here and now.*

Suddenly, the anti-wedding is only twenty-four hours away. Earl's brother, Johnny B., has driven down from Georgia in his shiny new truck, and Allie, Chase, and Samantha arrive on the same plane just in time for a "bubba-que" with Mullet and Earl.

Sheila's eager for Sam to meet Mullet. She's certain her intellectual friend will find him fascinating. Big mistake! Within seconds after his arrival, Mullet and Earl are into it. Bizarre yarns and tall tales pour forth, and as the vodka flows, both their language and their taste in stories grow raunchier. Too late, Sheila realizes she should have expected this. For some unknown reason, she'd assumed they'd tone it down for her refined pal; instead, they're going overboard. By the time the two Billy-Bobs have exhausted their repertoire of tasteless jokes and anecdotes, Samantha's patience looks to be tapped out. A tale of how someone evaded combat in Viet Nam is what really does her in. Out of deference to her friend, Sam hides her disgust, but Sheila knows it's there. Sick about the turn the night has taken, she wants it over and Mullet gone. To communicate this, she launches an abrupt, almost hostile clean up. A little startled, the raconteurs get the message. As the party breaks up, Samantha is out the door and on the way to her motel.

Why was this such a surprise? I knew these guys were loose cannons. How could I not foresee this happening? Of course, they felt they had to live up to their legends, especially with Johnny B. here!

Allie and Chase come in from playing at the neighbors. Pooped from their flight and hours of hide and seek, they're ready for bed. Johnny B., also exhausted, retires early. Earl is in the bedroom, getting undressed. Too many drinks and too much food have taken their tolls, and sleep is seconds away. From the doorway, Sheila says, "I have to wait up for Dan and Annette."

"Sweet pea, I know you're mad 'bout somethin'," he slurs before collapsing onto the waterbed.

"Yeah, but I'll cool down, so let's forget it."

"Nah, we better talk, I did something wrong, dint' I?"

The concern in his voice softens Sheila. "Earl, there's so much good about you, why did you have to show your nasty underbelly?" He rises up in shock, but she continues. "I wanted Samantha to know the man I fell in love with, not someone out of *Deliverance*!"

"Oh, spare me your Yankee snobbery!"

SLOW DANCE

"You know I'm no snob. And you can't tell me the way you acted tonight is the real you, because it's not. It's some fictional character you parade out to show off for folks."

Earl considers what she's said and decides Sheila has the advantage. First off, she's still pretty sober, and then there's all that adrenaline she gets when she's really pissed. "Look, blossom, I'm drunk and dog-tired. There's no way I can turn this around. You're probably right; we did have too much fun. But darlin'," he pleads in mock desperation, "please don't leave me at the altar!" If his words are meant to lighten the moment, they succeed. Sheila laughs and hugs her strange conglomeration of manhood, but she steps back before he can give her a kiss.

"Things will be better in the morning," she says, striding to the door. When Earl doesn't respond, she turns to see he's already sound asleep. She has to get outside, under the stars that steered her to this point. With nature surrounding her, she addresses the mass of tiny suns. "This is so not the side of Earl I needed to see tonight!" she screams in a stage whisper.

You're overreacting, the stars seem to respond in unison, *and yes, you should have seen this coming. Getting Mullet together with Earl and Johnny B. set the stage for back porch humor. To that, you added too much booze, et voila! You got what you deserved, so stop whining this instant.*

Sheila does stop, and as usual, she turns next, to God. *Lord, I'm certain you kept me from hitting the wall up North, and you gave me the strength to do things I never thought I could. Help me now; I feel marrying Earl is the right thing, but if it isn't, stop me before I make another mistake!*

Sleepy now, she continues to pray on the couch in the living room. A while later Dakota rouses her with his fierce watchdog bark. "Anyone awake?" Dan and Annette are tapping at the window. Seeing them together makes Sheila marvel that some divorces can actually be amicable.

"We missed a turn and have been lost for hours," Annette groans.

"Yep, we've seen most of north Florida," Dan adds.

"Hey guys, where've you been?" Earl's sleepy warmth precedes him. He kisses Annette, and taking Dan's hand in both of his, gives it a good shake. Then, in genuine spontaneity, he gives Sheila's brother a huge bear hug.

Here's the real Earl. This is the guy I love! At peace now, she eases to his side, and lets him put his arm around her. Earl, sensing reconciliation, squeezes her tightly. It's late, so Dan and Annette leave to find the villa they've rented. Earl returns to his waterbed and Sheila to the one she shares with Allie and Chase. Drifting to sleep, she's certain her prayer was answered.

The next day, Earl is the man Sheila had originally wanted Sam to know. The perfect tour guide, he squires their guests through the scenery of north central Florida. They visit the historic town of Micanopy and tour the Marjorie Kinnan Rawlings home at Cross Creek. The highlight of their outing is a walk in the pine-filled woods where Sheila and Earl's new home will soon be constructed. The groom is the perfect Southern gentleman all day. His good manners make last night's performance seem like a bad dream. This relaxes Sheila and the anxiety of what she's about to do gradually releases itself. As the sightseeing concludes, they return home with just enough time to get ready for the kick off of their life together.

Their preparations completed, mother and daughter appraise their reflections in the bathroom mirror. "Allie, you look like a princess in that dress!" The little girl's second-hand blue and pink print dress is a hit, so are the white lace socks she chose, herself, at the local Publix, and the pretty patent leather shoes, they'd found at Kids Wee Cycle. Allie beams, at the mirror, unaware of her mother's pains to keep all costs of this anti-wedding to a minimum.

"And Mommy, you look like a queen!" Sheila does a positive appraisal of her own, previously worn dress with an elegant lace jacket setting off a low cut chiffon sheath.

Bending to be eye level with her daughter, she asks, "Sweetheart, do you have anything else you want to talk about before we leave?" She thinks they've covered the waterfront about her remarriage, but she has to be sure neither child has any concerns.

As her brother had responded earlier, Allie says, "Nope!" and smiles her pixie grin.

Chase bursts into the bathroom, "Mommy, I don't want to wear a tie!" Sheila regards the son she's put through hell over the past two years. He's perfect in khaki pants and a powder blue shirt.

"You know what, buddy?"

"What?" he asks; bracing for a lecture.

"You look awesome just like that."

"All right, Mom!"

Sheila draws both children to her in a sandwich hug before their grand entrance into the living room where Johnny B., Earl's football buddy, Odum Dysart, and the groom, himself, applaud their entrance. Earl moves toward them. Placing huge hands on her shoulders, he gazes, no, he climbs into her eyes.

"You're so much more than I deserve," he whispers.

"You've got that right," she kids, then stepping back to appraise her groom, "My! You do clean up well! I guess I will marry you." Earl laughs as they go out the door, but he knows he skated by a close one the night before.

They arrive at the club in time to see Mullet and the Stitch and Bitches pulling up in a white Rolls Royce limousine. Each of the Bitches steps from the Rolls like a movie star at a premiere. Mullet, the last to appear, is regal in top hat and tails. In one hand is a container of Grey Poupon, and in the other, is a Mason jar of vodka. All the way across town they'd had the limo driver pull next to unsuspecting cars. "Pardon me," he'd say, holding up the jar, "would you care for some Grey Poupon?" The hilarity of the scene replayed itself from intersection to intersection. That, plus several glasses of fine champagne, has rendered the Bitches positively glowing with good spirits.

Inside the club, their laughter continues. All are regaled with Mullet's antics, and Sheila, fully in the moment, realizes this is exactly how she'd planned it. Earl's son, Ryan, strides into the room completing the perfection of the moment. On one arm is his beautiful wife, Chloe, and, in the other is their precious baby, Gillian. Sheila, Allie, and Chase rush to welcome the extended family they dearly love. Dan and Annette arrive, as do Alana and Jack Randolph, and Cass and George Church. Everyone's here, so they're herded onto the balcony where Sheila, Earl and Murph will stand with nature as their backdrop. Pulling Allie and Chase to her side, Sheila gives each a squeeze, and smiles up at Ryan, Earl's best man. At Ryan's side is Chloe, with the baby in her arms. Next is Janice, Murph's wife, and completing Sheila's circle of love are Johnny B, Samantha, Mullet, Odum, and the Bitches.

"Let's do it!" Earl proclaims, taking Sheila's hands in his.

Murph begins the ceremony with an invitation for everyone to join Sheila and Earl in the spirit of their love. Ryan, his family, and

Melissa McDaniel

Allie and Chase are brought into the loop as he weaves the importance of family into their parents' union.

Then, it's their turn. Sheila hasn't written and memorized the vows. For this marriage, she wants heart-felt spontaneity, so much so she hasn't allowed herself to ponder what she's about to say, not even once. Earl faces his bride, and begins, "Sheila, I've loved you since the first time I saw you. You're everything I've ever wanted in a woman, a friend, and a wife. I want to spend the rest of my life with you and no one else. I promise to love you with all my heart. Every day, in every way, I'll do my best to make you happy so we can we grow old together in the bond of our love."

Wow! Sheila thinks in the instant before it's her turn. *He put thought into that. My anti-wedding mood has rendered me totally unprepared.* She gazes into the teal eyes that started it all, and begins, "Earl, I, too, loved you from early on." *I tried not to but you entered my soul and I couldn't get you out.* "Like you, I knew we were meant to be together." *I fought it, but it was meant to be.* "And I wake every day in wonderment, realizing what it is to truly love a man. I will try, always, to bring joy to your life, and I'll be loyal to you until the day I die." *I'm no Carlene!* Then, to take it out on a lighter note, she winks, "And I promise to never beat you at golf!" Their vows exchanged, Murph pronounces them husband and wife, they kiss, and friends and relatives close in with hugs and good wishes.

Odum, Mullet, and the Bitches come up. "That wasn't legal, was it?" Odum asks, "Nah, you can't just marry yourselves, can you?"

"Wanna bet?" Earl displays the marriage license.

"I'll be," Mullet examines the license, "a do-it-yourself wedding. Maybe I'll try that someday!"

"Not totally do it yourself — we couldn't do it without Murph!" Sheila pulls Murph and Earl to her in a group hug.

"We did it!" All three are amazed at how simple it'd been. "If more weddings were like this, I might quit law and go into the business," quips Murph.

"You'd have to start charging money instead of booze," laughs Janice as she hands him his favorite drink.

Area Code, Sheila's favorite local band, plays "The Power of Love." It's a song she and Earl relate to almost as much as Bonnie Raitt's "Let's Give Them Something to Talk About." "That one you can play later," she'd told the band. The newly married couple moves onto the dance floor, and Earl pulls Sheila close. Nuzzled into him, she thinks about the road she's traveled to get to this point. *Three years ago, I was teetering on the edge of God knows what, and now I'm here, married to my split-apart.*

"How are you, really? Things O.K. with us, blossom?" Earl asks.

"I'm fine, and we're great!" Sheila responds with certainty.

More guests have arrived, so as the song concludes, they pry themselves apart to mingle. Enjoying the party are Wyatt and Katelyn McKee and their children. Katelyn is the friend who'd learned of Sheila's plight that Thanksgiving two and a half years earlier. Since then, her unconditional support has seen Sheila through plenty of hard times, and her thoughtfulness just keeps on flowing. She's even invited Allie and Chase for a sleepover after the reception. *That Katelyn is something! She instinctively knows that spending tonight with her kids will ease the strain of my absence.* An hour into the party, the McKees announce they'll be going because they have pizza and a movie waiting at home. Before they leave, Sheila pulls Allie and Chase close. "You two have fun now. Earl and I will see you tomorrow, O.K.?" Allie hugs her then runs happily back to the McKee kids. Chase lingers, and looking strained, he pulls his mother down to his level.

"Mommy," he says biting his lip, "don't make a baby tonight."

"Oh, my love!" Sheila exclaims, scooping him into her arms. "That will never happen. You will always be my only little boy, and I love you with all my heart!"

"O.K.!" Chase plants a big kiss on Sheila's cheek and runs to catch up with the others.

"How stupid of me!" Sheila whispers to no one. "In my perimenopausal state, it never occurred to me such a topic should be covered. Poor Chase!" To distract her thoughts, she goes to refresh her drink.

Leaning against the bar, she surveys the room with satisfaction. *This is as much a party for them as it is for me.* There's Sam and Dan, listening to the Pine Springs College football coach talk about their winning season. Alana, her first friend in Florida, is talking to Janice, her second, and Annette is on the dance floor with Ronnie Stokes, Sheila's Fourth of July river buddy. *Ronnie seems to have met his match; her moves flow into his and back again. Sexy people*

Melissa McDaniel

do have a way of finding each other! Speaking of sexy, Sheila thinks as she focuses her attention on the Bitches. Having found few single men worth dancing with, they've started their own circle. Striking in appearance, and fiercely independent, they are the finely chiseled products of their experiences. Just by watching them dance, it's clear these women enjoy music, laughter, and sex. And they certainly have no hang-ups about dancing with their sisters. Sheila runs onto the dance floor to join in. "Proud Mary" is pulsing out a beat that's unlocking all inhibition. Sheila notices Samantha standing nearby. "Sam, come join us!" Out she comes, and the circle opens to welcome her. *Rollin', rollin', rollin' down the river.* As they dance, they're careful not to knock over a Tom Collins glass someone (for who knows what reason) has left on the dance floor. All the moving and scooting around the object gives Starling an idea. She picks up the glass, strokes it suggestively, and sets it in the middle of the dance floor. Arms waving, she approaches the cylinder. With back arched, she moves seductively around it as the other bitches hoot and holler. One by one, each performs for the glass. Genevieve, ever graceful, moves sensually around it. Wanda shimmies, and Ramona does her famous 360-degree hip gyrations directly over the glass.

"Your turn Sam!" Sheila pushes her Yankee bud into the center. Sam, always the good sport, performs an impressive Charleston to everyone's cheers.

Now it's the bride's turn. Sheila moves into the middle of the circle, letting long repressed bumps and grinds find her hips. Eyes closed, she rotates her pelvis to throbbing drums as she anticipates the great sex she'll soon be having.

"You go, girl!" Ramona prompts. "Run with those wolves, darlin'! Just keep it coming!" The music ends and the Bitches share a group hug, reveling in the chemistry that binds them together.

It's time for the band to take a break so the sisterhood wanders toward the hors d'oeuvres table. On the way, Sam intercepts her friend. "Sheila, I just had a revelation! It's that I didn't know the real Sheila up North. She was nice and talented but that woman was restrained. It was as if there was something always holding her down. Now this gal," Sam's arms wave up and down to indicate the all of Sheila, "This anti-bride is a different creature entirely. There's much more that defines her. Don't ask me what it is, but it's larger than life." Sam steps back, again assessing the woman in front of her. "I think, down here, you're much more yourself than you ever were up North."

"You've nailed it, Sam!" Sheila confirms. "This is the 'me' I was born to be. The 'me' who was crafted by the wishes of others has finally died a slow and horrible death."

Sam's about to add something when they hear a fracas at a distant table. It's Earl, Mullet, Odom, and Jack going at each other.

"Are they angry or just fooling around?" Sam asks.

"They're not angry," Sheila informs her Yankee friend. "But I do predict a 'major drunk-front is about to move through this room.' That's the term Mullet uses to describe what happens after 'the imbibin' o' too much likka." Sheila laughs, wondering how many drinks her new hubby has had. *Not to worry,* she tells herself, *he's celebrating.* She flashes on the time Pine Springs College won a football championship. She'd watched her honey down several vodkas to mark the occasion. Earl seldom drinks like that, when he does, it is an observance of something significant. Unfortunately, it's a celebration that renders him shit-faced. *Oh well, I guess I should be happy he sees marriage to me as being equal to a championship!* From across the room, Sheila can see that the celebration has been complete. Fortunately, the evening is coming to a close.

As the valets jockey cars around, an extremely intoxicated Earl finds his way to Sheila's side. When his car arrives, she immediately climbs in the driver's seat. Getting the message, her groom obediently staggers to the passenger's side, opens the door, and falls into the passenger seat.

"Hey!" he says, eyes half-shut.

"What?" she snaps.

"I love you!"

"You'd better!" She puts the car in drive and eases past the guests who are joyfully cheering the newlyweds.

Chapter 54
Wedding Night

It's a quiet thirty-second ride to the golf course villa Earl rented for their wedding night. Sheila parks the car and is opening the door when her groom breaks the silence. "Darlin', there's something I've got to tell you."

This is it, my greatest fear! Now that we're married, he'll blindside me with something awful.

"Uhhhh," he drawls slowly, "you know when I dropped off our bags before we went to the club?"

"Yes?" *Why is he dragging this out?*

"It became apparent to me, I hadn't specified what kind of bed we wanted." Noting Sheila's 'get-on-with-it' scowl, Earl nervously continues. "Yeah...well, we have twin beds."

"You mean our 'bridal suite' is a room with two single beds?" Sheila laughs at the absurdity.

Earl also chuckles, too drunk to realize his bride is pissed. "Pretty bizarre, huh?"

"More than bizarre, it's surreal. Can we go in now?" she asks testily, but then, remembering a gift she left at the club, she says, "Wait, I have to go back for something. You go inside and get comfortable."

All the way to the club and back, she lectures herself. *This is your wedding night, hopefully your last wedding night. Don't ruin it getting pissy over the small stuff.*

Outside their room, her lecture continues; *keep this positive, with any luck all that vodka has made him wild with passion.* With a "come hither" twinkle in her eye, Sheila swirls through the open door. She has fantasized about this night, even bought the lace topped, thigh high stockings Starling said would be so sexy. She's looking good, feeling great, and ready for love. She's ready, and her groom is passed out.

There — taking up every inch of his single bed — is her new husband. He'd gotten down to his boxers and Ducks Unlimited T-shirt when the drunk-front moved in. She closes and locks the door, then turns to survey the situation. *He has no clue I'm here.* "Hark, what blob is this?" she shouts to prove her point. "Earl, my love, would you help me with my zipper? What? You can't find it? Well, maybe if you were conscious, darlin'!" She unzips her dress as minutes before she'd envisioned he would do. It falls to the floor, and she looks down at it, certain its first owner had better luck. Next she removes her Wonder Bra, the lace-topped thigh-highs, and silk thong panties. *What a waste!* On goes a white satin chemise, a gift from Genevieve at the lingerie shower the Bitches had thrown for her. *What would they say now? They'd wage odds on the future of this marriage, that's what! But they can't see me, and I'll never tell!*

There's no room on Earl's bed, so Sheila kneels beside it. "Hey stud!" she yells to penetrate his unconsciousness.

"Mmmmmmm?"

"Come on, big boy, I give you permission to ravage my body."

"Huh? Oh! Darlin', I love you sooo mush," he slurs before returning to oblivion.

Resigned to a sexless night, Sheila turns off the light and crawls under the sheets of her respective bed. With Earl's drunken roars as background music, she assesses the state of things on this night of nights. *It's not like I haven't had enough sex. I'm just disappointed, maybe even a little humiliated that I put such stock in our wedding night being special.*

Earl is suddenly quiet; he has stopped breathing. Sheila waits. One, two, three of her own breaths later, she leans across the space between their beds and slaps his arm. He takes a huge gulp of air. The following swats get harder as Earl's sleep apnea sets in. *So, where was I? Right: I'm bummed, and justifiably so. The blimp across the aisle has gotten so drunk we can't even consummate our marriage. And I'm lying here wide-awake, keeping swat-watch over a man whose body forgets to breathe. Oh Earl, how could you!*

She stews in the dark for at least an hour. Whenever the danger in Earl's halted breathing gets to her, she takes another swipe at her beloved. Finally, the monotony makes her drowsy, but before she can fall asleep, the snoring stops completely. The body on the other bed jerks and heaves itself up. The hulk lumbers to the bathroom, flicks on the light, and shuts the door. The toilet lid goes up, then, silence. Minutes pass; five, ten, when twenty-some minutes have elapsed Sheila rises to check on her groom. "Earl, are you all right in there?" No response. Slowly, she opens the door. The great T. Earl is sitting on the commode, sound asleep. His big, handsome head tilts to one side as the mouth she usually loves to kiss, purses open and shut in silent, tiny o's.

Feeling malicious, she wishes for a camera. "O.K. Earl, time to get back to bed. Come on babe, wake up. Let's go!"

"Mmmm'ah dead yet?"

"No, stud, you're on your honeymoon; now get back to bed!"

With Sheila steering, the newlyweds shuffle to Earl's bed. As he collapses onto the mattress, he warns Sheila to beware of the dandelions.

"What?"

"Dandelions, attack dandelions!"

Oh God! Now he's hallucinating, how much did the boy have to drink? This opens the floodgates on Sheila's adrenaline. Knowing sleep's out of reach, she lets herself free fall into the boiling cauldron of her brain. First, her thoughts channel to the corsage that had been delivered that afternoon, at the same time as a gardenia plant from Laura Tolafson. What a romantic thing for Earl to do, she'd thought as she'd opened the box. But it wasn't from Earl. She should've known!

"For the bride of my dreams, remember me when...All my love forever, Val." *Quick, get rid of the card,* she'd thought. But ripping it up and burying it in the garbage wasn't enough. The corsage had to go too. Wouldn't Earl think it curious for someone else to send her a corsage? Could she say Laura had sent it with the plant? But no, she could never wear Val's orchid as she was marrying Earl, no matter how lovely it would look on her dress.

How did he know an orchid would be perfect? He probably just ordered the most expensive corsage FTD had. Examining it, she'd thought how exquisite it would be just to hold it during the ceremony. *But that's exactly what Val wants; I'd be holding it and thinking of him. No! It's a trap.* Closing her eyes, she'd ripped apart the corsage, throwing all but the ribbon, tape, and wire into the garbage disposal. It was awful destroying such beauty. But what hurt more was the momentary joy and subsequent disappointment she'd experienced when she thought the corsage was from Earl. Sheila regards her heaving mound of drunken husband on the other bed. *There's the rub: Val knows how I crave romance and he's counting on this juxtaposition with my less-than-romantic groom to work in his favor.* She'd debated the merits of telling Earl about Val and the corsage. Maybe that would put an end to Val's pursuits, but no, he'd love a confrontation.

Sheila hadn't even bothered to wonder how Val knew she was getting married. He could have talked to Sam or Laura, and by now, she's pretty certain he tracks her credit card trail. At times, she even thinks he has her tailed. His card had said to "remember him when." *Remember him when I spend my wedding night awake and alone? O.K., Val, your corsage may have won on the short term. But for the long term . . . well, that remains to be seen.*

Chuck-Will's-Widow, the funny bird that's been shouting its name all night is quieting down as dawn gets underway. Soon, bright, cheerful sunlight streaks across the floor of the honeymoon villa. In contrast, Sheila — having spent her wedding night wide awake — feels cloudy and dull.

Earl pops up in his classic good mood. His perception of the night they'd spent on twin beds couldn't be more different. Sheila wonders if he even knows they didn't make love. What he does know is he had a terrible dream. He regales his bride with a story of being attacked by monster dandelions. *There's that dandelion thing again!* She makes her way to the bathroom. Cold water to splash on her face is the first order of business. *This will help,* she tells the mirror, then, focusing on the wallpaper framing her face, she knows in an instant. Yellow and gold tassels, like the ones she seen on expensive Hermes scarves, dance on a white background. *Behold Earl's dandelions!*

Nothing more is said about the peculiar wedding night. Earl goes off to play golf with the guys. Allie and Chase come home. Dan and Annette leave for the airport. Johnny B. drives off in his truck, and Sheila, Sam, Chloe, and the kids go to brunch. The rest of the weekend rolls out pleasantly. Since they've been together for two years, the newlyweds are more like an old married couple. Sheila questions if, from Earl's perspective, there's any difference, at all.

The answer comes when he arrives home from work Monday evening. The kids are in the backyard playing with Dakota, and Sheila's in the kitchen putting the finishing touches on a shrimp salad.

"Hey love!" she calls over her shoulder as her spouse enters the kitchen. Not hearing his usual "Hello darlin'!" Sheila turns to see what's up.

The teal eyes speak before he does. *This is my wife,* they seem to say. *This really* is *my wife!* His expression is softer, more loving than Sheila has ever seen.

"Darlin', I'm the luckiest man on earth." The reverence in his eyes, his voice, and his touch speak volumes.

"This is what I need," Sheila whispers, "the assurance that this marriage is important to you."

"Important to me?" Earl draws back in disbelief. "Only in the sense that my devotion to you runs deeper than anything I've ever known. I've never, in my entire life, felt so whole. This marriage isn't just *important;* it's the greatest commitment I'll ever make. It fills me with a purpose I've been seeking all my life."

Where has all this beautiful rhetoric been? Without knowing it, Earl has dissolved two years' worth of insecurity. Trusting now, in the strength of his commitment, Sheila's ready to embrace her new role as the wife of T. Earl Langley.

Chapter 55
Sevie

It's three weeks since the wedding and although she's truly happy with Earl, Sheila has started to pray incessantly for Charles to decide it's time for the children to be with her. Without them, the upcoming construction of their new home seems pointless. *How wickedly ironic, after all the harrying years of being everything to everyone, I finally have the time to devote to my children, but I don't have them!*

For the umpteenth time, she considers filling the void through some meaningful volunteer activity. *Dare I try again?* She remembers her woeful sobs while rocking an "at-risk" newborn in a local hospital. Even the nurses had been embarrassed! And when she'd volunteered to tutor at an elementary school, she'd be working with a child, when suddenly, her eyes would fill with tears, scaring the little boy or girl.

I'm just not the type to be without my kids. It doesn't matter that my grief is self-inflicted; it's as real to me as if they had been ripped from my world. It has changed me. No longer am I the positive "go-for-the-gusto" gal I once was.

The voice agrees. *Yes, you have changed. But even if you were to get your kids tomorrow, the ache of what you've done will be with you. You might as well accept that and forge a peaceful coexistence between your pain and the here and now. And for God's sake, put some joy into your life!*

"Put some joy into my life?" Sheila's pondering this when Dakota appears from nowhere. "Hey big fella how much do you miss your Mattie? Does she flit in and out of your doggie mind making you ache for her as I do for Allie and Chase?" The Labrador's licks seem to agree. "I miss her too, and God knows; so does your master. Maybe what we all need is the joy of a new little addition to this family. That's it, Dakota! For Earl's birthday, we'll surprise him with a puppy, a lab just like you. You'd like that, wouldn't you boy?"

The *Pine Springs Daily Record* has an ad for a breeder with four yellows, three blacks, and two chocolates. A phone call sets it up for her to get an eight-week old puppy on the afternoon of Earl's birthday. *If only Allie and Chase could be in on the surprise! But they won't be back until June. By then, the puppy will be four months old.*

Will you stop with this looking at the dark side? Even in your worst moments up North, you didn't see your glass so empty.

I don't know. This may be more of a band-aid than a cure, and Earl really wants a seven- wood for his B-day.

Oh, please! This will be the best seven- wood he'll ever get!

On Earl's birthday, Sheila follows the breeder's directions to the outskirts of Pine Springs. *Five acres and a doublewide seem to be the American dream around here.* One pine-paneled doublewide heralds a sign, "lab pups 4 sale." Sheila pulls onto a gravel drive where she's greeted by a Labrador frenzy. Two females, with the droopy tits of motherhood, vie for attention, while a male prances around with a huge branch in his mouth.

"Hi, guys! Are you the welcoming committee? Sit!" All three obey.

"Hey!" a woman's voice calls from a far off pen. There, on the dusty ground, sits the breeder, surrounded by puppies. A black is cozy in the curves of her crossed legs; a chocolate and a yellow are snuggled in each arm. The rest stumble around her in a kaleidoscope of puppy hood. The breeder explains that Clyde, their daddy, is the magnificent chocolate at Sheila's side.

"Throw him the stick he laid at your feet, he wants to retrieve it for you. He's one hell of a bird dog!" Sheila hurls the branch and Clyde flies after it, catching it in mid air. In seconds it is returned for an encore. "Molly, the pups' ma, is this old gal. I also have one left from Yella's litter. The ones with ribbons is already spoke for by folks in South Florida. My reputation for pups is statewide. I come out here and hold them to get them use to people. Come on in and see which one you want."

Sheila heaves another stick for the demanding Clyde, then opens the gate and moves in among the precious brood. There are three yellow females who haven't been spoken for. One by one she holds them. Each is adorable; it's going to be a tough decision. The last little female has been sleeping in the shade of a doghouse. As if on cue, her black eyes open. She yawns, and stretches the full length of her tiny, buff body. Still woozy from her nap, the puffball stands and staggers a few steps. Tripping over her own paws, she collapses and seems to be going back to sleep when something captures her attention. She rises again, and with every step, she picks up speed until she pounces mercilessly on a tuft of grass.

"That's the one," Sheila announces. "I like her spirit!" She doesn't know that spirit will instigate thousands of dollars of damage to antique quilts, custom-made drapes, a suede jacket, and a TV remote control. At this moment, all she wants is for the creamy little creature to be in their lives.

Money well spent, she thinks, writing the check that makes the puppy hers. With AKC paperwork in hand, Sheila carries the puffball to the car. Both Mom and Dad are by her side. "Did you come to say good-bye to your baby?" Clyde and Molly sniff their offspring. Molly swipes at the pup with .a gentle lick. Pop, losing interest, drops the branch at Sheila's feet. "Right, Clyde, you have your own priorities. She heaves the stick another time then opens the car door. Molly, with docile attention, watches her offspring disappear into the car. "Don't worry, girl, I'll take good care of her." The branch falls at her feet again, "Clyde, is this an obsessive compulsive thing?" For the last time, she sends it skyward and gets in the car.

As the vehicle begins to roll, the puffball braces itself against a movement it has never before felt. With stoic calm, she looks around, wondering where her puppy pen has gone. Ten minutes into the ride, the tiny creature decides to climb over the steering column and get under foot. "You're full of it, aren't you?" Sheila lifts the pup onto her lap, and as it nestles into the warmth of her legs, the first of a million rushes of love course through her.

As ever, Dakota rushes to greet Sheila as she enters the house. "Hey waggle butt! Here's your new playmate." Dakota winds the air suspiciously; something new has entered his territory. "It's O.K., she's no threat to you. You'll always be alpha dog."

The huge lab is actually quivering as he approaches the pup, now cradled in Sheila's arms. His nose gently investigates every inch of the tiny creature so stiff with terror.

"This isn't fair. Let's go into the yard." On the grass, the puffball relaxes some, and as curiosity sets in, she sniffs back at her new companion. When she decides to pee, the stud in Dakota is ecstatic.

"Ohoh, Birthday boy will be home any minute; we've got to get you ready." Sheila leaves them in the fenced-in yard to arrange for the surprise. *Let's see, make a sign; find a ribbon.* Just in time, all three are ready and waiting in the living room as Earl comes through the door.

"Hey darlin'!" Earl smiles and starts across the room

"Stop! Don't squish your present!"

Earl gasps when he sees the puppy. Although she's stepping on her happy birthday sign, the message is clear.

Sweeping his gift into two big hands, he nuzzles the silky softness. Through shiny, teal eyes, he asks, "Is this my seven wood?"

"Yes, and it's the only seven wood in the world that will love you back."

That night Earl, Dakota, Sheila and their new puppy, Sevie, curl up together for the first time. Sheila remembers how she'd envied Mattie's love-fests with her master. Now, she's delighted to share this man's love with both of their furry children.

Chapter 56
Can It Be?

On a perfect May morning, Sheila is in the backyard repairing the damage an armadillo caused rooting for food the previous night. One of the locals told her that long ago, a derailed circus train released the critter's ancestors into the perfect habitat of north Florida. Now thousands of armadillos happily call it home. *This is the ideal habitat for me too. I love it here. I love the people, the culture and sometimes the lack of it. But what I can't stand is being without Allie and Chase. Now that I'm respectably married, it's time to convince Charles the children should be with me.*

With new conviction, Sheila flies north. For this visit, she's staying with Lillian, the dear cousin-in-law who'd often felt the iron fist in Dora Ronson's velvet glove. One morning at breakfast, Sheila observes that things might have been different if she'd sought Lillian's advice when her mother was manipulating her so.

"I didn't tell a soul what it did to me to break my engagement to Ed. I figured the more I talked about it, the more I'd suffer. And, really, what would have been the point? My Dad was too passive to rally support for me, and my brother would never have encouraged me to go against our mother's will."

"I doubt I would have been helpful back then," Lillian says, "Maybe, I'd have listened, but I'd never have advised you to oppose her. The repercussions against me would have been too costly."

"I understand," Sheila says knowingly, then, in exasperation, "If only Mom hadn't loved me so much!" The anguish in her voice is almost palpable. "Maybe then she could have shared me with Ed!"

"Honey! You don't really believe that, do you? If she really loved you, why did she do everything she could to keep you for herself?"

"I think she didn't realize how much I loved Ed."

"She knew! I distinctly remember her saying how worried she was that Ed was 'the one.' I'm going to let you in on a secret; Dora Ronson was a mean, selfish woman, who always got her way, no matter whom it hurt. She pulled that anti-Catholic thing to get rid of Ed. She wasn't about to let him take her sweet, conciliatory daughter away from her. Sheila, you really must stop trying to legitimize her motives for wrecking your life!" Lillian grows quiet; wondering if she's being too harsh, but it's the victory of revelation she sees when she checks her cousin's eyes.

"You're right! She didn't love me so much as she owned me! I was her property, and until someone else came along, someone whom she could also own, she wasn't going to let me go. Poor Charles was that person!" Angry tears are forming fast.

"I'm sorry, honey, I didn't mean to get you started."

"That's O.K, you're not the first to tell me what a mean thing she did. My own, sweet Allie saw it for what it was. Last December, I drove the kids down to Chicago for a weekend package they were offering at the Palmer House. Both of them were awe struck by the lobby. They sat down, tilted their heads back, and just stared at the beautiful ceiling. Who says children don't appreciate fine art? Anyway, Allie asked how I knew about the hotel and I explained that the father of an old boyfriend had been in the hotel business. Well, you know how inquisitive Allie is! Soon, she'd learned we'd been engaged, and when she asked why we didn't get married, I told her the truth that my mother made me choose between her love and the love of the boy. With crystal clear insight, my nine-year-old declared, 'That was mean of Grandma! Mean! Mean! Mean!'

'Aha!' I thought, 'the emperor's wearing no clothes!'" "I'd denied that fact all my life. I knew Mom could be hard on others but I never thought she'd make me her victim. It has taken the innocent objectivity of a child and, your own insight to drive it home. The truth be known, she put Charles and me on a collision course with fate, not because she loved me too much, but because she loved herself more." Lillian nods; relieved Sheila finally knows the truth.

SLOW DANCE

"Uh oh! I have to go now, Lillian. I have an appointment with Allie and Chase's counselor in fifteen minutes. Please pray for us, pray that she'll say it's time they should be with me!" Sheila hugs her cousin goodbye and runs out the door hopeful of what the encounter will bring.

On the way into the meeting, she recalls Earl telling her, "Blossom, you do what's best for Allie and Chase. It's that simple."

After exchanging pleasantries with the counselor, Sheila makes her case. "Now that I'm married, and things are stable it's in Allie's and Chase's best interests that they live with me, right?"

"Actually Sheila," the counselor begins slowly, "it's not that easy. As I've told you, they're doing unusually well with their father. Your phone calls help tremendously, of course. The children tell me all about your conversations. They're a great source of stability, and I encourage you to continue to call them daily."

"As if anything could make me stop! Talking to them is my lifeblood! I wouldn't dream of stopping. What I've come here to know is how are things going with their father? What kind of job is he really doing?"

The counselor looks surprised, "I don't think Charles would mind my sharing this with you. He describes your allowing him to have the kids as 'a great gift.' He says he never realized how much he loves being with them."

"Is that so?" She manages in a shivering whisper. It feels like ice cold water has just trickled down her back. *Can it be? Are those the words of a passive father turned active? Have the kids provided him such sanctuary?*

The counselor drones on, describing every fun thing Charles does with and for the kids. Sheila sits in misery, half-listening, half-thinking. *Is this the man I left? I knew he'd do well by the kids but I never thought he'd so completely embrace the role. If he's sincere and the children are thriving, what does that mean? Oh please, don't tell me I should concede defeat!*

"I came here, hoping you'd say it's time for Allie and Chase to be with me. Your support would help me make a case that Charles will listen to. Does what you're telling me mean you think Charles deserves to have the kids, if, after all I put him through, he wants them so much?"

"No, I didn't say that. I think your guilt is making that assessment. Look, Sheila, I know what being away from your kids has done to you. Why are you always so conciliatory?"

"Conciliatory?" *That's the same word Lillian used to describe me just this morning.* "That's me! I'm a master conciliator. I was raised to yield to others, no matter what the cost to me. Always, I was to put the feelings of my grandmother, aunt, mother, and everyone else ahead of me. The one and only time I put my own feelings first was when I left my husband. But even then, I was so worried about Charles I left my children with him to ease his pain. Now that's worked out so well, they may never live with me again!"

"When were you first aware of this drive for harmony?"

"I've always had it. I was rewarded for it in school and then in my career. And when I left the kids with Charles, I was certain that, once he'd healed, he'd recognize the sacrifice I'd made. Then he'd reward me, too, by agreeing the kids should be with me."

"Do you see it as sacrificing for the good of others?"

"Look, I was taught that because I was the strongest, healthiest, smartest, prettiest, it was my responsibility to hold back, compromise, give in, do whatever I had to, to put the other person first!"

"Who taught you that?"

"Duh! Do you think it was my mother?"

"Do you feel you're stronger than Charles?"

"I've always thought that."

"Do you believe you helped him by leaving the children with him?"

"I don't just believe it, I know it! Don't you? It gave him a focus, a sense of identity, a crack at sainthood."

"What did it do for you?"

"Ha! Everything it did for Charles, it took away from me! I'm empty. I miss them so much I physically ache." Sheila takes a jagged breath, rubbing her arms and legs. "It's a dull pain that's with me every second of every day. I want them with me! Please, tell me what to do!"

"It's not for me to say what to do in regard to your children. But you're aware, aren't you, that at age thirteen, a child can decide to live with whomever he or she wants?"

"They should be able to do that right now! We all know they want to be with me. Why do we have to wait so long for that to happen?" When the counselor doesn't respond Sheila answers her own question. "What else can I do? Have them witness a long and ugly court battle I wouldn't win anyway? "

The counselor is silent. What she sees is a woman doomed to continue her cycle of conciliation. Finally she speaks, "Well, as I said before, the most important thing is to focus on making Allie and Chase's lives as stable as possible."

"You know I will!" Sheila stands abruptly; she wants to get away from this counselor who is no help at all. In the parking lot, she rests her head on the steering wheel of her rental car and lets the tears flow. *Can it really be I may never again live with my children?*

Later, on her return flight to Pine Springs, she fights even harder to comprehend the grotesque irony confronting her. *What I did for Charles will forever keep me incomplete.* The passive dad has turned active, and he'll do whatever it takes to keep the kids with him. His words, before she left for the airport, made that crystal clear. When she'd confronted him, saying that since she was now married, it would be best for the children to move to Florida, the effect had been the same as pouring gasoline on a brush fire.

"In your dreams, bitch!" Charles had snarled through a disfiguring smirk. "You don't have near the money to pay for the court battle I'd drag you through! Remember, you 'abandoned' your kids." So smug he'd been; he'd almost sung that last sentence.

Sheila had fought back. "Leaving them to be with their father when he needed them most was not abandonment! Sparing them the trauma of abrupt and uncertain change wasn't abandoning them!"

"You left. I didn't. No court will see it any other way!"

"Just think about it, that's all I ask." Sheila had tried retreating to a softer position, but it made no difference.

"Never! You made your bed, now go away!" Charles had slammed the front door in her face as Allie and Chase watched from a nearby window. She'd smiled and blown kisses hoping to alleviate the fear she'd seen in their eyes. Then she ran to the car before they could see her tears.

Recalling the scene makes her pray, *Lord, only you know what all this doing to their precious little souls. What memories of these incidents will impact their lives and affect their decisions? If we do go to court, will the hostility they'd witness follow them through life? No matter what we do, Chase and Allie will suffer.*

Now, as she flies away from them yet again, Sheila feels she's drowning in the almost certain realization that she'll never get her children. *If it's true, will life be worth anything without them? Damn it, God! Why couldn't you have put Earl's soul in Val's body? He's near my kids. He's funny, successful, and, at times, he seems to love me more than Earl does. Things would be so different if the man for whom I was willing to give up everything had been a Yankee!*

Inner Sheila can stand it no longer. *Forget about that! What saved you was getting away. You're closer to the real you in the South than you could ever be up there. Consider, for a moment, how you've changed, how far back to your original self you've traveled. Thoreau would be so proud!*

That's true. The past two years have been like a horrendous trip through the birth canal. A battered stranger has emerged, and although I can't put it on a résumé, there's more to the woman I've become than the work that defined me. There's more too, than the perfect daughter and wife roles, but will I ever be whole without my children?

Well, girlie girl, you'd better figure it out soon because not having them with you is a major threat to your mental health. If you're going to make it without them, you'd better start believing what you've always said, that you're with them every minute through your phone calls, cards, thoughts and prayers.

This internal dialogue helps Sheila pull it together before the plane lands. Earl rushes to meet his wife, wondering if the two weeks in Wisconsin have had a good or bad influence on her psyche. From her smile, he hasn't a clue as to the upset she's had.

Val, on the other hand, knows of her turmoil. Having had her tailed, he knows about the appointment with the counselor, and the subsequent tears as she sat in her car. He even knows Charles slammed the door in her face at their last encounter. These are positives in his book. They're signs she's unhappy, missing her kids, and crushed by the fact that they may never be with her again. In time, she'll come around. So, for now, he'll capitalize on her longing with flowers and gifts that say, "Come home, so Allie, Chase, and I can love you in person."

Chapter 57
Stabilizing

"You know I meant every word." Val's voice is a tender coo coming through the phone.

"I didn't read the note," Sheila responds sharply.

"Where'd you take my posies this time?" he asks, trying not to sound irritated.

"I threw them in the trash." Actually, Sheila plans to take the exquisite long-stemmed yellow roses to an emergency care clinic.

"Did you even look at them?"

"Nope!" she lies. Maybe someday, she'll hurt Val so much he'll stop this nonsense.

"That's all right. I know that no matter what you do with my gifts, the message still gets through."

As aggravating as his attention can be, he's one of only a few people who know the person she once was. It hurts to juxtapose his perception of her with that of the uninformed folks of Pine Springs. To them, she's Earl's trophy. To Val, she's still the passionate career woman and mother. For the past two years, he's hovered unseen, always there if she were to need him. At first he frightened her, in a stalker sort of way, but she has to admit, his ongoing cushion of support has been a comfort. And although she snubs him whenever or wherever he surfaces, he's relentless, "If it means outliving your redneck husband, I'll do it. I'm healthier and in better shape, so I can wait."

What if he does outlive Earl? What will I do then? To Sheila's shock, Val has gotten an annulment, just as he said he would. But even as a single man, he's attractive only as a friend. Earl is an impossible act to follow. If anything were to happen to him, she's pretty sure she'd go it alone.

In late summer, Sheila and her irreplaceable husband embark on the one project everyone says will put their marriage at risk. It's the construction of their dream home on the edge of a dense pine forest just outside Pine Springs. "It's a divorce trap, pure and simple," Wanda warns her at the Wednesday night Stitch and Bitch.

"She's right, you know," Starling concurs. "It starts with the plans, and soon a minefield of decisions looms before you. Everything from what kind of tile, to the size of the toilet seat is fodder for a fight."

"I doubt that'll happen to us," Sheila tells her gal pals, "It's as if this house has been preordained. From a book of two hundred fifty award-winning homes, we each chose ten favorites, then five, then three. The house we're building was on both of our final lists. It's a casual, country-style home. And what I especially like is that it resembles the Florida cracker houses I love so much." Sheila winks at Ramona who was the first to introduce her to the style of home the Florida cowboys (or "crackers") had made their trademark.

This gets a high five from Ramona. "Atta girl! I remember you saying you wanted a house like that, now, if you can just stay married through the process!"

In the early days of construction, things go so well Sheila scoffs at the Bitches' predictions. But one day, she does spot something. The pipes have been laid and a cement slab is poured over the floor of their soon-to-be kitchen. "What's this?" she points to a pipe on the outside wall.

"Well, darlin', we need to talk about that. Remember, the original plans had the sink over by the window and you said you wanted it over here?" he points to an area that will overlook the family room.

"I sure do."

"They missed the change and put it where the plans originally indicated."

"That's not what we wanted!" Sheila's upset. Of all the oversights to be made, this one ranks with the worst. Now the pipes are laid and it looks permanent, as in forever.

"I know," Earl agrees. "So we need to think about what we want to do. One thing to consider is, over here, we'd have a nice window to look out while doing the dishes, also at that other location, all our dirty dishes would be visible to our company if they sit and eat at the counter."

Geeeeez! Inner Sheila screams, *suddenly he's Martha Stewart, worried about aesthetics? No, he's siding with the good old boys who screwed up and now he's trying to get you to accept their mistake.*

"We made the change, right? It was written on the plan with our initials beside it?"

"Yes, but this is a really big change, blossom. They've laid the pipe and poured the floor. Does it make that much difference?"

The risk here is if Sheila stands firm she'll be perceived as a bitch by both the construction workers and her new hubby. What backlash will her insistence cause over the next few months? She looks from the current to the preferred location of the pipe. There's no doubt in her mind she wants the sink overlooking the family room, making her a part of everything, even when she's cooking or doing dishes.

For a second, she's back in the Lake Michigan house she'd found so isolating. Her children are usually in one end while she's far away in the kitchen. No! She won't let that happen again, not even if it means just standing with her back to the family.

Wait, her conciliatory nature argues, what would it hurt to be a good sport? Somebody will get in big trouble if they're made to change it. Sheila's about to concede when a lightning bolt strikes her consciousness, *If decades of conciliation created a life so intolerable I traded it for exile from my children, why ever would I cave in again?*

"No!" Her fierce response startles Earl. "I want the sink right here where we told them to put it, and if it's not changed, somebody's going to have a problem with me!"

"O.K., sweet pea," Earl says with more surprise than irritation. "I'll tell them to move it." Sheila finds it gratifying that her new husband isn't trying to dissuade her further. Although he sympathizes with the workers, he's ready to respect her wishes. Moments like this prove his commitment to her. And she, in turn, is growing more devoted to Earl than she's ever been to any man in her life.

The gestation time for the house of their dreams is four months. One of the workmen putting form to the lines on the blueprints is Rodney Barsham. Barsh, as he likes to be called, is a carpenter par excellence. The only thing he enjoys doing more than his work is talking about it. The intricacy of craftsmanship required by the house's long staircase is a source of great pride. "Darlin', you won't see a finer staircase anywhere around here!"

Sheila disagrees, "No, Barsh, not just around here; how about in all fifty states!" To her, this man is one of a dying breed. The long hours he spends at his craft are indicative of his values. Speeding up this job just to get on to another is not an option.

Getting to know Barsh and Pitch Kincaid, the construction manager, is a real treat for Sheila. She loves it when one or the other regales her with the "whys and what-fors" of their jobs. Either of them could have sauntered out of a Majorie Kinnan Rawlings novel — they're that authentic.

Probably, she's an even greater oddity to them. They must see her as a Yankee with peculiar ways and even stranger tastes. It's a puzzle that she wants natural wood when everyone else insists on the more formal, white molding. And what's with her insistence on huge, single-pane windows, not the latticework ones currently in style? She keeps telling them she wants to feel like the forest is indoors with her. Having fished, hunted, and lived their lives in the woods of north Florida, Barsh and Pitch don't see looking at trees as such a treat. But to this city chic, it's like going to church. Her quirky desire to bring out the natural beauty of everything further intrigues them. When the stone fireplace is masterfully pieced together, one of the stones bears a hole left by whatever critter inhabited it eons ago. Rather than have the hole filled, as is usually the case, Pitch decides to ask for Sheila's preference.

Just as he'd thought, her response is, "Please don't fill it, leave it exactly as it is. Something took a long time to make that hole, and it should stay as it is out of reverence for nature."

When it comes to the mantle over the fireplace, both Barsh and Pitch want to do right by Sheila. They show her a lovely pine mantle they've stained to match her molding. Part of its beauty is it's gracefully cut wooden brackets. They're almost feminine in their curves.

"With this, you won't think you're in a huntin' lodge." Pitch's pride in his thoughtful selection is touching, but what really tickles Sheila is that the hunting lodge feel is *precisely* what she wants.

As well as the construction of their home goes, the landscaping does not. One night, Earl appears with a look that signals trouble. "Blossom, I've got something to tell you." Sheila's brain assaults her with dreaded scenarios. *Earl is sick, he's lost his job, he's running off with Carlene.* With a deer-in-the-headlights look in her eyes, Sheila awaits the inevitable.

Seeing her fear, he assures her, "It's not life-threatening, just sad. You know the woods in our front yard? Well, they got more of trim than we wanted."

"How bad?" She envisions her woods with a buzz cut.

"They left six or seven trees."

Plumbing can be moved, concrete torn up and put down again, but a forest is hard to replace. After her initial gasp, Sheila surprises herself. "That's all right; such things don't need to be a big deal in the grand scheme of things. The kids are healthy and thriving. You and I are well and we love each other, and new trees can be planted with a lot less effort than it took to change my life."

Chapter 58
Carlene

Sheila and Earl move into their dream house in early November. Correction, Sheila and two handsome young bucks are the ones to move the newlyweds. Earl absolutely, positively has to go to work. With plenty of vacation days, and several months advance notice, he's somehow unable to take the time off.

"So, what's up with that?" Sheila had asked at the Wednesday night Stitch and Bitch.

Genevieve, licking the salt from the rim of her margarita glass had observed, "Most men think moving is women's work. Maybe it's a Southern thing."

"It's a lazy thing," Starling had added, "Earl owes you big time!"

Yes, he certainly does, Sheila's never worked so hard at such a lonely job. But moving day actually goes well, thanks to her adorable assistants. Three hours into the move, she's relaxed, enjoying their company, and treating them like buds. After six hours, she's giving them whatever she decides she and Earl no longer need. The junior-sized basketball hoop Allie and Chase have outgrown? "Take it." The old exercise machine she's never once seen Earl use? "It's yours! Here, do you want a bed frame, mattress, and headboard? How about some lawn furniture?" Soon, anything Sheila doesn't feel like moving to the new house resides in the back of the young studs' trailer.

Late in the afternoon, Earl pulls into the drive to see his wife lounging in the yard with two strapping young men. He hopes the empty beer bottles surrounding them tell only the tale of a job well done. Sheila knows her hubby's put off, but she could care less.

"This is our reward for a hard day's work," she announces in a toast to the guys.

Earl seems a little nonplused that his wife is being so casual with these kids, but when he walks into the house and sees everything set up and in its place, he's downright jubilant. He brings out more beers, pops one for himself, and leans against the truck to be regaled with their moving day exploits.

Sheila knows it was jealousy she'd seen flash through his eyes. She also knows he'd taken pains not to let it show. Just as Murph had said so long ago, Earl keeps that emotion to himself. It's as if he sees it as a sign of weakness. The most the great T. Earl reveals is when he makes a show of putting his arm around Sheila when other men are admiring her. It's his display of ownership. Funny, they both still harbor a tendency to get jealous. Is it because they love each other so desperately? Maybe, but Sheila knows hers is also in proportion to all she's given up to be with the guy. His innocent flirtations can drive her wild. And when other women are open about their attraction to him, she's ready to fight. In a way, it's a marvelous feeling. Seldom has she felt so alive, so infused with passion. But it's also a destructive thing that often turns her against Earl, triggering horrendous fights. Her thoughts on jealousy are magnified when she comes face to face with Carlene.

It happens when they're tailgating at the last football game of the season. Sheila notices Earl's face has turned to stone while Murph's sports a shitty little grin. They're looking past her at something or someone. Their gaze leads to a great butt in tight-fitting jeans. Instinctively, she knows this is Carlene, the woman who reamed and cleaned Earl's heart. She watches the temptress ease her way into the group. Some of Earl's friends, the ones she'd tried to seduce while still "loving" Earl, turn their backs. *What makes them so pious? Is it shame, embarrassment, loyalty to Earl, or the presence of their wives?*

O.K., let's get this over with.

"Hi, Carlene! I'm Sheila, Earl's wife," the subtext of which is, you may have broken his heart once, but he's mine now.

To her supreme satisfaction, Sheila sees Carlene's eyes flash with insecurity. *Yes, Carlene I'm a worthy foe, and if your appearance here is to reclaim Earl, it's not going to happen.* The woman's shaken confidence seems to grow as Sheila intentionally moves into her rival's space. Janice, noticing this, comes up to ease the strain. As she listens to Carlene and Janice talking, Sheila wonders how she and Carlene could ever have loved the same man.

Was it the sex that brought us both to Earl? Then she remembers Carlene's unfaithful brand of love. *Earl is too good for you, you tramp! Whoa! I almost said that aloud.* Before her contempt becomes too obvious, she feigns disinterest and excuses herself to join Earl. His arms encircle her waist, pulling her close, telling her she need not worry. But she does worry. The figure in tight-fitting jeans haunts her in the days to come

"So why does that woman threaten me so?" Sheila asks while lunching with Katelyn McKee and Daphne Post. Daphne is Mullet Moss's beautiful on-again, off-again lady friend. They're relationship has recently switched to the "on" mode, and Sheila hopes, this time, it will last.

"She threatens you because you're smart enough to know Carlene should never be trusted. I don't know why T. Earl put up with her for so long. It seemed the worse she treated him, the harder he fell." Katelyn's remarks, intended to soothe Sheila, accomplish the opposite.

"Isn't it sad we try so hard to be good sports when being manipulative and cheap works better?" Daphne sounds like she speaks from experience.

Katelyn agrees, "Carlene had that boy mesmerized. He was always standing at attention, just waiting for her command. And she was always showing up with some little bauble Earl had given her 'just cuz he loved her.'"

"Arrrgh!" Sheila can't stand this. "I don't ever get baubles. For my last birthday, Earl gave me a golf gizmo."

"A what?"

"I got The Greg Norman Secret. It's a wrist thing, supposed to improve my golf swing. One day I saw it advertised on TV and mentioned maybe I'd like it for my birthday. I'd meant, maybe as a side gift, but it was Earl's one and only present for me. That hurt. For weeks, I tried to figure out what that gift was saying."

Katelyn laughs, "Darlin', all it was saying was he wants you to be a better golfer!"

"Right," Daphne interrupts, "he probably thought it was perfect. Mullet's like that, our last breakup happened when I got a tackle box full of rubber worms for Christmas."

"Listen," Katelyn breaks in, seeing the worry in Sheila's eyes, "I've never seen T. Earl so happy. You've made a huge difference in his life. I'll bet he's thrilled not to have to bribe you for your affection."

"Thanks, but I'll always be insecure about that woman, with her deficit of scruples, what's to keep her from coming back for Earl?"

Sheila doesn't like it that her lunch partners have to think long and hard before responding. "She will be back," Katelyn announces with certainty. "She'll surface again, because the great T. Earl is better than anyone her sorry redneck will ever attract."

This doesn't help. How can she hold her ground against an oversexed tramp with a proven track record of "mesmerizing" Earl?

Katelyn sees her worry and rushes in with assurance, "Don't you fret, darlin', if she tries anything, T. Earl will escort her to the door. He wouldn't dare jeopardize what he's got with you."

"That's right," Daphne proclaims, "you're what he's always wanted, he told me so himself. Girl, you've got nothing to worry about!"

Sheila hugs and thanks her buds for their support, but as she leaves the restaurant, she's wondering when and where her nemesis will strike again. And this concern about Carlene is just one more layer on an already existing stack of issues. First, is the fact that when she left Wisconsin she committed career suicide; being twelve hundred miles away from Allie and Chase mandates a job with no restrictions about taking time off. Such a position doesn't exist in hard-working Pine Springs, and her little business representing local artists is flexible, but not at all lucrative.

O.K., her inner voice pops up, *so what's the big deal? You need less down here. While the lion's share of your income goes toward transporting you and the kids back and forth, you can still get by.*

This makes Sheila grind her teeth. *I've always worked. I was built to work!*

Were you really? You've never given anything else a chance. Is Ms. Career Woman afraid of becoming her mother?

Sheila considers this. *Too often these days, I find myself enjoying the things she used to do, like gardening, cooking, and decorating my new home. I remember wondering what my mother did with her time. Now I know...she enjoyed it! So, yes, I am afraid of becoming my mom, and I'm terrified of doing to my kids what she did to me.*

That won't happen: your children are happy and growing more independent each day. There's no way you can smother them from this distance!

What a thing to say! If I had my children here, with me, in this wonderful place, I wouldn't have to live vicariously through them. They'd have their lives and I'd have mine.

My, my, inner Sheila won't let go. *First, there's worry about losing Earl to some bimbo, then there are doubts about your worth without some high-powered job, all of which coexist with your endless self-deprecation about being without your kids. You're not much better off than you were before you swapped Richmond Heights for Pine Springs!*

Sheila sees the truth in the voice's observation; but as to how to make things better, she hasn't a clue. She must keep on keeping on, hoping and praying that, somehow, she'll find a truth in it all, something that will pull her through. It's around this time that something does happen to show Sheila the fallacy of her work-derived identity.

Chapter 59
Tina, Rocky, and Thoreau

Well, hello Tina! It is early morning, and Sheila's on the deck of her new home, reading the *Pine Springs Daily Record*. Dakota and Sevie snuggle at her feet, and a hot cup of coffee is steaming nearby. A photograph of Tina, the tireless volunteer, smiles out at her from the front page. *What's Ms. Dynamo up to now?*

No! Oh no, Tina! Reality crashes in as she reads of the woman's apparent suicide. She flashes on the last time they'd talked. As usual, the frantically busy woman was preparing to travel somewhere in connection with her volunteer work. And, as usual, Sheila had sensed an undercurrent that screamed *all is not well!*

What finally did it? I remember how I used to tell myself to keep up a good front for the sake of everyone else. Did you do that until there was no front left? People never had a clue how unhappy I was and I'm certain most of Pine Springs saw only a dynamic powerhouse in you. The article cites depression as a possible factor in your death. You wore your enthusiasm like a suit of armor. Did you think the fuller your life was, the less depressed you'd be? And did you find that you were so crammed full of obligation there was no time for yourself? Did you allow detail to fritter your life away? And then, did your superwoman bravado keep people from seeing your dilemma?

Her peripheral vision sees something move across the forest floor. In an instant, she's restraining Dakota and Sevie so her "pet" Black Racer snake can dart out of range. That done she returns to her friend's photo. *Tina, you paid such a price; I hope you've found what you needed. Is your serene smile telling me not to despair in the simplification of my life? Are you and Thoreau looking down on me right now, wondering if I'll ever get it?*

Sheila envisions her hero shaking his head. "You're the lucky one," he's saying, "you awakened to the dawn within and saved yourself. And Tina? Well, Tina's at peace, her quiet desperation is no more."

The memorial service is held in a school gymnasium. Several hundred mourners, many of whom saw something but did nothing fill the seats and line the walls. *Willy Loman would be impressed,* Sheila speculates, as she listens to the mayor praising Tina's eagerness to serve. "She gave and gave and gave," he says. *Until she gave out! And everyone took and took until Tina had nothing left.* Sheila, losing interest in the speaker, does her own salute. *Tina, they talk about you going to your final rest, I don't think you wanted rest. What you craved was freedom. You had to simplify, to undo the web of responsibility that entangled you. Well, Tina, you accomplished your goal in a big way and we're all down here saying "poor Tina" this and "sweet Tina" that.*

Someone nudges Sheila. It's Roxanne Beach, a woman Sheila has recently gotten to know. She's inched her way through the crowd to reach Sheila. Rocky, as she's known by her friends, is another overachiever.

The two women exchange sympathetic looks. Then Rocky whispers, "I'm pregnant!" Sheila turns to look into the young woman's eyes. In them, she sees the gush of creation she'd felt when she, herself, was pregnant. She hugs Rocky, marveling at the symmetry in the moment.

A few months earlier, Rocky had revealed enough of her life for Sheila to realize that she, like Tina, was a younger version of herself. She'd climbed high on the corporate ladder, was a tireless volunteer, and had elderly parents for whom she never seemed able to do enough. With her plate so crowded, Rocky had almost decided not to take on the additional demands of motherhood. "Do it!" Sheila had advised, regaling Rocky on the positives of having children. Not only had she believed Rocky would be a good mother, she'd also felt her friend's marriage was of the stuff that could survive anything.

So here Rocky stands, pregnant by the man she adores. *Now if only she can keep her job and the demands of her parents in proper perspective with her new mommy role. Maybe I can help her do that. I can tell Rocky what not to do; I'm an expert on that! Lord, if this is your role for me, I can do it. I'll serve as the career woman's walking, talking example of what not to do.*

Next to her buddy Thoreau, Sheila has always considered Einstein to be a worthy mentor. Back in college, she'd agreed with his thinking that the best way to teach is by example of what not to do. Inadvertently, Dora Ronson had embraced his theory; she'd taught her daughter what not to do when she interfered with Sheila's choice of a life partner. Now, as her own children grow, Sheila vows to never interfere with Allie or Chase's lives. *They'll follow their own hearts, not mine. And along the way I'll teach Rocky that there truly can be a virtue in selfishness. Although I've never been a meddler, I will periodically give my young friend an on-the-spot reality check, something I never did for myself.*

Chapter 60
Library Good-bye

The spirits of Thoreau and Tina fly north with Sheila when she next visits her children. Although she's still taunted by the blank page of her identity, their spiritual admonitions do help her focus on the gift she's been given. *Few people get the chance to connect with themselves as I have. This is something I shouldn't blow.*

For this visit, Sheila has been invited to stay with Phoebe, her friend from junior high and the attorney who probated her mom's estate. Phoebe's home is a townhouse packed with decades of acquisitions. Oil paintings, watercolors, porcelains, and sculptures are displayed on all the walls and in every nook and cranny. Her love of good things is obvious, but her most prized possessions are nine cats and one geriatric poodle. They're her family, her children, and the beneficiaries to her estate.

At her office this middle-aged attorney might seem crisp and perfunctory, but under her professional veneer is an intensely warm and fun loving person. She and her cats know how to play. Toe kissing, tummy rubbing, and neck nuzzling are all part of the rapture. Sheila's completely at home in the midst of her furry hosts, but it's her old school chum's company she enjoys most. Phoebe is an excellent listener, with an attorney's mind for detail, and a genuine desire to learn how and why relationships run amuck. She thirsts for updates on Sheila's dealings with her ex. And when Sheila laments over her mistreatment of Charles, Phoebe snaps her back to reality with, "So what that you let him down? What did he do to you when he had his affair? What was that? If he'd told you about it back then you wouldn't be in this mess now! You're the noble one here; you're the one who refused to live a lie."

They sit late into the night with Phoebe practicing her latent counseling skills. In the morning, she rushes off to her office and Sheila fetches her children for school. As she's done every year for four years, she drops them off at their respective classrooms, hoping, always, to see and talk to their teachers. It still is critical for her to be three dimensional to these people so vital to Allie and Chase's well being. They must be made to understand that she's doing everything she can to be a positive, active force in their lives.

Today, she decides the local library is where she'll spend the time between school drop-offs and pickups. Inside the old brick walls, she walks from room to room, looking for a cross section of people to observe. It's too early for most of the regulars, so she chooses to sit by a window where she can see Wagner's Hardware, her accomplice of four years ago. Trip after trip, she'd made to its UPS shipping department with boxes of belongings, packed with the future in mind. They were addressed to a T. Earl Langley in Pine Springs, Florida. Without fail, the clerk would wisecrack about the weight of the box, and Sheila would wince, silently retorting, *it only contains my life!*

This morning, when she'd picked the kids up for school, she'd stepped inside the foyer of the house that had been her home. The sensation of being immersed in her previous life had almost knocked her over. So much was the same! Knick-knacks, books, and artwork were exactly where they'd been when she'd left them behind, not from lack of caring, but because she'd wanted the children to have the comfort of familiar things when she wasn't there. Seeing it all this morning had made her heart stand still. Even now, years later, when she's truly happily married, she still mourns the death of the family, that abstract thing that's not so abstract after all. That unit of blood and circumstance hadn't been a consideration during those crucial months of decision and departure. In her mind, she'd seen herself leaving her husband, ending a marriage, and temporarily separating from, but never leaving, her children. The family-ness of it all hadn't entered the equation. *I didn't know what a creature it was, or that it would lurk forever in the loneliest part of my heart!*

To escape such thoughts, she leaves her seat to wander among the stacks of books letting their titles reach out to soothe her. An elderly woman is staring at her. Sheila smiles because she knows the woman is thinking that she looks familiar. *We're regulars, you and I. We're here because we have nowhere else to go. The books comfort us and protect our anonymity. They cozy up to us like mute friends, and we feel less chafed.*

She squeezes by the lady and continues her way through the maze of titles. Absorbing the books' silent dignity calms Sheila to the point that she can return to her seat. Maybe she'll write a letter to her cousin, Bootsie.

From behind, someone clamps two hands over her eyes. She's always hated this game. Now their owner will expect her to guess, and of course, she can't. It could be any of a hundred people she'd known in her earlier life. "I give up," Sheila whispers. The hands don't budge. "O.K. then, how 'bout a hint?" It comes in the form of a kiss on the back of her neck. Laughing, "Well, that narrows the field; you're either an old boyfriend, or... a secret admirer!" She yanks off the hands and twirls around to see whom else but Val?

"Ouch! You play rough!" he says massaging one hand.

Sheila watches as Adonis, in a business suit, seats himself on a wooden chair. He truly is a perfect ten. "You have to leave, Val, you look too good to be a library rat."

"Is that what you've become? A library rat?"

"Sounds like, 'Is that how far you've fallen!'"

"On the contrary, it's more like an evolution."

"Evolution?"

"Yes, sweet Sheila, seeing you intermittently as I do, it's as though I'm collecting snapshots of a metamorphosis."

"How so?" She's certain Val has no clue how she's changed.

"Well, for instance, whether or not you believe it, you're infinitely more relaxed, and in touch with the inner you. No longer do I get the feeling you're four or five thoughts ahead of yourself. You listen better, too." He pauses to remember the old Sheila. "You always seemed to be racing somewhere; the function of a plate too full, I expect."

Sheila smirks, "It's nearly empty now."

"No, it has different things on it, things you originally wanted in your life."

"I wanted my children in my life!" she snaps.

"Yes and their absence caused the greatest change in you."

"Not for the better!"

"And not for the worse, it has worn you raw; but it has also deepened you, made you realize life doesn't always go the way you think it will."

"No kidding!" Sheila starts to interrupt, but Val stops her.

"And unless you let that negative streak take hold, I predict this experience will have made you a finer person."

"Yeah, right," Sheila isn't buying it. This is just another of Val's attempts to get close.

"Few people know, as I do, what's happened to you these past four years. And no one, I repeat, *no one* knows the extent of your anguish."

"What do you mean?"

"What I mean, my dear woman, is that with everyone else you've kept up your façade, even, I think, with Earl. You portray yourself to be Super-Sheila, the woman who can do anything, be anything, but what no one knows is that you also feel everything. Lately, in our phone conversations, you've let me see what an abnormally sensitive creature you are. And it's not just your own feelings that rub you raw, but everyone else's as well. I do believe you hurt more for Charles than he does himself. Personally, I don't know how you stand it."

Val has hit home with this observation. How can he know this? It's as if he's climbed inside her.

"And your compassion, combined with the suffering it inspires, is actually serving you well as you search for the person you are yet to become. From afar, I've witnessed you coming to terms with the fact that the greatest sorrow in your life was actually self-inflicted. I know how you beat yourself up over having misjudged Charles's desire to keep the kids, and I've seen how near to the edge it has brought you."

Briefly, Sheila wonders where Val is going with this. But really, she doesn't care. His words seem to be absorbing some of the pain. She sits silently, wanting to hear more.

"I also know that while some people up here portray you as 'sitting on your derriere, doing nothing in Florida,' you've been growing into one of the strongest women I've ever known. For a long time, Sheila, you measured your self-worth by your salary or how much you were able to get done in a day. It's a million times harder to use the yardstick of your soul. At some point, years ago, you took that measurement and found it lacking. And, for trying to correct that, you've been viciously maligned by those who think they know you, and those who don't know you at all. I know Sam Scott and Laura Tolafson have stood by you. They understand the war you're waging to reclaim yourself. But I'm in utter disbelief at the people who choose to write off what you've done as a selfish and crazy deed. I guess everyone loves a scandal, and it's easier to condemn than look for the truth in things. Well, I say fuck them."

Gasp! Never, in all the time she's known Val, has Sheila ever heard him use that word.

"Really, this has taught me a lot, too." Reflecting a moment, he adds, "Like which people I don't want around if I'm ever brought under such scrutiny!"

They laugh. Sheila can't believe how good this is making her feel. As she studies his handsome face, she realizes he's located her yet again even though she'd given him no notice that she'd be in Richmond Heights, let alone at the library. "I appreciate every word you've just said, Val, I really do, but tell me, how did you know I was here?"

"Oh, the same way I know everything about you, like the fact that you've just purchased a cabin on the Santa Fe River."

It's true. The boon town of Pine Springs had become too populated for Sheila's rural cravings so she'd taken out a mortgage on a retreat that was to be all her own. It was to be her declaration of independence from all men. Really though, she never wants to be anyplace without Earl by her side. Her face grows radiant as she describes her "Cypress Delight."

"It's built on stilts, high above the Santa Fe. It's the river I first fell in love with when I moved to Florida. Marjorie Kinnan Rawlings would love it, and Thoreau would be so jealous! We have huge cypress trees and ancient oaks with festoons of Spanish moss. The river's so pristine you can see the bottom. Cranes, Great Blue Herons, Kingfishers, hawks, even wild turkeys frequent our property. Dakota and Sevie love it, but best of all are the people, true river folk, simple, independent, and proud, no airs about them!"

Sheila talks on, explaining how when she first saw the cabin, she knew she'd found a part of her that'd been missing. As she describes it, Val watches Sheila transform into the vibrant, "go-for-the-gusto" woman with whom he'd fallen in love many years earlier. The thing he's feared most has come to pass.

"You really have become a part of that place, haven't you? I can tell by the way you talk, you'll never leave it."

"It's what I've always wanted. Why would I leave?"

"I see." Val pauses, not wanting to complete his thought, but the time has come for him to face the inevitable. "As a result of your evolution, you've found the person you were meant to become. And I fear this new person needs me even less than the old one did."

For once, Sheila and her inner voice respond in unison. "That's right, Val. You're not the one for me. Earl is."

A long moment passes as the executive in Val struggles to be objective. He's invested years in this non-romance of theirs. He and his wife had even agreed to end their marriage so he's free and clear to do anything he wants. But what he wants, what he's always wanted, is to be with the creature beside him. How sad it is that as she has changed, he's fallen even harder for the person she's become. Unfortunate too, is her total commitment to that Southerner of hers, and he has proven to be equally as stalwart in his devotion to her. Maybe Earl is meant to have her after all. Val ponders this as Sheila endures the silence. She knows what's coming. It's time for this lovely man to exit her life and get on with his. She'll miss his long distance support. It was nice during her moments of doubting Earl, to know someone else cared so deeply about her. But that's all it has ever been. Val is a comfort, nothing more. He doesn't have her soul. Some other time, in another place, and without her ever having known Earl, she and Val may have gotten together, but not now, not in this life.

"Well, sweet Sheila, I finally understand. You may be what I've always wanted, but Earl, and all that he is, is what you need. I won't say good-bye. I'll check in with you from time to time but you won't have to dodge my flowers and gifts any longer."

"Thank you, Val." Sheila, suddenly sad, adds, "You've been a sensational friend, and I want only the best for you."

Smiling at the cliché, he understands he never had a prayer of winning her away from Earl. "Maybe, instead of same time next year, we could do same time in five years? I mean, if, in five years I find myself still loving you, I might drop by to see how you're doing."

"Val!"

"Don't worry, I won't be a pest. If nothing has changed, I'll go on my way."

"In five years you, yourself, should be married!"

"Maybe, maybe not."

Feeling his sorrow much too keenly, she grabs his hand. "Goodbye, you amazing man."

Val stands and looks down at the woman he'd felt so sure of winning. He touches her hair with one finger then bends to pull her face to his. Sheila tastes the gentle touch of the first kiss she's ever let him place on her lips. Before she can react, he's gone.

Chapter 61
Time to Live

Another four years has passed, making this the eighth anniversary of Sheila's departure. This is her thirty-eighth trip north to see Allie and Chase, and they've made about as many visits south. When she's not shuttling them wherever their teenage lives demand, she returns to the public library that serves as home base until she can be with them again. It's a weird existence they share, one with long periods of absence hinged to times of intense togetherness. Occasionally, she wonders if she'd known what it would be like would she still have left Charles. This morning she'd gotten a glimpse of what life might be like if she had chosen to stay.

During her last moments of sleep in Phoebe's guest room, she dreamed she'd gone to her job at Riel College. She was wearing her previously owned designer suit, the one that always seemed to say, "Don't mess with me." She'd needed the power look today because there was to be a tense meeting with her boss. It was the same drill she'd always had to endure when one of her employees had done something in a less-than-perfect way. It was up to her to absorb the blows, otherwise her boss would demand the employee be fired and one more qualified be hired at an impossibly low salary.

From that meeting, she'd paced through the day with the cool competence of a seasoned professional. Crises never bothered her; nothing did, because she didn't care about anything. On this occasion, she'd worked until well after 7:00pm, and why not? Neither of the kids would be home. They'd both called to ask if they could stay at their friends' for dinner, and even to finish their homework there. Was it her imagination, or were they trying to get away from her? She'd told herself not to take it personally, but she still worried. They'd been her best buddies, her playmates, the ones she could depend on to fill her life with excitement. Now, as teenagers, they were gone most of the time and the void they left was unbearable. Intellectually, she knew it wasn't good to hang on so. Wasn't she repeating her own mother's sin of living vicariously through her children? But it was too late, she'd even started to subtly try to influence them not to go too far away to college, "Remember, if you go to the University of Wisconsin you'll get a good education and have a fabulous time." The subtext of which was, please don't leave me by myself! But she was already alone in the big house on Lake Michigan.

She'd walked into the living room and turned the light on in the curio cabinet. The reflection in its mirror had tried to engage her; it wanted to remind her that everything it predicted had come true. But she'd refused to acknowledge it. Instead, she'd gazed out the window at her beloved lake. She missed her nocturnal visits to the beach, but those encounters had worn her down so much she'd finally asked a doctor to prescribe a sleeping pill strong enough to suppress her anguish. It was all about the choice she'd made that night on the beach so long ago. It had been there for her, the road not taken, the turning point, but she'd declined. How courageous she'd felt when she refused the lake's invitation to end her misery! And how virtuous she'd seemed in her decision never to see that Southerner again! She'd told herself she was doing the right thing, the decent thing. But inner Sheila saw it for what it was: she'd conciliated yet again. She'd sacrificed her spirit for Charles and the status quo, just as she had for her mother long ago. And eight years later she was paying the price, still in the house, the job, the marriage, and full of self-loathing for not having had the courage.

Charles had come home during her moments of reflection but she hadn't noticed. She was transparent to him as well. Eventually, they'd acknowledged each other as they'd moved, in their own thoughts, around the house. Sheila had sensed more than ever, a cool distance from Charles. It felt exactly as it had when he'd had his affair; could it be happening again? The man for whom she'd sacrificed her spirit? The one she'd tried so not to hurt? Had it all been for naught?

"Hey Sheila!" Phoebe had called up the stairs, "what kind of omelet you want?" Sheila had awakened from her dream thrilled not to be living the fate it portrayed.

Now, as she sits in her favorite seat in the fiction room of the library, she focuses on the ultra-modern building that replaced nostalgic old Wagner's Hardware. She feels as foreign to her hometown as that new building is to its aged neighbors. The driven career woman is completely gone. Long, casual hair and comfortable, old clothes are her style now. The work ethic that once dominated her days has given way to a "value-to-life" ratio. If she doesn't see the meaning something would add to her life, she either doesn't need it or she won't do it.

No job or paycheck will ever measure her worth again. In fact, Sheila's entire concept of money has changed. It has nothing to do with the woman she is or what she can own. To her, money is the means by which she stays close to her children. Her resources are committed to the phone calls, airfares, and hotel bills of their long distance relationship. Equally as important has been her investment in the quality of their experiences when they're together. *I can't give hugs and kisses over the phone. My smiles, winks, and pats on the back must occur on a time-lapse basis. I've deprived them of almost everything a mother can do. But a thirst for life and a passion for the new experiences it has to offer are the gifts I will give them.*

This was her credo through the years: every long weekend and school vacation they could spend together was devoted to the collection of experience. Travels across the country, to the Bahamas and Europe, have devoured her finances, but it has been worth it. Sheila hopes these adventures have expanded her children's experiences, imprinting them with an awareness of the vast world outside their upper-class suburb. She prays, too, that it will infuse them with an enlightenment that can transcend the confines of their everyday lives.

As Sheila has changed, so have Allie and Chase. They've grown; how they've grown! It's as though she's watched them move from sparkling morning to glorious afternoon. The transformation, however, has been far more complex than merely following the sun through the sky. Their growth has been hard-earned as they've struggled through each day of their uncharted lives. Learning how to live without their mother, and with a far-from-passive father, has made them strong.

As her children have grown and changed, their place of primary residence has not. Allie, now fifteen, could not be stopped from moving to Florida if she were so inclined. But a wonderful group of friends and the opportunity to attend an outstanding high school aren't worth trading for an unknown. For Sheila, it's a sad reality, but in her heart, she knows it is right. What Chase will do remains to be seen, but she suspects he, too, will opt for the bird in the hand. And that's fine because it's about what's best for the kids, not her.

One constant that's only for the better is Sheila's love for Earl, and his for her. As she had foreseen in the beginning, theirs is a love that will not be stopped. Neither Carlene, nor Satin, nor Val could come between them. Nor will she let the torment of her guilt sabotage their love. Over time, Earl's devotion and the good counsel of her inner voice have reduced her crushing remorse to a dull, constant ache.

Very soon, she will be fifty years old. Two decades of her life she lived a lie, and in this last one, she learned the torture of telling the truth. Now that she and the inner Sheila have merged to become the person she was meant to be, it's time to live.

Chapter 62
Slow Dance

"I want it in writing that there are no alligators in this river." Laura jokes nervously as she dips her toe into the cold Santa Fe.

"I've never seen a gator near here," Sheila tries to reassure her.

"What's that mean?" Sam prompts.

"Well, any river in Florida could be a gator habitat, but the locals say this water's too clear for them to set up housekeeping."

"That's right," drawls Lou, Sheila's river buddy from that first Fourth of July. "What they like is black water." Seven Yankee faces look clueless. "Black water's all dark and weedy. You know...like a swamp?"

"This water's crystal clear." Sam observes, "I see straight to the bottom!"

"It's so clear gators don't like it cuz they can't sneak up on their prey." Ramona says this as she uses her arms to imitate a gator's jaws snapping shut.

Annette and Barb venture in then stop. "It's freezing!" Barb exclaims, "This is way colder than my lake in Wisconsin."

"It's a constant seventy-two degrees; it just seems cold compared to the ninety-six-degree air. Come on in, everybody. Let's try to get launched on our tubes at the same time." Sheila shoos everyone into the water.

Erica and Kelly— her buds from the professional association through which she met Earl — follow. Sara, her Nashville bud, and Phoebe, her attorney pal, close ranks behind. Hopping confidently on their tubes are Katelyn, Chelsey, Janice, Alana, and Cass, Sheila's first friends in her new life. Miranda and Jenna from her country club job are here, so is Daphne, Mullet's fiancé. Even Rocky is here with her four-year-old daughter.

"Whoa, this current's strong!" Erica proclaims as she takes off on her tube. The Bitches, all experienced floaters, laugh at their Yankee counterparts as they tether an inflatable dinghy loaded with adult beverages and a boom box to Sheila's tube. Then, as simultaneously as possible, this colorful armada of the female "Who's Who" of Sheila's life takes off with the current.

This "float" was Earl's idea. He organized it in celebration of Sheila's fiftieth birthday. Knowing her conviction that experience should take precedence over possessions, he figured the ultimate gift would be to get Sheila together with her buds, in the place she loves most. Earl, Allie, and Chase float one hundred feet ahead. What a pretty sight fifteen-year-old Allie is! The cute little girl has given way to a breathtaking beauty. Chase snorkels nearby without the aid of a float. He's done this so many times he knows how to let the river do the work. At thirteen, his good looks foreshadow the handsome man he will become. Suddenly, he submerges, fins kicking furiously against the current. A few seconds later, he pops to the surface with one hand waving an old green bottle as if it's rare treasure.

"Here Al, catch!"

"Yuk! It stinks!" his sister complains as she stashes the booty in a mesh bag. "Earl, you take it!"

She tosses the bag to the man she and Chase lovingly call their "bonus dad." On a huge inflatable raft, complete with arms and a back, Earl looks as though he's sitting in his recliner. He catches the treasure with one hand and stuffs it in beside him.

"Hey, blossom!" he hollers back to Sheila, "Tell the girls to look strong, buzzards ahead!"

"What does he mean... buzzards?" Annette asks, hoping it's not what she thinks.

"Look up." Sheila points to black specs circling high in the sky. "They're scouting for lunch."

"Are those really buzzards?" Phoebe asks.

"Yes, and so are they." Thirty more of the huge black birds are roosting in a nearby cypress tree. They're warming themselves in the sun by stretching out the full breadth of their wings. It's a haunting sight that Sheila loves every time she sees it. Today, however, she'd rather watch the seven Northerners as they grow quiet and sit tall.

Cass paddles fast to grab on to Sheila's tube. "I like your friends!"

"Knew you would!" Sheila beams, remembering how, on that trip to New Orleans, Cass had reminded her of her Northern pals.

Winking at Sheila, she joins in on the teasing. "I wouldn't stare at the buzzards as we go by. They don't like it and they're liable to swoop down at you." In unison, the Yankees redirect their gazes. The Bitches hoot and holler at this, telling Cass she's mean, but all the while loving it.

"Actually ya'll are a little too fresh; they like dead meat, road kill, and such." Genevieve clarifies.

"Yes, they'd love to gnash on one of my exes!" Wanda laughs.

"Look at those turtles!" Kelly points to a tree trunk with a dozen turtles sunning themselves. A few plop off but enough remain to provide one of the idyllic scenes so familiar to the Santa Fe. A great blue heron completes the picture by landing nearby.

"Sheila, this is entirely too beautiful to be real. It looks like a movie set. Where did you get the heron? Central casting?" Sam laughs, but she's truly envious that such beauty is an everyday occurrence for these lucky Floridians.

"Oh my God! What are these crazy fish doing?" Erica screams as several sleek, silver fish make six-foot arcs all around her.

"Must be mating season for the mullets," Janice observes. "Erica, they think you're hot!"

"Horny little guys! Can you eat them?" Annette wants to know.

"Some folks do, but if you eat them during mating season, you won't get any sleep!" Ramona jokes.

"Mmmmm! Where can I get some?" Kelly asks, thinking of her husband.

"Hey Daphne, isn't your fiancé named Mullet?" Sam inquires, remembering the good old boy's back porch humor on the eve of Sheila's wedding.

"He sure is," responds Daphne, "Some folks say he looks like a mullet, or maybe it's because he makes his living winning fishing tournaments." Then with a wry smile, "Personally, I think it's because he's just as horny as his namesakes!"

Melissa McDaniel

Starling laughs, "I can see it now, Mullet performing six-foot arcs around you in his hot tub!"

Miranda and Jenna float up. They're discussing the spectrum of real estate parading by. Some shacks are the disheveled fish camps of generations past, their owners having grown too old or too broke to keep them up. They're juxtaposed to the new, pseudo-rustic cottages like Sheila's. In a way, she grieves for the river natives who have lived for generations on the same properties. She's sad, also, for their children who, because of the gentrification of their rural paradise, may soon be forced to sell.

"Don't you be thinking about developing this place, Miss Miranda!" Sheila kids in a drawl that's becoming second nature.

"Not to worry, Sheila, the tree huggers are in your corner on this one." Miranda starts to explain about environmental restrictions when Jenna interrupts.

"Hey, Sheila, you could get that rich suitor of yours to buy up all the property. Then it won't ever be developed."

"What rich suitor? Have I missed something?" Katelyn can't believe there'd ever be anyone for Sheila other than T. Earl.

"Oh, along the way there was someone who thought he could dethrone Earl. But he's gone and won't be back, at least for a year or so, maybe not ever."

"What do you mean a year or so?" Katelyn asks, still concerned.

"Now, Katelyn, you know that middle-aged hunk is irreplaceable." Sheila points to the man reclining on his easy chair raft. Whatever he's saying is putting Allie and Chase into hysterics. Peels of laughter dance across the water.

"Well, I should hope so," Cass cuts in. "Cuz you two are a couple for all time."

"Like Scarlet and Rhett!" Genevieve chimes in. "Nobody ever thinks of you without thinking of Earl and vice versa."

Sheila smiles; that's nice to hear. As a couple, she's always felt they were invincible, even when she'd been her most insecure, she'd never really considered bailing out. She notices Phoebe and Barbara floating together. The intensity in Phoebe's eyes tells Sheila she hearing the story of Barb's reconciliation. Earlier, Sheila had noticed that Barb's sparkle is back. Evidently, she'd made the right choice in returning to Ron.

"So Ms. Branford-Langley, I'm sure we'd all like to know: would you do it again?" Ramona is the one bold enough to ask this question. It's something each of these women has wondered, but dared not ask.

It's a question Sheila would never allow herself to answer. Lately though, as she and her inner voice have merged, she's started to confront the yes and no of it all. Gazing at the happy threesome floating in the distance, she realizes it's a picture of what she'd originally prayed for; Allie, Chase, Earl and her, together, as a family. But sadly, this family happens only on long weekends and vacations.

Her friends are still waiting for an answer. Their anticipation seems to be punctuated by the throbbing beat of a Righteous Brothers tune on the boom box. Finally, Sheila puts into words what her inner voice has known all along. "On most days, I think I did the right thing, and on others, I worry I didn't. But I've never once doubted that Earl is the man for me, or that Pine Springs and this river are my home. Beyond that is the truth — that it was the inevitable thing. I had to take my life back, and, although the ache of what I did to Allie, Chase, and Charles will torment me for the rest of my life, I know from here on out, it is my life. Nobody's scripting this part for me, and it's my responsibility to make it have been worth everyone's pain."

As she concludes, the boom box throbs, *now it's gone, gone, gone...whoa, whoa, whoa!* And Sheila recalls the night at the roadhouse, the jukebox, the sensuous beat of the Righteous Brothers, and her long, slow dance with destiny.